PURPLE HEARTS

PURPLE HEARTS

A NOVEL

C W SMITH

TCU PRESS FORT WORTH, TEXAS

Library of Congress Cataloging-in-Publication Data

Smith, C. W. (Charles William), 1940-
Purple hearts : a novel / by C.W. Smith.
p. cm.
ISBN 978-0-87565-362-4 (alk. paper)
I. Title.

PS3569.M516P87 2008
813'.54--dc22
2007028177

TCU Press
P. O. Box 298300
Fort Worth, TX 76129
817.257.7822
www.prs.tcu.edu
To order books: 800.826.8911

Book and Jacket Design by Pentagram Austin

AUTHORS NOTE

ANYONE CASUALLY CONVERSANT WITH AMERICAN SOCIAL HISTORY DURING WORLD WAR II MIGHT RECOGNIZE A RESEMBLANCE BETWEEN THE FICTIONAL EVENTS IN THE CLIMAX OF THIS STORY AND THE RIOT THAT OCCURRED IN BEAUMONT, TEXAS, IN LATE JULY 1943, WHEN, ON THE RUMOR THAT A WHITE WOMAN HAD BEEN ASSAULTED BY A BLACK MAN, WORKERS AT THE PENNSYLVANIA SHIPYARD STORMED THROUGH TOWN BURNING HOMES AND LOOTING STORES AND KILLING SOME CITIZENS AND INJURING SCORES OF OTHERS. (THE NUMBER OF FATALITIES IS IN DISPUTE, AND LOCAL HISTORIANS CLAIM AFRICAN AMERICAN VICTIMS WERE UNDERCOUNTED.) FOR THOSE INTERESTED IN LEARNING THE FACTS OF THE ACTUAL INCIDENT, SO MUCH AS THEY ARE KNOWN, EXCELLENT SCHOLARLY SOURCES CAN BE QUICKLY GOOGLED. ANY SIMILARITIES BETWEEN THE HISTORICAL EVENTS AND THOSE DEPICTED HERE ARE STRICTLY INSTRUMENTAL.

Books By C.W. Smith

Novels
Thin Men Of Haddam
Country Music
The Vestal Virgin Room
Buffalo Nickel
Hunter's Trap
Understanding Women
Gabriel's Eye

Short Stories
Letters From the Horse Latitudes

Nonfiction
Uncle Dad

To the memory of Jesse P. Ritter, Jr.

ONE

GEORGIE KARACEK'S CELLMATE watched him flail on the floor like a landed trout. His butt went *thumpety thump* on the varnished pine. It was way past taps. Their MP was at the duty desk up the hall.

"Serrrrrgeant?"

"Wha'?" The sergeant had a jowl packed with hoagie.

"Karacek's havin' a fit."

The cellmate leaned farther over his top bunk. Georgie's spine now arched into a rigid bow, and he started sort of crab-dancing heel/head, heel/head, drumming on the wood. If he was faking, it was pretty strenuous stuff.

Georgie's eyes rolled back, showing only whites. He was the color of a turnip.

"Damn, Sergeant!"

A *sqwonk*! of chair-scoot, then the noncom stood outside worrying the lock. He swung the door and, holding his riot stick, leaned over while standing back from the convulsing private, as if Georgie were a puddle of something he meant to keep his boots out of.

"Hey, Karacek!" He poked Georgie with the baton as Georgie's bowed form locked tight, then, howling his terrible, incomprehensible aria, Georgie trembled and quaked, at last sank flat to the floor. He sighed. His clenched fists bloomed slowly open to show pink palms.

A spot the size of a saucer darkened his lap. The cellmate once had KP with Georgie. You could flim-flam the amiable fellow into doing your work, but you had to bear the malarkey about that wife, and he didn't care who heard him quoting poetry. And one time he froze on the cargo nets and they had to pluck him off like a June bug from a window screen.

The sergeant prodded Georgie's shoulder with his boot. "Private Karacek!" he boomed.

In a moment, Georgie's eyelids parted.

"Tonus and Clonus," he groaned.

At the West Garrison hospital, you'd have thought it noon, not midnight, the way lights blazed, and nurses, orderlies, patients, and doctors came and went while the lame or lazy snoozed with arms flung across their eyes. But it was always that way everywhere now. *The enemy never sleeps!* the posters warned, so nobody else could, either. Catch a few winks and next you know the Luftwaffe's ripping up your roof. Being hardly forty miles from the Pacific meant getting rousted out in the dark and hustled down to the shore in the rain to repel a Jap invasion. Between the units dragging in from punishing night hikes to reveille calls at three-forty-five for breakfast KP, the camp knew no difference between night and day.

Dimly he was aware they asked if he'd had measles; having apparently said yes, he was bunked between two live cases. He lay groggy from the seizure while a medic with a clipboard interrogated him. Outside in the street deuce-and-a-halfs coughed and cleared their diesel throats amidst a chorus of shouted orders as a battalion clambered up through olive-drab proscenia burdened with everything they'd been issued, off to Ord or Oakland or San Francisco to board Liberty ships bound for the Pacific.

For a brief spell he slept, though once a nurse shook him awake and poked a thermometer in his mouth, then, reading it, sneered, "You don't look sick to me," and strode off.

An MP showed up as Georgie was staggering into the legs of his fatigues. The MP had a toothpick secured between his teeth. Silently he watched Georgie button his trousers. Being under his scrutiny felt like being observed picking your nose. As usual, it hurt like the dickens to move. Tender bruises glowed like big juke box buttons all over his body and his calves had golf ball knots where he'd cramped. A swelling on the back of his head oozed clear fluid into his palm when he cupped it. His pants had dried but stank of piss. Thank God he hadn't crapped them.

Dawn glimmered pale out the window. The ambulatory patients had lined up for mess. He could smell bacon from somewhere in the building, and his stomach lurched.

"Let's move it, goldbrick."

"I haven't had breakfast, sir."

"Don't sir me, Private! I'm not a fucking *officer*!"

"Sorry."

They left the building with the corporal behind him, his baton cocked at parade rest. When they reached the sidewalk, the MP's coffee-graveled baritone came at his nape *hup tooup threeup fo*, and Georgie skipped once to take the beat. Across the Salinas River the sun burst over the Cholame Hills and the sudden orange flare disclosed lively tableaux—half-tracks clattering on pavement in the company street, a trio of WACS in nurse's togs floating by in a swoony fog of banned cologne and steadfastly averting their heads, a convoy of troop trucks roaring out of the motor pool, a platoon, slung rifles shouldered, tramping across their path at a crossroad while the MP kept him marking time. Guys in the ranks shot him sidelong glances of curiosity or contempt.

When they marched past the stockade, Georgie pitched over his shoulder, "Uh, where we going, Corporal?"

"Shut up, goldbrick."

"Firing squad?"

The corporal popped him sharply right atop that lump. He winced, sucked air through his teeth. They marched on in silence. Several times the MP ordered him off the footpath to mark time when anyone in uniform approached, so their progress was halting. They appeared to be heading toward HQ at the far end of the loop. Georgie's unit was billeted in tents across the river, and, as much as he hated the desert heat and the dust, he longed for his simple narrow cot.

"Corporal, can I ask you something?"

The MP grunted.

"Am I going to a court-martial? Reason I ask is I haven't shaved or brushed my teeth or combed my hair, and I'd like to put on fresh fatigues. If we—"

Another *whack!* to the noggin.

"Ouch! Damn, Corporal, it was a civil question!"

4

The MP marched him up the steps of HQ, which looked like the camp's many other rudimentary frame structures, though the approach up the graveled walk sported a border of indigenous succulents whose names he didn't know. Inside, at the end of a very busy hall, he was halted outside a closed door where another MP stood guard. Georgie's escort handed papers to his counterpart.

"All yours."

To his departing back, Georgie called out, "Thanks for your forbearance." The corporal ignored him, but the new warden clapped him hard on the shoulder to drive him to a pew-like bench and growled for him to hold out his hands. He was cuffed with them in his lap. This new MP was a staff sergeant with black eyes nested in wrinkles like those of an ancient tortoise. His sleeve had a half dozen hash marks.

He wagged his finger at Georgie.

"No funny business, Private."

The mode of the warning seemed oddly avuncular, but then this old dog probably joined up when Georgie was still in diapers. Georgie nodded, eager to please. The MP went through the office door and closed it. During the hour he sat he kept tucking his feet under as people strode by continuously—hatless murmuring officers and non-com company runners or high-division couriers in cyclist's boots, sashaying attachés, WAC clerks in flirty skirts, most bearing file folders and striding the hall with earnest intention as if lives at either distant front depended upon their efficient dispatch. It made you want to stand and salute.

At length the old sergeant returned, unlatched the cuffs, took him gently at the elbow and guided him through the door. Soon as they'd cleared the threshold, the MP bellowed, "Teennn-HUT!" and snapped to as an officer entered.

"At ease, Sergeant. Your prisoner's mine now. You're dismissed."

For a bit Georgie stood at attention staring at a framed photograph of Roosevelt on the wall. Around that photo and another of General Patton were arrayed plaques with painted unit crests for the 77th Infantry Training Battalion (Georgie's present unit), the 26th Artillery Brigade, and the 7th Armored: the famous black-bordered triangle showing a half-track slashed by a lightning bolt. The officer's wooden desk was an Independence Day parade entry, its corners festooned with miniature American and regimental flags, and two clean ashtrays fashioned from the butt ends of artillery canisters.

Without moving, he tried to watch as the seated officer—birds on his collar points—leafed through papers. Maybe his.

His stomach growled loud as a freighter's creaking hawser. He considered apologizing. He held himself erect so stiffly that his calves were about to cramp again, and he hadn't drawn a good long breath since the officer had entered.

The colonel looked up, frowning. "You're Private George Karacek?"

"Yes, sir."

"Stand at ease, soldier."

"Yes, sir." He exhaled, shifted his feet apart, let his head loll a little on his shoulders.

"Sleeping on guard duty and failure to obey a direct order."

"Yes, sir."

"You understand these are serious offenses?"

"Yes, sir."

"You understand why, soldier?"

Georgie could easily produce at least one why but wasn't sure it was the correct one, or the one solicited, or even if he were supposed to propose one at all.

"I think so, sir. You don't want the enemy to come upon you unawares. And you can't let people choose to obey or not."

"Exactly. So why didn't you stay awake three nights ago at the ammo dump at zero two plus thirty hours? You didn't mind if the enemy came upon us unawares, as you put it?"

A trick question. Automatically Georgie worked the math to convert to the civilian clock, as if the trick lay in that puzzle rather than in the beat-your-wife mode of it. Meanwhile, the colonel rose and strolled to the windows. He was bald with a monk's grey fringe horseshoeing his skull. He wore the wireless-rimmed spectacles of a bank clerk. He leaned into the window as if expecting someone in particular to walk past. Camp Roberts boasted the largest parade ground in the nation—four football fields in length—and always, when you looked across it, a dozen recruit platoons were practicing close-order drill separated from one another by what seemed acres of space and so distant they looked like gliding rectangles of green. The focus of the colonel's attention, however, was local.

"Sir?"

"Report there on my desk from the infirmary says you had an

epileptic seizure in the stockade last night. Do you have epilepsy?"

His face bloomed hot as a blast from a stove door swung open. "Sir, is *that* what happened to me?"

The officer peered harder into the pane at his nose then suddenly raised a knuckle and rapped sharply on the glass. A dome of glossy auburn hair bobbed across the sill; the colonel's left eye twitched, he flashed the passerby a "V" sign. His jaw muscle stretched as if he might be puckering, and Georgie thought too late to check the reflected face for that. Apparently the case of Private Karacek was but an *entr'acte* in a soap opera of fraternization.

"You tell me." He turned, mission complete, and took his chair. Now he seemed deflated, even disgruntled. Before Georgie could reply, he went on. "Lucky for you I'm a doctor as well as an officer, so I'm somewhat familiar with the condition. Nobody your age—you're, what, thirty—would be surprised by this. Don't bullshit me, soldier. I don't know how you got almost eleven weeks into training without anybody knowing, but we do now. No point in denying it. You got your choice. You can have a dishonorable for that nap you took and for refusing to snap to when the sergeant of the guard ordered it—which if truth be known you were probably in a *petit mal* state of *absawnce* and he didn't know that—or you can take a medical and go back home where you belong."

The colonel pulled a smile to one side of his mouth as if he intended to be taken as a kindly, understanding fellow, but Georgie heard *back home to the gimps and nuts and girls.*

"Aw, sir! Please! Okay, yeah, I've had it since I was six. I didn't mention it when I joined because I hadn't had a grand mal in a good while, and I was hoping it wouldn't matter. I was—"

"*Wouldn't matter!?*" The officer snatched up Georgie's file and tossed it down for emphasis. "You were carrying live ammo in your M-1, soldier! What happens when you have a fit and jerk the trigger? You think any trooper wants to be in a foxhole with you while we're taking fire and you have a fucking *fit*? You think anybody can count on you for *anything?*"

That stung deep. He might crack wise about the Krauts using redheaded nurses as distractions, but he tucked that one away. "I take your point, sir, about handling the rifle. But there's plenty else I can do. I know radios and dogs. I can type, too. Either something like that or limited service, sir. And I was thinking about working in the mess. An army fights on its stomach, they say, and I can man a griddle. I—"

"That's what we use those colored troops for."

"Sir, I'm not too proud. I want to serve my country." He tried to capture the colonel's eye, but the officer had uncapped a pen, rolled the chair snug to the desk, and his wrist and elbow were carving a scrub-woman's gigue in the air with his hurried cursive. Deaf.

"Sir, I want my family to be proud." Georgie's chin trembled minutely. Last night's fit was a whopper and left crud gumming up his system. No food since four o'clock yesterday. His eyes watered. He grit his teeth to squelch a rising tide. *For God's sake! Buck up. Do not blubber!*

"Sir," he said, "I *need* for my family to be proud!"

The colonel looked up blankly as if he'd disposed of the case but had forgotten the private was present.

"Go home to your wife, son. She'll be delighted to see you."

TWO

SCARCELY TWENTY HOURS LATER he was cuddled by a leather wing chair in the lobby of the Paso Robles Inn. Though it was going on ten P.M., the place swarmed with military personnel. The line for the phones stretched from the booths down the hall to the lobby's entrance. He was in no hurry to claim a place. He hadn't composed his news to Sylvia and his mother, and he wasn't sure that a person who'd mustered out shy of graduating had a right equal to anyone who had. Up in his room, he'd donned his khakis wondering if he were authorized to wear them now, even though his uniform was so bare of insignia, except for the unit patch on his shoulder, he might've been taken for a milkman. He'd put it on it nonetheless, half ill-at-ease, half-defiant (not his fault!), reminding himself he'd passed the tear gas test and had lain still in the hole he'd dug while a tank ran over him. Qualified with the M-1. Just *two* more weeks, easy weeks compared to those before them, and he'd have completed the required thirteen.

In the lobby among dozens of uniformed soldiers he felt blissfully part of the herd. He wanted Sylvia to see him in it at least once. Being in uniform painted all with the same broad khaki brush; it erased everybody's history, lifted the lowly, cut the mighty down to size. Strangers glanced at you and the word "soldier" popped to mind, and they believed you to be much like every other dog-face. Donning it for the first time eleven weeks ago, he'd felt a tectonic heaving inside, immensely pleasurable though also frightening because it was so powerful and strange. In the uniform, he *disappeared* while at the same time was transformed into someone utterly conventional, and he hadn't realized he'd been looking for it all his life. When he stood in formation his third eye gazed down upon the platoon, the company, the regiment, the brigade, and he took pleasure in being a dot in a matrix, like a newspaper photo, a single dot in a pointillist's picture.

No one here knew his history—the fits, the eccentric upbringing by an overprotective mother, the spell at Sonyea—but the matching khaki pants and shirt, matching one another and matching everyone else's, didn't *mask* his true self, he believed. The uniform the U.S. Army had issued was the outward sign, to him, of his own belated maturation. He was married now. He was ready to take on the responsibilities of being a normal man, a normal patriotic man, when his country called normal men to service.

He'd wanted to give his bride the gift of having married a brave soldier.

Looking like everyone else, but acting accordingly? That was much harder to master. He was accused of having a *philosophy* that prevented conforming—"Private, do you think you're someone special that you can't ________?" Keep in step, iron your clothes, shine your shoes, clean your rifle. What he had was fuzzy focus, a penchant for skylarking. He'd been a world-class lollygagger all his life. If the colonel wished to call it a symptom of his epilepsy, that was generous—and there was something to it, sure—but truth is that often what transpired in training groups of ordinary men would bore the tits off a hog. Hour-long lectures on things you could grasp in a second. The pointless waiting.

He eyed the lines, considered leaning against the wall and inching along it, anyway, and when he got to a booth, he'd either be ready to talk or not. Sylvia had written about the notice the army sent back to the *Enterprise* when he arrived at boot camp. Nobody would be surprised to hear he'd washed out. But nobody he'd ever known in Port Farview would've imagined he'd lie still in a hole while a tank ran over him. Nobody had ever seen him trim and fit; the U.S. Army had double-timed thirty pounds of pudge off. His waist was four inches tighter, yet his coat size had soared from a 39 to a 42, his shirts from a medium to a large. He'd been the shape of a pear, sometimes an apple. Now he looked more like an upright chunk of tree trunk, he believed. The uniforms he'd originally been issued were tight across the back and blousy through the waist, the pants belt-pleated from being cinched to fit. He'd never come in first and there'd been times when he'd straggled in last from a run or a hike or the obstacle course in the desert heat, and now and then he incurred the wrath of fellow recruits by shouldering arms right instead of left or by mooning during a lecture and getting caught—but on the other hand he quietly helped two illiterate boys from Georgia write letters home, and they stood up for him.

He didn't quit, didn't fall by the wayside. Okay, the time on the cargo net, maybe, but he was bushed, not *defeated.* During a field exercise their platoon was strafed by fighters dropping sacks of flour, and one bounced and hit him square in the chest and bowled him over, slammed him to the dirt. Knocked his wind out. The referee declared him a casualty. What surprised everyone was that he got back to their bivouac on his own two feet without hitching a ride in the medic's jeep. They laughed when he straggled in coated with flour.

He *kept up.*

Nobody in Port Farview would believe that.

Nobody here could know that was a miracle.

So it was especially bitter to have his old nemeses Tonus and Clonus crow victory again. The seizure he had second week here came after lights out and his toes had curled so he'd stumbled to the latrine before toppling over unseen. Reveille woke him on the concrete floor. Dilantin might've carried him clear through boot, but he couldn't ask the medic for it without tipping his hand. He'd dreamed he might go a good long stretch without seizing, though he'd only fooled himself: quitting your medicine and subjecting yourself to stress was a recipe for a four-course grandy.

In the phone line, he slipped out his wallet. Her face with those big brown eyes and heavy brows she plucked to thin arches conjured a reliable mix of tenderness and fascination, underscored by pride of possession. A quicker cadence in his pulse. Her ample springy haunch yielding to his palm, how she kissed with her big soft lips open, nothing he'd ever known before, not even enough to dream of ever having it. She was So. Goshdarn. Beautiful! Mrs. Georgie Karacek! Incredibly his, improbably his! Half his reason for joining up had been to propitiate the gods for this wholly unexpected stroke of luck. Never had a girlfriend, now he had a *wife!* Being her groom was so rich an experience that he could only feel secure about it by, paradoxically, depriving himself of that. She made him so deliriously happy that he needed to keep a distance—she was the fire he stood back from to get warmed through and through.

"That your old lady?"

The corporal looking over his shoulder gratified Georgie by uttering the question. He was holding his wallet open like a book.

"Yeah."

The corporal's rusty brows did a hubba-hubba squiggle.

"She looks like that movie star, can't recall her name."

"Everybody says Ava Gardner."

"Yeah. That's her. How long you been married?"

"Three months, two weeks, and four days."

The corporal clucked his tongue, winked.

"Damn! That's tough luck, fella."

This ordinary young American male couldn't possibly imagine Georgie's profound satisfaction to be envied for capturing such a bride and pitied for having to leave her bed. It was on his tongue to say he hadn't been drafted, but he stopped himself. Saying he'd volunteered might seem sanctimoniously patriotic and also perverse. At any rate, it would require more justification than he cared to give now (or maybe cared to consider).

"You headed home?"

"Yeah." Georgie smiled, folded over the wallet's wing, feeling lordly with the power to cut short the corporal's vicarious enjoyment, and slipped it into his pocket. He wanted to come clean in case the corporal presumed that Georgie was in transit between duty stations, but mention epilepsy and the corporal would back off ten feet in case it were contagious.

"How 'bout yourself?"

"Yep. Kansas City. Got a thirty-day furlough then I report back East." He grinned, narrowed his eyes. "Not supposed to say just where," he murmured sotto voce. Clearly the hush-hush orders were parity to the pleasures Georgie had awaiting him at home.

When he eventually reached a free phone booth, he calculated it was two A.M. in Texas. He hated to awaken her so rudely but was way too het up to sit on his news.

He gave the operator the Port Farview number. The phone rang on the other end. He pictured it on the spindly stand by the bathroom door, the hall dimmed for the night with only the small sconce near the foyer lighted, Sylvia in her burgundy silk pajamas, her limbs akimbo, probably just now hearing the phone's insistent jangle in her tousled-haired head, oh, she'd smell like fresh bread if he put his nose to her bed-warmed nape right now, fresh bread and old cologne.

The phone rang on, steadily nagging someone to look alive, answer up. Maybe she was at Elizabeth's house with his mother? Not likely.

He was afraid the operator would cut him off, but there arose a great rattle, the phone lifted then apparently dropped to the floor, picked up again, some scuffling.

"Hello? Karacek residence!" a breathless female voice declared.

Who the heck is this?

"I have a collect call to anyone at this number from Georgie."

"Georgie? Uh, oh! Mr. Karacek! Gosh, operator, hold on a second. No, wait, I'll go get her—"

"Anyone can accept the call," the operator said, but the addle-pated party had dropped the receiver with a *clunk!* and dashed off.

"Sorry, operator," offered Georgie. It came back now: Sylvia had written that an old friend's daughter was coming to stay since her mother now worked nights in the bomber plant in Ypsilanti and the father was long gone.

Much clattering and *clokking*, as if the girl were barehanded juggling hot pipe wrenches, then, "Gosh, operator, can you wait a sec? I'll go look for her—"

"Honey, can you just accept the call?"

"I, uh, yeah, sure," she said, then, "Is it okay?" and Georgie knew she was asking his permission.

"Yes. Please," he said.

When the operator left them, Georgie said, "You must be Mary Kay."

The girl was too rattled to converse. "I'll go find Sylvia, Mr. Karacek. Okay?"

She left again. Find Sylvia? Puzzling. Their bedroom was only steps away from the phone stand. Obviously she'd already looked there, hadn't she?

He heard footfalls as the girl ran down the hall, then the back screen door opening and slamming shut with a familiar screek and *whap!* that sent his heart zinging. Home! His cheek on her bare breasts. Sitting on the back porch in the swing listening as she sang *Oh sweet and lovely, lady be good …* while she stood in the yard stretching up to pluck a garment off the clothesline and fold it. Good God, he adored her!

He'd all but forgotten how much pleasure he could derive from watching her glide about the kitchen or sit in the parlor darning socks, locks of black hair the sheen of crow-wings falling over her face, her mouth puckered and her brow all screwed up as if it were a bewildering puzzle. No matter how worked up or worried or irritated or restless he felt, when he looked at her face he went all calm deep inside.

Thud thud went the girl's feet on the flooring. Must be barefooted. The receiver snatched up.

"Robert said he saw her going out the back and down the alley probably just taking a walk around the block she does that sometimes when she can't sleep, I'll go out front and see if I can catch her," she reported in a rush then was gone.

Outside the phone booth, the Kansas City corporal roped his arms into a bumper across his chest as he waited for Georgie to finish. Five-minute limit on calls, said a sign on the wall. Georgie'd used most of his. He screwed himself into the seat a bit more so his lips couldn't been seen and worked his jaw.

Robert? The boarder Sylvia had taken in—she'd only mentioned it once, but his mother had sure gone on and on about turning the house into a place for tramps and delinquents. The boarder was probably living in the garage apartment.

Then he heard Sylvia and the girl clambering into the foyer, the girl saying she hoped he was still on the line and she was sorry it took so long and Sylvia's rich alto *Oh honey I'm so glad you answered I just needed a breath of air* musical, lilting, with a nervous excited laugh threaded through it, then—

"Georgie?? Is it you?"

"Hi, hon!" he yelped, swung toward the corporal and jabbed his forefinger at the receiver as if to say *got her at last I know you'll understand if I'm on a minute more.*

"Georgie! Are you okay? Did you get hurt? Is everything all right?"

"Oh yeah! Honey, I'm coming home!"

"Home? Really? Oh, darling!! That's ... that's *wonderful!* But I thought you had two more weeks! When will you get here? How long can you stay?"

"I'm leaving early tomorrow morning. I should get into Houston day after tomorrow, I think."

"Oh, honey! We'll have a big party. Have you told your mother?"

"No. I didn't want to call her this time of night. I'll do it first thing tomorrow morning." His mother wouldn't be a bit happy to be second in line to hear this news. She'd sure let him know that, too. "I've gotta go now. Guys are waiting."

"Oh, Georgie, I'm so … so *glad!*" she gushed. She sounded happy, yes, but also anguished, as if his return would relieve her of a burden his absence had caused. She started mewling and snuffling. He couldn't hang up while she cried, of course. Her sobs warmed his heart, and tears stung his eyes. That his presence or absence could cause such powerful storms of feeling in a woman who was not his mother or his sisters was a new experience, a richly satisfying one.

"Honey," he murmured.

She snorted herself back into control. "Sorry, sweetie. How long did you say? What can we plan on doing while you're here?"

How long. He'd hoped she'd forgotten she'd asked. He opened his mouth to say he'd been discharged but saw the ruddy-haired corporal frowning and tapping the crystal on his watch.

"Thirty days," he said. "It's a thirty-day furlough."

Never Beyond This Shore

HERE at the sea's edge is as near to Jim as I can go.

Other women have gone farther than this. There were women on Corregidor; women have gone to Ireland and Australia and Iceland; women have been lost in the Battle of the Atlantic.

But I know I would be foolish to dream of serving as they have. For a woman to go farther than this shore demands a special skill, complete independence—and I have neither.

No, my task is here, here in the little storm-tight house that sits back from the cove, here with my son.

And if I become discontent with the seeming smallness of my task, Jim's words come back to steady me. "I'm leaving you a very important job, Mary. Until this war is won, there won't be any more evenings when we can sit by the fire-side and plan our tomorrows together. It will be up to you to make the plans for the three of us. "Mary," he said, "keep our dreams alive."

★ ★ ★

MAKE no little plans, you who build the dream castles here at home. When you try to imagine the future, after he returns, be sure your imaginings are full of bright and cheerful hues, for that world of tomorrow will be resplendent in things you don't know—never even imagined. Allow for wonderful new developments in such fields as television, fluorescent lighting, plastics. And leave a flexible horizon for the marvels that are sure to come from the new science of electronics. When you're dreaming of your better tomorrow, count on us. General Electric Company, Schenectady, N. Y.

★ ★ ★

THE VOLUME *of General Electric war production is so high and the degree of secrecy required is so great that we can tell you little about it now. When it can be told completely we believe that the story of industry's developments during the war years will make one of the most fascinating chapters in the history of industrial progress.* 952-346K-1

GENERAL  ELECTRIC

THREE

U-BOATS WERE HUNTING with impunity, and the day Robert left Washington swimmers at Virginia Beach gawked when a freighter exploded offshore and bloody chunks of seamen bobbed in on the tide. Union Station's blue-bulbed interior was as raucous as an aviary as he elbowed through the throngs. After an hour he got a ticket west but had to stand until Baltimore, where he got a seat and dug out *See Here, Private Hargrove.* But then a herd stampeded aboard and he gave his seat to a girl who looked sixteen and pregnant. He sat on the arm. She was off to Long Beach, California, to live while her hubby was out in the Pacific. The way she said "out" Robert knew she pictured him alone in a rowboat and nothing but water on the horizon. She hoped housing wasn't so tight in California.

To cheer her up, he said, "The other day I heard that a fellow drowning in the Potomac was screaming for help, someone came running and said, 'What's your name and where do you live?' And the drowning fellow said his name was John Jones and that he lived on such and such street, so the Good Samaritan went off fast as he could to that address and told the landlady that Jones had drowned and he wanted to rent his room. The landlady said, 'Sorry, I've already rented it to the fellow who pushed him in.'"

Smile of a tired person—it died on the vine. She yawned, tilted her head against the seat like someone trying to float on her back, and so he turned away to let her sleep. Since the windows were black-masked shut, the air was hot and rank. Many passengers stood or perched on their valises. Small children were propped upright, their knees half-buckled and their arms draped over maternal thighs, or they nestled in their mothers' laps; a GI nearby spelled one mother by dandling her toddler on his hip. Though he saw a few marrieds, all elderly, it struck him that they'd all been uncoupled: soldiers, sailors, flyboys, pregnant schoolgirls, unescorted mothers—all traveling without mates. It made him sad but less alone.

To stretch his legs he wormed down the line to the baggage car, where three GIs were playing poker on a casket. They glanced up when he ushered in track noise, and he tapped the brim of his fedora. One gave him a hard look. A heavy shade hid the one big window. They were lighting their game with a signal lantern; it turned their faces red.

"Game open?"

Private Look said, "Where's your uniform?"

He had curly black hair, dewy lashes, and the virtuoso smirk of a street-corner loiterer who ape-calls your daughter.

"Sorry," Robert said. "Docs in three cities turned me down. My brother's at Fort Bragg."

"Long as you ain't yellow," said a corporal. He dipped his copper-topped head toward their makeshift table. His freckle-peppered hands were big as catchers' mitts.

"I got a job waiting in Port Farview, Texas—oil company. I'll be keeping you fellows in fuel."

"What'd these docs tell you?" asked Private Look.

This raised his hackles. He was tired of justifying himself. Shame was partly why he was leaving Washington. Did Look think it was easy to see his friends in uniform?

"Bum leg." He tapped his left knee.

Private Look swigged from a bottle of Cobbs Creek. "What's wrong with it?"

"Ante's two cents," said Red.

The light from the lantern burned on his face. "Polio." He avoided Look's face. He sat on a crate, straightened his left leg, and dug coins from his pocket, and, hoping to end the inquisition, tossed two pennies onto the blanket-draped casket.

"Five card stud." Red dealt everyone a card face up.

The play went on a while—he got up and down a buck or so—until at the end of one hand everybody had folded but he and Private Look.

"Whatta ya say, Polio?"

Robert's hand was marginal—a pair of sevens in five-card stud with one down card coming. Look's up card was a six. Robert bet two cents; Look met and bumped a nickel. Robert checked Look's face, met him and bumped another.

"Call you, Polio." Look tossed in another nickel.

"Last one down and dirty," said Red.

As he was dealing, the vestibule door banged open. The conductor stuck his head in. "Cumberland's coming up, boys. Ladies in the station have got hot java and doughnuts for you." He saluted and slammed the door.

Three of spades.

"Check to the big money," said Robert. "Let's hear your bet."

The train slowed and rattled its couplings, jolting them a little.

Look bolted up and slipped his wallet out. "Ten bucks." He slapped the bill down. A week's wage for a coal miner. Now Robert was sure he was bluffing. The train released a long hard whistle like a pent-up breath, and they nosed into the outskirts of the Cumberland station.

"Okay, here's mine." Robert laid two fives on the bill. It was a reckless bet, but he'd been goaded.

"What you got?"

"I called you."

The private picked two cards from his hand, set them on the bills. "Pair of sixes."

Robert spread his cards on the casket. "Sevens is all I got." He didn't reach for the money.

"Well, I . . ." The private peered into his hand. "I got another. . ." He flipped through the three cards. He glared. "What the fuck?! I had another six!" He said it as if Robert had stolen the third. Robert tried not to laugh.

"Forget it. Take back your money." Robert picked up Look's ten and offered it.

"Fuck no! I had three sixes!"

"Maybe last week."

A khaki blur, then something solid slammed his nose and pain shot through his head like a giant ice cream headache. Windmilling, Look clambered over the casket and poured himself all over Robert, cursing and flailing away; they tumbled backwards and Look scrambled onto his chest where he sat astraddle and pounded Robert's head and face. Robert vised the soldier's balls in his fist and wrung them while he gouged Look's eye with his thumb, then Look's buddies yanked him off.

"Fucking 4-F asshole! Yellow chickenshit! We get our asses shot off and he stays home and rakes in the dough!"

They wrestled him through the vestibule door. Robert's nose was gushing blood, so he pressed his handkerchief to his nostrils, tilted his head back. If they hadn't pulled Look off he felt as if he'd have kept on whaling until one of them was dead.

Being called "Polio" rubbed him really raw. But he'd learned early on how to walk with only a little hitch in his gait, something it took people a while to notice. It didn't keep him from most things. He made a fair catcher and hit his share of homers, but he was slow and clumsy around the bases. But too bad the draft board docs were sharp-eyed. He'd gone all the way to Philadelphia looking for a blind one.

In Nashville he waited hours; in Memphis he spent the night slapping mosquitoes while lying on the terminal's lawn. A guard at the door to the ladies' lounge kept drunks from disturbing mothers with children sleeping there. These facilities were Jim Crow, too, even out on the grass, and Negroes in uniform no matter their rank drank from the coloreds fountain.

To save time, in Texarkana he rode a bus for hours and stepped off in Port Farview at three-thirty A.M. He lay on a station bench with his head on his bag, and at first light washed up at a filthy sink. He'd gone two days without a bath, though he did don a clean but wrinkled shirt. He bought a local paper, *The Enterprise*, and skimmed it while standing in line to take a counter stool at the depot diner. He'd already studied up a bit on the small port town on the Neches River before leaving Washington; it was the hub of a coastal complex of oil refineries and chemical plants, and a shipyard on an island off the port was turning out warships. He'd figured housing would be tight, and the classifieds didn't yield much. Today's front page brayed a story about a melee aboard a city bus between white and Negro patrons, and an inside editorial urged citizens to be patient in the face of trying conditions. "In these days of scarcity and sacrifice, just remember that there is a war on, and even if it seems there's a lot less elbow room everywhere you go now, think of your sons and brothers and fathers overseas."

After greasy eggs wolfed while feeling the next fellow's hot breath on his nape, he walked in a humid heat that put cold blotches in the armpits of that clean shirt. He located the Magnolia headquarters near the port amidst acres of racked pipe and oil-soiled machinery.

His new boss was a low-keyed gent who said he'd be fishing away his golden years if the war hadn't called him back.

"What happened to your face?"

"A soldier thought I ought to be in his uniform."

"Thought maybe you got into that mess."

"What mess?"

"Our coloreds always been a peaceable lot. But war biness has brung the trouble-makers—too many folks and too few places to light."

Robert had the feeling he was being warned, though whether the fellow suspected he might be a perpetrator or only a victim wasn't clear.

On a used business envelope the old boy wrote the address of a woman willing to take a boarder. "She kicked one out, though. Watch your step, son."

This second, more useful, warning led him to expect an elderly widow who'd ask him to read Scripture while she crocheted. Robert told him he meant to work soon as he found lodging, and, leaving his bag, he followed his directions and eventually reached a pleasant avenue lined with overarching sycamores that dappled the herringboned street with light. Two-story Victorian homes adorned with gingerbread molding stood hip to hip like happy bovines behind white picket fences. Most had flags in their windows, and along the curbs the turf had been planted with beans, tomatoes, and onions in victory gardens.

The house he sought looked typical. Two speckled mutts lying under a shrub got up to sniff him. On the glass front door a "V-Home" poster said those inside *follow the instructions of the air-raid warden*; those here *conserve food, clothing, transportation and health*; they *salvage essential materials*; they *refuse to spread rumors designed to divide our Nation*, and they *buy War Bonds and Savings Stamps regularly*. Beside it a service card—a single blue star in a white rectangle with a red border—showed somebody here had gone to war.

How would they like a 4-F boarder? Well, Clark Kent had failed his physical, too—his X-ray vision had caused him to read the eye chart in another room.

He heard a woman singing—*Oh sweet and lovely, Lady be good … Oh, lady be good*—in a rich, strong, self-confident alto. A collie waddled into view behind the screen and aimed its nose at him. Then footsteps sounded and a woman appeared gripping the green handle of a dust mop. A red kerchief was bound around her black hair. She was wearing an apron. Housekeeper, he guessed.

"Excuse me, but I'm looking for—" he consulted his notes. "A Mrs. Karacek?" He said Car-EH-sick but wondered if it weren't CARE-uh-check.

"I am she. It's Sylvia."

"Oh! Maybe Mr. Frank Jackson called you? I'm—"

"Oh! Excuse me! You came sooner than I expected! I was just cleaning the room! Please come in."

"Thanks. I'm Robert Goforth."

"Welcome, Robert."

He faltered moving over the threshold because she extended her hand into his path, held high and brandished like a pistol. Her hand was large with soft skin but firm muscle, and she gripped his like a hearty good fellow. She was almost his height—5'8"—in pumps, and he'd guess her age at thirty-five. She smelled of furniture polish. She was strikingly attractive, with arched brows plucked thin, large brown eyes, high bold cheeks and a strong nose, maybe part Italian or Cherokee. Her wide, full-lipped mouth had dimples like parentheses halves on either side.

She stood the mop in the umbrella stand. "This is Mollie." She nodded at the dog. He murmured "Hello, Mollie," feeling like an idiot. Leading him through the foyer, she smiled nervously. He smiled back. Under her apron was a rayon house dress featuring tropical flowers. She had a nice full figure. He walked close enough for her to keep him under surveillance and kept smiling. They went up the stairs with her hugging a wall lined with framed photographs and talking over her shoulder, him down a step off her port beam. Her rear was wagging in his face. The collie whimpered below, and she halted to say, "No, hon, you stay there." She smiled. He smiled back. "My husband's dog. There's others around, too. This poor old thing can hardly get around now. I know she misses him as much as I do."

They started up again, and she said, "I have to tell you I was expecting someone older."

A nice way to say he was draft age. "Well, I was too."

She laughed. "What did Mr. Frank Jackson tell you?" A lilt in her voice put ironic quotation marks around his name, and one brow arched upward lent her a remotely dangerous air. She had a saucy edge, he could see, and he liked that. She could take teasing and give it back as well, most likely.

"He said you'd kicked somebody out, and he told me to behave myself."

"My goodness! How flattering!"

He laughed. "I think he was referring to this," he pointed to his shiner, "which I got in the wrong place at the wrong time."

"Well, as for that boarder, I'd never had one before and my mother-in-law insisted it had to be a girl. Listening to her was my first mistake. Anyway, I'm still working out the rules. Have you boarded in many homes?"

"No. This is my first."

"I guess we'll make it up as we go along. My husband signed up in February, and, believe me, his pay doesn't go far. We need the money, and people need places to stay." She pointed up the stairs. "You'll have his old boyhood room. I've cleared a lot out, but I need a couple hours more to finish."

"I'll be happy to help."

"That's not necessary."

She opened a door in the upstairs hall, and he would've stepped into the room, but she was still talking, blocking the way. It dawned on him that the character of his landlady would be as important as the room.

"I'm eager to have a man to talk to now and then. With the war on and all … Well, the women I know are a comfort, it's true, but . . ." She smiled. "Oh, never mind! I'm afraid I'll scare you off with my jabbering!"

Nervousness apparently produced a need to babble and flitter-flutter her hands about; when he was self-conscious, he got quieter, which only made things worse. He forced himself to respond to set her at ease.

"Oh no, I like to hear talking. My mother and my aunts go on like magpies. It's music to my ears. Things would be awfully dull without it."

The room had nine-foot ceilings and windows on two sides. A roll-top desk with a swivel chair, a single bed, and along the interior wall a long table with a stool. Atop the table stood cartons and three small aquaria whose glass sides were marbled with mineral deposits. The room smelled like old cheese and dust.

"It's very fine. You sure it's not needed?"

"Oh no! My husband said we ought to have a nice place for a guest, meaning his mother, but I told him that I'd bet a dollar to a doughnut that she wouldn't set foot in it while he was away unless she heard that

I was running a cathouse."

"You're not close, then?"

"Oil and water, believe me. She's lived around here since day one and thinks of me as a 'foreigner.'"

"I noticed that you don't sound Southern. Are you a Midwesterner?"

"No. Quite a bit of the Northeast, a slice of Chicago, and Florida all mixed up. My father was Greek, my mother Irish."

"Greek and Irish—that's a stormy combination."

"Oh my word, yes! My father said it was like living where there was no spring or fall. They had to have a drama, and if they couldn't find one, they'd make one. How about you?"

He pointed to his black eye. "I seem to get enough drama without looking for it."

She chuckled. And patted his forearm as if to console him for the injury. "No, I meant where are you from?"

"A little town in New Jersey."

"That name Goforth sounds teddibly English." She winked.

"It is. But I'm no tea-sipper, Sylvia. My ancestor came over without a pot to pee in, if you'll pardon the expression, and probably running from the law. I'm the first to graduate college, and my parents worked as hard for it as I did. My brother's in basic at Fort Bragg now, and my mother's a clerk at a Woolworth's. My dad was foreman in the Fulper pottery plant in Trenton before the crash, but now he's learning machine tools at a munitions factory." He was, in other words, as red, white, and blue as they come.

"Well, you have an honest face, anyway. Let me show you the rest of the house."

Another room upstairs was Sylvia's sewing room: two Morris chairs with reading lamps and a work table under windows that faced the street, a Victorian fainting couch on which perched an empty bird cage, and an electric Singer of recent vintage. On the worktable lay tissue templates to a pattern and swatches of material pinned to them. She pointed to the rolls of black material mounted over the windows. "You see the black-out curtains? I had two sets, but she stole one when she left. This is the only room I use at night when there's an air-raid, though sometimes I get under the dining room table. Oh! And my sand buckets are on the back porch. Flashlights and first-aid gear are in the kitchen."

On the way down, Sylvia called out names to the photographs lining the staircase wall. One series showed her spouse at various ages, and at the bottom, he was in uniform—a pudgy, gap-toothed, cherubic, curly-headed fellow in eyeglasses who might've been a cross between a Renaissance Gabriel and a Little Rascal. It wasn't the usual warrior portrait—there was such incongruity between that happy baby face and the seriousness of the khaki, it was as if he'd stuck his head through the hole of a photographer's mock "soldier" set-up. Robert found it hard to picture them as a couple and saw no photo of them together.

As they entered the kitchen, a yellow Bakelite radio on the counter was playing Jimmy Dorsey's "Tangerine," and she immediately stepped to it and twirled the volume down, though not without a little sashay using a curvy hip to mark the last audible beat.

"I suppose we should discuss the meals. I hope you don't mind I'm Catholic—I mention it because I don't eat meat on Friday. And I never was much for fish."

"I've been observing Meatless Tuesday since the war started. I don't see a problem switching to Fridays. I don't expect you to feed me, anyway. What I can't get at a café I can fix on my own, if you'd set aside a corner in your icebox."

She beamed a sideways grin and waved toward the drain board laden with plates, glasses, pans, and food containers. "You can guess how the inside of my icebox looks, Robert. To be honest, I hate cooking for one person and I hate eating alone even more. If you'd take your evening meal with me there'd be no extra charge—it's cheaper sometimes to cook for two. We'll get you a ration book and you can let me use the stamps. I'm a little new at it, but I bake pies and cakes when I can get the sugar and the lard, and if I don't get help eating them I'm afraid I'll look like an elephant when my husband comes home."

Sylvia Karacek was a far cry from that dreaded elderly widow, and something inside him released, like a drawstring undone, for the first time since leaving the East Coast.

"Sylvia, I'd be honored to share your table, and I insist on paying for my board as well as my bed."

"Good!" She clapped her hands girlishly, gripped his forearm as if it were a tennis racket, gave it a hearty squeeze. "I'm so glad this is working out! You've no idea how worried I've been. It was so awful before!"

"Me too!"

In the dining room stood dark walnut furnishings, which she dismissed with an airy wave as they passed, then they went into the parlor—a sofa, two wing chairs, and a chintz easy chair with a hassock. A side table held a cup and saucer and a newspaper. The upright piano had sheet music open on its rack. "I heard singing earlier—was that you?"

"Yes, guilty as charged!"

"You sounded very professional—do you perform?"

"Oh, no. I once was with a touring troupe and hoped ... well, you know, things change. But I'm in a community group, and we're planning a variety show for a War Bonds rally, and we are desperately, I mean *desperately*! in need of male voices, male bodies! Can you play or sing?"

"Well, not so anybody would want to hear me."

"In a chorus, then? We have comedy sketches—have you ever done any acting?"

"I had a fiancée once."

She reared her head back to guffaw. This time the hand did a *slap*! on his arm as if to say you card!

"Can you stand still long enough to take a cream pie in your face?"

"Well, from the looks of my mug I'd say I'm not too swift at ducking."

"Seriously, now—will you consider it?"

"Of course."

She tapped her knuckles on a closed door as they passed it, saying, "My bedroom," then they came to the bath. A folding wooden rack stood next to an open window, and the rungs held women's white cotton briefs and brassieres, a half slip, garter belt, a pair of stockings, and a girdle. Despite the claims on the front door, she'd apparently not entirely heeded the call for rubber salvage—along with auto floor mats, bathing caps, beach balls, worn-out tires and suspenders, jar gaskets, and garden hoses, the president had asked women to give up their girdles.

"I would've taken these down, but they're damp," she said with a tinge of embarrassment. "We have a clothesline out back. Which I had a very hard time impressing upon my boarder. There's a washing machine on the back porch. I won't do your washing but I'll be happy to do the linens, of course, so long as you're not too fastidious—I don't iron my sheets."

"I've never slept on ironed sheets except at a hotel. I'm very used to taking care of myself. I've been batching it for some time."

"No girl back home to cook and clean for you? A nice-looking fellow like you?"

His eyes shot to the mirror hanging above the basin. Purple-blue eye, red nose still swollen, a day-old beard and his hair in greasy strands. He looked like he'd been hijacked in an alley while sleeping off a binge.

"I appreciate the flattery, but no, the girl is gone."

Back into the foyer, they'd come full circle. Between them there'd arisen a bright vapor of good fellowship issuing from their mutual relief to have found in the other someone so agreeable.

"Oh, I forgot to ask." She twinkled her brown eyes. "Do you take a toddy now and then? In moderation, I mean."

He laughed. "Guilty as charged."

"Do you dance?"

He blushed. "No. Afraid I'm too clumsy."

"Oh, I bet I could teach you. My poor hubby spent his life as a wallflower until I came along, and now he does the rumba like he was born in South America."

"He may have more talent."

They stood another moment; his mind churned to find something clever to prolong his interview.

"Do you have any special requirements?" she asked.

Had she somehow guessed about his leg? "Special requirements?"

"Oh, protection from cat allergies. A need for Ovaltine at two in the morning?"

He laughed again. He was a laughing fool; everything that was said seemed to inspire it. "Well, none of those. I'd like to use your telephone now and then."

"Fine."

"And do you have any special requirements?" he muted his laugh to a chuckle, though he was afraid he sounded lewd.

She blushed. "Can you fix things?"

"So long as it takes a saw or a hammer or a screwdriver or a plumber's helper or a pipe wrench. I'm lost with electricity."

"You wouldn't mind doing little repairs from time to time?"

"Not at all."

"So it's a deal?" she asked. "Forty dollars a month? And we can take something off for the handy-man things."

"Yes, fine." The price seemed fair, considering the shortage of housing, and God only knew what the diner grub was like here. They shook again, this time playfully, as if poking fun at their own formal need to clinch the deal, and it afforded a rich pleasure to have her hand clasping his. A current ran back and forth.

"I told Mister Jackson I'd work the rest of the day."

He was still clutching her hand, though, pumping to give the appearance of shaking it. Now she flushed and jerked hers away as if he'd been licking it, closed her fingers with a tiny smile, and slipped her hand into her apron pocket.

"So you'll be back by six or so? We'll have dinner, then."

"Well, please don't go to any trouble. My first day, I don't know what to expect."

"I understand. If you're not back right then it will keep, I'm sure."

"Well, thank you again," he warbled.

"Thank *you*!"

FOUR

HIS TRAINER DROVE THEM on back roads in dense pine groves and swampland from one oil lease to the next. They measured and recorded the outflow from a well into nearby holding tanks and made certain each pumping jack was functioning properly and was turned on and off on schedule. It was not hard work—it required some math, some writing, some common sense and experience about machinery, a lot of driving.

At six-thirty Wiggins stopped at a pharmacy on the courthouse square to get a stogey. Robert followed him in to buy his hostess a good-will offering. A comely nurse on the cover of *Life* caught his eye, so he took it. He was coming back late, even though he'd told her he was uncertain when he'd return. He hoped she'd eaten and had kept the food warm and he could wolf it down off the stove-top. He was exhausted, and what he wanted more than food was a hot bath and to doctor his nose so that he could breathe through it. Clean clothes. A full night's sleep in a bed.

Wiggins offered a lift, so Robert told him he was staying with Mrs. Karacek and gave him the address.

"Say, now *she's* a looker, ain't she!"

"She's pretty easy on the eyes, all right."

"You solve the mystery of what that gal sees in Georgie besides his money, you lemme know, hear?"

"Why, what's he like?"

"Thirty and was still living in his mama's house and working as a delivery boy when she showed up outta nowhere. His family's rich as Croesus. One daughter's hell on wheels and the other's downright peculiar. Georgie has fits. It's a wonder the army took him. Never even had a girlfriend before this one come to town."

"Well, he may have virtues nobody but she knows about."

Wiggins had to slalom down the cobblestone on Acorn Street because so many cars were now parked along both curbs that only the center lane was clear, and twice they pulled into a driveway to let a coming vehicle pass. On the parkways men in shirtsleeves stood smoking or tended gardens.

"Didn't use to be this way. Too many people for a town this size now. You hear about that squabble on the bus the other day? Ship-worker got into it with a nigger, couple dozen got pitched into the hoosegow 'fore it was all over. Me, I wanna get out West where a fellow's got some space. I seen pitchers of Los Angeles where the streets are so wide you could hardly chunk a rock across them."

And no doubt paved with gold, Robert thought, as they veered to the curb at Sylvia's. He thanked his driver, got out, and went up the walk with his bag in hand and the magazine tucked under his arm.

It was twilight. The two hounds now bounded up to stand with him at the door, shoving at his knees to get their noses wedged into the screen. He rang the bell. The collie waddled into view to appraise him through the mesh.

"Hello, Mollie."

"Come in," he heard Sylvia call. When he tried to knee the dogs aside to keep them out, they scrambled past and raced through the foyer and down the hall. Sylvia glided in from the parlor. Her long hair had been caught in a bun, disclosing a strong neck and, in turn, accentuating her soft, fleshy chin. She'd taken off the apron and was wearing white high heels, a bright yellow cotton dress and a string of pearls with matching ear clips. She looked, well, breathtaking to him.

"Robert, you can feel free to come and go. *Mi casa es su casa.*"

"Thank you. I didn't know if it was okay for the dogs to come in."

She laughed. "I try to keep them out myself, but Georgie always let them have the run of the house, so it's hard."

"Does he breed them?"

She grinned. "Not on purpose. It's more like collecting. They're all strays. One ran off when he left, and frankly I'd just as soon they all would."

He held out the magazine. "I picked this up for you."

"Why thank you! That's very thoughtful. I guess you'd like to clean up before you eat?"

"Yes! Please!"

"Take your time. It's a casserole—it'll stay warm."

His windows were open, and a breeze thermaled up the staircase and through the room. The long table had been cleared and wiped with polish, and on it stood a vase with red and yellow zinnias. The bed had been made with a yellow chenille spread, and on the desk was a small wicker basket holding two apples and a pear; beside it neatly stacked in a pyramid were two red wash cloths, two red face towels, and a red bath towel. He sighed, deeply.

The steamy vapors in the hot tub loosened the clots in his nose. He shaved twice because he hadn't shaved well in days, using a razor blade he'd had now for three weeks, his own tiny contribution to the war effort. Six hundred razor blades were the equivalent of one .30 caliber bullet. If everybody in the country saved one tin can, that's enough metal for thirty-eight Liberty ships. He could tell Sylvia that 2300 pairs of nylon stockings would make one parachute, and fifteen pairs, one artillery powder bag. Thirty of her old lipstick tubes could make twenty rifle cartridges, and one pound of kitchen fats would yield one pound of black powder.

He carefully rinsed out the tub and basin. He put on clean clothes. As he came down the stairs, voices arose from the parlor, and Sylvia stepped into the foyer. She whispered, "I'm sorry—do you mind?" and dipped her head toward the parlor. She was blushing furiously. He shrugged.

A thin blonde with eyeglasses was seated on the sofa wearing a beige hat and dress and brown pumps; across the room a tiny older woman in a dark blue suit and hat bobby-pinned to tightly curled gray hair perched on the rim of the wing-chair cushion. Her small sharp features put him in mind of a ferret. He recognized the women from the family photos. On the coffee table was a teapot of white china, with two matching cups and saucers.

Sylvia's arm moved to indicate him, but he curtsied up and said, "Good evening, ma'am. You must be Mrs. Karacek. I'm Robert Goforth, and I want you to know I'm grateful to have a room here thanks to Mr. Jackson over at Magnolia and your daughter-in-law." He smiled at the younger woman to include her. He presumed she was one of the daughters her co-worker mentioned.

"Well, your gratitude aside, we're not used to having boarders. After our last one, I was very uncertain about giving my permission," the mother said to him but kept her gaze fixed upon Sylvia. "And to be frank, Mr. Goforth, I still haven't decided and I'd appreciate not having my say-so treated lightly!"

"Of course!" he said, though he had no idea what she meant.

Sylvia said, "Evelyn, Mr. Goforth hasn't signed any agreement and I never dreamed of asking him to until you'd been consulted."

That seemed to pacify her. Robert's impetuous leap had caused the trouble, he saw, though Sylvia hadn't mentioned that his boarding was contingent upon anyone's permission.

"I don't want to seem presumptuous. I'm just glad for the chance, that's what I meant. No one said things were settled."

Sylvia and he waited mutely and the blonde sat frozen while Ferret Face inspected the rim of her china cup before setting it into the saucer with a tiny clink.

"What happened to your face, young man?"

He considered walking out to rent another room.

"A soldier hit me."

"Why, if you don't mind my asking?"

He did, and he let a pause say that for him. "I suppose because he'd been drinking and he was scared of what might happen to him overseas, and when he found out I wouldn't be going he took it out on me."

"No doubt someone had talked him into joining against his better judgment."

"Evelyn, don't say things like that!" Sylvia burst out. "You agreed!"

"Perhaps I shouldn't have."

"What is that supposed to mean?"

The blonde passed him a stricken glance, as if appealing for help.

"That I should've been a better mother." The woman tagged both her daughter and him with her gaze as if tallying her allies or the number of spectators.

Sylvia turned to him. "Mr. Goforth, would you excuse us, please?"

He went out onto the front porch. An elderly woman in a faded Mother Hubbard stood in her next-door driveway pointing a garden hose on a potted geranium; she didn't see him, and she was craning her neck into the light flooding onto her from the Karacek's parlor. She caught him looking and jerked her head about.

"You the new boarder?"

His first impulse was to step across the driveway and introduce himself, but her question sounded like an accusation, so he just nodded.

"Tell her that half Walker done grunted in my zail-yahs again."

The anger was clear, if not the content, so he nodded again and stepped off the porch. A notion about this place was emerging. Had this old woman been elder Mrs. Karacek's neighbor for long? Possibly Mrs. K had looked down her nose? And then moved off? And now the neighbor was getting her revenge by reporting violations of the code of gentility. *Your tenants are dragging down the neighborhood!* The older native homeowners maybe were accustomed to an orderly world in which Negro servants did their domestic duties and didn't run off to work in defense plants and the white trash stayed where they belonged, as well. Now these hordes of *strangers* rushed in to rent their rooms, park on their streets, keep odd hours, and play their music all night, drink, shout, let their dirty urchins run wild.

It hurt his pride to be someone whose presence was supposedly detrimental to the good reputation of the household. He'd hike through the neighborhood on the chance somebody had put out a room for rent sign.

Feeling sorry for himself, he passed broad porches where families were sitting in wicker chairs enjoying the evening. Through lace curtains he saw them at dining tables breaking bread. He felt homesick, but twilight often did that. His Claire-injury started hurting. Did she ever regret jilting him? He wondered where she was right this moment, but that only conjured an image of her in the arms of a newly minted ensign in dress whites.

The collie was tailing him, shedding bats of honey-colored fur that wafted and settled like trail blazers. He walked until the pavement collapsed into a country lane with barbed-wire fences on both sides enclosing pastures where white blotches on the hides of the grazing cattle glowed softly in the dusk. Then he retraced his steps. He was past being hungry. His head pounded and his breathing was shallow.

No lights were on in the parlor. "Hello, Sylvia? It's me, Robert." She'd told him *Mi casa es su casa* but apparently it wasn't *her* casa.

Getting no response, he went into the foyer and looked into the parlor. She was sitting on the sofa. He eased down into the wing chair.

She sighed. "Oh, I'm so sorry you had to get involved in that! I had no idea she'd come running when she got the news."

"Is it okay for me to be here?"

"Yes, of course! It's my house! I'll have whoever I wish living here, by God!"

He waited. He sank deeper into the chair. He was melting into his shoes; a wave of nausea swept over him. He must have looked faint, because she leapt up, rushed over, took his hand to hoist him up.

"Oh, you poor boy! I know you must be famished—here, let's go eat!"

Later—deep in the night, he thought—he was roused from a sweaty wallow of sleep by someone savagely shaking the foot board. He swung up in alarm and saw a bulky form hovering over him, heard sirens and a call from down in the street, "Get those lights out!"

"Robert! Wake up! We're having an air raid!"

Groggy, he looked at his watch: eleven. He'd been asleep less than an hour. As he stumbled to his feet, she was darting down the hall. He followed her to the dining room. It was dim. She shined a flashlight into his face for an instant then away. He saw yellow spots against a navy blue backdrop.

"Quick, let's get under the table!"

His body was miles behind his brain and his brain was miles behind reality. Half-asleep, he obeyed—Sylvia seemed to be moving at a tremendous speed, her words sharp and quick. They got on their hands and knees. The table was too low for them to sit, so they reclined on an elbow.

"Do you think we should listen to the radio?" she asked.

"It's probably only a drill. Haven't you had them before?"

"Yes, but each time I think this could be it. It's the refineries and the shipyard. I'm scared! Oh, I hate the war!"

"Neither the Japs nor the Nazis has a plane that could reach us here except from a carrier in the Gulf, and it would've been spotted *weeks* ago."

Of course, rumors launched planes from submarine decks, and who knew what German buzz bombs could do? But maybe she hadn't heard this so he kept quiet. His elbow hurt. "Why don't we sit in the parlor? So long as we keep the lights out, we'll be fine. If we hear bombs, we'll come back in here, okay?"

She followed him. In the parlor a little ambient light showed an outline of the sofa, and he led her to it. She scooted close. It was dark in the street; he heard talking out there, then a vehicle with blackout lamps cruised by slowly. He listened for sounds in the sky, heard only crickets.

"Doesn't seem like anything serious."

"Yes. I feel silly. But I'm just an old scaredy cat. And I hate being that way. I try to talk myself out of it, but my fear doesn't respond to coaching."

Her flank was warm against his arm. She was fairly wringing his right hand with both of hers the way girls do on a roller-coaster or in a frightening movie. He could smell her perfume and her long unloosened tresses brushed his bare shoulder. He was fully awake now, and he relaxed to enjoy this unexpected intimacy.

"I don't think you have any reason to be afraid here."

"What about an invasion by land?"

He shrugged. "We'd hear them coming. It's still a few miles to the Gulf, isn't it? Besides, I believe there are army posts nearby."

"But what if they manage to get here?"

"You have a gun in the house?"

"There's an old hunting rifle in the foyer closet. I guess there are bullets for it somewhere."

"I'll stand in the door with it," he joked. "They won't get past me."

"Don't make fun of me."

"Then don't be hysterical." He didn't know how she'd take that.

An "all clear" siren went howling up over the trees, and vehicle engines started out on the street. Lights from their head lamps flickered wildly over the parlor walls. She rose, leaving a cold space, and he followed, standing as close as he dared.

"Well, thanks. I feel a lot better with you here."

"You're welcome."

"Well, good night again."

He wanted to shake to feel her warmth again. She lifted her hand to reach the one he held out, and her lapels parted. Her negligee showed the tops of her breasts beneath the robe. While they shook her gaze caught his—“Oops!” she said—and her free hand rose to draw the long pink collars closed.

FIVE

Robert seemed to be a magnet for information about the Karaceks. By the time he'd worked at Magnolia a week, he'd been pumped full of gossip by secretaries and coworkers who knew the family and who apparently expected a *quid pro quo* by way of insider dope on that new bride of Georgie's. He learned that they were among old monied Port Farview families who attended churches with names boasting the adjective "first," families whose ancestors chartered the Port Farview Country Club and whose fortunes derived from lumber, oil, rice, cotton, and real estate. Georgie's paternal great-grandfather helped found the town after the Civil War and owned a thousand acres of the Big Thicket, several saw mills and a short-line railroad to serve them. Georgie's maternal grandfather owned the first bank in nearby Kountze County. Both families boasted land on which oil was found soon after the Spindletop gusher in 1901, and the boom of the last decade had brought even more prosperity. Though his father died of the Spanish flu when he was eight, his mother had ably managed the family's oil leases, agricultural real estate, a lumber yard, and four family homes in two towns. Evelyn was admired for her grit and intelligence as well as for her elegant garden luncheons, though Robert caught the hint that other women her own age and social standing felt she was a tad overbearing.

Of course she had their sympathy as well. Her oldest, Marianne, always peculiar, was at forty a frail devotee to Mary Baker Eddy, and she never seemed to be out in the world unless accompanying her mother. The librarian Eliza Shier reported to people that Marianne claimed to be writing poetry *for* Emily Dickinson as the "vehicle" of the dead poet's efforts to speak to the living world. The middle child, Elizabeth, was a wild thing in her schoolgirl years and was thrice carted bodily home by Port Farview constabulary who knew not to jail her for public drunkenness. She regularly pilfered items from stores, and the proprietors had to call Evelyn to retrieve the goods. She had no interest in even a horsey college for young ladies such as Sweet Briar where the most stringent demand might be the tuition. She flung herself freely into a dalliance with the high school's football coach, which cost him his marriage and his job—"and that was a damn shame 'cause the 'jackets had a good shot at district that year." It left Elizabeth with a desire to spend six months in Paris to "get away from people giving me dirty looks all the time," she was heard to say.

Eventually she married a plodding land man and gave birth to two children and was now pregnant with a third. "That's *supposedly* why old Miz K moved up to Kountze—to hep her," said one source. Since her schoolgirl days she'd gained weight and lost her considerable sex appeal. Her experiences hadn't humbled her one whit, it was said. Her manners were every bit as coarse as those of a roustabout's wife, and she screamed at her obnoxious children across the floor of the Port Farview Country Club dining room, where they regularly made the Sunday after-church buffets, arriving so early in their Cadillac and so half-dressed *everybody* knew they'd just gotten up and had skipped the services at St. John's Episcopal. She ate multiple plates of food, though she sent her six-year-old son or her husband through the line for the second or third. She treated Clarence like a dog or a servant.

Then there was poor Georgie. The little fellow had his first fit the first day of the first grade of school, and Ol' Doc Waller advised Evelyn to teach the boy at home. Ol' Doc Waller believed that the daily life of the epileptic had to be free of stress and strain. Rough and vigorous recreation was discouraged in favor of quiet pursuits such as collecting, reading, writing or other arts.

He couldn't play with other little boys. Evelyn put him on a high-fat diet presumed to be beneficial, and from that first seizure until adolescence, nobody could recall his leaving the Karacek's property without an adult escort aware of his condition. Marianne and Evelyn dedicated themselves to teaching him, and as a result of their tutoring, "they say he knows as much as a good many who went up to A&M."

Robert unfortunately didn't have much to report about Georgie's recent bride. Or much he cared to report to a curious, gossiping public ear.

They'd established a routine. Around six Sylvia served dinner, plain but filling fare. They often had a potato, though for butter they had to substitute a brick of lard beaten into a palatable texture in a mixing bowl with a pat of yellow coloring. (His job, and he guessed it had been Georgie's.) They'd have an egg or chicken, now and then some pork. They enjoyed squash, onion, and pole beans from the garden that he helped weed, water, and defend from squirrels, moles, mice, jays, crows, and a hundred kinds of bug and worm and bee.

Sylvia had a sweet tooth, so they usually had a cake or cookies or fruit pie she made by studying a *Ladies' Home Journal* or *Good Housekeeping* laid open on the kitchen table. He feared getting fat, which seemed ironic and even shameful considering the war made food scarce. But Sylvia always said, "I really shouldn't eat this." It eased her conscience and permitted full enjoyment while any morsel remained. When finished, she'd complain that she felt fat. That was his cue: "Not fat, Sylvia. Like Jane Russell, if you don't mind my saying—just voluptuous."

After dinner, some nights she'd bustle to rehearsal (to her disappointment, he declined to join the troupe). On Thursdays her St. Anthony's auxiliary assembled packets of shaving articles, chocolate bars, and soap. Sometimes a friend called and she'd go to the movies or to the Red Cross station to roll surgical dressings or work at the USO canteen at the train station. Otherwise, evenings they'd listen to Gabriel Heatter or to her dance band records—Artie Shaw and Glenn Miller and the Dorseys were favorites she'd saved from the salvage calls since shellac was a needed war materiel. While she hummed or sang along, she wrote to Georgie, or they played Chinese checkers or rummy. Sometimes they read, each to a chair in her upstairs sanctuary. If she were in a jolly mood, she'd play novelty tunes—they shared a bemused liking for the dopey Tin Pan Alley war hymns: "Praise the Lord and Pass the Ammunition" or "When Those Little Yellow Bellies Meet the Cohens and the Kelleys" or "To Be Specific, It's Our Pacific."

But if she were blue, she'd want to be alone, and "The Moonlight Sonata" seeped up the stairs like a melancholia-inducing gas. When moody, she drank red wine from a juice tumbler, and though she never slurred, she chose her words with a care that suggested translation, and a subtle dip showed in her walk as if she was reaching from one stepping stone to another.

Her room was below his. Once he was awakened by a rhythmic cooing, like a dove's call. When he realized the source, he was jolted into an agony of arousal, and he hurried to catch up. But she soon heaved a groaning sigh. He plunged on alone, conjuring up a hoarded cache of glimpses—the breast and a rosy upright nipple behind the pink lapels, her skirt lifted so she could, unaware of his gaze, adjust her stocking tops—but before he could beckon a blissful spasm he heard her weeping. He tried to shut it out; her sorrow spoiled his desire, and he doggedly staggered over the finish line like a runner who'd already spent his energy.

He wanted to comfort her. But his scenarios turned tawdry as his hands moved from petting her shoulder to fondling her breasts. He didn't dare console her. He couldn't trust himself. For one thing, he deliberately nursed his yen for her as an antidote to his sorrow, and, having done it well, it wouldn't be easy to hold back. She aroused an itch in him. Claire was a genteel aristocrat; she was a skinny blonde neurasthenic, high-strung and flighty. Sylvia was an earthy parvenu. Claire had class; Sylvia had sex appeal. Sylvia had married up, he thought, which was what he'd been trying to do and loathed himself for it. She'd succeeded but he hadn't, so he could condemn her while envying her triumph. Because she was unavailable, his passion seemed safely contained, only medicinal.

Did she know the torture he endured? She was a "touching" person, and he'd never been one, nor had anyone in his family. Her fingertips on his collar to adjust it seared the flesh on his nape. A lash caught in his eye, and Sylvia had him lay his head in her lap while she dabbed at it with a tissue, and he kept fibbing—"I can still feel it"—because her arm was across his forehead, her breasts brushed his cheek, and his head was pillowed by her spongy pudenda. He wanted to turn over and plunge his tongue into her crack. It horrified him to experience these sweeping spasms of desire because they seemed so tainted with irritation. His recent injury at the hands of a woman made him wary and half-angry with all of womankind even while he knew that to be irrational and unreasonable.

Sylvia stroked his arm, pat his shoulder, pinched his waist playfully. He never returned these jocular caresses; he was afraid to. He was also afraid that she'd think he was offended by this tactile Morse Code of affection. He was like a dog who longs to be petted but can't voice the desire and can only crudely approximate a human gesture—the forepaw wildly flagging the air, the dance around the feet of the master, the wagging tail. He hovered within her arm's reach in case the mood struck her to touch him. He presumed it was as natural and unconscious to her as breathing; she loved her husband.

He seethed with jealousy when she and a widow friend from church brought home traveling servicemen. They'd serve cookies and coffee, then they'd shove the dining table to the wall and fox-trot and jitterbug them across the floor. Sylvia's hands, her fingertips, flit from their forearms to their shoulders to their biceps to their chins.

No, not an overture to a symphony: only a lyric standing alone. One drunk flyboy dogged her into the kitchen and tried his luck, and he heard her declare, "Hey, Mister! We'll have none of **that**!" She always shut down her domestic canteen before midnight, and they'd drive them back to the station. He'd lie awake picturing her wheeling the big '38 Lincoln along the darkened streets with a half-drunk soldier melted into her flank while they merrily warbled their way back to war.

These soirees were reported to Mother Karacek, who invariably telephoned soon after, but Sylvia told her that she treated those boys the way she hoped someone would treat Georgie. One evening she returned from rehearsal with a Negro sergeant, his wife, and their infant. They'd been bumped off a train to make room for white passengers and were sitting exhausted on a park bench near where she rehearsed. They'd planned to spend the night there. She gave them her bedroom, and she slept on the chaise longue in her sewing salon.

She fed them before Robert got up and drove them to the station. As he was coming home from work, Mother K's new black Packard was wheeling away from the house. The tip of old Mrs. Malone's nose and fingers showed around the edge of her curtains. He asked Sylvia what had happened.

"Oh, I do feel a little sorry for her. Her whole world is coming apart at the seams and she's powerless to stop it. She did go on and on about having those Negroes here last night, and I let her blow off steam. She can say what she wants. The minute she turns her back I'll do what I damn well please!"

"That's the spirit!"

She chuckled. "The thing that irked her the most was hearing where they slept."

"I think you like to get her goat."

"Oh, I think I do, too!"

When Sylvia danced with those fellows, he ached with envy. Dancing had always been agonizing because he felt and looked clumsy, and at many a dance he'd sat sidelined while his date whirled gaily in the arms of somebody else. Taking lessons would permit his left palm to caress Sylvia's warm right one and his right hand to stroke the small of her back (maybe even lower!), to say nothing of bringing them breast to breast and loin to loin, and so, after working up his courage, he brought up her earlier offer to teach him—"not the samba or the rumba, though, because I can't even do a basic fox-trot, yet."

She was pleased, and he took a heavenly lesson in fitting his form to hers. "Oh, my goodness, Robert! Not so close! You'll squeeze the breath out of me! We're dance partners, not mating pythons!"

His fickle lust astonished him, but it did banish thoughts of Claire. He wondered if he weren't besotted because he was alone and far from home (even 4-F civilians could be lonely, though it wasn't socially acceptable), and his hormones were singing like drunken sailors in his blood. It disconcerted him, put him off-balance. He spent too much time thinking about *playing house* with her; he was the hobby-hubby, the surrogate spouse, the faux father. He yearned for his due in his mock marriage, though enacting and managing that seemed beyond hope. She was married and loved her husband, and he was no slick seducer. Self-conscious about his body, his meager experience consisted of visits to whorehouses with soused-up pals and two fretful, hurried bouts with Claire; one the night they declared their love, and the other the night she stuck the knife in his back.

What did he offer Sylvia? He spied her seated at her salon work table with her right cheek laid in her large palm, slumped into her dumps.

He stuck his head in the door. "He's all right, Sylvia, really. Everybody says the men don't have much time, and, besides, you yourself said he's not one for writing."

She sighed but didn't look at him. "Yes, that's true."

"Really. Don't worry. It's like my brother—he'd as soon eat a plate of horse manure as take up a pencil and paper!"

She twisted her head; a spaghetti of gray glimmered in her dark hair. She smiled like a patient who wants to be cooperative but whose heart isn't in it.

"Georgie's about as bad. But I did send a box and it'd be nice to know if he got it. I worry about him more than I'd worry about some men. Like you. I doubt I'd worry about you."

"Well, I thank you for that!"

She chuckled. "Oh, I mean that some men are so *capable* of taking care of themselves! It was a compliment. Georgie has trouble following instructions and he tends to go his own way, and I'm afraid they won't be very patient."

"The army's famous for getting all kinds of fellows to go along. Why don't you send him a letter with a bunch of questions such as 'Did you get my box?' and 'Do you miss me?' and a check-off slot for 'yes' and 'no' and 'maybe' and 'don't know?' and include a stamped envelope?"

She grinned. "That's very good, Robert. Now I see the value of a college education."

He hoed weeds, thinned onions and lettuce; without being asked, he refastened and painted loose porch boards. If climbing on a ladder was required, he gladly did it. He saw to it that the sleek Lincoln had its fluids checked and the tires inspected. He carried out the trash. If something needed taking up the stairs, he told Sylvia to leave it at the bottom. He competed against her precious Georgie, though he never knew what the husband's duties had been—whether because of modesty or privacy, she didn't reminisce much about their life together.

He brought small tributes of his appreciation—he traded a farm wife a gallon of gas for a pound of home-churned butter; he bought a box of cream-filled chocolates after he heard her tell a neighbor they were her favorites; he brought her *Life* and *Colliers* and *Ladies' Home Journal*; he brought her Pears soap and Woodbury bath powder. Once he was tempted to buy opal earrings he thought would suit her well, but the gift seemed too personal and expensive, so he bought an Xavier Cugat record for her and Georgie to dance to when he came home, since they were fond of Latin steps. She was touched.

One night they were in her upstairs salon and she was writing a letter. The radio was whispering some dreamy ballad. She'd moved it up there so that an unannounced visitor wouldn't find them being companionable in the parlor, he suspected. Seated at her table she was wearing black slacks and a white blouse and her hair was up in a red bandanna. Her bare soles—the toenails painted bright red—were propped on the lower rung of the chair. Her mother-in-law didn't like to see her in slacks, but he did.

"What do you tell Georgie in your letters?"

"Just about my days and nights."

"What do you tell him about me?"

She smiled. "Not much. I did tell him about the dancing lessons. I don't want to make him too jealous." A corner of her mouth curled up wickedly. "Only a little."

"Is he the jealous type?"

"Not really. Not like some I've known, believe me." She went on writing. "I have my ways of convincing him I'm a good girl," she said with a sly smile.

"How's that?"

"I remind him of things I do with only him."

When he didn't ask what, she said, "Of course, it's probably only the censors who get an eyeful of *that*!"

"I didn't know they censored that kind of thing."

"Well, if anything gets cut out, I know Georgie can mentally fill in the blanks, anyway."

"He's a lucky fellow."

She went to eight-thirty Mass Sunday. Late Sunday morning, still dressed in a suit and hat and gloves, she drove to Kountze to have "dinner" (the local term for the mid-day meal) with the "horrid" Karaceks. She always came back cross and tired, immediately changed into her robe and lay down in her dark bedroom for a while. She'd emerge groggy and say something such as, "My God! That woman! She drives me nuts! I wish the Japs would come shoot *her*!" She'd heat a can of Campbell's tomato soup and they'd listen to "The Shadow" and to Jack Benny and "The Army Hour." They'd turn the cups of their week upside down and let the dregs drip out.

Sunday night in bed always meant meditating and summing up for him. Like a child including everyone in his prayers, he reserved a slot for worrying about his brother Jimmy, scheduled to ship out. Did Jimmy worry? Since he wasn't a soldier, Robert didn't know. He wasn't a fiancé, either. Nor was he Sylvia's lover. What did he want? What did he hope for? He'd traveled far to get away from all he knew, and, predictably, it had made him homesick and lonely. He wished he had a Claire to write him like Sylvia and thousands of wives and sisters and sweethearts and mothers were writing their absent warriors. The songs spoke to them: "I'll Be Seeing You," "We'll Meet Again," "Saturday Night Is The Loneliest Night of the Week," and "He Wears a Pair of Silver Wings." He longed for an attractive woman to worry about his welfare, to yearn to have him at her side, to passionately dream of "doing those things that I will do only with him."

He decided that his interest in Sylvia just wasn't healthy. He needed to meet a girl, if not for a serious romance, then at least to dilute his obsession.

Did Sylvia know any unattached young women? They'd finished supper, and she was clearing the table. She aimed a peculiar frown at him.

"Why do you ask?"

She sounded so brusque. Maybe she believed that a 4-F fellow had no right to court and distract a home front girl who might be sending her absent guy her best thoughts and prayers.

"Why? Well, I'd like to ask somebody to the movies or to dinner."

"Are you afraid to be seen in public with me?"

The knife she scraped his plate with glinted in the light.

"Gosh, no! I presumed you were afraid to be seen with me! It's your reputation at stake. I have none to protect."

She sighed. "Yes. You're right. I don't want anybody to ring up that damn woman and start nasty rumors. Sorry." She set his plate in the sink with a *clank*. "To tell the truth, I'm jealous to think somebody has somebody to go to the movies or dinner with."

"That's natural."

She twisted a faucet, then a column of hot water blossomed into steam in the sink, and she bent over it. He wondered if his question had gotten lost.

"I was thinking that you might know someone *personally*."

"Hmm. Do I know someone?" She peered at the ceiling as if it were engraved with the faces of the homeliest, dullest females she knew. That she would begrudge him this small pleasure because her husband was gone irritated him.

"It's okay. Never mind. A girl at the office is pretty friendly to me. I haven't heard her mention a fellow. Maybe she's willing."

"What's her name? I might know her."

"Marjorie Sinclair."

"Marjorie Sinclair! I certainly do know *her*! I'm afraid her parents are very particular about the company she keeps. I know her mother from the canteen."

His face felt flushed. "What's wrong with me that a parent might object to?"

"Oh, you're an Easterner, a newcomer. Yankee. Those for a start."

"Couldn't you vouch for me?"

"My word wouldn't mean much. I'm under a cloud of suspicion myself."

"Really? Why is that?"

"Georgie's mother poisoned the well when she saw he was interested in me. I heard she's told people I traveled with a carnival or that I was running from the law, nonsense like that. She went all out to discredit me. I honestly don't think she can believe that any healthy, grown woman would take an interest in Georgie. She's told everyone in town that I'm a gold-digger. I don't want their damn money!"

He was dogged about his point. "So you think Marjorie's mother believes that and would hold it against *me*?"

"Something like that, yes."

"Why don't we try before we presume rejection?"

"You want to ask Marjorie Sinclair out you can do it without my help!"

Her fist held a long wooden spoon and when the heel whacked the counter the brown shaft shot up rigid with a quivering orb on the end. The outburst surprised him.

Sylvia washed two glasses, rinsed and set them in the drainer, then she twisted her torso, showing him her curvaceous bosom, and raised the apron hem to wipe her hands.

"I'm sorry. I didn't mean to be sharp with you. Why don't I sleep on it and I'll bet I can think of someone." Her smile was patronizing, and he turned sulky.

He shrugged. "Okay." He'd still ask Marjorie.

He had weeding to do before the twilight gloom grew too thick, and as he stood to push his chair into the table, she said, "I'm sorry my company's not enough for you."

"Your company is *very* sufficient for me, Sylvia!"

"I understand—of *course* you need your own friends here! I should've volunteered to find someone already—it was very selfish of me not to think of it before you had to ask."

"It *worries* me that your company is so sufficient for me," he blurted out, afraid he was saying too much but determined to prevent her from feeling that he was deserting her from a *lack* of interest. "That's all. I don't think it's a healthy thing for your company to be so, so *sufficient*, like I said."

"I *do* know what you mean, Robert." Her hair swished and skirted her soft olive nape as she turned her head; her calves flexed as she rose on her toes to water a potted African violet in the window. "I've had the same thoughts myself."

He had to bolt the room he was so frightened—had they just confessed to a mutual interest? He shouldn't presume: "same thoughts" might mean she'd noticed his infatuation and agreed that *his* interest in *her* was unhealthy.

Once outside, he wished he'd had the courage to ask for clarification, though he didn't know where it would lead them if she'd meant she'd developed "unhealthy" feelings, too.

The next morning, he intercepted Marjorie in the hall. She was a short, full-fleshed blonde with a pug nose, bow lips, and a cutely winning smile. She was fun to yak with and her bosom was appealingly apparent beneath almost anything she wore.

"Uh, hey, Marjorie, I've been wondering if you'd like to go out to dinner and the movies with me Saturday night."

"What's playing?"

"I don't know. I haven't looked. You going to turn me down if Robert Taylor's not in it?"

"Nope, you dope! Just curious. Can my kid sister come, too?"

"Uh, yeah, sure."

She stiff-armed him on the shoulder and knocked him against the wall. "You moron! I'm not bringing my baby sister, for crying out loud! I don't even have one! Boy, did I get you going!"

"Do you need to check with your mother?"

"Are you nuts? I'm twenty-one years old!"

Marjorie's ready assent and her indifference to parental permission suggested Sylvia was too suspicious of the local opinion. He wanted to tell Sylvia before the grapevine did, but this was delicate. He needed to couch this report so that she didn't feel foolish.

"I have good news for you." In the twilight he was thinning onions while Sylvia worked two rows over on the okra plants that had just borne their first pods.

"What's that?"

"Not everyone in town listens to Georgie's mother. Marjorie agreed to go out with me. I guess her mother's opinion of you is better than you think."

Rustle of her skirt as she worked from one plant to the next; cicadas in the trees ratcheting away; a dog barking a few doors down, a child yelling somewhere. He couldn't tell if she were storing this information away with serene equanimity or brewing a witch's potion.

"When are you going out?"

He fine-tuned his ear for her inflection, heard a faint undertone of resentment.

"Saturday."

"I won't bother making a meal for us in that case."

"Oh, sure! That's why I'm telling you now."

Snip, snip, snip—the okra pods tumbled from the stalk as her scissors went up it.

"Where do you plan to take her?"

"Thanks to your good cooking, I don't know much about the cafés here. Could you recommend one?"

"I suppose you want it quiet and cozy and romantic."

"Oh no! Bustling and crowded and cheerful's what I had in mind."

She chuckled—with relief, he thought. "They'll all be crowded, believe me! Let me think about it."

They worked in silence.

"Does Marjorie still live with her parents?" she asked.

"I don't know."

"What movie will you see?"

"I guess that Bob Hope picture with Dorothy Lamour—*Road to Morocco*—if it's still playing."

"Did you remember our troupe is performing in the park Saturday night for the war bond rally?"

"Oh! Thanks for reminding me! That'll be perfect. What time?"

"Around eight."

"Fine, then we'll plan to eat before."

After a pause, she said, "If you wouldn't mind telling me, I'd like to know if she's still living at home."

"Sure."

Another row, more seedlings plucked, more stalks gelded by her scissors, then Sylvia said, "You know, I never brought it up because it never occurred to me, but we never discussed your having guests in your room."

"No we haven't."

"I never brought it up because—well, you remember I'd presumed you'd be older? And I never imagined you might want to date a girl such as Marjorie."

He wondered what "such as" meant but kept his mouth shut. She stepped outside the upturned turf with the air of someone lifting her boots from the muck of a stable and posted herself on the grass with her fists on her hips.

"I'm afraid I'll have to ask you to refrain from entertaining girls in your room, Robert, because—"

"Oh sure," he said easily.

"—Because with Mrs. Malone on one side over *here*—" she waved, broadly, even wildly, to the west—"and the Dickensons over *there*—" jabbing a finger twice in the air—"and God knows any Tom Dick or Harry strolling down the alley could look up and see you carrying on, and I—"

"Oh no, fine, that's fine. I don't intend to bring—"

"—I do not want anyone carrying tales to Georgie's mother even hinting of any impropriety here in this house! God knows—"

"I have no intention of bringing Marjorie—"

"—I've had trouble enough with that woman without some boarder of mine doing God knows *what* with a girl like *that* up in his room!"

Their raised voices bounced off the garage when they stopped abruptly. You'd have thought he'd already turned his room into a notorious brothel stocked with tramps for a clientele of drunken soldiers and shipyard workers. He was perplexed—hadn't she claimed she didn't give a damn about Mother K's opinion?

"I wasn't aware until now," he said, slowly and quietly, " that there might be objections to Marjorie's character, Sylvia. Our discussions about her had to do with the cloud of doubt hanging over *our* heads. I'm a stranger here. If you felt that by going out with her I would stain your reputation I wish you'd have told me sooner." The evening light had died into a violet dusk that made it hard to discern her features. "Is there something I ought to know?"

"Oh, I'm such a horrible *bitch*!" She whirled on her heels and walked toward the house. "She's fine! Sorry!" she called out. She strode faster and faster then broke into a run up the back stairs, hoping, he thought, to get through the door before bursting into tears.

SIX

From her darkened bedroom, Sylvia peered through the blinds as Robert worked the garden in the twilight. He'd rolled his sleeves up. His arms were tan and sinewy, and she knew without looking that his hands were large and sturdy, fingers strong enough to tighten a bolt. He didn't mind getting them dirty. She had thoughts about them she didn't like but couldn't easily put out of her head.

Upstairs she sat at her table with a gold-nibbed Parker she'd discovered in a drawer and a piece of stationery embossed with "Sylvia Karacek" in gold; the cream-colored paper was thick as parchment and scented.

Dear Dot,

Well, yours truly's in the dumps today. My guy's been gone six weeks now, though it seems like forever. He doesn't write much, but I guess they don't give them much time, you think? I'm still having knock-down drag-outs with his mother about nearly everything under the sun, and I think I told you about what H____ she raised about getting another boarder? She's about over that, though, because I pointed out a half-dozen repairs he'd made to the house and that pretty much shut her up. Georgie's the world's sweetest man, but he's not the type to pick up a tool and use it. He does okay if you stand over him, ha ha ha, but he likes to gab too much to stick to anything. And now that my boarder's paying rent I don't have to ask her for anything, and, believe me, she and I both like it that way. I could tell you tales about marrying money, hon! I know you must think I'm just rolling in it and eating bon-bons all day and ordering servants to fetch my coffee, but, believe you me, it's just not that way. Georgie has to beg for every scrap from Evelyn, and it galls me no end. It's like taking out a bank loan every month for her to give him the part of the trust that's legally his to begin with.

But I don't want to be crying in my beer. I can hear you laughing anytime I catch myself sounding like I'm having hard times.

But I am lonely, dammit! It's not fair I turned out to be the one stuck here and he went to California when I was on my way there when I got stranded here! Yeah, I know—he'll be shipping out to God knows where (probably in the Pacific), and I'll be safe and sound, so I shouldn't complain. This house is beautiful and I love living in it and I love shopping in stores where the family's known and people treat me with respect. But I am lonely. (I said that already.) I worry sometimes about what lonely women are tempted to do. I know you hear about it all the time and read it in magazines.

So—here's what I'm thinking. My boarder is staying in Georgie's old room now, but we have an apartment over the garage that hasn't been used in years. You told me that Mary Kay is a handful for you these days because you have to work nights then days at the bomber plant, and she's on her own too much and you're both having to live in that tiny trailer? Well, I'm thinking of moving my boarder, Robert, out to the garage apartment, and then Mary Kay could come and take Georgie's old room or his sister's, which is across the hall and is just sitting empty. It has some nice white wicker furniture, too, that I know a girl like Mary Kay would appreciate. It would be wonderful to have her around—she's my godchild, after all—and it would give the two of you a breather from all your fighting. If you wanted to pitch in a little each month for her board, that'd be swell, but you don't have to.

Are you still seeing that guy Clyde? It's nice to have a regular man, isn't it? When Georgie was here, I came to depend on him just to listen to me whine, and he was always thinking of ways to please me. He's the world's sweetest man, and I love him to pieces. I started going back to Mass and confession since he joined up, to get some Heavenly insurance I guess you could say. I worry about him all the time already, and he's not even out of basic training yet!

Call me collect any time and tell me what you think about my plan!

Love,

Syl

SEVEN

THE "MARJORIE REPORT" CAME REGULAR as the war news from Sylvia. Robert learned: 1) Brother Bud was an infantryman, and her mother said Marjorie should write him more; 2) After graduation Marjorie went to business school in Dallas but flunked out; 3) Marjorie spent too much on clothing and records; 4) Yes, she still lived at home but wasn't as much help around the house as she should be, especially now that her mother was bookkeeping at a sawmill; 5) Her father gave her an Elgin wristwatch with a 24k gold case for her twenty-first birthday, and she lost it within days.

He said, "Oh?" or "Huh!" It seemed a marvel—Marjorie's mother, so recently among Sylvia's detractors, was now her bosom buddy. If these conversations were inspired by their date, what was Sylvia saying about him? He wouldn't ask. By now he knew the cost of this date would exceed the pleasure gained, unless Marjorie proved eager to teach him the *Kama Sutra* in a single night.

Working Saturday morning spared him from hearing, say, that Marjorie had contracted syphilis. When he got home at two, Sylvia and a comely fellow trouper were upstairs working on costumes in a cloud of Old Gold smoke. The radio blared (was this irony?) "Got a Date With an Angel" when he looked in. Sylvia's pal, a pretty redhead with long slim legs and no wedding ring (why hadn't Sylvia suggested her?), was miming a soft-shoe while Sylvia circled her, pins pinched between her lips, checking the fit of the fetching blue tap pants and a rhinestone-spangled red jacket.

"Hello!" he yelled. He waved a salute.

"Robert! Stay out of the bathroom!"

"I'm not in it!"

The redhead smiled. He winked at her.

"Hi! I'm Robert." He stepped forward, but Sylvia jockeyed between them.

"We're busy."

When the pal left at four, he found Sylvia at the piano studying her musical score.

"Okay to use the bathroom now?"

"What? What time is it?" She glanced at the grandfather clock. "Oh my God!" She riffled pages of the score.

"I'll only be a minute." He started to go; she bolted up, spilling leaves of the music onto the floor, and he helped retrieve them.

"Don't use it long!"

He handed her loose sheets. "You've been rehearsing a lot and you're really talented, Sylvia. I know the show'll be super."

"Oh I hope so! I'm so nervous I could *explode*!"

"Sit down." He pulled her to the easy chair. "Breathe slow and deep—"

Her bosom rose and fell, rose, rose, and fell. With his palm to her forehead, he pushed her back into the cushion.

"Close your eyes and breathe slow-ly and deep-ly. Ten times."

Standing by the hassock, he counted aloud and dragged the pace. He tried not to watch her lovely breasts swell and sink for a few counts then decided what the hell. After "ten" she said, calmly, eyes still closed, "You're very smart, Robert. Thank you. I'm not normally so in a tizzy about being onstage, but it's been awhile."

"You're welcome." He waited a beat. "Who's your friend?"

Her eyes shot open. "My gosh! I can't have a friend over without your ogling her?"

"Never mind. Since she was with you I thought her character would be beyond reproach, anyway. I'm trying to please you."

She sighed. She closed her eyes and inhaled again. "Aren't you sorry you ever laid eyes on me now?"

"No."

She smiled. "Betty's a grammar school teacher. She told me you were devilish handsome. She also said you looked like the kind of guy who can't be trusted." She opened one eye and cocked it at him. "She has a fiancé overseas. '*He wearrs a paiirr of sill-ver wings,*'" she sang.

"Just his luck."

"Poor Robert."

"So you do feel sorry for me?"

"Yes. And I know I've been on a toot about Marjorie. Please don't let me discourage you. She's really a ... a good old-fashioned girl at heart."

"I don't plan to marry her. Or anybody."

She was silent for moment. "That's how it starts. You hear people say, 'Oh, I saw her across the room and knew in my heart she'd be the one!' But that's not true for ninety-nine out of a hundred. It's about as true that people say, 'I'd never marry her in a million years!' And then they're standing at the altar."

"I'm not completely green at this. I was engaged once."

"Don't tell me you saw her across a room!"

"No. She got prettier each time we met at the water cooler."

"Aha! What happened, if you don't mind my asking."

He endured an explosion of images like a speeded-up montage—Claire on her horse, Claire chewing on a lipsticked soda straw, Claire toying with the hairs on his nape. His stomach lurched; he swallowed.

"Oh, people change."

"Excuse me for prying." She clapped her palms over the knees of the chair. "I'd better eat before I get sick. You don't want to eat too much and you don't want to eat too little before a show."

She put out her hand for him to tug her upright, and he did. Then, standing, she smiled warmly. "I feel better. I always feel better after I've talked to you."

"The feeling's mutual."

He bathed, shaved, Ipana-ed and Brylcreem-ed. His date was at six, and he planned to use the company car and not log his Saturday overtime as recompense. At five-forty-five he was crossing the foyer when Sylvia called out, "Robert? Could you help me?"

He'd been in her bedroom only once, to fetch a scarf from her bed. He'd gotten a quick impression of enticing scents, glittering vials, heavy walnut chests and a four-poster bed, clothing piled on chairs, underthings spilling wantonly from drawer mouths.

"Yes?" he said at the threshold. The room was zebra-striped by the half-closed Venetian blinds. A peculiar chemical smell wafted to his nose. She was standing on a straight-back chair wearing a Carmen Miranda outfit—a wide, pleated black skirt decorated with red and yellow rickrack and a hem that struck her knees. Her white peasant off-the-shoulder blouse had ruffles and enough elastic for a Jeep tire.

"You like my costume?" She rotated on the chair to swirl the skirt. "It's for my Latin number."

"Nice."

"This stuff—" She held up a bottle. "We're painting our legs instead of ruining good nylons. See?"

She drew the hem upward and gave her glistening legs a frowning scrutiny, turning one this way and that. "It works pretty well. From a distance you can't tell it from real stockings."

"It would fool me."

"I need help with the seam."

She bent to hand him an eyebrow pencil. "Just draw a line up the back of my legs like a stocking seam."

She turned so her calves faced him. Her curvy rear bobbed at his eye-level. His heart pounded.

"Can you do it with me up here? I'd lie on the bed but like the song says, 'It decants on your pants.'"

"No, this will be okay, I think." His hand was trembling. "Are you sure you want me to do this? I'm … I'm not much of a draftsman."

"My stocking seams are never straight, anyway."

"How far up do you want it?"

"I'm doing something like a can-can, but not as racy. Go as far as I did with the paint."

She lifted the hem to show where she'd stopped. Above that, in the dark recess, the snug arcs of white briefs. It was hot and sweat prickled his hairline.

"Okay," he croaked. "Here goes."

He touched the pencil tip to her skin above the heel of her pump, then slowly drew a squiggly line. Her skin twitched like horseflesh tickled by flies.

"I'm not very steady."

"Don't worry."

He cupped his free palm around her shin to anchor her leg and his drawing hand; he put the point to her skin and moved it up to the back of her knee. His knuckles brushed her skin. She shuddered and flinched, giggled.

"That tickles!"

His hands crept slowly up from her knee and under the skirt until he couldn't stand it and pulled them away just before he reached where she'd stopped painting. He was afraid the sweat on his hand would smear the paint; he was afraid that if he went another centimeter he'd start babbling and licking her thighs. He was stiff as a porch post.

"Okay for," he said, clearing his throat, "that one."

She peered over her shoulder and ninety-degreed her calf to inspect it. "Oh, that's good!"

He swallowed, took a deep breath, tried to will his senses numb, and made a quicker job of the second leg, clenching his jaw, taking pride in the workmanship, the clean Zen-master stroke up her calf and knee and thigh, flicking lightly with the pencil at the top to make her shiver again and say, "That tickles, too!"

"Done."

"Wonderful!" She whirled and fanned his face with the wide skirt hem, then beamed down at him. He had no idea what was next. She had him in a trance. She spaded both hands before his eyes red nails up, waggled them, impatiently, and he finally understood she wanted him to help her down. He started to take her hands but she set her palms flat on his shoulders and so his hands went automatically to her waist; she crouched to jump, he lifted—

"Alley-ooop!" She leaped daintily in the air. When she landed, she stumbled and lurched into him, laughed, bussed him wetly on the cheek.

"Thanks, Robert! You're a brick!" Her breath was sour-sweet with wine. She fidgeted with the waistband of her skirt.

"Well, break a leg."

She gave him a twisted grin. "Have a good time with Marjorie."

In his idling car he breathed slow-ly and deep-ly to the count of ten to make his swelling go down. It would be hard to keep his mind on Marjorie. He wondered if Sylvia knew. He bet she could've gotten Betty to draw those lines before they went on. What if he went inside and told her how he felt? *Oh Robert, I've been having those same feelings!*

And then?

He'd launched this effort to get his mind off Sylvia, but when he pushed one way he got tugged from the other. Ring-around-the-rosy: to forget Claire, he let his itch for Sylvia go unchecked; to squelch that, he was going out with Marjorie. He told himself he was probably confusing his lust with Sylvia's intentions—just because he wanted her didn't mean that she'd caused it or welcomed it. Maybe he needed a cold bath and a flogging with wet weeds.

EIGHT

MINUTES LATER, HE WAS SEATED in Marjorie's living room waiting for her to appear. Marjorie's mother set a plate of cookies on the coffee table arranged in a V. "They're made with molasses, a Fanny Farmer recipe, and Marjorie just baked them to send a box off to Bud." Robert was caught between robbing the heroic Bud of one more homemade cookie and refusing mother's hospitality (and a sample of her daughter's homemaking skills), so he took the cookie.

To his relief and her credit, she didn't ask why he wasn't in uniform. She seemed more interested in Georgie. How often did he write home? What did he say of his experiences? (It dawned on him later that she could've questioned Sylvia, given their alleged intimacy.) He hedged and said that he wasn't sure how often Georgie wrote.

"You could've knocked me over with a feather when that boy up and joined. Earl says it might make a man out of him."

If it doesn't kill him first. "They say it does that."

"He always was a strange bird. High-spirited as all get out, but now and then he'd do something peculiar and folks would scratch their heads. Boy was prone to fits, too."

"Is that right? Mrs. Karacek doesn't talk about him much except to say she misses him."

"Well, sure she does! He always was the *sweetest* boy, and he sometimes looked so forlorn it'd break your heart! If you see his mother, please tell her I'm prayin' for him just like my Bud."

"How could he join? I mean, with the fits and such?"

"I'd say he didn't tell them. They say Miz Karacek was about to go raise Cain with Congressman Martin but he talked her out of it." She gave him a prim smile. "That's the mother, not the wife. That's who we call Miz Karacek. Sylvia, I'd say, was all for his going."

"Sylvia is worried sick about him, too, Mrs. Sinclair."

"Of course she is! I meant she was all for his doing what made him happy." In case he thought she was a liar, she added, "Of course. That's what I meant.

"Oh, *there* she is!" tah-dahed Mother. Marjorie now leaned one shoulder on the kitchen door frame, languidly cudding her gum. With her fingertips she dabbed timidly at a white flower fixed to her hair as if it were a recent injury.

She yawned. "Georgie Karacek's a fruitcake, Mom."

She had donned a cotton shirtwaist dress, white with small red roses like cat's paws dipped in blood; it also had that shorter, save-material hem ordered by the War Production Board, and her pink knees were cutely dimpled. She looked sunshine-fresh, a flower with a flower.

At the Magnolia Hotel's White Blossom Room they lined up to be seated. Their frazzled duration waitress was a chubby teen whose prior training was probably serving tea to her dolls. The sugar bowl on the table was empty except for a slip of paper saying "Sorry!" The girl handed only Robert a menu, the size of a *Life* magazine, but Marjorie balked at the antiquated chivalric custom and demanded her own.

"Holy cow!" said Robert. "What's 'Nigger Chicken?'"

"Just plain ol' fried chicken," Marjorie replied blandly.

"So why don't they just call it that?"

"Gosh, beats me. It's pretty good, though."

"Does it come with Klan-fried potatoes?"

Marjorie cocked her head at him. "Don't be a wisenheimer. I dunno about back East, but our colored folk love us and we love them."

"If you say so."

"That woman Georgie married used to work here."

No wonder Ferret Face was in an uproar. That explained Sylvia's touchiness about "propriety."

"Was she a waitress?"

"Lord no. Too uppity. Hostess. You'd think she was, uh, you know, that famous hostess—"

"Pearl Mesta?"

"Huh?"

"Never mind."

They went on. Over the meal, they chatted, and he asked how she liked her work. She said, "Ma'd have me doing all the housework if I stayed at home. I sure like having my own money and buying my clothes!" But when she got hitched, she'd quit—"The man I marry won't want me to work."

"You have someone picked out?"

"Hell no. I'm writing three fellas overseas, but I'm not 'khaki-wacky' no matter what Ma says! There's just too many stories. You know what happened to this friend of mine? She met this boy in flying school in San Antonio and she got all worked up about becoming an officer's wife and they got married, but then he flunked out of flying school and got, what?, demoted I guess, and they sent him out to Utah to work on the engines—he's a mechanic!—and she had to go live in the desert and him nothing but a corporal." Marjorie shuddered. "And this other girl I know, she has this friend who was engaged to a fellow then when he got shipped out she didn't hear from him for a long time, but then he wrote to her from a hospital and told her he'd been wounded. He said he wanted her to come visit, so of course she did, and when she got there she found out what he hadn't told her yet."

A spark of glee played behind her grey eyes, relishing the suspense. "You know what it was?"

"He was a German spy?"

"Shut up. No. He didn't have the heart to tell her he'd had his arms and legs shot off."

"How'd he write that letter?"

"Don't get technical! You know, a nurse or something."

"Didn't the girl realize it wasn't his handwriting?"

"Oh, you're being a moron just to spoil the story!" She reached to swat his head with her menu. "Anyway, how'd you like that?"

"I wouldn't." An ugly thought popped to mind. One thing he hated about being jilted was having to learn how small he could be.

"You know what's strange? Ma doesn't want me to go with soldiers, but her son's one! I tell her think about poor Bud in a strange place and not knowing any nice girls or families—wouldn't she want somebody to bring him home for a Sunday dinner? And she says, 'Yes, but that's Bud.' And I say, 'They're all somebody's Bud, Mom.'"

"That's astute of you."

"I hate hypocrites. Don't you?"

"I dunno. Some of my best friends are hypocrites."

She chuckled. He was relaxed, full of good cheer partly because he was fairly sure they wouldn't date again, though he wished her well. This was a diversion. He hadn't forgotten what happened in Sylvia's bedroom. For Marjorie this only meant a night out, a free dinner, a companion at least as interesting as the half-read magazine to which she might otherwise be condemned.

When they left the hotel, Marjorie said, "You gotta hold my hand."

"Nothing would please me more, but why do I gotta?"

"In case mother sees us. Or one of her friends."

"Why—"

"Figure it out, dummy!" She slugged his bicep with her knuckle, no doubt something learned from Bud. The jolt shook the flower from its bobby-pin anchor, and she fussed with it as they went along.

"You want her to think I like you."

"Bingo!"

"I do like you—I asked you out, didn't I?"

"Oh, she's in a big hurry."

He took her hand and they strolled past the courthouse that commanded the square with its pigeon-peppered monument of General Lee on a horse, saber upraised, Marjorie swinging their arms in a big pendulum arc. During their dinner, the sky had lowered, and a cloud ceiling looked faintly orange as it reflected the city lights. The already humid Gulf air was closer, stickier. Traffic streamed by in the dusky streets, and headlights caught their faces as if in a photographer's flash.

"A hurry? To—"

"To get me out of her hair. And not hitched to a soldier. You ever listen to 'Amanda of Honeymoon Hill?' It's Ma's favorite soap opera. It's about a girl from the wrong side of the tracks who marries into an aristocratic Southern family."

"She's really off-base if she thinks my family is either Southern or aristocratic."

"Don't worry. I've got no plans for you."

"That's good. I'm ... well, I guess you could say I'm spoken for."

"Oh yeah? A girl back East? That figures." She flung away his hand. "You lousy two-timer!"

She swung her head to see his face and cackled, "Had you going again! God, what a chump!"

He sidled over, bumped her hip, slid his arm around her warm waist and tugged her close. "If you see your mother, let me know and I'll give you a great big sloppy kiss. You know, just for the show."

"Very funny. Don't get fresh."

She slipped her arm around his waist. Feeling her hip brush his as they walked made him appreciate the wisdom of his original goal. She tried to teach him to skip like Dorothy on the Yellow Brick Road, but it was too much like a dance step for him.

Along the street bordering the park, soldiers from nearby camps had parked an armored car, two Jeeps, and a display of captured Japanese small arms. They'd set up a .50 caliber machine gun in a sandbag emplacement. A crowd of boys and men huddled around a three-striper who worked them like a car salesman—putting them one by one behind the machine gun as if for a trial spin.

They ambled companionably into the park. The air smelled of popcorn and cigars and the raw sizing from the big green canvas tent behind the gazebo. On the lawn milling about in a merry hubbub of murmurs and laugher were native Port Farview-ites and visitors from nearby villages, oil roustabouts and roughnecks, shipyard workers, farm families in patched clothing; many had blankets and wicker picnic baskets, and several roving concessionaires hawked soda or ice cream, peanuts, and popcorn.

They eased along the back where Negro families had quietly taken up unobtrusive places on the lawn, swivel-hipped through the crowd and then down to the front. Marjorie said, "Find me something to sit on, Mister—I don't want grass stains on this dress!"

He took off his ancient seersucker blazer and laid it lining-side down on the grass.

"Aww! You're so sweet!" She plopped down cross-legged, and the soft nubs of her knees poked out from the hem. She smoothed out a sleeve for him to sit on.

"Gimme a coffin nail, won't you?"

"Sorry." He pat his shirt pockets. "I quit for the duration."

"That's patriotic. I admire that."

"The good ones are too hard to come by. Don't you know there's a war on?"

"Go bum one."

"Does your mother know you smoke in public?"

"Uh-uh! She'd wring my neck!"

"Aren't you afraid she'll see you?"

"Naw, heck, she's still at home."

"But what about holding my–"

"Gee, you really are a dope!" She grinned. "How'd you get through college?"

"Cheated."

"You—? You're a liar."

"Had you going, didn't I?"

"Ha double Ha."

Then folks toting horns and drums and violins came ducking through the flap to the green tent and inspired applause and whistles from the crowd. They took seats in chairs below the gazebo's stage; they were followed by the rotund mayor, who told borrowed jokes about Lana Turner's sweater and Bob Hope's nose. Then a Baptist preacher who looked twelve asked them to pray for all the boys in the service; a matron in an old hat big as a pterodactyl aria-ed "God Bless America" in her best Kate Smith imitation and, dripping with sweat from her brow and chin, moved them to join her lustily. Marjorie had a vigorous soprano with unerring pitch, and she wasn't afraid to exercise it.

Various civic leaders pitched Defense Stamps and War Bonds, then a Boy Scout leader asked for volunteers for a scrap drive, and a head nurse pleaded for blood donations. Then a flyboy came forward to a tremendous standing ovation—a hometown favorite, said Marjorie, he'd played football at A&M—and told the crowd how much their letters meant, and with everyone's support with War Bonds "we'll whip the Japs by the end of the year!"

Business concluded, a barbershop quartet (with a female tenor wearing a false moustache) gave them Gay '90s nostalgia ("Down By the Old Mill Stream"); an ensemble that included an accordion and a wash-tub bass sang "Let's Find a Feller Who Is Yeller and Beat Him Red, White, and Blue" (to which he cringed), and they segued pal Betty's appearance in the blue tap pants and spangled red jacket to do a soft shoe with them. He thought her legs bore stocking paint, too, and he wondered what lucky soul had drawn lines on hers.

Sylvia's full troupe then followed—an old fellow dressed in a bowler hat and a green checked suit told ancient vaudeville jokes. And in the comedy skit that parodied an old silent movie melodrama (*I can't pay the rent! But you must pay the rent, etc.*), the vaudevillian-now-villain got the pie in his face, thrown by Betty as the mother of the damsel in distress.

Then Sylvia came forth to do her "South of the Border" number, and, while he wasn't surprised by the quality of her singing, her poise onstage and her pleasure in performing were new to him, and it struck him how much she was in absolute possession of, and was master over, her body, like a dancer. Her fake stocking seams looked straight. He almost mentioned it to Marjorie.

They stopped at a table to sign up for a bond, then followed the crowd away from the park. They walked past Pinkham Hardware with its blackened windows and one light burning over the cash register, past the old livery stable the United Daughters of the Confederacy had turned into a museum, then they continued on the brick sidewalk under oaks whose leaves left tattered shadows from the street lamps at their feet. The air had grown still and something like artillery rumbled far in the distance. He hoped it would rain. A wet trickle down his ribcage itched, and his shirt collar was soggy against his nape.

He absently hummed "South of the Border."

"You ever been to Mexico?" Marjorie asked.

"Nope."

"Bud and his friends went down to Nuevo Laredo. I heard they went to whorehouses, but he wouldn't admit it."

"You want to go?"

"To a *whorehouse*?"

"No, no. Mexico!"

"You couldn't pay me! I bet you'd like to go."

"Why do you say that? I'm a nice young fellow, haven't you heard?"

"Oh, yeah. Besides, you've got your own spicy señorita, right?" Marjorie broke loose and held her hands overhead to imitate playing castanets, singing, "I met a pretty señyor-ee-ta down Mexico waaay. ."

"That what you call yourself? The Spicy Señorita?"

"No, not me, dummy! Georgie's wife."

"Hey, don't even make jokes like that, Marjorie. People love to gossip and next thing you know they're all sure something's true that's not."

"Okay, don't get so excited."

"Sorry. It's just that she's married, and she's concerned about what people say."

"Okay. But it's only natural that people talk."

"That doesn't make it *right.*"

"I meant only natural considering," Marjorie insisted.

"Considering what?"

"Well, there's how they met, for instance."

"How did they meet?"

"She was living in the hotel, it was just last fall, but got kicked out for palm reading fortunes in her room and what not so then she started doing it out at the Bide-A-Wee tourist courts and Bud told me him and a bunch of his pals got drunk and went out there on a lark one night and had their palms read ha ha ha. And that's how she met Georgie, too."

"Palms read ha ha ha?" Her snide suggestion annoyed him. But he couldn't resist pressing her for more. And hated himself for it.

"Yeah, you know."

"Spell it out."

"Use your noodle, for God's sake."

He decided to ignore the nasty innuendo. "Well, palm reading—so what. That's harmless."

"Are you a moron? Three weeks later they were married and then she kicked old Mizzus Karacek and Marianne out of the house that they'd been living in for forty years and then zip! Georgie was off to the army. You think stuff like that doesn't make people talk?"

"Maybe she saw in his palm that he needed her. Maybe Mrs. Karacek would rather live with her daughter while he's away. I hear Elizabeth's pregnant and is having a hard time."

Marjorie rolled her eyes. "Maybe she looked in his face and saw a sucker."

"Oh, come on, Marjorie! You just don't know her. She's a very … honorable woman, and you can tell people I said so."

"Okay." She smirked. "I'll say you said so."

The car was parked down the way at the curb, and he realized he had no plans for the rest of their date. He wondered what she expected.

"I guess the same people talk about me, too?"

Marjorie shrugged. "Sure."

"What do they say?"

"Just the usual." She skipped beside him, smirking—torturing him was fun.

"What's the usual? I'm not used to hearing Southern housewives gossip."

She laughed outright. "You're a spy. You're a Jew. You're a rich man. You're a swell. You're hiding from the law. You're her lover. You're a fairy. You've got a wife and children back East. You're 4-F because you're mental. And, oh yeah, you're an old boyfriend who's come to help her pick the whole lot of Karaceks clean."

"Boy, that's inventive! These people ought to write fiction. I won't say anything about any of that crapola except this—I swear on the Bible I never laid eyes on that woman before I came here to take this job and that *nothing* has happened between us that I couldn't describe in public." *He assisted his landlady, Mrs. Georgie Karacek, in preparing her costume for this evening's performance.*

She took his hand. "Swell."

Had only jealousy inspired this? Even so, it revealed the Port Farview collective mind, and the information about Sylvia surprised him. Where and why had she learned palm reading? He could see why such a person might inspire speculation in a small town. Also that gossip's true poison lay in its contagion—now they had *him* wondering.

He was so annoyed he wanted to get away from Marjorie. A lady wouldn't have told him what gossips said. A cold bath was more appealing than anything likely to happen between Marjorie and him now.

But once he had the car headed toward her house, Marjorie said, "I can't go in this early. My Ma will think something went wrong and I don't wanna listen to her hound me all night. You got any hootch?"

"Not in the company car."

"Let's go to Jigtown—we can buy a bottle pretty cheap."

"Your mother won't hound you if you come in smelling like a distillery?"

"I'm free, white, and twenty-one, Mister. I'll have a drink if I feel like it. And she'll just think we had a good time."

"Considering my unsavory reputation, I hope she doesn't think we had *too good* a time!"

"Don't worry—you won't. So she won't. Wish this car had a radio! I know, let's sing!" She broke into "Don't Sit Under the Apple Tree With Anyone Else But Me," and insisted he join in, so he did.

NINE

MARJORIE NAVIGATED HIM PAST the ancient wooden colored high school and to the outskirts of town where a refinery loomed out of the dark horizon backlit by flaming torches and coils of gassy-smelling steam bumping against the cloud ceiling, out farther until they thumped off the pavement and onto a sandy uncurbed road. They passed a sawmill where, even on a Saturday night, a saw screamed as it burrowed its furious head into a stubborn knot. Any corner you turned in this nation day or night you found yourself at a vortex of commercial energy.

"There's where Mom works now."

They cruised on in a cocoon of headlamp light; the loblolly forest leaned in upon them, but now and then a tarpaper shack with lighted windows heaved out of the gloom, with auto hulks propped on stumps glowing like metallic jack-o'-lanterns. Negroes strolled beside the lane, the men in jaunty hats and pastel-colored shirts with sweat patches under their arms and the women in shiny dresses walking barefoot in the sandy berm and carrying their shoes. Over the trees bony lightning flickered. The moon was swallowed by clouds.

They reached a roadhouse, doors and windows open, pumping out light and music and laughter like an anchored calliope. A parrot outlined in blue neon hung over the door. On a sandy parking lot cars shared space with a brace of patient mules harnessed to a wagon. Patrons stood by the door passing a bottle, their cigarettes winking orange. As his engine died, a shrill guitar riff sailed into the clouds.

"Go around to the kitchen door and ask for Sam."

"What do you want?"

"Whatever they're selling. It differs."

This seemed like a lot of trouble to get a little liquor cheap, but he padded in the shadows on a bed of pine needles to the back. A yellow rectangle appeared in the wall when an aproned man swung open a door. He sat on the stoop, lit a cigarette. Robert said, "Hello!" so he wouldn't be startled.

"I'm looking for a Sam."

"What anybody need a Sam for?"

"Whatever hootch he's got on hand."

He flicked away his cigarette, and that made Robert say that if he had any butts he'd buy some, too. He came back with a jelly jar and a half pack of Chesterfields and told him two-bits.

Back in front, the Negroes were gathered before Marjorie as if she were a choral leader or a coach. The white carnation at her temple shown with a cold glow like that of a lightning bug. She was smoking a cigarette Jack Benny style, her upheld wrist languid as a starlet's. The Negroes cut their eyes toward him then back to her. One rough-looking buck looked him square in the eye then let his gaze meander beyond them.

" … let her know Mr. Bud misses her good home cooking. He tells me every time he writes, Lucy."

"Yes'm, Miz Marj-ree," said a slight woman.

"And you tell her Ma said soon as the war's over and she doesn't want to work in a factory she can come back to our house." You'd have thought Marjorie was offering a lifetime's free lodging in the Waldorf-Astoria.

"Yes'm, Miz Marj-ree."

"And how's your brother?"

"Lee Roy?"

"Yes. Has the old truck. Always whistling."

"He fine, Miz Marj-ree."

"I hear he joined the army."

"Yes'm."

"Where is he now?"

"Alabama."

Somebody emitted a short, sharp laugh. Someone else said, "Alabama, yeah, uh-huh!" They stirred slightly then fell silent. They seemed to mark time, waiting for him and Marjorie to leave. He stepped up.

"Why, there's Mr. Robert right now!" She grinned. "Sam treat you right?"

He held up the jelly jar. She beamed at the crowd as if their procuring this hootch linked them in a grand enterprise.

"Mr. Robert here works at Magnolia and lives at the Karaceks' house. Robert, this is Lucy. Her sister worked for us, and that's Abner, he plows our garden every spring—Abner, you still have that old horse with the J brand on his hip?"

"Yes'm, Miz Marj-ree."

"And Sara Jane who worked for my grandmother, and Bobby Clemons, is that you there? Used to hep my granddaddy shoe his mules, iddn that right, Bobby?"

"Yes'm, Miz Marj-ree."

"And I think your nephew used to work for Miz Karacek, iddn that right?"

"Yes'm, Miz Marj-ree."

A faint undercurrent of humor hummed through the group like a pedal tone. Marjorie's ostentatious familiarity was, he guessed, designed to show him how chummy white and colored were down here.

"And I have Roebuck to thank for the butt." She took a last drag from the cigarette, blew the smoke vaguely in their direction presumably to show her appreciation, then ground the butt under her platform sandal.

"Now I want y'all to be sure to come around on Christmas Eve, you hear?"

He heard murmured "yes'ms" and "thank you ma'am" and "sho' will" then one baritone edged through it, chuckling. "What *fo*?"

"What for?" Marjorie leaned, squinting, toward the crowd. "Why for punch and gifts, what else? You think we're gonna put you in chains, Walter? That is you, iddn it?"

"Maybe so, maybe no."

"Ooo, you one bad nigger," somebody said with a laugh.

"Oh, I know that's you," scoffed Marjorie. "I haddn seen you in a coon's age. Where you been keepin yourself?"

"Jailhouse."

"He been in *Flaw*-ri-da, Miz Marj-ree," said Lucy.

"What they have you in jail for, Walter? Is this about that scrape on the bus? I heard you was in on that."

"Sassin a nosy white woman, maybe."

Marjorie grinned. "She must not of had much gumption if she had to call the law to handle the likes of you."

"I reckon not," said Walter.

Having tussled the truculent Walter to this draw, Marjorie bid them all good night, and they strolled off. Back in the car, he showed Marjorie the Chesterfields.

"Oh good!" She rummaged in the glove box for matches. "That one I got off Roebuck was garbage weed or something." She lit up, exhaled with a grateful sigh. "You're not so worthless after all. Did you get anything to mix the lightnin' with?"

"Your spit."

"Works in a pinch." She uncapped the jar, pursed her lips as if required to kiss a corpse, and swigged.

"Whew! Man oh man, I bet this stuff kicks like a shotgun. Sam must've made it in a horse trough."

"Let's hope not." Was she a regular customer? She had no apparent fear of being seen here. He took a slug that swelled in his stomach like a bowl of burning bile.

She took two more big swallows. "Now we can go home," she gasped. She started singing "They're Either Too Young or Too Old," which included the line *I can't sit under the apple tree with anyone else but me.*

At her curb, he lifted his door handle, but she said, "Hold it! What's your hurry? Got a hot date?"

"No. I didn't want to be presumptuous."

It was after midnight, but lights were on in nearby houses, and people were strolling the sidewalks. A radio played faintly. The air smelled of electricity and rotted wood, and a cool damp breeze had sprung up from the west.

Marjorie's house was dark.

"Looks like nobody's up."

"You kidding? She's sitting behind the curtain. If we get in a clinch, she'll jump up and turn on the porch light."

"So we don't need to worry about getting carried away."

"She's the air raid warden for our block. She's very vigilant."

She laid her head back, closed her eyes, hummed "Begin the Beguine" and he remembered Sylvia swaying on the stage, her skirt above her knees and then the ghostly feel of her thigh in his palm. The yoke of Marjorie's dress exposed the tops of her breasts. He thought she wanted him to kiss her. To his surprise, he did want to.

"I'm tight already."

"This stuff's got my head spinning, too," he said.

She took his kiss willingly but put nothing into it. Her breath was copper-ish from the cigarette. He was in a mood to find the boundaries. He slid his palm under her skirt and caressed her knee. Her mouth opened a bit. A drop of rain plopped hard on the roof. Someone with a dog on a leash walked by, whistling. Within a minute they were kissing hard; he was about to fondle her breast when the wind kicked up and blew a loose paper into the car, then the rain came in big drops that splatted on the windshield so hard he feared it was hail. They rolled the windows up.

"Wow!" she said. "That's *rain*!"

They returned to their earnest kissing. He was clumsy and too sudden with his hand, and she steered it to her waist.

"Gimme a cigarette."

He took one, too, his first in a good while.

"I'll neck with a guy who's spoken for, but you won't get nothin' else," she said when he'd lit them.

"Hey, I'm a gentleman. What if I just broke up with her?"

"You'd lie just to feel me up? Boy, am I flattered!" She cackled and whacked his thigh with her fist. "Heck, no guy's ever tried *that* one!"

They kissed again, but the lighted cigarettes in their hands distracted them, and her flower tumbled into her lap. They tacitly decided to smoke. The nicotine made him woozy.

"Thanks for asking me out. I've kind of wanted it since you showed up at the office."

"Really? I'm flattered."

"Hope I didn't do myself a disfavor by letting you know."

"How so?"

"Don't be a moron! Girls are supposed to play hard to get."

"We still have our clothes on."

"Ha double Ha! Truth is I don't know how to act any more. I'm not as wild as I seem. But I'm not the nice girl my folks raised me to be, either. If the war hadn't come along I'd probably be married and have a baby already."

"That'd be fast work!"

"You know what I mean. I'd be a whole lot like my mother only younger. I don't know what's in my future now, so when somebody handsome and... *deb-own-air*," she mugged for a mocking effect, "comes along, part of me says here's my chance and another says things like that don't matter now."

"What does?"

"Whatever the moment brings, I guess. I've got a friend, Melinda Showalter—she's in New Orleans working in a plant that makes ducks—you know, amphibious vehicles? She keeps writing me to come live with her. She's making a bundle and she says it's all a great big party, the Quarter and Bourbon Street and a million gobs on shore leave. She's having the time of her life. She says last thing in the world she'd want would be a husband. But it's not just for that. I want to *do* something that will *help*."

"I know what you mean, believe me. Why don't you go?"

"I'm on the verge." She rolled the window down far enough to toss out the burning butt, and he followed suit before she cranked it up. Then she kissed his cheek. "I haven't told **anybody**, not my Ma and not my boss."

"I'll keep mum."

"Thanks." She cocked the rearview mirror to inspect herself. "I'm a mess. I look like we did everything in the book. That ought to make her happy."

TEN

Getting home was slow, as the downpour swamped the one poor wiper and he couldn't recognize landmarks in the rain. At the house he dashed for the porch, slipped off his shoes and socks so he wouldn't muddy Sylvia's floors, and let himself in.

"Sylvia?" he hollered.

"On the back porch. Come join me."

He put on sweat pants, an undershirt, socks, and slippers, then he dug his flannel robe from a box in his closet. He heaped his sopping clothes on the bathroom floor.

Sylvia was in the swing, still in costume. A gutter downspout behind her spewed a noisy torrent onto the walk. Mollie crouched under the washing machine tubs, whimpering. Three other mutts lay calmly on the porch near the door.

"I love it out here when it rains." She hoisted her wine glass. On a table by her knees stood another glass and two wine bottles, one empty, the other half full. "Have some wine."

"Thanks!" He poured a glass and took a swallow. It warmed him. She scooted aside, so he eased down next to her. She swung her end a little with her toes, so he let his end move too.

"This will be so good for the garden."

"Yes," he said. "Sylvia, you were great! If you were nervous, it sure didn't tell! You looked like a real professional!"

"Thank you. I thought it went pretty well, too, even if I say so myself! Thanks for coming."

"My pleasure."

"I was just sitting here thinking how much I'd missed being in front of an audience. There's just something about it, you know. All those eyes, they just seem to be bathing you with adoring looks even when they don't like you!" She laughed, and he laughed with her. "When I was living in Chicago, I used to go the movies at least twice a week. I get the feeling here that if I go to the movies by myself, somebody'll think I'm a loose woman. And if I went with a friend who is male, it'd be worse. This town seems awful small sometimes. I guess I need a girlfriend. In Chicago, I'd just drop in after my shift sometimes before I went home. For a quarter you can see the latest picture *and* a stage show! And they've got these movie palaces like the Oriental—oh, they're like castles, truly like castles! I saw *Gone With the Wind* there three times in one week!"

"'Frankly, my dear, I don't give a damn!'"

Sylvia laughed. "I skipped a morning of work to catch a matinee that third time and caught hell from my union steward."

"Where were you working?"

"Place on South Franklin—sewing buttonholes. Never again, I hope."

"'As God is my witness, I'll never go hungry again.'"

"'Not even if I have to cheat or steal or'—what is it?"

"'Lie.'"

"Kill, I think." After a moment, she chuckled. "Oooo—a diamond ring! … Rhett, do buy a great big one!"

"Sounds like you miss big city life."

"Oh. Yes. I do. I really do. I don't think I realized it until Georgie left. I've just been so much on my own. I keep thinking about some great times I had up there going to a floor show and dinner. I saw Jimmy Dorsey and his band with Helen O'Connell in the Panther Room of the Sherman Hotel."

"Why'd you leave?"

"Well, I guess I'd say I didn't like the company I was keeping."

She rubbed her bare arm briskly. The screen protected them from the rain, but the breeze gusted in chilly huffs, and the costume's peasant blouse bared her arms and shoulders.

"You need a wrap?"

"I am too cool, but it feels marvelous!"

He wanted to pull her close, warm her with his arm around her, but he didn't know how to show it.

"Let me know if you're too cool."

"All right. And did Marjorie enjoy the show?"

"Oh, it was all she'd talk about after."

"I'm sure!" she scoffed. "And was she everything you wanted or expected?"

He laughed. "Well, hardly. I didn't want much and I expected little. She took me to a Negro joint to get some homemade hootch. Then we sat in the car at her house and just yakked until the rain came." He was torn between assuring her that he'd been "faithful" and making her jealous.

"Sounds cozy—parked in the dark car, the booze, the rain. That car's got no radio, though. Maybe you should've taken the Karacek carriage. Those nice soft plush seats. It would've been perfect for you."

It hadn't been offered, of course. "Now, don't get started," he said. "I doubt I'll date her again."

"We'll find someone better."

"Maybe I'll stick to being a lonely bachelor. It's safer."

They swung in silence, each lightly touching a toe in unison on the floor as they arced to and fro. The front passed and now the rain fell steadily but without the wind; the light above the garage door thrust a hooded triangle downward into striations of glittery crystal. She shivered a little. He had to respond.

"Here—" He raised his arm in an outsized gesture as if it were a mechanical instrument he was taking off a shelf to utilize, then he laid it stiffly across her shoulders. "Better?"

"Ooo, you're warm!" She collapsed into his flank.

"You didn't go to a cast party?"

"They're all poop-heads. And the person who put on the party's a teetotaler. Can you believe it? I wanted to *celebrate*!" She looked at her empty glass. "I had two of these before you got here."

He poured her glass full. An unexpected ray of hope glimmered on his horizon.

"Here's to your successful show!"

They clinked glasses and drank. Then she sank into him and dropped her head to his shoulder. Her breast eased against his ribs, and her thigh pressed his. He could smell perfume in her hair. He was annoyed to go hard for what seemed the umpteenth time today.

She sighed theatrically. “I’m really mad at Georgie tonight.”

“Why?”

“For not being here. I know it’s not fair, but it’s how I feel. I wish he could’ve seen me perform. I miss him so much. He’s so much fun, like a wacky puppy, and I miss that, and I’m mad at him for taking that away. He’s not like a lot of other fellows, either. He’s happy just holding you.”

The more she praised her poor dear Georgie the more it irritated him.

“I can understand that. Most men would probably feel the same about you—lucky for whatever they get. You’re beautiful and smart and warm.” A stinging pressure swelled up in his eyes. That moonshine and this wine had gotten to him if he was feeling this sorry for himself.

She must have heard the break in his voice. She took his hand. “You’ve become such a dear friend, Robert. You say the nicest things to me. You always lift my spirits.”

“I *mean* them, dammit.”

The rain had slackened, pitter-pattering on the leaves and making a *dink dink dink* in the downspout. Water stood shining in the garden rows and the tomato plants were bowed and bedraggled. Their garden, now. One night, on a neighbor’s recommendation, while Sylvia held a flashlight he poured trickles of salt on big slugs chewing their lettuce, and the slugs writhed and dissolved like the wicked witch in *Oz*. They made faces and she grabbed his arm, yipping, “Oo! Yikes! It’s awful!” wrinkling her nose, then they roared with laughter.

Sylvia said, “I wish he knew how hard my struggle is, too. I write and pour my heart out to him, and he just can’t or won’t respond. They say you’re supposed to stay upbeat and help them remember the good times so they’ll have something to fight for, but it’s a two-way street! If I didn’t have those photos I couldn’t even remember what he looks like! I truly wish I weren’t an out-of-sight, out-of-mind person no matter how hard I want not to be!”

As she wept softly, he patted her shoulder. He knew what she was afraid of now. He saw he had a chance, too, and that made his heart pound. He was glad Georgie had neglected her and hated himself for that. Life would be much simpler if it were Marjorie he wanted. He hugged her close, feeling both tender and aroused, drawing her breasts against his chest, smelling the rain and perfume in her hair. His right forearm lay across her lap, and he could feel her hips moving with the swing's slow arc under the thin cotton skirt. He ached so he felt sick.

"Oh, Sylvia," he whispered in her ear. "You're so good, you're such a fine, fine woman!"

"Poor Robert," she murmured.

"Sylvia, please let me kiss you!"

She didn't answer; he moved his palm to her cheek and gently raised her face. Her eyes were closed. He kissed her mouth, very softly, as if she were sleeping and he was afraid of waking her, and she neither resisted nor participated. Her lips were very soft, and kissing her made him lightheaded and drove his blood down into his blue ache. He broke off from fear he'd pass out.

"Oh, Sylvia, I want you so much."

She was quiet, then she said, "It's been a long time since I felt wanted." She laid her head back and canted it toward him. She smiled. He'd set his hand lightly on her lap and she squeezed his fingers.

They kept swinging, and she kept milking his hand and smiling. He knew then she couldn't say, "Yes," but didn't want to say, "No," either. She closed her eyes and hummed. If one kiss stole home safely, would a second? He kissed her again. She kept her hands together in her lap and her body still, but moaned quietly through her nose. Then suddenly her mouth burst open into his. She kissed him back as if she were a paraplegic whose sole means of communication was through this rubbery wide mouth. He'd never had a woman put so much passion into a kiss. She thrust her breath down his windpipe, she licked his lips, the tip of his tongue, still without moving any part of her body; she kissed the way someone ending a long fast would devour a ripe peach in private.

She broke off and looped her arm around his neck, yanked him so tightly and so close he couldn't move. She hooked her chin over his shoulder.

"We have to stop!"

"Yes. Okay. I'm sorry."

"Don't be! I'm. . .flattered. It feels good to be needed. I need you, too." Her breath huffed against his ear.

"It's a two-way street?"

"It's a two-way street."

His joy overflowed and before he could check himself he'd planted his mouth on hers again. She said *mmmmp*!—he surprised her—then twisted her face so that her mouth was smeared against his cheek.

Then she wrenched herself away and struggled up from the swing. "I think it's time we said goodnight."

In her absence, he sat stewing. He felt *used* and tricked. Was she that jealous that he'd had one date with someone else? She must have known she'd worked him up this afternoon with that stocking seam gimmick, then when he came home she had that second glass waiting, then she'd sat against him with his arm around her and didn't say no when he kissed her.

The memory of the kiss stirred him again. And made him angry—damn him for thinking with his pecker! Nobody held a gun to his head and said *Sit down! Drink the wine! Kiss the woman!* He could've made plans to see Marjorie again and eventually desire for her would purge this itch for the *wrong woman*!

On the other hand . . .

Poor tormented Sylvia ached for her dear Georgie. She was lonely and vulnerable; she'd had her stage triumph and missed him with a particular sharpness; she'd had too much too drink, and the rain had been a sweetly sorrowful spice for this melancholy stew. He'd come along with his overheated need and didn't care how weak she was. He'd taken advantage of it, forced himself on her.

Georgie was off fighting for them—not knowing a 4-F gimp was assaulting the wife he cherished so much he'd risked his mother's wrath to marry her and maybe his life to please her. Somewhere, tonight, he was thinking of her waiting at home, lovingly turning over their sweet memories.

Georgie should damn them both to hell!

He tapped on her bedroom door but there was no answer. He went upstairs to go to his room but through the open doorway of her salon she was silhouetted as she stood at the window looking down into the front yard.

He tapped on the doorframe. The room was dim but when she turned light from the street glinted on her cheek.

"Sylvia, I want to apologize. I'm really sorry. It was my responsibility as a man to behave myself, and I took unfair advantage of you in a weak moment. I let my feelings for you carry me away."

After a moment, she said, "You always say the right thing. It puts me off balance. You think right now I want to hear that you have, have *tender feelings* for me?"

"I guess if you don't want to hear that then I don't always know the right thing to say."

She sighed, as if annoyed. "This fellow I was with in Chicago, he was a big gruff Cossack, and I never heard him say more than a half dozen words at a time. I could sure read his face, though. You learn to do that. It's how you protect yourself—you read the face. Especially Josef's eyes. They were so light you could almost see through them right into his head. One look when he came through the door and I'd know I was in for hell for the next few hours, and I'd know maybe even before he did when he was going to belt me. I just didn't know whether it would be only a slap or two or this would be the time he killed me."

"Why on earth would you stay with such a man!" he burst out. He wanted to murder the bastard.

"It just went from day to day, year to year, and you don't notice the time passing. And he never acted that way until later. He wasn't crazy, only mean as a dog when he was drunk. Sober, he was a good enough fellow."

"But he started out being *nice* to you?"

"He was pleased to have me. You might not believe this, but I was once a very beautiful woman."

"Oh, for crying out loud, Sylvia! You're still a beautiful woman!"

Her smile flickered across her mouth. "Your question was why. He helped me when I needed it. Badly."

"So you stayed with him just for that?"

After a pause, she said, "Not *just*, Robert. He paid for my son's funeral when I was dead broke, and he did it without my having to ask. And he was just a working stiff like me. He found the burial plot, arranged for the service."

"I'm sorry." He wanted to ask what her child died of but restrained himself.

"I am too." Her voice was shaking. "Then everything turned sour and I had to run to get away. Georgie doesn't know about him."

She sighed deeply. He didn't know what to do with this information—not the "big gruff Cossack," but that she'd told him and not Georgie.

"What you and I did—I'd hoped never to do something like that in a marriage. I wanted one thing in my life to stay clean and simple and pure. Georgie's the kind of person makes you want that."

Georgie and his unassailable character! Robert wanted to tear his own hair out. His eyes were stinging and his face was twitching; he was afraid he was about to embarrass myself.

"Do you think I should find another place to live?" He felt gallant making the offer but at heart he was only bluffing.

"Well, I am thinking, you know, that it might be a good idea at least for you to move into the garage apartment. It'll protect us both from temptation."

"Yes. Thank you." He'd willingly pay whatever penance was necessary to keep the door open for another transgression.

ELEVEN

HE'D WON A REPRIEVE. As soon as the garage apartment could be cleaned she'd get help moving furniture up to it. She told him that she'd invited the daughter of an old friend in Michigan to come stay a while and that she'd be taking Georgie's sister's old bedroom upstairs.

He made himself scarce; she made herself scarcer. You'd think he had leprosy. Sunday after Mass she was out doing Good Works, and when she returned from her volunteer work on Monday she announced that she'd taken a job sewing powder bags nine hours a day, five and a half days a week.

"Father McNally told me to stay busy." They'd crossed paths on the front porch; she was on her way to the train station's USO canteen for the evening.

"You'll feel better knowing you're doing your part," he offered.

"Yes. I've been far too vain and selfish." She was wearing a matron's rue-colored dress.

Would she give her wages to charity? Next morning and each morning thereafter a car pool driver honked and she went down the walk at six-thirty in fetching bell-bottom slacks, deliciously snug across her rear, her hair in a polka-dot bandanna, and her lunch in a big wooden purse with a painted rooster on the side. After work Tuesday, a note said she'd left a sandwich in the icebox and that she'd gone to the hospital to work the Red Cross blood drive. Clearly their nice, conjugal suppers were over. He missed her terribly. And Marjorie had left for New Orleans.

He gave a pint of blood just to see her. She was wearing a blue smock and a little cap. She hardly noticed him. A Negro mother was giving blood because her son was overseas. Sylvia's Red Cross supervisor insisted on segregating her blood from Robert's. Sylvia got hot. "Dammit, blood is *red* no matter who it comes from!" The supervisor said it was a strict Red Cross policy, and Sylvia said, "Well, that damn sure doesn't make it right!" He was proud of her.

Friday he was late coming home. On the porch Mollie was whining at the screen, and when he stepped around her, Sylvia hollered, "Don't let her in!"

In the dining room, Sylvia was wearing a blue snood and old paint-smeared overalls over a man's T-shirt and had apparently scrubbed every square inch of flooring—the overall knees were sopping and baggy.

"You wouldn't believe the dog hair I've cleaned up!" Holding the scrub brush, she swabbed her forehead against her sleeve. "There's food on the stove, but when you've eaten, I need help moving the furniture and rolling the carpet back in the parlor, if you wouldn't mind."

"Sure. Just let me change."

So they would apply elbow grease to balm her Catholic guilt? The week-old memory of their kissing was to be thoroughly scoured. Going upstairs, he smelled linseed oil and the banister was sticky. Outside the sewing salon stood a bucket and mop and a wastebasket overflowing with scraps of material and papers. She'd not touched his room. He changed into old khakis and an undershirt. Downstairs, he found a grilled cheese sandwich covered by a plate in a cast-iron skillet, and he wolfed it in three bites chased with milk. In the parlor, she was grunting and heaving the sofa to scoot it out from the wall.

"For God's sake, Sylvia, let me!" He rushed to take her place, and she stepped back, panting. It took them both to move the sofa, the oak secretary, and the two wing chairs into the dining room. He ignored the ache in his bad leg. The hassock, coffee table, magazine racks, the lamps and their tables they handled separately. Going to and fro they passed in the archway, and her demeanor was taciturn and grim, as if they were gathering articles condemned to be burned in an *auto-da-fé*.

They rolled up the Oriental carpet—dust clinging to the cross-hatch weave flaked off in sheets—and dragged it into the hall.

"Filthy!" exclaimed Sylvia, fists on her hips, surveying the floor of the emptied room. "Just filthy!"

"That Mother Karacek!" he said. "What a pig!"

She ignored his levity. He stood by like an attending nurse while she ran the Hoover, and when she stopped to move the plug, he said, "Call when you're ready to put things back. Do you want me to help mop?"

"No. You go on."

He got a cold Dr Pepper from the icebox and sat brazenly in the swing on the back porch. His leg hurt. He was working his troubled calf when Sylvia came out, wiping her nape with a towel. Strands of hair had slithered from under her snood to dangle cutely across her brow, and she kept futilely tossing them back with her fingers.

"Whew!" She smiled weakly. She noticed his massaging hand. "Are you all right?"

He considered telling her about his polio then decided spilling the news now would seem manipulative. He said, "Have you been working this hard since you got home?"

"More or less. I'll finish the upstairs rooms except for yours tonight. I've hired a man to help tomorrow." Her nod went up to the garage apartment, which, perversely, he had yet to inspect.

"What's up there now?"

"Just junk. A good bed, though." She looked away. "I want you to have the easy chair from the sewing room and your desk and the chest. And if there's anything else you need, just tell me, Robert. Please."

Your bed. With you in it. He succumbed to a childish impulse to resist this plea to be pacified. "Whatever's there will be fine. No need to bother yourself. I'm only working until noon tomorrow. I can move my own things."

He swilled the last of his Dr Pepper and they set to work rearranging the furniture in the parlor. Next day, Saturday, they both worked half days, but when he got home early afternoon her hired fellow—the Negro from the roadhouse named Walter—was already hefting items up the stairs. He pitched in. It evidently amused Walter to be paired with the weakling from a Charles Atlas ad. Walter easily hoisted his end of something, then, as Robert huffed and groped to get a purchase, he waited with a smile lurking under the bill of the cap he wore low over his eyes. They moved the five-drawer chest down one flight of stairs and up another. They removed the drawers and the roll top from the elephantine oak desk. As they clomped, grunting with it, down to the first landing, the thing slipped loose, and Walter yelled, "Whoa, damn you!" and one wild sweep of a corner sent half the portraits clattering off the wall. On this trip even smug Walter grimaced, and crystalline sweat gleamed along the rim of his African-blue jaw. They had bruises and strains after wrestling it one step at a time up the staircase beside the garage.

They took a break with cold Dr Peppers and sat on the floor. Out the window, he saw Ferret Face's Packard pull into the drive.

"Uh-oh," Robert said. "Here comes Big Mama."

Walter laughed.

"That woman's nothing but trouble," Robert said.

Walter shrugged.

"Sylvia told me you and her husband Georgie go way back?"

Walter smiled. "Back to the day. Out at the farm."

"Whatta you think about his bride?" It was rude to put Walter on the spot, but he was dying for information about the loving couple.

"She nice enough."

"Damn, Walter! You're a cagey fellow."

Walter grinned. "Loose lips sink ships, Mistah Robut."

Mistah Robut. Or was it Raw Butt? And Robert had thought because he was willing to break into a brotherly sweat with Walter that Walter'd drop the country coon act and treat him as an equal.

"Sylvia tells me you got into a squabble on the bus with a couple rednecks. She says they started it but you and another fellow got arrested. A soldier."

"Thas about it." He leaned against the wall and pulled a cigar stub out of his shirt pocket, lighted it. Walter looked at him again, less guarded he thought, though maybe he wondered where Robert was leading him. Robert raised his brows an inch, and Walter went on. "Disturbin the peace. We got thirty days and a fifty buck fine."

"That's rotten."

Walter nodded.

"When I saw you out at that joint in the woods, they said you'd been in the jailhouse. I wondered."

Walter nodded again. *Wonder all you want*, that head bob seemed to say.

"So that was what you all were talking about?"

"Un–huh."

"I guess Marjorie didn't know."

He smiled. "I reckon she don't read the papers, Mistah Robut."

They heard the Packard start. He hoisted his form off the floor, stiff in the joints already. He knew no more about Georgie but he believed he'd made an inch of headway with his pal. At least Walter wasn't afraid now of making a sly remark about Marjorie to him.

They finished within the hour and Sylvia paid Walter. As he boxed up clothes and books he meant to cart to his new digs, late afternoon turned toward suppertime. He thought he'd try his luck at getting time alone with her.

He found her standing on the porch by the double-tubbed washer. Her back was to him; she was looking out to the garden. "Sylvia?"

She didn't turn; she dipped her head and one hand heel went to her eyes to swipe sideways.

"What's wrong, Sylvia?"

She sank her hands into the rinse water. "Evelyn."

"What's her problem now?"

She flicked away gnats swarming her face. "She told me no lady ever associated with her family had ever worked for wages in a factory, and if I needed money she'd give it to me."

"I can't imagine you taking her charity."

"You know me better than she does."

She heaved up a dripping sheet from the tub and stuck a corner in the wringer. He turned the handle while she guided the sheet into the rollers and held it free of the draining tray as it emerged.

"She said she'd heard stories about you and me and that she was tired of telling me I had a responsibility to the family's reputation." She glanced at him quickly then away. "She insists that you leave."

"What'd you tell her, for God's sake?"

"I told her it was my business but that you were moving out to the garage to avoid any misunderstandings. And I told her about Mary Kay coming to stay." She took the sheet they'd just put through the wringer and started it on another pass. "I said I hoped that would quiet any such talk."

"Aw, these small town gossips can kiss my bee-hind!"

"Yes, I know! And I agree. Except . . ." She sighed and her deep brown eyes rose and met his gaze steadily with a hint of resistance. "Except this time you and I know there's more reason for the gossip. And knowing it made me feel dirty." Her lip line was a crisp slit and she kept watching her busy hands. "I really *loathed* feeling that she had good reason to be high and mighty with me."

"I'm sorry to be somebody who causes so much trouble for you."

"You can make it up to me."

"How?"

"Help me hang out these sheets."

TWELVE

My dearest darling Donnie,

Oh gosh I miss you! There's a really big hole right where my heart is, and it would fill to the brim if we were together. When I think about what Mom put you through I could die with embarrassment, but I know because you love me you don't blame me. I love you, my darling, I truly do, and it will last through all our trials—promise!!

I try like the dickens to look on the bright side. Sylvia (she won't let me call her Mrs. Karacek) is supposedly my godmom, and she's been super. I don't know what Mom told her (I'm afraid to ask). I was expecting she'd treat me like a juvenile delinquent and crack the whip, but so far she's been like a big sister, very understanding.

I wanted to go home to Gran but Mom was too mad to send me where I wanted, and I think she was afraid of what I'd say when I got there. (I really miss her, too, but I sure won't tell her yet!) Anyway, Sylvia's husband is in the army, and their house is a big two-story mansion with a big front porch and a nice yard with a garden plot and a garage and even an apartment over it where a boarder stays. Even though every night I feel weepy and sorry for myself to be away from you and living among strangers, I sit myself down and count my blessings.

Number 2 is (hey, bet you can guess #1!!) I've got my own room! It's upstairs and has windows that look out over the back and side yard, and the big oaks right outside shade it so the morning sun filters through, making my room cool and nice with shadows. There's even a lock on the door! And my own bed, too. With no one in it but me! (Of course, some wonderful fellow sneaks into it while I'm dreaming to hold me in his big strong arms!) I have a dresser with a mirror!! And a chest of drawers with nobody's stuff in it but mine. And a closet! For the first time, I have more spaces to put things than I have things to fill them! I can put my favorite pictures on my nightstand—guess who is closest to my pillow!

Blessing number 3 is a piano! All my life I've yearned to learn, and soon as I saw it in the parlor I about dropped my suitcase on my toes! Sylvia's taught me a little, and I'm already playing "duets" with Robert the Boarder (hereafter referred to as "RB"), songs like "Heart and Soul" and "Blue Moon" and this boogie-woogie tune where I play the walking bass line. Sylvia works at a war factory sewing and doesn't have much time, but she says she'd buy me lessons. I can't let her do that, but I'm looking for a job after school and will buy my own. I can't wait to start taking! Next time you see me, I'll play "It's Been a Long, Long Time" for you. You know the words? "Kiss me once and kiss me twice and kiss me once again ... it's been a long, long time ... " Oh, dear. Now I'm getting all weepy again. (Sorry about that tear drop right on the ink.)

Blessing number 4 is I have a girl friend already! Linda lives five houses down and goes to high school here, too. She's a cheerleader and very popular but not stuck-up, and she's been really nice about letting me eat lunch with her and her friends in the cafeteria. It's hard being the new kid, especially in the middle of the year. (I'm waaay ahead in algebra and waaaayy behind in Texas history!) Just like in Ypsi, "old" kids stick together and feel superior. Linda's an "old" kid, but because of my super personality (ha ha just kidding) she lets me be her pal. She has black hair and gray eyes and a really cute figure, but no I will not send you a picture! I have to worry about those college girls you're around every day. We both like Beechnut gum and Robert Taylor and swing music, and we both read *The Song of Bernadette* at the same time but didn't know it! She slept over and we "played" nuns like we were ten. We took turns being the Mother Superior, and we made my room into a cell and lit candles. What really touched me was that when we were talking about whether God was a spirit or a man or a woman or just all the molecules in the universe put together, she said she was glad to have me as a friend because she couldn't talk like that with her old friends. They'd think she was a drip. It pleases me to think that even though I came along last I have a small part of her that nobody else does. (And I did get the message to keep mum about such stuff!) She thinks it's really neat that I've lived other places, which makes me feel like a world traveler (would you believe she's never heard of kielbasa?), and she loves my so-called Yankee accent. She wants us to start a troop of the Victory Girls here like I was in up there. I guess she thinks I'm an outlaw character, what with living away from my "parents," and for all I know Mom sent a flyer down before I arrived: Beware of Wild Child. Anyway, having her as a friend is about the next-best thing to having you. (And, yes, I've told her about you and showed her your picture. I hope you don't mind! I just had to let somebody know about the man I love. She said she thought you looked like Robert Payne! I told her I wouldn't tell you that because it would go to your head.)

I have blessings to ten, but I won't tell you the others yet. I'm afraid you'll think I don't grieve about leaving you. Do you miss me? I hope so! But I also worry that's selfish—if I really really loved you, wouldn't I want you to be happy? I hope you'll write me at least once a week. I don't know how long this will last—I know you'll be off to the service after graduating next year, so God only knows when I'll see you again. If Mom gets over being so steamed, I will beg on my knees and be the world's best daughter if she will let me come there for Christmas. But I've got to toe the line here so that Sylvia will send her good reports.

Can you tell I am trying to stay cheerful and make the best of things? What buoys me up, Donnie dear, are my memories.

We were in the drug store and you were calling your mother and I was standing in the door of the phone booth and you winked and said to her, "Guess what, Mom—I've got a gal." Then she must've asked who I was and you said, "She's cute as a button and really sweet—I know you'd like her." Then when you hung up you said that when she and your dad came to visit you'd introduce me. Once we were standing in line at the movie and that really cute girl who is in your Latin class came up to you with her friend and started talking—well, I should say flirting!!—with you, and you said to them, "I want you to meet my girlfriend, Mary Kay." I know these memories aren't really romantic like the guy and the gal canoeing in the moonlight while he croons to her, but they stick in my mind 'cause they were moments when I knew you treasured me. And I remember silly little stuff like secretly spending the afternoon in your room studying and eating popcorn made on your illegal hot plate and how you always held my hand like I was six when we crossed the street.

Oh jeepers! I'm a mess! If I don't stop watering this letter I'll have to start all over!

Please write to me soon soon soon. I am dying!!! to hear from you!

All my love to my darling Donnie Dearest. . .

Mary Kay

♥

THIRTEEN

THE BREEZE THROUGH his window carried a honeysuckle fragrance that inexplicably threatened him with melancholy. He'd finished letters home and had started one to his brother. The more he tried to boost Jimmy's spirits, though, the bluer he was to be sidelined on the bench.

The landing floor creaked. Probably Mary Kay. Sylvia said, "If I'm looking for her, she'll likely be with you!" He said that he didn't encourage her, and Sylvia replied, "Well, you're just irresistible, Robert!" with fond mockery. He'd been properly civil but aloof to Mary Kay, and Sylvia protested far too much—was she trying to divert his attention? So far as he could see, Mary Kay's fellow in Michigan occupied all the space available for the role of adored male.

The screen door squeaked open.

"Knock-knock."

"Come in," he said, though she was already hovering over the threshold.

"No—'knock-knock.' It's a knock-knock joke—you start."

He kept writing to show she was intruding.

"Come on. Don't be a goon—start the joke."

"Okay. Knock-knock."

"Who's there?" She laughed. "Pretty damn funny, huh?"

"Ha double Ha," he said, imitating Marjorie. "Don't curse. It's not becoming."

She strolled in, scrutinizing his quarters, sniffing like a cat.

"What're you doing?"

"What's it look like?"

She strutted to his chair and bent over his shoulder. He smelled Beechnut gum. A hank of blond hair swung into view. She was wearing a white cotton blouse with the tails loose and chocolate stains on the lapel.

"Looks like a map of worm tunnels."

"My handwriting's not that bad."

"Who're you writing?"

"None of your bees-wax."

"Aw, come on, tell me! Is it your girl? "

"I don't have a girl."

"You have a fly on your head, instead."

Something tickled his left ear and when he swatted at it he saw the broom straw.

"Don't be pestiferous."

"*You* don't be obstehooteous."

"What?"

"Look it up."

"Where? In your head?"

Behind him, she yawned hugely and smacked her lips.

"What about Sylvia? Is she your girl?"

"Don't be ridiculous."

"So who's the letter to?"

"If you have to know, my brother."

"Is he army or air corps—is he an officer?"

"Sorry to disappoint you—he's a dogface pfc."

"Why would that disappoint me?"

"I figured anybody who reads movie magazines would only find a dashing pilot officer acceptable."

"I don't read just movie magazines! I read *Forever Amber* and *Song of Bernadette* just this week! And you're cynical. What if I have a yen for the proletariat?"

He looked at her. Yen for the proletariat*?* She could be brainy even while acting like a goofy tomboy. She could add a line of figures in her head almost instantly and still whine like a ten-year-old that nobody *ever* wants to do anything with her. She worked crossword puzzles that exasperated him. She claimed she won an Ohio-wide spelling bee at ten.

She had a pert nose and wide-set light blue eyes. When she read she wore glasses, and without them the blue in her eyes washed to watercolor. Her mouth was wide as well, with pale thin lips able to work that width to best advantage by offering a wholly different aspect on either end, a bit similar to Sylvia's—in part because she'd picked up Sylvia's mannerisms. Her present grin was saucy on the left side, with the right side standing under to prop it up.

"Are you a Communist?" he asked.

"You said I'm still a child. Whoever heard of a child Communist?"

"I never said you. . ." Realizing she'd baited him, he turned to the letter.

She sat on his bed and bounced as if it were playground equipment. "Why aren't you in the army?"

"You're very nosy."

"Come on. You can tell *me*. Aren't we friends?"

Mary Kay's tone—insolent and bantering—wasn't right for the deeply troublesome subject, and he was caught between embarrassing her by taking offense and tossing it off.

"I work in a defense-related industry."

"Gee, I know that! I mean do you want to go?"

"Yes, very much."

"Me too. If the war's still on when I finish school in two more years, I'll join the WAACs, and I'm going to be a cryptographer or maybe an aviatrix. I love those words, don't you? Cryp-TOG-rah-fer. A-vee-uh-trix! I could say them over and over. They're like mouth calisthenics. They have women pilots now—you hear about the WASPs? Donnie's going to the air corps—he's in ROTC training. The women can't fly combat missions but they ferry planes across the country so men don't have to do it. I'm interested in aeronautics. I was in the Civil Air Patrol in Ypsilanti."

"You told me."

"It won't kill you."

"What won't?"

"To hear something more than once."

"True. And it won't kill you to tell me something only once."

"You're a smart aleck."

He wrote, *There's a wacky teenage girl living with us now.*

"So what do you think of my plan?"

"To be a crypTOGrapher or an A-viatrix? I'd be proud of you for helping your country."

She was quiet for a bit. She lay across his bed, head and arms draped over the edge, idly trailing her fingernails on the floor and writing in the dust. She yawned. "If you really want to go, why not just quit your job and sign up?"

"Why not just quit school and sign up?"

"Don't be a goon. I'm only fifteen, or I would. But you could."

He went on writing, though with his teeth clenched. She got up and stood at the west window—the light turned her visible curl of ear pink throughout—bracing her palms on the sill and flexing her arms, arching up on her toes.

"Don't you have anything to do?"

"Yes. But you didn't answer my question."

Now he *did* want to shame her. He laid down his pen with a theatrical flourish. "Okay. Last December I went with some pals to a recruiting office. They all passed the physical. I didn't. End of that story. Don't you think I *want* to be with them? Do you think it's easy looking like an able-bodied man and knowing people are asking why their sons and brothers and husbands and fathers are risking their lives and I'm still here? Don't you think that bothers me?" His voice was trembling. He wasn't holding back—she needed a lesson in manners. He almost added that he'd been so humiliated he'd fled a thousand miles from home. "If you'd thought about it you could've guessed I have a good reason and being treated as if I didn't is insulting."

Her gaze stayed out the window. She was blushing, so he'd stung her, but she wouldn't collapse like a tent with remorse.

"Now I guess you'll ask why I failed the physical."

She met his eye, then quickly looked away. "No. I won't ask you anything else! Gee! Okay?"

Uneasy about wounding her, he said, "My leg."

"Besides, I didn't mean *that* question."

"What question, then?"

"About Sylvia. What's wrong with your leg? I've never seen anything wrong. Oh, hey, I don't mean *they* wouldn't think so! I mean, you know, I could never tell."

He might have been a friend complaining about feeling fat and she was trying to talk him out of it.

"I had a disease when I was a kid and one leg's a bit shorter."

"Polio—like FDR?"

"Yes. It doesn't keep me from doing anything I want to do, but I couldn't convince them of that. They're too damned stupid—pardon my French—to see that I could point a gun and pull the trigger good as the next fellow."

She peeled away from the window, circled behind him, then grabbed his neck and hugged him awkwardly but quickly, leaving a fleeting impression of her long tan arms across his chest and her cheek against his.

"I apologize for prying."

"You're forgiven."

"About not being in the service." She giggled. "But I still want to know about Sylvia. Linda says Sylvia's quite dashing and much too chick for people here. I heard her husband's kind of . . ." She twirled her finger at her temple.

He resumed writing. "Never met him. And I need to finish this."

"So you're taking the Fifth Amendment! The jury will presume you're guilty."

He snorted. "Of what?"

"Of being Sylvia's secret boyfriend!"

"Hey!" he glowered at her. "She's married! And she's very serious about her marriage vows! She misses her husband. Don't kid around about this."

"Okay. Colly, don't bite my head off!"

"Well, you need to be careful about what you say to people."

"Loose Lips Sink Ships. I stand corrected."

"All right. Now don't you have something you should be doing?"

"As a matter of fact, I do!" She picked up a soiled shirt he'd left lying on the bed. "I came up to borrow this."

"What for?"

"Sylvia wants me to help in the garden and I need something to wear."

"That one's dirty."

"Why get a clean one dirty?"

He shrugged. "Up to you."

She left and he finished the letter. It worried him that Mary Kay was so alert to the undercurrents because it would disturb Sylvia to know it. To him, with Mary Kay on the premises, a game of hide-and-seek might commence. Mary Kay had become their chaperone, but this might allow Sylvia leeway to rebel. He existed in a state of perpetual arousal—Sylvia was so near and yet so far, as a corny song might say. When they were all together, Mary Kay's presence thwarted even his adoring gaze, and a smart and sensitive kid might easily detect *sub rosa* messages.

He planned to mail the letters downtown before reporting for duty at the scrap collection center. As he was leaving, Sylvia was in the kitchen washing dishes. Under an apron she had on the rayon dress with big red flowers against a cream-colored background.

"Where are you going so dressed up?" He moved against her back and sniffed her nape. "You smell good."

"Shh!" She winced away.

"She's upstairs. She's going to the scrap drive with me."

"Oh, Robert, for God's sake, it's not her!" She stamped her foot. "Saying that is really an insult, you know that?"

"Sorry."

"I'm starting to wonder if you really mean it when you say that. Actions speak louder than words, you know—and don't give me that bull about being carried away!"

His face was hot. He knew he'd violated their pact, but the compulsion to test her limits had been irresistible. She was glaring at him; he turned away, shamed but feeling an injured pride.

"Got it loud and clear. Tell Mary Kay I'll wait in the car," he tossed over his shoulder.

He had permission to use the company vehicle for this patriotic duty. He waited in it, trying to calm himself. Thing is, he told himself, if she hadn't put so much into that damn kiss he probably wouldn't be so tempted to press her. But that kiss told him what she really felt.

He tried to shake it off. Down the street Mary Kay's pal Linda and her father stood in their yard each raking cut grass, and he remembered doing that with his Dad before he went off to Rutgers, remembered how Jimmy and he helped and usually wound up turning the garden hose on one another and finally him. That memory of a time before all his personal turmoil and the upheaval of the war boosted his spirits.

Then Mary Kay came out wearing blue jeans and bobby sox and saddle oxfords and the dirty white blouse, and something about her girlish, forthright innocence warmed him even more.

When she got in, she said immediately, "Sorry for asking about the service. I didn't know it was a sore subject."

"It's okay. I tell myself that we all have a part, only mine isn't very glamorous or dangerous."

"I knew this midget, Alfie, back at Willow Run. He and his cousin work inside the wings on B-24s. They hire midgets because nobody else can get inside there and rivet."

"I guess I'm in the same category."

"Oh no! I didn't mean that! Gosh, I've got my foot in my mouth today! I meant everybody can contribute."

As they passed Linda and *père* Mary Kay hailed them heartily, yelling, "We're going to the scrap drive!!" Linda waved back.

"You think she's cute?"

"Yeah, she's attractive."

"She's thinks you're dreamy. Just don't tell her I told you, for God's sake."

"Dreamy?"

"Yeah. Would you go out with her?"

"She's a high school girl, Mary Kay."

"So? My fiancé's a college man and I'm just a high school girl."

"Why do you care?"

"Sylvia told me to cheer you up."

"Did she say why I needed to be cheered up by a fifteen-year-old?"

"She said you were sometimes sad."

"Isn't everybody?"

"Yeah. But—" She shrugged.

"Well, truth is, I was engaged before I came here, but the girl called it off."

"Gosh, that is sad! Sure hope it doesn't happen to me."

"Me too. I'm sure it won't."

"If you don't mind my asking, did she say *why?*"

When Mary Kay asked very direct questions in such a forthright manner, answering them was irresistible. No point getting your back up.

"She said the time wasn't right, with the war coming. But I think she loved another fellow more and it took being engaged to me for her to realize it."

"Oh, that's awful!"

"You think so? I try to see the silver lining. I'm glad that she realized her mistake before we got to the altar. Also, now I have to wonder just how much I wanted it, too. Or why I wanted it. Her."

"Oh don't say that! That's really frightening."

"Frightening?"

"Well, heck yeah! I mean you guys were supposedly in love and you had a wedding planned but now it turns out that neither one of you really wanted to do it? It's like this car here is going down the road but nobody's driving it even though I think *you* are, but it turns out you don't even *know* you are. You really think people are so, so *oblivious* to what's happening to them or why?"

"Oh yeah."

"Well, that *is* scary. I'm afraid that whatever power I have to make Donnie care for me depends on my being *right there* where I can erase any negative impressions or second thoughts or bad feelings he's having. I imagine him telling people about me and maybe he feels embarrassed about my age. I can be charming in person, though, and make people forget, I think I can anyway, well, I *know* I can, I mean, why else would he have taken up with me? But I can't be charming by long distance, and even though I've tried really hard in my letters, sometimes it feels like too big a job. I just know he's going to wake up and ask himself why should he be tied down to some *kid* who isn't even there when he's about to go off to war. I just do *not* know what *I* have to offer. He says he can be himself with me, he says college girls are looking for husbands who will support them like princesses and he feels like they're judging him every minute, and I'm not that way."

Or, he thought, Donnie doesn't worry about your judging him. "That sounds like a good reason to love somebody—that you can be yourself with them."

"Yes, but it's also good to try to be the better person that being around someone you love makes you feel like being."

"Does he make you want to be better?"

"Well, I always want to be more mature. I try to act older at least."

He smiled. "So he has no earthly idea how silly you really are?"

"Oh ha ha! No, he knows. And when I'm silly he gets this expression—I wish you could see it!—Here!" She mimed the look women give infants encountered in public. "He just thinks I'm adorable!" She cackled.

"The fool!"

"Oh, indubitably!"

"What's your mother think about your engagement?"

"Sylvia didn't tell you why I'm here?"

"She said that your mother said you were too wild for her to handle."

"Do I seem that way to you?"

"Not so far."

"Okay, then. So now you know why I'm here."

"She wanted to break you and Donnie up?"

"She said she couldn't imagine him being interested in me except for one reason and the last thing she wanted was to be looking after a bush child."

"Mmm. Bet that smarted."

"Yep. Especially—" she teared up suddenly and turned toward the window. "Especially since he's always a *perfect* gentleman. She suspects me of being a tramp because *she's* one."

"Now that's a harsh thing to say about your own mother."

"Yeah, well ... the shoe fits. I wish my dad were around, I bet she wouldn't act that way."

"Do you know where he is?"

"Oh, yeah. He's a captain in the air corps."

"That explains your interest in aviation."

"Yeah."

They drove on in silence; he stopped at the post office, and without being told Mary Kay got out and deposited his letters in the night slot. He wondered if she'd caught her mother *in flagrante delictu* with a 4-Fer. And had been sent away because of that—ironically, to a home where a 4-Fer was working hard to diddle the wife of an absent soldier. It chilled him that she might find them out—her disgust and indignation would be ferocious.

As they rode on, she chewed on a thumb nail. "That stuff about my father being a captain in the air corps? It was bunk, Robert."

"Really?"

"I turned over a new leaf since I got here. I try not to lie to myself about things."

"You weren't lying to yourself, were you?"

"Well, I start wishing really hard and then it sticks in my head and turns into a fact. Then I tell it. But I do know the difference."

Sylvia had said Mary Kay needed the attention of men; now he knew why. "That's good. So what's the real story?"

She shrugged. "I dunno. I kind of remember him from when I was two or three."

"You never heard from him after?"

"Uh-uh. For all I know, he *could* be in the air corps."

"True. If you like, he can be in the air corps when you're with me. I wouldn't mind."

She beamed. "Thanks. But no thanks. Like I said, I swore off lying."

"It's fine if you change your mind."

"Maybe I'll tell Linda. What do you think?"

"Are you afraid she'll stop being your friend?"

"Yeah. She has two parents and she's lived in that same house since she was born. Her dad works and her mom stays home and cooks and cleans and takes care of Linda and her baby brother. They go to church. They all sit down and eat dinner every night, and they take vacations together. If she thinks I don't have a father ... ."

"You'll be trash."

"You got it, Nostradamus."

"If Linda thinks that, she's not much of a friend."

"I guess. But I'm so grateful to have one I'll even settle for one who looks down her nose at me."

He laughed. "Now *that* is really pathetic!"

She grinned. "Isn't it?"

The scrap center was in an abandoned blacksmith barn. Volunteers were mostly women, but there was always a handful of men too old or boys too young and those like Robert: felons and feebs, cowards or cripples. He went out in an old Model A truck. An old man drove and another fellow and he walked along curbs picking up galoshes and twine-wrapped newspapers and balls of aluminum foil and old saucepans and heaved them into the truck. His partner had no apparent infirmity other than a peculiar air of preoccupation that required them to whistle him back the way you do a dog when they finished a block. The old fellow had one good eye, and drool from the chaw in his cheek oozed brown lines down his chin like a Chinese goatee. Grandson was at Pearl

Harbor but wasn't scratched, he said. He's at the Great Lakes Training Center now. *Lee*-roy there, his Mama done had two others join and she told the gummit to keep this one at home to look after her. Like as not he'd a shot hisself in the foot, anyway, and not on purpose.

He told the old fellow about his brother. It afforded him a meager reflected glory. It was humiliating to be lumped with other rejects even while contributing to the war effort. He knew this humiliation was unjustified and even inappropriate; it insulted his fellow volunteers, and he had to choke it down, argue it into a corner. They all felt it. Fellows working at the center told you right off the bat they had bad eyes or flat feet or TB, and they'd love nothing better than to be at the front. They'd expect you to justify your exemption. It got competitive. My exemption's bigger than yours.

Mary Kay and two girls sorted clothing to be sent to refugees; they all chatted amiably and even collectively sniggered when some yokel tried to flirt. Despite Mary Kay's worry about fitting in, it was hard to imagine she wouldn't be accepted—she was neither shy nor abrasively forward; she was warm without crowding your boundaries and could easily carry on a conversation. He had no doubt that she'd led a Victory Girls troop in Ypsilanti, and it was easy to see how a guy six years her senior might find her appealing. She was immensely *likable*.

On the way home he told her about Drooly and *Lee*-roy and had her in stitches. She told him that her coworkers were in her home economics class, where they had garnered a sterling reputation as composers of vegetable casseroles, and they'd sewn their own aprons and embroidered them with little spoons and bowls. "They thank I tawk FUH-nee," Mary Kay said.

Back on Acorn Avenue, Linda's yard was absent of folk. Looking was irresistible—he was eager to have his dreamy self admired, but the empty yard had no such high opinion of his desirability. Mary Kay said, as if reading his thoughts and making light of them, "I wonder if her mom'll let her go out tonight with Harley Wilkinson."

"That's her current beau?"

"She thinks he's a drip but he's a senior and has his own car."

"And that's sufficient to stake a claim?"

"Oh, she's not as shallow as that makes her sound. Besides, her mom thinks she's too young to date. Her mom's real strict and old-fashioned."

He wondered what Mom thought of her daughter's best pal being engaged at fifteen, but tact kept him quiet.

"So my taking her out was purely hypothetical?"

"Oh, there are ways to get around rules and regulations, Buster."

"That there are, kiddo."

To the soldier I didn't marry

I'VE WAITED five hours for you, Dave. It's too late now to go to the Marriage License Bureau.

But that doesn't matter, because I know you won't be coming at all. I may as well take off the blue feather hat you've never seen . . . and try to stop thinking of you, grim and helpless, staring from the transport's deck at the water widening between us.

You'd warned me: "Someday I'll sail. Just like *that.* I may not even be able to phone you. But you'll be my wife, and an Army wife keeps her chin up."

Well, Dave, I didn't quite get to be your wife. It'll be a long time before I set out our International Sterling for breakfasts-for-two. But my chin's up, all the same . . .

I'm going to fish Mrs. Hascom's letter out of the wastebasket. I'm going to write her: Yes, I will take my nursery-school job back, please . . .

You see, darling, in these last few hours I've done a lot of thinking. I've had it brought home to me, pretty forcibly, that I can't sit out this war. *I've got to help hurry you back.*

I realize, suddenly, that it's *me* the government means when it asks women to pitch in here at home. Women like me must take all kinds of jobs—often thankless, inconvenient, unglamorous ones. Those jobs must be done. We're the ones to do them. If all women felt about their men as I do about you . . .

Anyhow, I'm packing tomorrow, and I'm taking along our International Sterling to *keep* me feeling like a bride-to-be. Somehow, it's a little piece of the life we're going to have. The War Bonds my salary buys will help complete our set—after Victory.

Go get that Victory, Dave. And then come back and collect one bride.

Because International is working full speed on war production and making less sterling, your jeweler may not have all the pieces you want.

But no American complains about shortages. He knows that until victory is won, bullets are more important than butter knives . . . surgical instruments more vital than spoons.

So buy War Bonds with your money . . . earmark some of them for International Sterling after the war. International gives you the lifetime satisfaction of knowing . . .

—that your sterling was made by the world's foremost silver house . . .

—that your pattern was designed by International craftsmen whose predecessors were creating spoons of coin silver 100 years ago . . .

—that pieces created by these craftsmen have been exhibited in leading art museums.

FOURTEEN

"Ferret Face rough you up?"

Sylvia peeled the damp cloth from her eyes, sat up on the sofa.

"I don't know why I bother being nice."

"How'd she get along with Mary Kay?"

Robert leaned against the archway. He had his hat in hand, hair slicked back. Clean white shirt, pressed slacks. How long had he been there?

"What time is it?"

Robert craned his head into the dining room. "Grampa says almost six but he's always slow."

Sylvia rubbed her temples. Her brain was foggy; she must've dozed.

"Where's Mary Kay?"

"Linda's," he said. "She told me to tell you they invited her for supper."

"That kid. In town only weeks and already she's had more invitations than I've gotten in six months."

"Tsk tsk."

"I'm not jealous. I'm happy she's doing so well." She dragged herself up, pushing on the sofa arms. She was still wearing her church dress. "I need some coffee, how about you?"

Robert hesitated. "Well. Okay."

Sylvia righted the percolator from the drain tray and filled it, loaded the basket and set it on a burner. Robert didn't sit at the table but instead leaned on the doorframe. This leaning *irritated* her. Looked like he might bolt any second.

"You can at least set your hat down."

He tossed it onto the table.

"So was she civil to Mary Kay?"

"I should say so! She went on and on about how pretty and sweet she was, and she promised to take her shopping for school clothes and never mind it's over for the year in less than a month. You could've knocked me over with a feather—what a stinking hypocrite! Here she gave me the business about turning the hallowed homestead into a boarding house for white trash and now she's playing the grand duchess!"

Robert chuckled. "Surely that's better than treating Mary Kay like dirt."

"Of course! I'm just saying it looked suspicious. With me it's all threats and lectures, as if that'd do a bit of good, and with her it's all sugar and spice. Comes to the same, in the end. She's only looking for a lever to lift you with."

"How'd Mary Kay take it?"

"How do you think? She's a teenage girl who never had a single advantage and a rich lady wants to buy her clothes?"

"Well, having them on a good footing can't be all bad, Sylvia."

Sylvia caught his little smirk. Something flared in her and for a second she thought she might swing the skillet at him. She wouldn't bite. Actually, she was relieved that Evelyn hadn't embarrassed them by catty remarks, and she was a little gratified—okay, begrudgingly—that Evelyn wanted to help Mary Kay, whatever the motive.

She took a long breath, and they waited in silence for the coffee to perk. Then she steered the chuckling percolator over two mugs she'd set out. When she brought them to the table, Robert bent to pick his up.

"For pity's sake, Robert! It's not going to kill you to sit and talk to me for five minutes."

Grinning sheepishly, he eased into a chair.

"I bet I look like Hades."

"You look beautiful as always."

"I haven't even washed my face since six o'clock this morning."

She fingered a strand of hair, tried to swing it in view but it hurt her neck to crane her head. She'd napped wrong. And, more irritating—he looked especially handsome. Rested, tanned, his hands strong but his nails clean.

"I said you look beautiful as always."

"Don't say it that way."

"What way?"

"You said it like 'yawn yawn etcetera etcetera and so forth.'"

He was quiet a moment. "You're hard to please today."

"It's Sunday evening. Evelyn Karacek always ruins my Sundays. And I have war work to look forward to tomorrow. And the next day. And the day after that. I almost wish she'd fought harder to make me quit."

"I thought you liked having work, your own money." His lips twitched into a half-smile so slight she knew he didn't want it seen. "I understood Father McNally prescribed it."

"I do." She met his eye. "He did."

He shrugged. He moved his mug from his knee to the table. He was about to get up.

"But the irony's galling."

"What irony?"

"I married into one of this town's wealthiest families and I'm still working like I have all my damn life. And I'm the only female member of it doing that. Neither one of his sisters has to lift a finger to provide for a family."

"So you're the only one making a contribution, Sylvia."

"Yeah." She gave him a weary salute. "Buy war bonds."

He laughed. His legs swung to the side.

"Hey, stick around. I'll rustle some grub."

"Gotta go."

"What's your rush?"

He shrugged. Then blushed.

"You've got a date! Who is it? Marjorie back?"

"No."

"Anybody I know? What's her name? Where'd you meet her?"

"Now, Sylvia, I won't trouble you with all that. It's just a casual chat."

"You can have a casual chat right here!"

He rose. "No, I can't. I wish I could, but I can't."

He carried his mug to the sink, rinsed it, upended it in the drainer basket. She wondered if "can't" was meant as a dig. Sometimes he liked to punish her for how she struggled to stay faithful.

"I'll give you a post mortem, okay?"

"Have to do, I guess."

Leftovers, she thought as she watched him stroll out of the kitchen, donning his fedora, *a man on his way to something or someone who'll brighten his day.*

She sat at the table as dusk seeped in like fog. She felt too weary to turn on the light because that would initiate a chain of activity she had no energy for: changing out of her dress and slip and stockings and girdle and into slacks, a blouse, and slippers—too early for a nightgown—washing her face, combing her hair, making a meal, sitting and eating it alone, cleaning up after, dragging up the stairs to her sewing room to sit like a good wife and write to Georgie about her week, keep up his spirits—every war widow's patriotic charge—when her own were flat on the floor. She usually told him news of his family she'd gleaned from these grueling Sundays; she presumed it made him feel good to think she was in regular contact and took an interest, but it was hard, so hard sometimes, not to whine to him about how Evelyn treated her.

She hadn't told him she'd gone to work as a seamstress for Uncle Sam because she was afraid he'd react like his mother, and she sure couldn't tell him the pay was not as important as how idle hands were the devil's tools. Robert's hands, anyway.

Lucky girl. Probably another secretary. Free, white, and twenty-one. Must be nice. Robert picks you up in that company coupe and takes you dancing at that roadhouse—hey, that fella didn't know a tango from a tuba until she taught him, how's that for gratitude! Even just sitting at a table sipping a cocktail and listening to a band would sure beat wallowing in the gloom over cold coffee. Maybe he'd take this girl to the Sky View Room. Back when she was hostess at the White Blossom, she'd sneak upstairs during her breaks and linger just inside the door when touring swing bands came to town—Harry James, Woody Herman, and Russ Carlyle. The Sky View Room couldn't compare to, say, the Empire Room of the Palmer House, where she saw Hal Kemp's orchestra and his show of "12 Terrific Tigresses." But the Sky View was among the few night spots on the road between Houston and New Orleans to boast glass-globed candles on tables spread with white linen. Windows on two sides faced east to the small port with its berthed oil tankers and the glimmering island of the Penn shipyard, and south to the Gulf, though to see ocean water would require peering across fifteen miles of soaring refinery tubing that coughed a billowing chemical miasma into that view. Late at night, Sylvia would often seek a pretext to deliver a message to the manager or make an inquiry about reservations on someone's behalf just to linger and listen to the music and watch the dancers. She'd burn with envy when the songbirds took the spotlight. It would just tear her up to have to creep about in the shadows like some pitiful match girl while on the stage—a tiny stage, even, such as the Sky View had—the spotlight gleamed on the singer's spangly dress and the diamonds in her ears. And all the while she felt that she had as much talent. Maybe more than some of them she heard. Like Helen Forrest, prime example! Some people get all the breaks, others just have to plug along, and it just did not seem fair.

Once, on a weeknight when no band was booked and only a half dozen tables were occupied, she talked the manager into letting her play the piano and sing. He said he liked Cole Porter tunes so she quietly chirped a background accompaniment to the murmur and clink of cutlery with "Anything Goes" and "Let's Do It!" and "Just One of Those Things." He liked her but couldn't pay her, he said, and she said she appreciated the chance to keep sharp and maybe she could do it *gratis* again? How much do you appreciate it? he asked, so she never went again.

No, not the Empire Room, for damn sure. But some young kid from a small town like this would probably be impressed by it and think her escort had a lot of *savoir faire* to take her there.

Robert's a college man and acts like a gentleman when he needs to—that would set most small-town girls' hearts to fluttering. Dark eyes with long lashes and the way his lips are always curved into a grin that might or might not be a smirk, and when he looks right at you you're never sure what he's thinking though you suspect you might not have all your clothes on. He's the kind girls say is "devilish handsome," meaning his looks alone might make you tempted to do things you shouldn't. He'll wrap that girl around his finger, have her starry-eyed and swooning. He's the kind of fellow you never quite trust but you sure want to give him a chance to test you.

Definitely not the marrying kind. Not if you have your wits about you, which you don't when it comes to it. Raymond was like that—see what you get.

You got Anthony. And then Josef.

As she was sinking into a funk so deep the only way out was slitting her wrists, the phone rang. On the way, she turned on the foyer chandelier light, and when she answered, she saw her shadow dash to the end of the hall and out the door.

Mary Kay wanted to stay at Linda's until ten.

"Is it all right with her mother?"

"Uh-huh. We asked already."

"What about homework?"

"We're doing it together right now."

Was it permissible to say "no" because you wanted company and were jealous?

"I don't know, Mary Kay. It seems like imposing."

"Oh, please! Her mom doesn't care—honest! I'll let you talk to her."

"All right." She meant "all right you can stay," but Mary Kay misinterpreted and went to fetch Linda's mother, who had a virtue name—Faith? or Hope? The prospect of playing Concerned Mother hiked her spirits. She was never certain what these small-minded, small-town people here thought of her, and the opportunity to impress a local of apparently sterling character with her own worth shouldn't go unexploited.

"Hello?"

"Hello, this is Sylvia Karacek, Mary Kay's godmother—"

"Oh, yes—"

"I insisted she put you on the line so I could make sure she's not a bother."

"Oh, no! Why she's just a dah-lin gurl! We're pleased to have her."

"Well, thank you. We're pleased she's found a friend in a girl as nice as Linda."

"That's real nahce of you to say."

Having basted one another with proof of their excellent manners and judgment of character, Sylvia hoped that Linda's mother might invite her over for coffee or lunch. As she considered making an offer herself, her job loomed as an obstacle, and not merely a practical hurdle: did FaithHope's opinion of women war-workers match Evelyn's?

"Thank you," Sylvia finally said. "I hope we can meet soon. I'm afraid that being a new bride and all, I've been remiss about meeting my neighbors."

"Oh thad be jus' *duh-light-ful,*" cooed Faith or Hope. "And the neglect is all on mah side, I'm afraid. I hope we can meet soon too!"

Though both yearned for a meeting, they'd apparently have to wait for a third-party intervention. Little was left but to say good-bye. Sylvia stood in the pale fringe of the chandelier's light with the dead receiver in hand thinking she could call Doris, though that was always unsatisfactory—you had to leave word at the trailer camp office to be called by her. She wanted to talk *now.*

She strode through the house and flicked on lights in every room, turned on the radio in the parlor loud enough so that anywhere in the house she could hear laughter from "Fibber McGee and Molly," if not the jokes themselves. She changed out of her dress and into her negligee and robe, washed her face and combed her hair, turned off the radio, opened a bottle of burgundy and carried it and a glass upstairs.

She sat for an hour or so sipping the wine at her writing desk, a sheet of her cream-hued, monogrammed stationery under her elbows and the gold-nibbed Parker uncapped at the ready but utterly reliant on a hand that couldn't stay in its traces. Dearest Georgie. Your mother made a crack about how strong I look since I took a factory job. My fingers and nails are so ugly I had to sit on them the whole time I was at Kountze today. I am invisible to Elizabeth, anyway, so thank God for small favors. Our boarder upsets me no end, gets under my skin, I am paralyzed when he touches me, and I know I should give him the boot because it's playing with fire to be around him, but I don't because he needs a place to stay and we need the rent money and if you believe those as reasons then you're as foolish as I am.

Hard to write when what you really had to say could not be said.

Dearest Georgie,
I have really great news! It got to where I simply could not sit at home like a lazy no-good-for-nothing while my wonderful fellow is off making a sacrifice—I felt awful not being useful, so I took a job. It's at Carson's Mattress Factory, only now they're not making just mattresses. Since I had experience as a seamstress in Chicago, they put me in charge of girls who're just learning, and we're sewing powder bags. I'm an Instructor! When they

get proficient at that, we'll all move up to parachutes!

I hope you don't mind, honey. It makes me feel good to know I'm doing my part, and also it keeps me from having to ask anybody for money. Your mother has raised a little fuss about it, and she hinted today that she might tell you. I hope you get my letter before hers, that's all I've got to say. I haven't been hiding anything, I swear.

She heard the front door open: must be ten on the dot. Mary Kay was a good kid; it was hard to imagine what Doris meant by "incorrigible," though much of it related to Doris's fear Mary Kay might wind up pregnant.

"I'm back! Thanks, Sylvia!" Mary Kay jutted her head into the room; her gaze flitted to the bottle—almost empty now—on the desk beside her glass.

"You're welcome, hon. Linda's mom seems real nice. What's her name?"

"Prudence. She is nice. And you are too!"

Sylvia smiled, but it was to Mary Kay's back—she had no need to linger and chat. After a moment, she heard Mary Kay's slippers flapping in the hall as she went down to the bathroom. Anthony would be her age. It was deeply satisfying to have Mary Kay stay with her, though often a pang knifed her heart because of the link to her own child. It irked her that Doris took Mary Kay for granted or spoke as if she were only a burden.

I'm getting rent from Doris for Mary Kay, too, now, so between your pay and my job and our boarders, we're doing really well on our own, sweetheart. It makes me proud of us to know that.

I'm just like Greer Garson in *Mrs. Miniver,* Sylvia thought. Keep the home fires burning. It was important to make sacrifices. It would be nice to be out dancing and dining and having cocktails, but that was for people with less mettle and starch. It would be nice to be in the Sky View Room and be free, white, and twenty-one, like a Magnolia secretary, a whole bevy there for him to pick from. He certainly didn't take *her* to the Sky View. Kissing him in the swing. She shouldn't have drunk so much. Shouldn't've drunk *anything.* He promised to behave, but when they practiced dancing here in the house . . . . It's true what the Baptists say—you get *all mixed up* with your partner, that close, your legs tangle together and you're belly to belly and breast to breast and you're moving together to the beat, the scent of him all in your lungs and your head. She suspected if she were to let herself go, he could get her more hot and bothered than she'd ever been.

Of course single gals like those Magnolia secretaries never have to worry about cheating on anybody, only about getting knocked up. Those girls are tramps, anyway, most likely!

Right now they're parked and are necking in that company car. Somebody ought to tell his superiors, surely *that's* not an authorized use of the vehicle! Let alone one employee doing that to another employee—must be against the rules as well, got to be. Must be nice to flout the rules and regulations and just scratch your itch when and where you want, no qualms or quibbles.

She'd worked herself into a familiar nocturnal mood where it seemed the perimeter of her life strained to contain the feelings bursting in her. That Georgie was now in California and she was stuck here seemed an especially cruel joke. She'd given up her plans and her dream of *doing something* with her talents out there, thinking that she would be safe and secure here for the duration, nestled in the bosom of a family who could provide for her but also blessed with having Georgie as a companion, a friend, someone who adored her and lavished his time, energy and attention on her.

Then he'd gone and left her here not only alone but *stuck in place.* In that *desertion* he turned out pretty much like all the other bastards she'd fallen in love with.

Tonight she couldn't sit still but had nowhere to go. She turned on her Victrola and played Benny Goodman records, but she had to keep the sound down because Mary Kay had gone to bed and tomorrow was a school day—that seemed the umpteenth restriction in her narrow life, even if she told herself she welcomed the chance to be a "mom" again. She finished off the bottle and talked herself out of opening another, but that too seemed just another oppressive limitation.

She was house-bound. The injustice burned bitter in her soul.

Now she was alone and had to work in a factory! What had she gained?

She lay back on her Victorian fainting sofa and had herself a cry; it seemed to help, but the sound of her own mewling irritated her no end and cheated her out of the pleasure.

Around midnight she saw Robert's company car creep to the curb in front and park. He passed under the street light on his way down the driveway, and he had a saucy little bounce in his step. She wanted to stick her head out the window and curse or fling something at him.

She couldn't go on living like this.

FIFTEEN

He was at his bathroom mirror in his BVDs when someone tapped on his screen door. He'd seen the light on in her sewing room and had been tempted to pass through the house but sat on it hard. Better in the long run to keep his hands to himself. He already regretted climbing all over her in the kitchen the day before. That kind of thing tore her up. She'd agonize for days.

He slipped on slacks and, barefoot and in his undershirt, he went to the door. She lurked on the fringe of the porch light; she wore a robe but her hair was brushed out nice, she had on fresh lipstick, and when he smelled her wine breath and perfume through the screen he had half a mind not to let her in.

"I forgot to give you some mail last night."

"Okay, thanks. Come on in."

He stepped back. She opened the screen, handed him a solicitation from the Rutgers alumni association and a Dear Joe Blow letter from Hartford Life. He leaned toward his desk and chunked them right into the trash, thinking *she comes half-loaded to my door already undressed for bed—God, does she think I'm made of steel?*

"How was your date?"

Oh. Post-mortem. "Come on in," he repeated, though she was standing inside. "Sit down." He waved toward the room. Other than the desk chair, the bed was the only place to sit. She sauntered to it and perched on the edge, legs crossed, elbows locked and palms flat behind to prop herself.

"I'd offer you a drink but I don't have anything. There might be a finger of that homemade hootch Marjorie and I got, but I use it mostly as a substitute for kerosene when I burn the trash barrel."

She laughed. "No thanks."

"What do you want to know? And why?"

"My, you sound so suspicious! I'm not the F.B.I.. Since I'm a poor homebody I want to hear how people are having fun. Vicarious enjoyment."

Since he'd this minute come in and meant to undress, wash up, and go directly to bed, he hadn't turned on any lamp but the overhead in the bathroom, and the room was dark but for a wedge of light pale as Swiss cheese from the half-opened door. It struck across her upraised knees and gleamed on one shin. He stood near the bed.

"I went to church."

"That's a good one."

"No kidding. I took your pal Betty to Sunday night services at the First Methodist."

"You took Betty out? But she's engaged!"

"Why would that prevent her from having an escort to church?"

"Since when does a Protestant service last until midnight?"

He laughed. "I thought you weren't the F.B.I.. If you want to hear this, don't cross-examine me."

"Okay. I apologize. Go on, please. I guess."

"We went to dinner afterward. Then we talked for a couple hours."

"In her apartment?"

"No. What kind of girl do you think she is?"

"I'm beginning to wonder."

Tormenting Sylvia was more fun than being on his date, but she'd never learn that. "We sat in the car."

"I see. Well, I can certainly picture *that.* Does your boss know about it?"

"Are you going to rat on me?"

"No. But I am surprised about Betty."

"Are you disappointed in her?"

"She does go on about her fiancé."

"I got an earful, too, you know."

She laughed. "Bet *that* was a damper!"

He said, "Well, she did cry out his name but at the moment it happened I couldn't have cared less."

That shut her up. After a moment, he sat beside her but left a foot between them.

"You're really a cad to say that."

"Thought you wanted the gory details."

When she didn't answer, he said, "If it's any consolation, the whole time I was with her I was thinking of you."

"Robert," she murmured. And reached to pat his arm. "Thanks for that, even if you don't mean it. I've had a rough night."

"What happened?"

"Dark night of the soul, as they say." After a beat, she sighed. "I decided it was wrong for you to go on staying here."

He looked at her face. She wore the doleful expression of a Christian martyr from an ancient painting.

"Should I pack this minute or do I have a grace period?"

"Oh, you *know* why I'm saying that! Don't be sarcastic!" She started weeping into her hands.

He handed her the clean handkerchief from his hip pocket. He was tired of this drama over so little it hardly amounted to more than hanky-panky under the mistletoe at an office Christmas party. Maybe more, but not much. To him, anyway.

Then he got it. She was letting him know in advance how she intended to punish them for the sin she wanted to commit right on the spot. She wasn't in an uproar about a peccadillo from a week ago or yesterday: she'd calculated the payment for the larger transgression still on her list. She vows to remove temptation from within her reach; he vows to move and stay away—then they're free to enjoy the sin they've passed judgment on in advance and meted out the sentence for.

He got up, shut the landing door, and clicked off the bathroom light. He sat and scooted close and held her while she snuffled and wiped her eyes with her fingertips.

"Honey, it's okay," he murmured. "I know it has to be done. It's hard, that's all. I don't blame you."

She leaned toward him. He could smell her, feel heat radiating from her body.

"Do you remember that night in the swing?" he whispered in her ear. Her head bumped his chin. "That kiss made me a goner, Sylvia. I wish it wasn't true, believe me."

"Shh," she said.

Down in his gut he felt stubborn and balky, blindered, his nose fixed on the road ahead. "Don't you care for me at all?"

"I told you I do."

"I don't know if I believe it."

She sighed. "I want to tell you something I've never told anybody. You can't make too much of it, but I want you to know. About Georgie and me."

She forced him to prompt her. "Yeah? What?"

"Please don't misunderstand it. He's … he's not … Oh, dear. This is so difficult to tell. Especially to someone like you."

"Someone like me? What does that mean?"

"I only mean someone who is so, so *passionate.*"

When she didn't go on, he tried to help. "Are you saying he isn't *passionate?*"

Her head bobbed. "It's because of his condition and his medication. But he's a wonderful person. He's kind and sensitive and thoughtful. He's also very *compassionate.* And funny. He's a pleasure to be around. He never went to college but you'd be amazed at how much he's taught himself."

He'd heard enough. He was determined to be so "passionate" she could never live without him. He twisted and insinuated his face into the crook of her neck, his lips against her beating vein. "Poor Syl," he murmured. "You're so sweet, too sweet, and dear. I want you to be happy." He laid his palm across her thigh. "You're the kindest person I know. You've been so good, so true. And I know it's been hard." He nibbled up her neck and probed her ear with his tongue, and she cringed and squeezed his hand, bent her head away.

"Don't, Robert! Please don't."

"Oh, Sylvia, honey—it's the last time we'll ever be together. It breaks my heart—don't you know that?"

"It's hard for me, too."

"I know. All I want is to lie beside you." He lay on his side and tugged on her shoulder to collapse her back across the bed. She reclined on her elbows for a bit then surrendered to gravity and sank into the mattress. He draped his hand across her stomach and she put hers over it, to control it, he guessed. He eased his hand slowly out from under hers and trailed his fingertips up the underside of her breast. Her hand stalked his, trapped his fingers. But didn't move them away, only held them stationary.

He lifted that hand, licked and sucked her fingers, the soft scooped crevices between, until she made a fist and shoved it under her back. But he could relish the taste of any available part, and he tongued the inner crook of her elbow and, peeling back her lapels, the tops of her breasts. He kept murmuring he adored her, that this was their last night. He knew she couldn't say yes and didn't want to say no, and though she struggled by lying passive, her body betrayed her.

She took his touches and kisses with passive abandon at first, as if surrendering her body to circumstances but withholding her approval, then that passivity contained an undercurrent of interest, as if she'd noticed a tingling nerve and sensations where their lips met. After an interim long enough to satisfy herself and presumably him too that she had struggled with her conscience, she let herself go. She helped by not resisting, and eventually his ears were brushing her inner thighs as his head and mouth moved to and fro, and moments later her jogging heels were hooked on the backs of his legs. Plunging into her, he blubbered into her damp neck, she moaned then murmured something indistinguishable, and as he got into a rhythm and sang *darling darling,* she called out, *Oh yes honey oh honey oh oh Ohhhh!!*

He didn't know how long they babbled, but soon she went rigid then groaned and writhed under him, and he turned inside out.

As they panted in each other's arms, a knock rapped his door. They were instantly electrified. He leapt up, scrambled for his drawers, yelled, "Just a minute! Be right there!" forgetting that with the lights off and the late hour, the knocker might presume he was asleep; instead, he sounded as if he'd been awake. Even as he was hopping into his underwear he was aware of the timing—the knock followed right after their *passionate* duet—and he wondered if the knocker had waited for it to stop.

He cracked the door and tried to look sleepy. He knew he looked disheveled.

"Robert, sorry to disturb you, but I can't find Sylvia!"

"Yeah? What's the problem?"

"There's a phone call. Collect. From her husband in California, I think!"

"Uhh. Maybe she couldn't sleep and took a walk around the block. She does that sometimes."

"Oh. What should I do?"

"Tell him to leave a number and she'll call back."

"Okay. Sorry."

He watched as Mary Kay ran down his stairs and into the house.

"Quick thinking," said Sylvia.

It sounded like a reproach, as if she was too righteous to lie that glibly.

"I didn't know what else to say."

"Do you think she'd been out there a while?"

"I don't know." He reached to embrace her, but she put her palm to his chest.

"I think I might've been … *talking.*"

"I love you."

"I think she might've heard us. She said Georgie was on the phone? I've got to go!"

"Sneak into the alley, walk around the block and come in the front door."

"Yes. You were quick thinking there." Now she sounded grateful one of them kept a cool head.

"You're welcome."

Hours later, the floor under his bed rumbled, and he shot awake and lay wondering where he was and where the thrumming came from, then he grew alert—a wan lavender light suffused the room, his watch said 5:40, and he realized that Sylvia had cranked up the Lincoln. Suicide by asphyxiation zipped across his mind, but no—headed for early Mass, no doubt. She'd surely spent a sleepless night. The Lincoln backed slowly north toward the garage door, then the tires crunched leaves on the concrete driveway strips. In the near distance, dogs arfed like they'd treed something. His bad leg throbbed. Wincing, he rose and stretched.

Then a *YIPE!* like a strangled bark shot up, followed by a hideous howl of an animal in pain. A car door slammed and Sylvia's voice rang out, "Oh my God! My God!"

He dashed to the window. The Lincoln was halfway up the drive with the driver's door flung open like a broken wing, and Sylvia in that rue-colored dress stood at the rear bumper with hands clapped to her cheeks. She shrieked, "Oh my God!" Something light-colored jerked spastically behind the rear then vanished. It alternately bayed and screeched. At the mouth of the driveway in the early morning light a fellow with two Scotties looked on. His dogs yapped and lunged frantically on their leashes, and the fellow hollered to Sylvia, "Better put that dog out of its misery!"

He ran in his bare feet down the stairs and across the damp grass to the driveway.

"Oh, Robert, help!"

Mollie lay on her flank between the strips furiously spurring herself around in circles with one back leg while the other trailed bloody and useless. As she barked she spewed blood from her snout.

"Did you run over her?"

"I don't know! I don't know!!"

He bent closer to the twitching collie, gritting his teeth, his heart pounding, while the fellow with the Scotties yammered at them from fifteen feet away like a Satanic cheerleader, "You better put that poor mutt out of its misery!"

"I was backing up, and I was upset and I wasn't watching," moaned Sylvia. "I felt a big bump and then poor Mollie. Is it her leg? Is it just her leg?"

Her hips were canted strangely, but her condition was hard to assess because she was convulsing and yanking her hindquarters about by pawing at the ground with her forelegs, frantically digging herself through the twig and seed-ball littered turf toward the underside of the car. Her limp hindquarters smeared red glistening streaks on the grass, and her efforts stretched open the broken leg so that gristle and the slimy white bone sheath glistened under the blood.

"I think her back's broken."

"You better do something!" the fellow yelled again.

He whirled and yelled, "Okay, goddamnit! We hear you!" Old Mrs. Malone stood at her parlor window clutching her cat in her arms. Sylvia was in the shock that paralyzes, but he was sailing into the one where you act without deliberating. He ran to the front steps, vaguely relieved to be away from the pitiful howls, and he darted through the door thinking *when horses break their legs they have to be shot;* he flung open the door to the foyer closet and pawed through the garments until he spied the old shotgun muzzle up against the wall. Soon as he grabbed it he realized it had no shells, so he marked time, dancing his fretful idiot's jig of indecision, his heart thudding against his ribs, momentarily stymied, and meanwhile the dog went on baying.

He rushed back outside with the shotgun and sprinted up to Sylvia.

"Don't look!" He spun her to face the garage. He whirled back to Georgie's mutt, now lying partly under the bumper with its side bellowing like a sump pump. He loomed over her with the gun helplessly wondering what next, and the fellow on the drive yelled, "Shoot him! Damn! Shoot!"

He swung the weapon around, clutched the muzzle and lifted the butt over his head. Then he cleavered down, but out of squeamishness he faltered and checked the swing so he only whacked the mutt on its ear. It yowled louder as the blow bounced its head off the ground.

He gritted his teeth, sucked in air and locked it in his lungs, pleaded *please don't move, damn you!* Then he swung down as hard as he could and cracked the poor thing's skull open like a coconut.

They got the old mutt buried by the garage before it was even full light. Mary Kay slept through it all and they told her the dog died in her sleep.

SIXTEEN

IN EL PASO, Georgie hauled his valise into the station to don his uniform. Two soldiers bearded in Barbasol were at the sinks in khaki pants and undershirts, and they said howdy. Their air of camaraderie relieved him—it probably wasn't illegal to wear the uniform with a medical discharge, but the absence of campaign ribbons and those blank sleeves might raise an eyebrow.

He wanted Sylvia to see him in it. Though Houston was hours away, he didn't want to wind up changing on the train. Also he enjoyed the reflected glory: when the train left El Paso, he lied like a dog to a cute kid from Arkansas with short red hair newly curled about her ears. He became an artillery spotter, a fellow creeping into enemy territory armed with pistol, walkie-talkie, binoculars and a map. Oh yeah, sure, had close calls, everybody does . . . .

She got off before Houston, taking the pleasure, leaving the guilt. He might fool her, but could he fool his mother, Marianne, Sylvia—or especially Elizabeth? Seeing him in uniform, his sis would bray like a donkey and call up the times he'd larked about the front yard in a Nosferatu cape.

No—he wasn't an imposter! But what was he? Certainly not a hero or even a potential warrior—he wouldn't be sent to the front and thus play on his family's fears. There'd be no scenes where he warns, brow all knitted, "If I don't come back . . ." and his wife protests, "Hush! Don't talk about it!" Of course they didn't know he'd been kicked out; any drama of his potential doom would be mounted on a false premise.

He wished he hadn't lied so impulsively about the furlough. How could he undo it? Summoning the courage to confess that he'd been booted out of boot was made doubly hard by the satisfaction of knowing he *had* served creditably and that they were *proud* of him. To be defeated, once again, by his body—that was especially bitter.

It seemed that each time he'd imagined he'd outwitted, outworn, or outgrown his illness, it reared up and smacked him. Thank God at least Sylvia was such a compassionate person! So patient and kind. Being with her had muted the *What If* song that had run through his head throughout his life, but now it had come soaring back from around the corner with a new stanza or two.

What if you're on guard duty somewhere in the Pacific and the enemy creeps up on you and you're twitching like a headless hen because there's a thunderstorm inside your skull and they just laugh and stroll right past you?

Then the old refrains came rushing back, the oldie-goldies, reprise of the Top Forty from his earlier days:

What if you're walking downtown alone and you get dizzy and your aura falls over you like the big *bwana's* tiger net and you suffer a *marked constriction of your visual field,* a camera shutter closing, then you fall down right in the road?

What if a truck comes along that second and you keel over into its path? The tires crunch your skull and leave tread marks in your face, crunch your skull like a robin's egg you see lying on the walk yellow yolk sticky oozing from it, the bumper'd whack your shin oh that would hurt wouldn't it? Like somebody hitting you with a baseball bat smack across the shins.

What if you're talking to an ordinary kid who comes along and he doesn't know about your auras and fits and you say—"'Lo, how's it goahn?" and he says about the same, and he adds, "Hey, let's go down to the river and mess around," meaning see who can chunk a rock the farthest, or who can stick his arm down deep in the water under a log and catch a catfish barehanded or in the shallows turn over rocks for crawdads or get sticks and look for snakes or poke around dried mud flats where the water went down after a flood and look for swell junk like old keys and tin cans or limbs of dolls or hunks of crockery, or dig a cave in the riverbank to make a clubhouse, or go with no plans just gliding from one moment to the next the way kids do sniffing out fun from wherever it might be hiding? Let's say you go along, Georgie. *What if* you aren't but just around the corner and your feet start that strange Lindy on their own and your newfound pal says, "What the hey, fella!??" Or you get down to the river with each minute gone by stitching you guys together like he's not even noticing you're a pink blob who wears glasses, and you can show him how to skip a nice flat stone across the water like Walter showed you—except when you get into your wind-up, the strange calliope music roars in your head and another sun pops up alongside the first, making it awful hot, next thing you know this new pal's saying, "Hey, fella, you sick or somethin'?" *What if* then instead of helping you he runs off and you pitch headlong into the water, huh? *What if* that happens, huh? Or he runs off yelling, "Hey, this kid's having a fit down by the river!"

And all come a-runnin'—Hey, big show!

What if you're in water over your head and you black out?

What if you're poking a stick at a moccasin or a rattler with your pal and suddenly you collapse like a playing-card house or fall like a kite when the wind stops, and that snake bites you on the face? (It's sort of like an inner weather, a tornado coming on a sultry afternoon, the skies glowering, the wind rising, the rain pelting, and all you can do is go for shelter quick as you can.)

What if you're riding a bike?

What if you're sitting in a theatre?

What if you're ordering a meal in a café?

What if you're talking to a girl?

What if you're talking to a girl you see at the library and she has no idea about your aura, your cry, your fall, your tonus, your clonus and excretory release, and you say, "'Lo, how's it goahn?" and she smiles back, and you say, "Wanna go get a soda or a sundae with a cherry on top?" And she goes right along as if she doesn't care you're a big pink whale with skin like a baby's butt because you never get to go outside and you wear goggles and you stutter, and you think *Okay, so far, so good!* as you stroll along the walk. Turns out say she's just arrived here and doesn't know that you have a history of toppling over on the spot and doing a St.Vitus dance on the pavement and then crapping your pants and yowling, and you're thinking *By Golly! Maybe this time* … and you go to Emerson's Drug and sit on a stool like a lot of other kids are doing and never mind that they *do* know your history, but you can just look them steady in the eye because, you know, this new girl, well, since she doesn't know the history, maybe you actually no longer *have* a history. And, okay, let's say, Georgie, that you manage to get her into Emerson's sitting on that stool, and you order and then you both swing on your stools slurping your single soda with two straws so romantic and your forehead's touching hers and her fine silky hair is gossamer stroking your fat cheek and you can see the little sweat beads glisten on her straw and her red lips part and her tongue slides along the length of it, and you can smell her powder the way Elizabeth smells when she comes out of the bath, and her lashes are long and her eyes glittery and twinkling with the delight of being so close … . But then your shoulders and your head want to do a drum roll on that tin ceiling and next you cough up a glob of milky soda in her face. *Splat! What if,* then, huh? *Gosh, honey, we knew you were new and if we'd had a chance, we'd a warned ya!*

What if you're handing Elizabeth a spoon to stir her custard? And she doesn't see you careening toward the handle of the pot over the burner?

What if you have a fit and *never come out of it!* And you get sent to a hospital where they put you in a locked room and let you foam at the mouth and shriek like a banshee for the rest of your life?

What if Mama finds stuff on your sheets?

She sent Georgie for a man-to-man talk with Ol' Doc Waller. She considered him the font of medical wisdom as he'd practiced medicine in his two-story home at the corner of Pine and State since before the turn of the century (he had told Georgie several times, "I spanked your Mama, boy!")

He removed Gower's book on epilepsy from the shelf and, fairly shaking it at Georgie, asked him if he knew that young patients who couldn't control themselves were sometimes castrated for their own welfare, that certain, uh, *foul practices* could contribute to his frailness, and that if his disease were to progress it might lead to severe mental instability?

In lieu of castration, Ol' Doc Waller recommended, and performed, a circumcision to reduce the amount of "unhealthy stimulation" Georgie might experience. He also suggested that Evelyn send him to a colony in New York composed entirely of epileptic patients.

"No, it's not a madhouse," Ol' Doc Waller assured his mother.

Doctors at the Craig Colony were reluctant to encourage their patients to marry and bear children. They believed that epilepsy was genetically connected to other afflictions of the nervous system such as hysteria, and to alcoholism and madness, although the precise nature of the link remained murky and in dispute. Where epilepsy was found in a family, one often (though not necessarily) also located genius and madness. Patients at Craig Colony could name the pantheon of epileptic, possibly mad geniuses: Vincent Van Gogh, Napoleon, the Russian author Dostoevsky, Mohammad, Peter the Great, and others. They took consolation in these names, though they were warned against delusions of grandeur (*I have epilepsy; ergo, I am a genius!*) and were cautioned not to aggravate an incipient unhealthy mental state by imitation.

They believed the condition to be incurable, Georgie learned, except where the cause of the seizures is organic, and they believed epilepsy was progressive and degenerative. The extent to which patients eventually succumbed to a chronic vegetative state (or to its opposite, a highly excitable "visionary" or hysterical condition) varied widely from one to the next and was related, they believed, to the age of the patient at the onset of attacks, frequency and severity of attacks, and the patient's surroundings.

Debate went on about the effect of the sex act upon a patient. While some believed sexual stimulation precipitated seizures, others held that "the acrimony of accumulated semen" might also serve as an irritant. The most frightening prospect for Georgie had been learning from Ol' Doc Waller that oophorectomy was a treatment, but most doctors regarded castration as a remedy for only the most recalcitrant cases.

This was more or less the medical fog in which Georgie was enveloped upon arriving at Craig Colony in Sonyea. (Ironically, Sonyea either meant "sunny place" in Iroquois or it was an acronym for State of New York Epileptic Association, depending upon whom he asked). He became one of 1,000 patients residing, studying, and working in over 100 buildings spread about a 2,000 acre campus originally built and inhabited by Shakers, a campus bisected by a stupendous gorge carved by Keshequa Creek with bluffs some 200-feet tall.

He felt both lost and at home. It was one thing to live in Port Farview where you were the only visible epileptic (rumors abounded of course, but he never saw anyone else have a seizure); it was quite another to be among so many where seizures were common as sneezes, and it was astounding to realize the disease came in as many variations as there were individuals afflicted by it, many more exotic and florid than his own, with aural and visual hallucinations, *déjà vu* and *jamais vu,* and the "big and small" sensations of Gulliver and Alice—macropsia and micropsia. This was both comforting and disconcerting. It meant that when your nerves suddenly scrambled and your blood ran backwards and lightning crackled in your brain and you fell and flopped about, no one would be shocked or disgusted. But it also meant that when you were blessedly enjoying the placid sunny weather of your system between hurricanes, it was impossible to forget your affliction because some patients who shared your quarters and your classrooms might have, say, two dozen fits a day.

As if the Shaker sensibility had embedded itself in the woodwork of the buildings and the flora and fauna, the patients were segregated by gender and lived on either side of the gorge, females in cottages with floral names (Dahlia, Clematis, Daisy, Heliotrope), men in more robust-sounding domiciles named after sturdy hardwoods such as Oak, Walnut, and Hickory. The campus was a self-contained world, with a gymnasium, a store, dining halls, a church, several infirmaries large and small, and, unlike Ol' Doc Waller, the doctors at Craig were more liberal in allowing their patients to engage in dances and theatricals and sports, and they had outdoor picnics on the Olmstead-designed Lower Green. They studied in classrooms; they were given light industrial or vocational training in shops, and they worked about in the kitchens and blacksmith shops and orchards.

Georgie soon developed a crush on a patient he met one spring afternoon when they'd both been called to Letchworth Hall to attend to business. Winifred "Winnie" Manning was from Michigan and had red hair; she was as tall as Georgie and had a competitive spirit that drove her to claim her seizures would make his seem like little *frissons* of terror or maybe the way you shiver when the bath water's cold. He said he'd had a fit in front of his first grade class and crapped his pants, and she said she'd had one during her sister's big church wedding and did the same—and was wearing a dress. Well, he'd knocked over a big grocery display of canned beans once. But she had flailed and kicked a dining table during a Christmas dinner and the centerpiece goose went crashing to the priceless Oriental carpet. Etc. Winnie was hard to best. That a girl could even play this game with him was thrilling. Half the crush he had on her was really an infatuation with the novelty of their situation.

They both longed to experience whatever healthy young men and women might. They knew that their normal counterparts could spy on the horizon such wondrous promised marvels as courtship and marriage; to those fortunates blessed with health, future intimacy with a mate was like an exotic unfamiliar city known to be a certain stop on the itinerary of the future. It outraged them to be told time and again that their condition precluded mating and that getting "stimulated" would be detrimental to their inner calm and that reproducing would pass this affliction along to their children.

Taking the risk of seizures, they feigned spooning their Pheno two days in a row so they'd be energetic and alert enough for the mission they set for themselves. On a sunny afternoon they strolled down through the grounds past the old Shaker Cemetery, then turned west, sneaked off the property, and, hiking through the woods and pastures, they stumbled across an abandoned hunter's cabin a stone's throw from the Genesee River. They were *not* running away from Craig Colony, they insisted later—it was a wonderful place! They meant only to have an adventure, they claimed, like ordinary boys and girls! To be explorers, to be free from being treated like babies with monitors and chaperones and hovering nurses and cottage mothers! That's all!

Winnie's subsequent pelvic examination proved otherwise. Then everybody knew their goal had been to stay gone long enough to lose their virginity.

"It was like trying to defuse a bomb or something for both of us," he told Sylvia on the first night of their honeymoon. "Or maybe like being told something's hot and don't touch it but you have to anyway. We dragged the old mattress off the bed and onto the floor and we sat Indian-style knee-to-knee for a bit. Then we held hands and, you know"—he laughed—"kind of waited for the other one to go *boom!* That went okay. We were both grinning so hard I thought we'd twist our jaws out of joint. We kissed, just a peck. Then we waited. It went okay. So we did it again and got away with it again. So we decided to kiss and just kind of hold it steady and see if that would pass. She had to tell me to close my eyes because looking at me was making her cross-eyed and dizzy and that was too much like what happened before she seized, you know, but we sat there leaning forward into each other's lips I dunno maybe five minutes until my back and neck were starting to burn, so we let up. So good so far. We were nervous and really giggly and jumpy, and her face was all pink in a way that set her freckles off. She told me that if she had a fit that I should just keep on going ahead, but she was just kidding, and I said well, okay, but what if I start having one too and there we'll be just locked together like a couple of mutts in the road but out of our heads just thrashing around the room here, that'd be one hell of a thing like a World Wonder or something. Too bad somebody's not here to capture it with a motion-picture camera. We kept making jokes like that so we could maybe shuck off the picture of that in our heads. But we got to feeling pretty confident about that kissing, so we went at it for a pretty good while, and it got to be maybe more fun than I could remember ever having. I was thinking maybe we'd been lied to. Looked like we could keep that up all day and night without anybody coming to any harm."

"I hope this story has a happy ending," said Sylvia. They were lying in the bed of the honeymoon suite in New Orleans' Roosevelt Hotel. She had come from the bathroom with a new silk robe swathed about her nude form and with fresh cologne behind her ears then slithered out of the garment and between the sheets. He was lying in the bed with the covers up to his chin. "Try not to break my heart with it, okay?"

"The happy ending is I'm here with you." He inched closer to her under the covers. "We got into that state where you're pretty darned proud of yourself for doing something scary and are just starting to feel cocky but still you know you've got a way to go and you can feel that fear creeping up on you. She said we ought keep going so long as it's going so well. I said 'whew, okay, if you say so. What's next?' 'I think it's petting,' she said, 'or maybe fondling.' 'What's the difference?' I said."

He turned his head toward Sylvia. "Do you know?"

Sylvia reached to turn out the bedside lamp. "I'm not sure. Maybe it's above or below the waist."

"Huh," said Georgie. "She said you did one with your palm and the other with your fingers. She took off her blouse. I was afraid to look at her. She put my hands on her, uh, chest while I looked at the ceiling. I started sweating and I could hear my heart thumping in my eardrums and I got short of breath. It wasn't exactly like something bad coming, really, but it was strange and I didn't know if it was good or bad. I could hear her sort of panting, too. 'You okay?' I asked, and she said, 'yeah, yeah, just keep going,' like I was digging away at a splinter, and I said 'you sure?' And she said 'we're gonna get this thing done even if it kills us.'"

Sylvia laughed.

"Anyway, after a bit her hand comes over and she starts groping around down below my belt. I was about as, uh, *excited* as a fellow can get and a little nervous, but then we started kissing again while my hands were on her chest and then she, you know, was fiddling around down there and reached her target."

Georgie burst into uproarious laughter; he sounded a little hysterical. Sylvia laughed too, though she wondered if she should.

"What's so funny? What happened?"

"You can probably guess."

"You had a seizure?"

"Oh, no! Not then. It was, uh—"

Sylvia chuckled. "Oh, I get it. You were a sixteen-year-old boy. I can guess."

"Yeah, it was about the best *seizure* I'd ever had."

Georgie went quiet for a bit. Sylvia rolled over on her side toward him. She put her palm on his belly. He flinched.

"Then what happened?"

"Well, we took a breather. We'd brought some bread and cheese and a pear and we ate that and congratulated ourselves on how our experiment was going. When it got dark we set to work again and it was a little easier feeling our way along and stopping for breath and sort of checking as we went. I don't want to be ungentlemanly and tell too much but sooner or later, you know, we got to where we set out for. Or close enough we got a good look at it."

"Did you. . .were you *okay?*"

"Yeah. Winnie had a whopper of a *grandy* the next morning, though, and hit her head on a rock and that gash bled bloody murder, scared me spitless. We stopped it best as we could and hoofed it to the road and got a ride into Mount Morris and the hospital. They came over to get us from Craig and they were hopping mad."

He remembered that as he and Sylvia lay quiet for awhile. He thought how upsidedown this was: he was the shy bride.

"Can I touch you?" Sylvia whispered.
He chuckled. "You can sure try."

SEVENTEEN

In Houston, everybody was eager to see him. Marianne, Elizabeth, Mama, and Sylvia made a grand to-do about his uniform ("Oh, Lord, will you look at how handsome he is!" crowed Mama). Even Elizabeth, hugely pregnant, treated him with respect, and Clarence kept saying he wished he wasn't too old. Cringing in their ardor, he flushed hot; they thought he was being modest.

His mother said they were all going home to Kountze for a dinner and reunion with the family and neighbors. This kind of declaration had always sparked conflict between her and Sylvia. Anxiously he watched Sylvia's face, but she was smiling so complacently, he wondered if they'd managed a truce.

Driving in a light rain, Elizabeth and Clarence and their children went in their Cadillac; Georgie and Sylvia and Marianne rode with his mother in her Packard chauffeured by a liveried Negro Georgie had never seen. Georgie asked about his mutts, and Sylvia told him Mollie died just three nights ago from old age and they'd buried her by the garage.

"Did you mark her grave?" asked Georgie.

"No, but I can show you where. But Buster and Billie are eager to see you."

"How about Pester?"

"I'm afraid he's run off."

Georgie sighed. "He always was a free-range pup. I expect I'll run into him somewhere. I've missed my hounds."

They sat hip to hip; she held his hand and slid her arm over his shoulder. She acted *the most pleased* to have him back. Her linen suit and the creamy silk blouse pinned at her throat with a pink coral cameo were new to him, and he guessed she'd dressed to appease his mother's notion of respectability. She'd put on a few pounds and looked like a prosperous mature woman; she was wearing her hair shorter along her jaw and a few silver threads hid in the bangs, but her cheeks were rosy from the heat. He'd all but forgotten the moist beauty of her mouth and her deep dark eyes and how her saucy grin hinted a promise of play. Her hands were very warm holding his. He was happy to be received so joyously; he was abloom with a rediscovered pride of possession, and relished the thought that once he dropped the pretence of "going overseas," they'd plan a future and he'd revel in his life with her.

Just before dinner, he changed into civvies. When he came out of the bathroom, Sylvia was lurking in the hall, and she stood a rigid finger to her lips, pulled him through a door and closed it. The messy clutter of books and dead flowers and the smell of votive candles meant it was Marianne's room.

"I miss that uniform already, soldier boy."

He shrugged. "Sorry."

She put her mouth to his and they kissed until he pulled away.

"Welcome home, darling." She pressed against him, her arms looped around his nape. He had his nose to her neck, and her Chanel #5 made his head reel.

She glinted a wry grin, eyes lively and dark. She squeezed his bicep.

"I can't get over how *good* you look, Georgie. You're so *hard.* Promise we won't be staying *here* tonight. I brought our car over so we wouldn't be stuck."

He got an inkling of negotiations that had apparently preceded his arrival.

"All right." To keep her eyes off his, he drew her close. She was warm and fleshy, substantial, and he liked how her body gave him the impression that if he pushed on her, she could resist, be anchored by her will and her weight. But hugging her seemed awkward, as if he'd forgotten how.

They went to the table with the conspiracy of their renewed bond. To his relief, no one interviewed him, and he listened while they told him their news, and Clarence offered a toast to him and other brave fellows. Marianne had to spoon-feed Aunt Mary and he couldn't tell if she recognized him or not. His mother had seated him opposite Sylvia, to thwart their intimacy he presumed, but Sylvia's stockinged toe caressed his calf. Elizabeth's boy Calvin did ask if he had brought home a gun, and Elizabeth—clearly on her best behavior—said, "Why no, silly, Uncle Georgie couldn't of got one in his bag!" and Georgie offered up a description of the M-1 he'd been trained with. Elizabeth wanted to know if he'd seen any Hollywood movie stars. No, but he'd seen a USO show with Tallulah Bankhead, and Elizabeth asked what was she like in real life.

After the dessert plates were cleared, his mother said, "Georgie, I've made a bed upstairs if y'all would like to stay tonight. I'm sure you're tired, and the weather's turned nasty."

Sylvia said, "Why, we thank you very much for the offer, Evelyn, but I don't like to be away from home overnight. I'd feel terrible if something happened."

"Of course. But surely your *boarders* can be trusted to look after things for one night."

He watched them stare each other down. Sylvia blinked.

"I wouldn't feel right asking them to."

"One night," said Evelyn. She turned to Georgie. "What's one night out of thirty? But never mind, do as you please." She leaned a little on the *you* to separate him from Sylvia, and he squirmed, looked out the window. A storm was gathering strength in the northwest; the day had been muggy and gray, with a sultry breeze—tornado weather. She had a point there. It would be an hour's drive in bad conditions. He did have thirty days. He actually had three hundred or three thousand days, for that matter, though no one knew.

Illusions he'd harbored that Sylvia and Mama had made peace now fled. They'd battle over every minute of this faux furlough. His mother watched, waiting for his response. He felt sorry for her; she looked drawn, older, and she'd plastered her worry ruts with powder but had only accentuated the mask of withering motherhood under it. He'd done this: *Georgie, my God, you're going to make me old before my time!*

He'd give her credit—despite her efforts to have his recruitment annulled and her bitter criticism of what she believed to be Sylvia's role in it, she had surrendered. She was pleased by the son before her eyes—fit, the fat shaped into muscle, his bearing and manner befitting a young male who'd undergone military training.

"I think I wanna to go home to Pee Eff," Georgie said. Sylvia smiled sweetly but, wisely, said nothing.

"Well, if you feel *that* way."

Actually he was thinking of his old room with the terrarium and books, his desk and crystal radio set, dogs sleeping at the foot of his single bed. Poor old Mollie. Dogs. They had no politics. Same to them if you got a bad conduct discharge or a Congressional Medal of Honor.

Departing from the foyer was hard as walking out of a river when you're hip deep in soupy muck. Mama would wound him for his choice.

"Oh, honey, before you go, write down the name of your army outfit."

"How come?"

"For the newspaper. I want to call Ed Williams and let him know you're home on furlough. You know they put those notices in."

"Mama. It's. . .it's just a *furlough.* It's not like I won a medal."

"I don't care! Some people might want to pay their respects."

He laughed. "I didn't die!"

She glared until his mirth had drained. "If it's all the same to you, I care what people think of the family. When we have *some* reason to be proud, we need to give people the opportunity to let us know they appreciate us."

He got it. *When we have some reason.* Because in the past you've given us so many to hide our heads.

"Fine. I'll call him myself if it makes you happy."

"No, you should do it for all of us. And yourself. For your wife."

He eased out the door frowning. He'd have to jack up this pretense of his furlough as he went into Kline's and Emerson drug, Larry at the counter saying *Saw in the paper you were home for a furlough, Georgie,* and he'd have to act as if being home were temporary. Damn that lie! Nobody would be surprised to hear he'd washed out. It would be true to his character and to his history. Failure wasn't uncommon. People left for college and flunked out or went off to make their entrepreneurial mark and slunk home with their tails between their legs, and they got razzed or treated with indifference or sympathy. Girls went away on visits to relatives that lasted the length of human gestation, and most people allowed them to stand upon their stated reason—my auntie needed a nurse. Behind their backs it was another story, and they knew it.

"I hate making a big to-do about this," he muttered as he and Sylvia hurried arm in arm in the gusts down the slippery walk to the Lincoln.

"Then don't."

Sylvia had driven only a block when the rain fell hard peppered with hail, and she pulled over. "You drive, Georgie. I want you to wear the pants in the family from now on."

He hesitated. Her second sentence put too much symbolic weight on the first. She wasn't tired; she wasn't out of the mood for driving, nor was she nervous about the rain—this was a ceremonial change. From now *on* hinted at their life before he left and a subsequent turn.

He stepped gingerly around the car's long hood clapping his hat to his head and feeling the sting of icy pellets, replaying her remark and its undercurrent of restlessness. Collapsed into the driver's seat, he clenched his hands around the wheel, toed the brake, the clutch, then experimentally slid the gear shift back and forth. The rain and hail were pelting the windshield and he wanted to put the wipers on but he couldn't recall where the switch was. He groped and found it. Then he put the car in low, but the calf on his clutch leg quivered, the rear wheels spun and slipped sideways before catching, and his heart leapt into his throat. He concentrated on steering the big car along with the traffic though it made him anxious to match that speed. The street led to the highway out of town, and though gas was rationed and it was close to midnight and pouring, traffic seemed heavy, and probably a good many drivers were drunk.

"God, I am so happy to have you home with me!" She scooted up next to him, gripped his bicep like a fireman's pole. She laid her head on his shoulder.

"Oh, am I, too! Gosh, it seems so long!"

Then she quietly cried while he negotiated the road. His shoulders knotted in a hot ache as the rain and wind rocked the car and the headlamps of oncoming vehicles exploded in blurry orbs on his windshield. She was happy to see him home; these were tears of joy. He didn't know how to respond. He'd been away, and was now having to relearn how to manage both this large chunk of moving metal and this "wife" he'd abandoned for months. Between his inward cringing and his outward flinching as lights from other cars jabbed at him, he was antsy, sweating. He had been back on Dilantin since mustering out at Roberts and hoped for the best.

She blew her nose and sat up, looked down the dark highway where their headlights laid two yellow poles ahead into the glittering rain.

"What did you miss the most about me?"

He laughed. "Little stuff. Like waking up in the morning and finding you there beside me in bed. Hearing you sing to yourself off in some other room. The way you talk to your African violets." It wouldn't be gentlemanly to wax eloquent about conjugal pleasures, but he added, "Kissing you. My lips got lonely."

She laughed. "And I missed how you make me laugh."

She snuggled closer and dropped her palm onto his thigh. A thrill rippled from it. But a tingle of fear zipped along there too. They were on edge a bit, probably just from the absence, but then again he had the odd sensation she was a stranger and he'd lost the sense of knowing her. The facts of their past connection—the courtship, marriage, their domestic life—seemed at odds with their present unfamiliarity. As if their life in the past had ended there. That frightened him. Away from home, he'd recognized that thinking about reuniting with Sylvia made him anxious, a little afraid, but of what he couldn't say since it wasn't logical. He'd relished his memories of their short life together, but in the safety of distant time and space. That a man would desire distance from his wife was a subversive concept frequently expressed in comedic form: hubby waves *he ain't here* at the bartender who's got the phone in hand, ha ha ha. Men were *supposed* to enjoy recreation with other men—hunting, fishing, bowling—over being with their wives. Having been more or less under house arrest during most of his childhood because of his epilepsy, Georgie had never belonged to a tribe of fellows like a sports team or a lodge or the Boy Scouts, and even though a recruit platoon was not exactly a club, the *maleness* was daunting. His emotions seemed paradoxical, contradictory; he'd grown up among women but didn't feel wholly comfortable having a wife; he joined an army of men who seemed to relish being absent from their women, but he took no pleasure in their company because he didn't know the passwords. What did the tribe respect and admire in another man? They respected other men who treated women with disdain and derision; they respected other men who lowered their antlers and got to cracking no matter who hoofed his way into the ring; they respected the biggest bullies, the cagiest cheats.

They drove in blinding rain.

A gust blew a wet curtain against the windshield; he danced too hard on the brake and the car fishtailed before aligning itself.

He grinned. "Sorry. Maybe you oughta, uh, not distract me." Her hand had slid over the lump in his drawers, and it was slowly writhing awake.

She set it back in her lap. But she lifted his right hand from the wheel and moved his palm onto her thigh. She'd pulled her skirt hem up; he touched bare flesh, the rim of her stocking top.

"How'm I gonna shift?" he joked.

She grinned. "Between us we'll get it done."

"But we'll be home soon. You know?"

"Yes. Sweetie, couldn't we be alone first? Let's stop at a tourist court, okay?"

"Aw, I don't mind driving. We'll make it okay, I promise."

"It's not that. I was thinking how wonderful it would be for just us to be together tonight. I want you all to myself before I have to share you. It'd be naughty! Like playing hookey. I want to show you what I've saved for you."

"What about the house?"

"That house has stood half a century."

"Wouldn't the boarders wonder where we are?"

"I told Mary Kay we might not be back tonight. She can fend for herself. She's very capable."

"How about that fella over the garage?"

"Mister Goforth? Doesn't matter. He'll be out soon. He's looking for another place."

"How come?"

"Why? He has a bad leg from polio. It hurts to climb the stairs, he said."

"Guess it's just as well."

"Why?"

"It looks better not to have a bachelor around when the husband's not there, I think."

"I'm sure your mother does, too. What'd she tell you about my boarders?"

"Nothing. She wasn't trying to stir up trouble."

"Oh, of course not!"

This thing between his mother and Sylvia—man oh man it made him want to stick his fingers in his ears and sing *la la la la la la la.* But as much as their tension made him cringe, he recognized a need for it deep down. If his mother and Sylvia weren't fighting, he'd be powerless.

He glanced at her; her face was averted, her hanky balled in her fist; she was supposedly entranced by the dark, windswept stands of pine. As a peace offering, he said, "Maybe you can get another boarder. I don't care what she or anybody says."

She leaned close and kissed his cheek. "Thanks. I'm sure I can put the room to good use."

Minutes later, she pointed ahead. "There—on the right." COURTS burned in blurry red neon in the rain. She spoke as if they'd settled the issue, so he pulled in and parked near a cottage with an OFFICE sign.

The door jingled, his glasses fogged from the humidity, and he had to wipe them on his sleeve before groping along a counter that seemed unattended.

"Hello!" he called out.

Behind the counter sat a Morris chair with a chrome ashtray on a stand beside it, cold cigar butt lying there like a dog turd. Sign on the wall. *In God We Trust. All others pay cash.*

He could tell her No Vacancy. If they were home, he'd feel stronger, more relaxed. There'd be things she had to do. Distractions. Here, though … A room in a tourist court was little more than a bed with roof and walls. But he did want to please her. The trouble was she'd proved to him months ago that he could perform, but it seemed ages since he'd been onstage, you could say. Jitters. And then there was that time he'd had that awful fit right on top of her.

His hands were sweating.

"Hellooo!" he hollered a second time.

An old boy with a corncob pipe clenched in his teeth came out of a back room and hobbled to the counter.

Georgie said he and his wife needed a room. He added that he was a serviceman on furlough.

"Lemme see." Using the pipe's mouthpiece as a pointer, he went down a ledger column. The bit leaked a trail of brown slime onto the paper. "Two people. Young feller and his *missus.* Maybe I do. Not sure, though. 'Posed to be a holdin' her."

"How much would it be if you had it?"

"Well, they go for four bucks most times."

Georgie tugged out his wallet. He gave the clerk a five. "Tell you what—that's for the room and something for your trouble."

"Number twelve. Up and left early Lord you wouldn't believe the names they was chunking at one nother, not fit for Crus-chun ears. It ain't been cleaned since, but any port in a storm, eh sailor?" He winked.

Five bucks! The war had made people ferocious greedy. It was sickening. And if previous tenants had "up and left early" they'd likely paid the room up through tomorrow noon and the old bastard was doubling on it.

Still, though, he strutted back to the car. The room that she wanted had become a trophy, a pelt laid at her feet.

"Any luck?"

"He had one he was slow to give up. I don't think he believed we're married."

"The nerve! How'd you convince him?"

He raised his hand and rubbed his thumb against his forefinger. "A little sin tax."

She laughed, cocked her brows in mock dismay. "Sin tax! Oh dear! Now I can't show my face!"

He grinned, then squinted through the steamed-up windshield as they crept over the mud in the courtyard. "Don't worry. *He's* not gonna say word one or he'll be eating it!"

"Mmmm. My hero." She pushed a red-rimmed pucker into the air between them, and he tapped it shyly with his lips. No point in telling her the geezer's seventy. If she thinks he's a Charles Atlas After, so be it.

Low-watt bulb in a naked fixture on braided wire. It stank to high heaven of cat piss and cigarette smoke and rank five-and-dime cologne, and the ashtray on a nightstand was heaped with red-tipped butts. A squad of empty Jax bottles on the bureau, lamp beside them tipped over and rested on its shade; a pennant of loose wall paper waved at them from the far wall, there was that much damp draft. The bed clothes were in a furious tangle and one pillow was on the floor, where it might have been flung.

"Mercy," sighed Sylvia. "Pig sty."

"All he had."

"Oh I'm not blaming you!"

While he stood rocking from foot to foot, she set the linens in order, then, slapping at the sheets, said, "I hate bed bugs!" He thought bed bugs might be the least objectionable item clinging to the sheets given that a man and woman had just smoked and drank and fucked and fought so recently on them. He plucked the pillow up and slapped dust from the slip and found the second under the bed. He considered mentioning that the clerk said the previous guests had fought and left early, but a wave of superstition squelched the impulse. He didn't want the ghost of their unhappiness to linger any longer by calling attention to it.

"That should do it!" She beamed, chocking her hands on her waist. "I don't think we need that ghastly light now."

He hit the switch. After a moment shapes manifested in the dimness.

"I'll change," she said.

She was a moving gray shape against a charcoal background, then "click" the bathroom light came on and the door was swinging shut. Enough light seeped under for him to drape his coat and shirt, then his trousers over a chair back. He climbed into bed still wearing his undershirt and socks.

It's very clear / our love is here to stay. … Not for a year / But ever and a day. …

Sometimes her singing seemed an expression of well-being, the well from within bubbling up, but was she really feeling that happy to be with him in this filthy room after wrestling his mother for his attention? Or was she chasing away the gloom?

"Scat!" he hissed to the ghosts who'd drunk the Jax and smoked the butts and slung the pillows.

She came out of the bathroom saying, "Make room, soldier!"

Her full satin slip glowed in the dark as she moved like an apparition, then she lifted the sheet and slid into the pocket like a runner coming into home plate, burrowing next to him, flinging one solid heated stockinged thigh over his loins and clutching at his flanks with her open hands. She lay her warm cheek on his chest.

"Ahh! At last! I'm so happy to have you back!"

"Me too." He patted her shoulder lightly with the tips of his fingers, the way you'd pet a bereaved acquaintance. "Except, uh, I'm a little … scared."

She lay still a moment. "Don't worry, Georgie."

It struck him suddenly that the couple might've merely fought their way to the nearest honky-tonk, where they'd drunk themselves into a truce, and now were staggering back to this bed to celebrate.

"I can't help it."

She sighed. "I know. Just. . .just lie here for a while. Nothing has to happen. Be patient with yourself." After a moment, she added, "Thanks for indulging me about the room. You're the world's best husband."

He knew she meant to stroke his ego. He appreciated that, but it was too transparent to be effective.

"I don't want you to be disappointed in me any more. For any reason."

"I wasn't to begin with."

"I wanted to be your hero." He was glad the room was dark; a stinging welled up in his eyes and he clenched his teeth to stanch it.

"I know. You are!" She wept quietly at about a *pianissimo,* snuffling and dabbing at her nose with the tail of his undershirt. Then came a steady crying at a *forte,* her breath hitching up quick between *boos* and *hoos,* and before long the aria had sailed into a full-blown *fortissimo* with her sobs *glissando-ing* and the metronome picking up its steady step, and the wretched melody clambered up and down a rocky minor scale—she was turning inside out on him, deep deep breaths and then long groans and whickering and whimpering, and meanwhile he murmured *there there* and helplessly patted her shoulder.

"Everything's going to be all right. I promise, honey."

She snuffled down to a halt, sighed raggedly, swallowed. "I'm crying because it's such a relief to be with you!"

Her cool fingers trailed across his belly. That would be the opening note, he knew, in their operatic duet. He'd mark the measures anxiously until the bar loomed up for his entrance.

The wind had picked up, and the draft in the room was a breeze against his scalp. At least that air swept this room of the stench of beer and sweat and cigarettes and semen; the fresh air smelled faintly glacial, of snow and a hint of juniper in the far-off Rockies the wind blew out of. He turned his near ear toward the window to listen intently. He'd swear a woman was shouting or cursing, and a man answered in anger. Only the sound of the storm, he guessed. By morning it would've passed, but that was hours away.

HEY JOE, LOOK WHAT AUNT MARY SENT ME...

AND DO I LOVE MILKY WAYS!

Yes, aunts and uncles, mothers and fathers, sweethearts and wives all over the country are sending delicious Milky Way candy bars. They know their boys will thrill to the taste of the delightful pure milk chocolate coating, the smooth creamy caramel and the luscious chocolate nougat center flavored with real malted milk . . . a taste treat found only in a Milky Way. Just think what a whole box of delicious Milky Ways would mean to your boy now!

EIGHTEEN

GEORGIE CONTENTEDLY WHEELED the Lincoln under a beautiful June sky washed of the mustardy miasma of Port Farview's industrial complex.

Sylvia said, "Georgie, did you notice how many servants your mother has? I hate to gripe, but I'm the only one doing war work. I also take care of the house and the yard and this car and manage the bills and look after Mary Kay while you're away, and, honey, I don't think it's right for your wife to seem like a poor relation. It's insulting to you, and it makes me feel they're looking down on me."

"Mama doesn't have servants."

"Really? What do you call Jemma and those girls who waited on us at the table and that driver and the Negro boy rooting about in Evelyn's flower beds?"

"They're *help*."

She snorted. "Oh. They volunteer."

"'Course not. It's just we don't use that word."

"Okay. Couldn't I have *help*, too?"

"Can we afford it?"

Sylvia fell mute a mile or so, presumably toting figures. Finally, she said, "That's another thing, Georgie."

"What is?"

"It's demeaning that you're not allowed to manage your own money, *our money.* I know you've long been in the habit of taking your *allowance* and not demanding more, but, sweetie, as the adult son, don't you think you should learn to manage the family's affairs? Shouldn't Evelyn treat you as a successor now? She acts as if Clarence has more right to that than you do."

She was spoiling a fine mood. Last night—best ever. She'd soothed his jangled nerves patiently until he forgot to be afraid. He lay still while she straddled him and went slow and easy and brushed her breasts across his face. Recalling it, he went stiff and could hardly pay attention.

"Besides," she continued, "What if something happened to you? I mean, God forbid, Georgie, but would you really want me depending on her charity?"

"No, definitely not!"

"Could you talk to that family lawyer?"

"Lester Pratt? What for?"

"Maybe just for information. For instance, do you know what your father's will said about when you came of age?"

Whew!! Sylvia might be right, but he'd sooner eat chicken dung than go behind his mother's back. "He left everything to her, far as I know."

"Surely you don't expect to take handouts all your life?"

Georgie shrugged.

"I mean . . ." she sighed. Running out of steam, he saw with relief. "She should put you in charge of *something* soon as you come back. She should treat you like a *man,* that's all."

And I should act like one, he thought. She was right. But checking with Pratt on the sly then demanding his mother *promote* him seemed impossibly difficult, even if necessary. He'd have to break such a daunting task into stages, and the first might be foot-dragging, followed by denial of urgency, then by outright procrastination.

"You're right, Syl." He spaded his hand between her warm thighs and grinned. He should give her *something.* She was burdened with responsibilities. If she knew he was home for good, of course, she might not feel so overwhelmed. But she might also be more insistent that he act.

"What kind of help you want?"

"Well, Mr. Goforth was doing the yard and helping me garden, but since he's moving this week, I won't be able to handle it myself, and I don't think it would look right, either, to be cutting the grass and such. Maybe we could hire a couple. They'd take the garage apartment, and he could drive the car and work in the yard and she'd cook and wash and help in the house. Oh, it would be *such* a relief, honey."

"I suppose so," he offered reluctantly. "Might be hard to find somebody with the war and all."

"What about Walter Jenkins and his wife? I hired him to move furniture, and when I was living at the Bide-a-Wee you used to bring me meals Thelma fixed, remember?"

A wave of nausea rushed over him, and he breathed it back. He'd sure hire Walter to help trim trees or fix a board or loose pipe—he was more savvy at plumbing than most white union men—but make *servants* of him and Thelma? It made him shudder.

"Uh, they got a kid. Scooter."

"There's room for three up there."

"Walter likes to come and go."

"You could ask him, though, right?"

He sighed. "I really don't want to."

"Why not?"

"It's a long story."

She smiled and patted his thigh. "I'm a good listener."

"Well, for starters, when he and I were fourteen, we were swimming in the river down at the farm. His cousin Rayette was with us. That was when Mama had sent me down. Elizabeth and Marianne were having fellas at the time. Elizabeth in particular was afraid I'd have a fit in front of some yahoo she was dating."

"Surely your mother didn't say that."

"Well, it was a typical treatment for young epileptics at the time. Get 'em off somewhere bucolic and serene and calm. But Aunt Mary and Uncle Horace worked me like a damn mule. I guess that was good for me, and maybe Mama did think it was best, I dunno. Anyway, it's the first and only place I had any pals, kids my age who'd play with me. Walter's uncle Samuel was our chauffeur and another uncle was a tenant farmer for Uncle Horace."

He drifted off as images flickered by, but Sylvia said, "You were swimming."

"Oh. Well, I had a seizure in water over my head and Walter pulled me out."

"He saved your life."

"That he did."

"Wouldn't that be all the more reason for giving him secure employment?"

"Well, ordinarily I guess it would."

"So?"

"So like I said, it's a long story. It's hard to explain. I don't want to lord anything over him, you know. I do feel a need to pay him back—not only for that but for a lot more. But not that way."

"Could we hire somebody else, then?"

He glanced at her. She did look tired. "I'll ask around."

"How about an ad in the paper?"

"You don't know what you're getting. Better someone people know. Mama won't outright poach, but you do hear when somebody unhappy wants to work for another family."

Sylvia had no idea how complicated this was. Evelyn did refer to her maids, her cook, her gardener, her chauffeur as *servants:* Georgie called them *help.* His relationship to them was thickly brambled, his feelings confused. Since his mother had always hired and fired, he thought of them as *her* servants; he enjoyed the illusion of transcending this unegalitarian aspect of his family. He had long considered himself as a kind of foreign visitor within it: though he didn't approve of having Negro servants whom one treated as inferiors, being a foreigner, he was obligated to quietly concede to his hosts' barbaric custom. To call them "help" did make it seem voluntary, and the term upended the power ratio: one *needed* "help." The help needed nothing.

Walter Jenkins' Uncle Samuel had been the Karaceks' chauffeur when Georgie was a child. Samuel was also a lay Baptist preacher whose congregation included Negro tenant cotton farmers. In the summer of 1919, Samuel and other Negro leaders sought out brokers in Galveston to buy their cotton directly, bypassing white middlemen who paid them less than white farmers. The local newspaper called the organizers "socialist agitators," and, on the night of July 11, 1919, a band of white men rampaged through a Negro neighborhood and burned down a dozen homes, including Samuel's, abducted and beat him and ran him out of town. Georgie had only a child's memory of his father leaving the house with the heirloom shotgun and warning Evelyn and the children to lock themselves in an upstairs bedroom. Evelyn was armed with a butcher knife "in case those folks run wild." Through the upstairs window, the orange glow was visible over the trees. For years Georgie had believed that his father had been like Zorro that night, riding out to bring justice and to prevent good people from coming to harm, but eventually he learned that his father had been among the men who worked Samuel over with an iron pipe and left him permanently crippled. He also knew that Aunt Mary's cracker husband Horace ("Uncle Aitch") had led a trio of night-riding goons that waylaid Walter on a country road near the family farm and beat him for little more than his refusal to hand over a Victrola record Uncle Horace had found offensive.

Rayette and Walter were dear friends back then, cherished all the more for being rare. Walter and Rayette attended the Negro school in town, but when they were out they angled for perch and catfish with Georgie, or they went to their self-proclaimed kingdom atop a Caddo mound, where they put on plays made up on the spot.

They hunted with Uncle Aitch's shotgun. Uncle Aitch told him not to let the niggers handle it, but Georgie always let Walter shoot and even Rayette, once. She was so skinny the kick flung her back to the ground and she never wanted another chance.

They peed in the woods.

They tormented toadfrogs.

They took turns listening to Georgie's crystal set radio.

The sat on the stoop of the smokehouse and drank RC Cola.

They pitched horseshoes.

They bet on who could spit the farthest.

Walter taught him how to light a fart with a kitchen match and Rayette walked off disgusted, saying, "You boys don't have any home trainin'."

They listened to Ma Rainey on Ray's Victrola. They heard Bessie Smith's "Down-Hearted Blues" and walked the path along the river singing at the tops of their lungs. *Trouble trouble I've had it all my days/ It seem like truh-bel goin to follow me to my grave ...* .

They read stories aloud from *The Brothers Grimm.*

When the weather was hot they swam in the river in their underpants. Rayette was lean and tall as Georgie, with wide square shoulders and stringy arms and legs. The boys teased her about her Caddo mounds, though they were no bigger than lemon halves. Her skin was the color of Karo syrup, so Karo was Georgie's nickname for her, though sometimes Walter called her "Beanie" for bean pole; Walter was Hershey, and Georgie was Tater, but Walter also called him Fish after they saw a fit. *Man, you floppin' like a fish outta watuh!* It scared them, they said. Walter said Mamaw told them that fit meant Old Scratch had put a blue demon inside, or maybe a haint crawled under your skin, Georgie, and Georgie sulked and said, "You don't believe that old stuff, do you?" Rayette said, "You got to eat some of this here mud," dropping to her knees and scooping up stinky black goop from the bank of the summer-lowered river. She stuck it under his nose. Georgie sneered. "What is it, blue demon poison?" Rayette said, "Uh-haw." Sighing, Georgie sampled it but spat it out when they burst into laughter.

Georgie looked at Sylvia. She was humming faintly, watching the flat coastal plain with its pastures of golden waist-high grass toss like waves in the breeze. She seemed happy. He wanted her to have whatever she wanted that lay within his power to grant her.

"About Walter?" She turned to him and smiled, a little vacantly, and he could tell he was calling her back from somewhere distant—and pleasant, maybe. "It was a golden time back then, that's all. But things happened that spoiled it all, things my family did to his. He's never held it against me and he's never said I owed him for pulling me out of the river, you know? But anyway, I will see to it that you get some help, for sure. I promise."

She leaned across to smack his cheek. "I'm going to prove to you I'm worth it."

NINETEEN

My dearest Donnie,
Hooray! Got your letter! I was practicing piano when I heard the postman at the door ask Sylvia if Mary Kay Wainwright lived here, and I about bowled her over to get it!

But (frustration!!) soon's I clutched it in my sweaty fingers Sylvia's husband asked me to walk to the drug store with him (I got a summer job! More later. . .), then when we got back Sylvia had lunch ready, then Linda came so we could plan our Victory Girls troop, and we had supper at her house, and then I ran home around dark only an hour ago, and I finally (pant! pant!) had a chance to savor your letter in private!

My answer's hot off the press. Is Melinda the one with the freckles in your Latin class, the one you say is so darned smart? The one I met outside the movie? If so, yes, dear Donnie, she'll make an adorable ornament on your arm at the ROTC graduation formal! I know that dance is important to you cadets, and it really kills me I can't see you in your dress uniform (does it have a sword?), so please! have a picture taken, even if Adorable Melinda the Red-Haired Genius with Cute Freckles has to be in it, too! I'm sure she'll have a beautiful gown—tell her green satin would look wonderful with her skin and hair! (Wait—tell her to wear a welder's cap and coveralls to honor ladies at work!)

Just kidding. I guess I sound jealous! You know what I really appreciate? That you said of all the girls on Earth, if it were possible you'd take me! And you explained that no cadet could attend without accompanying a lady, and that regular officers from Selfridge Field would be there with their wives. I really do understand, Donnie Dearest! And you didn't have to remind me that Melinda irritates you. Doesn't she also have calculus with you? I remember you said she argued with your professor about how to arrive at solutions. You also said she and your sister were pals. So I know she's from your hometown and you'll be more at ease at such an important event with someone you know, even if she gets under your skin.

So have a wonderful time, darling! (sniffle! sniffle! honk!) Send me a program! I want to know what the theme is for the decorations and the menu (and what Melinda does wear), and which orchestra plays and what songs, and all that. Send me a dance card with your name in every slot, so I can pretend I was there. And, oh yeah—when I say describe what Melinda wears that includes jewelry and shoes. Gloves and hat and wrap. You'll think that's silly, but I mention it because a fellow might not think to add those things. She'll have a purse, too, okay? We call such a thing an "accessory" as in "accessory after the fact," ha ha ha.

But enough! Go! On that night, I'll listen to the radio and dream I'm at the Ypsilanti Armory dancing in your arms! Just think of me, my dearest darling!

As for here—lots has happened since Sylvia's husband got home Wednesday morning. Things are going on here that make me sad and nervous, but I'm not going to burden you with hearing all the dirt. Suffice it to say (doesn't that sound fancy) that Mom pitched me out of the frying pan into the fire. But don't worry.

I was glad to finally meet Georgie (Mr. Karacek) for more reasons than one. He is a really nice guy! On our walk to the drug store, he told me he was happy to be home and that I was welcome to stay as long as I wanted. He also asked if I wanted a dog! I've never had a pet except for Gran's evil-tempered old tom, so I was thrilled to say yes.

I found out he has epilepsy (don't worry—he's not crazy and it's not catching!). He's funny, and he likes to sing and acts goofy with Sylvia, and what really hurts is to see how happy she seems to be, too. I haven't heard her laugh so much since I got here.

And you might remember that boarder? the one I called RB? Well, he's moving out this weekend, which will make me breathe a little easier, to tell the truth. (Sorry to sound so mysterious. I am okay, really, it's nothing to do with me.)

Oh—one more thing about Melinda then I promise to shut up. She'll have her hair done special. You won't have ever seen it that way before (or ever again, if I can help it ha ha ha! Just kidding!), but please add it to the things you are required to describe as per our contract to take her to this darned dance. Don't just say it was "up" or something pitifully vague like that. Ask her what it's called (hair-dos have names), and there may be instruments up there to keep things tidy—combs or pins or even tiny flowers!—and please include them in your account. I hate to be such a pill and I hope you understand. Hearing all about it helps me feel better about not being there.

Anyway, yesterday Sylvia put on a nice homecoming dinner for the four of us. We had baked chicken and sweet potatoes and fried okra and a pecan pie that someone who works with Sylvia brought as a welcome-home gift. Everybody was on their best behavior. Mr. K got out his ukulele, Sylvia played the piano, and we sang corny old songs like "Down By the Old Mill Stream," then we listened to *Stage Door Canteen* in New York while Mr. K and RB smoked stinky cigars.

I have to write a pen pal overseas tonight before taps, as you fellows say. I hope you're not jealous that I write fellows in the armed services. I believe it cheers them up to hear from anybody back home, even if it's not someone dear. Like I've told you, Corporal Mills tossed me his address out of the back of a truck when I was crossing the street in Ypsi, so it's not like we're from the same hometown or I was bosom pals with his sister.

Oh, dear. Just thought of something else. I hate to bring it up, but I can't rest easy until we clear the air. I was wool-gathering about that night, and I pictured you and Melinda and Freddy B and his date getting in his car and going for a late supper after the ball, and you and Freddy B have a sip from a flask. Nothing unusual about a couple college fellows having a nip or two to keep the spirits high on such a big night. You're sitting beside her in the back seat and it's cozy and it's a beautiful night with a soft breeze and the stars all twinkly, and you're both a little tipsy, and she's so happy to have been like Cinderella tonight that she leans over and

GIVES YOU A KISS YOU DO NOT ASK FOR!!!

Please remember that you do not have to return it! I know this sounds silly, but I have to draw the line somewhere. No kiss goodnight at the door, either. Even if it's like a brother-sister kiss. It's not necessary. Please don't think I'm being childish (oh, damn it, I know I am anyway!), but I can't help feeling this way.

Gosh, I've done it again. Please pardon my outburst. I got off track. Anyway, school's just out, and I'm supposed to start work Monday at Emerson Drug. Mr. K introduced me to the owner, Mr. Emerson, and he hired me on the spot—sweeping and washing soda glasses, putting things on shelves and the like. I can make a little money to call you. How I yearn to hear your voice, even if it's telling me what a dumb little kid I am, and even if you're lecturing me about which is the proper fork. (I'm grateful for all you've taught me about being a sophisticated grown up!) Anyway, I'm hoping that maybe my birthday present will be a call from you. (You DO remember my sixteenth birthday is coming?) Tell the operator it's the Karacek residence on Acorn Street in Port Farview, Texas.

I better stop now and get my beauty sleep. I'm supposed to go fishing tomorrow morning with Georgie and a

Negro pal of his, and I've never fished before. I'm excited about it.

I hope you're not upset by all my requests regarding Melinda's apparel on the Big Night. I feel silly making so many. So I might as well tuck this last one into the stack—please do not say anything to her about this! I'd be completely mortified! I don't want her to think I object to your going together or that I worry about it. If you were to reveal that you're making notes to send to me, then, you know ... Well, I guess being a man (a real man, by the way!) you don't know. Take it from me that it will not help the situation one iota for you to let her know in any way shape fashion or form that I want to "hear all about" what she wore and everything else about that night.

Oh honey I love you love you love you and this is SWAK SWAK SWAK!

All my love from your most faithful girl,

MK

P.S. Oh, her nails, too.

TWENTY

THE MEN GOT HUNGRY, propped their poles with stones, then bantered about rounding up firewood. They decided the tenderfoot should do it, and Mr. Karacek told her, "Don't get nothing smaller than your leg or longer than your arm," and Mr. Jenkins said, "Be sure it's dry," and Mr. Karacek said, "With a nice feathery bark," and Mr. Jenkins said, "Oak's best so don't git nothin' else."

"Is that it?"

"Hmm," said Mr. Karacek. "Don't come back with less than a full load."

"How will I know?"

"A full load is one you cain't carry," said Mr. Jenkins. In full sunlight his skin was almost purple, like a blackbird's back. He wore ragged coveralls and a red shirt under, and a straw hat. The day had turned warm and humid, but at dawn when they arrived, fog lay over the river. Puddles stood in the ditches and hollows from last night's rain.

She was hungry, too. Sylvia had fed them bacon and eggs and toast, and Mr. Jenkins made grits (new to her and too soupy), but Mary Kay's appetite was surprisingly sharp.

"If I can't carry a full load and can't come back without one, then I can't come back."

"It's a conundrum."

"Hurry yousef up too, girl," said Walter Jenkins. "We need our coffee hot."

"We'll set things out meanwhile."

"Just be looking, though."

"'Less you tarry. I might start. Maybe Hershey'll give you some if mine's gone."

"I didn't bring 'nuff for me *and* no hungry little white gal," said Mr. Jenkins. "She look 'bout hungry 'nuff to chaw off a man's laig. If Tater don't save you none, you ain't *got* none!"

"Too bad that crappie she caught is too bitty to cook up," said Mr. Karacek.

"You guys gave me the very worst place!"

"Don't have nothin' to do with that," said Mr. Jenkins. He shook his head sadly: *child just can't learn!* "You don't hear them fish."

"Hear them?"

"Thas right," said Mr. Karacek. "You hear fish don't matter where you stand."

"What do they say?"

Mr. Karacek had taken a red oil cloth out of his knapsack and was spreading it on the ground while Walter Jenkins arranged cantaloupe-sized stones in a circle.

"Talk fish talk," said Mr. Jenkins.

"Sounds like this—" Mr. Karacek hummed and vibrated his lips with his finger to pantomime the "babbling idiot." He and Walter Jenkins burst into laughter.

"All right, wiseacres."

She scouted up wood, Billie and Buster and J.J. leaping ahead and thrashing through the underbrush. All morning the men had teased her. She loved it. If a woman poked fun this way, it would seem mean-spirited, but this was clearly a *ritual* among males. She accepted it good-naturedly and sassed back a little to prove she wasn't harmed. Ten thousand times in her life she'd yearned for a father, and it was never more poignant an ache than now, when she could imagine being in the woods with him. It made her hate Linda, though Linda had never mentioned her dad's taking her anywhere other than to lessons or school or on errands. Still, though, sometimes Linda must get him all to herself.

She carried back an armful of sticks. They'd rolled a big log close to the stones to sit on and had lighted a tiny fire. They didn't razz her about the wood; she stepped to the fire and laid a branch across the stones.

"Don't use that green one—or that damp 'un: they'll smoke," Mr. Karacek instructed gently.

She nodded, placed an old dry stick over the stones and watched as the flame flared up bright. She piled her load away from the fire, set two more sticks on it.

"You got a good fire goin', girl. You might of earnt some lunch."

"Be outta your sack," said Mr. Karacek.

"Heck no! You white folks gotta stick together."

"Tell you what—I give her a bit and you do too and that oughta be enough. She ate 'nuff breakfast to last most folks four, five days. She can't need much more now than half a cold sweet tater."

"Thas white of you."

Mr. Jenkins dipped his hand into an old pillow case and brought out smaller parcels—clean rags wrapped around wax-papered squares of yellow cornbread already buttered and slathered with molasses, a glass jar of field peas with chunks of "side" and peppers swimming in it, a turnip, and three fried peach pies; when harvested, Mr. Karacek's knapsack gave forth pieces of fried chicken—liver, back, wings, legs, ribs, breast halves, and thighs—three boiled yams, an apple, a hunk of yellow cheese. Here she'd imagined that hunters and fishermen ate jerky and hardtack!

Mr. Karacek also had three tin plates partitioned like diner-ware and tin cups and utensils. The men sat on the log with their plates in their laps, but she sat Indian style on the ground, though the moisture seeped into her blue jeans. She ate a chicken leg and two hunks of cornbread and a cup of field peas and one whole yam, two slices of apple and two bites of cheese, and even took one nibble of the raw turnip (uh-uh!) Walter Jenkins cut with his knife and passed. Then she had a whole peach fried pie—she'd never had one but now believed she could eat her weight in them.

Mr. Karacek boiled water in a saucepan, lifted it off the fire and sprinkled coffee grounds into it. After it steeped, he dashed the surface with cold water to settle the grounds and carefully decanted the coffee into cups. She declined one by making a face. She was about to pop.

The dogs had waited patiently, sniffing about the camp in a large circle and alternately standing about like beggars, and finally Mr. Karacek rewarded them with scraps and a raw chicken liver. Mr. Jenkins took something from his pillow case wrapped in newspaper and tied with string. He slid down to sit back against the log. The package contained a long cigar butt. He doctored it by licking the loose ends of leaves then cleaning the end with his knife blade, held the renovated stogie up to inspect it, then lit it with a flaming twig.

He lay his head back against the log and puffed. The smoke drifted up into the sunlight. The woods were still. Now and then the fire snapped, little puffs of air blossoming in the burning wood. A crow cawed. From far away there was a *thok!* of an axe.

"Zatacubano?" asked Mr. Karacek. He too had his eyes closed and was reclining against the log.

"Um. Lasun."

They fell quiet. She wondered if they'd sleep. She liked how they didn't have to talk every minute. She wanted to fit in; she didn't want them to think she was a chatterbox. Or that she was weak, a girl who couldn't take it.

She waited as long as she could, then, knowing she was in for it, she asked, "What does a person do when they have to use the bathroom out here?"

Of *course* they hee-hawed like jackasses.

"Hold it till you git home," said Mr. Jenkins. "Thas what we do."

"Really?" It wasn't possible to hold it one more minute! They were razzing her.

"If it's uh 'mergency, you make do."

"Is there a special place? Like a latrine?"

This was funny, too.

Mr. Karacek waved grandly at the forest. "Anywhere you like." He turned to Mr. Jenkins and grinned. "Remember how Rayette hated to pee in the woods?"

"She wadden that way till a snake bit her hiney."

"Very funny."

She picked her way through the thick damp brush along the bank then went under the pines on a forest floor spongy with dead needles. The air was very still, and the loudest sound was the tiny *whisk* made by her blue jean legs sweeping across branches. A fly buzzed. Buster wanted to follow so she had to shoo him back.

Once out of sight, she lost the need to be picky about a place and, behind a big tree trunk, she trampled a patch of long grass, glanced about for snakes and spiders, pulled down her jeans and underwear and squatted to pee.

She toed dirt over the spot. Then a strange lassitude overwhelmed her and she sank standing back against the tree and peered through the foliage into the empty blue sky. This primitive necessity in these surroundings stirred something in her, drew it over her like a cloak. She hardly knew these other two humans. And they were men, adults. She was young, a girl, and she was a thousand miles or so from anyone who knew her. The trip had taken three days by train. She might as well be in a foreign country.

Oh, Mom! How could you do this to me!

If the earth should open at her feet and swallow her, those men would *tsk tsk tsk* then resume fishing. Neither would know how to contact her mother—Sylvia would, sure. But even when her mother was told *your daughter just fell into a hole,* she would cry real tears for a few seconds and then crocodile tears for days on end so people would feel sorry for her that she had such a daughter who'd lose herself that way. Nobody in Port Farview would know to tell Donnie unless they found his one letter where he asked about taking that girl to the ROTC ball, and what would they conclude? If they asked her mother to tell him, she'd say she would but wouldn't. Gram would care. She wished she were at Gram's house right now.

Golly! What a melancholy place these woods are! They make a person positively morbid! Quit feeling so sorry for yourself! Don't you know there's a war on?

She played Indian maiden on the way back, creeping softly through the underbrush so that not even the woods would know she was present. The men were still drinking coffee and were talking in earnest when she broke into the clearing; they looked at her as she padded up and eased onto the log. They grew strangely silent and she presumed she'd interrupted a conversation they couldn't continue freely with her there. Not something naughty, something serious.

"I see you didn't get et up by critters," said Mr. Karacek. He was smiling politely. Mr. Jenkins's cigar had gone cold in his mouth.

"Nope."

The silence this time was awkward. She prevented them from talking, but they didn't feel free to send her off. She was about to announce she was going off to fish when Walter Jenkins lifted himself to his feet, stretched and peered into the woods.

"Anyhoo," he said to Mr. Karacek. "Thas the las' time anybody gone do *that* to me." He winked at Mary Kay. "I'm goin' back to work! Them fish is talkin' again."

She was dying to know what they were discussing but it would be prying to ask. She expected Mr. Karacek to go too, but he poured the last of the coffee into his mug. He looked at her.

"Walter and me go way back."

"Did you grow up together?"

"When I was your age I lived here at the main house for a while. We used to fish right here. Walter's Uncle Roy was my Uncle Horace's 'cropper. His cousin Rayette was about our age, and we used to play sunup to sundown. We were all good pals back then."

"Is that where those nicknames come from?"

"Hershey and Tater?" He laughed. "Yeah. But."

He stopped, looked downstream where Mr. Jenkins was moving along the bank. "Things happened down here. I had to go back to town. My family, uh, well … I didn't see him and Rayette for a good while, then I went off to a sanitarium in New York and when I came back he was up north working. Until last fall, I hadn't seen him in years. Then we kind of took up where we left off. More or less."

He sipped from his coffee. "He's been in jail down in Florida since I joined up. He didn't much care for how they treated him. That's what he was talking about."

Her heart skipped. A criminal!? "Why was he in jail?"

"Working with union men."

"Is that against the law?"

He gave her a rueful smile. "If you're colored and it's in the South, the fruit growers don't like it one little bit."

"My mom's in a union. Everybody who works at Willow Run is. Negroes, too."

He shrugged. "Roosevelt had to get the law passed for everybody to get fair treatment in the war plants or Randolph was gonna march on Washington and embarrass them. Lot of places the unions are last ones wanna see coloreds on their roster, believe me."

After a moment, Mary Kay said, "Thanks again for introducing me to Mr. Emerson at the drug store."

"You're welcome. You'll make pocket money, anyway."

They watched Walter Jenkins work his line, the cold cigar jutting from his lips. He slow-stepped downstream two-forward one-back, the bamboo pole dipping a little, springing up.

"You fitting in, you think?"

His question startled her momentarily. "Yeah, thanks to Linda. She's a really good friend. We're … Hey, I have an idea! Would you talk to our Victory Girls troop about being in the army?"

He sighed. "Well, I'm flattered, but I was … I *am* just a lowly private."

"But you could talk about anything. Like how important it is to get mail. Or about the food. I just want the girls to hear it from the horse's mouth."

He smiled—sadly, she thought. "The food?" He chuckled and shook his head. "It was plentiful."

He wasn't encouraging. Maybe he was modest. He had a round face with gold curls hanging over his forehead and big lips that showed a gap between his front teeth, and with his glasses and his friendly demeanor, he looked harmless and vulnerable, too. It was hard to believe he was older than Donnie. Donnie had to shave his black chest hair to keep it from sticking out over his necktie.

"Okay, so how about a soldier's daily routine?"

He sighed. His foot was jittering against the ground. "If I told your troop about *my* daily routine it would sound like whining, and that sure wouldn't inspire them to help fellows in uniform."

She smiled. "Gee, now you've really aroused my curiosity!"

"Oh, you know—there's the old hurry-up-and-wait. You get orders to do things that don't make sense and you're not allowed to question them."

He was so much the opposite of a bragger! "When you go back, will it be to the Pacific or England?"

He was quiet for so long she wondered if he'd heard her—or was he imagining being in the thick of the battle?—but then he said, "I dunno."

"I guess they wouldn't allow you to say even if you did."

"Probably not."

"Would you like to get letters from me?"

He laughed. "There's nothing I'd love better, Slim."

She blushed. She'd never been nicknamed, though Donnie did call her Cutie Pie.

"I'm writing some other fellows." She added, without thinking, "I'll keep you up on everything that's going on at home."

"I'd like that."

Maybe that'd be how to reveal her secret. She pictured him in a foxhole opening her letter and reading it. The trouble was, in the movies such a letter was a harbinger of death.

TWENTY-ONE

Dear Donnie,

It's Thursday, June 18th, 11 P.M. My sixteenth birthday. Also, in less than forty-eight hours you and Whozit will be at the ROTC ball. Lucky for her.

Here's something pathetic—people here don't know today's my birthday! I wasn't sure all week, but, gosh, you don't want to broadcast it—you might as well put in a gift order, even if you don't mean for people to buy something! All a person wants is to have people acknowledge your special day. (Even if they have to read your mind to find out.) Especially on a SIXTEENTH BIRTHDAY!! Especially if YOU'RE A GIRL!

When nobody mentioned it by Tuesday I thought they were cooking up a surprise party. Surely Mom would tell Sylvia. Since you'll never see this, I can tell you my daydream without fear of mortification. You went to my mother (in your uniform), and you told her I wasn't a kid now and you hoped she'd relent and let us be together because you love me so very dearly and want to spend the rest of your life with me. You told her you're afraid that once you go overseas, something could happen, so won't she please let me come back to Ypsi? She is very impressed by your maturity and by how handsome and manly you look in your uniform. Then you tell her that my most fervent desire would be hearing from you both on my birthday, so Mom says, "We can do better than that!!" (So long as you're wishing, go whole hog.) "We can go down there and bring her back! Together!" Then she says how wonderful it is to have such a nice young man dependable and strong and promising and handsome and educated be connected with our family, how proud she is of me for having sense enough to choose you!

That's about as likely as a herd of purple cows walking from here to Borneo.

Excuse me while I go puke.

No kidding ... (A little later ...) Well, I knew that wouldn't actually happen. I'm not that stupid. But I am pretty stupid, considering I encouraged you to take Whoizit to the dance and I'm wondering is this why you forgot my birthday? A pretty stupid person tells her gee-dee fiancé fine, go ahead and take a beautiful redheaded goddess to the ROTC ball! Gee, why would it matter to me?

Pretty stupid but not so stupid I actually believed you and Mom would voluntarily be in the same room together.

But I did believe one of you would call me. I did think somebody would send a letter or a card.

Is that asking too gee-dee much?

Since the day's not officially over for fifty-five minutes, somebody could prove me wrong. But I'm sure as h—-not holding my gee-dee breath!

I won't send this because I'm raving like a lunatic. Could be Mom's in the hospital unconscious and you've been sitting by her side so faithfully the hours slipped away before you had a chance to call. (Ha!) Or Mom worked a 24-hour stretch. Phone lines in Ypsi are tied in knots.

(This is still later!) Oh, talk about ironic! As I was writing "tied in knots" the phone rang! Sylvia and Georgie were in bed and she took forever to answer it. Sylvia yelled my name and my heart leaped! I about killed myself galloping down the stairs. Sylvia grinned and said, "Why didn't you remind me it was your birthday!" Like I'd put something over on them.

I about knocked her down to grab that damn phone out of

her hand, because I just knew it was you!

But it wasn't. As you know. It was Mom, but I was pretty darned happy to hear from her! She claimed to be calling from a friend's house, but it sounded noisy and she stopped to put coins in the phone, so it was probably a bar. She had to work late. She said she missed me. I think she really does. I heard tears in her voice, but it could've been from drinking. I was so happy I didn't even ask about coming home. I told her my good news—I have a friend, and people are very nice to me. School is ridiculously easy, I like my job, and our VC troop is a roaring success. (Linda twisted her old friends' arms to join, but that's okay.) I've got a dog named J.J. I'm learning to take care of. I tried to sound thrilled to be here. Maybe she'd get jealous and want me back. Of course, my coming back's got nothing to do with me and you or my state of mind—it's whether she's got some bum like Clyde who wants a place to sleep and freeload for meals.

Gee, I sound bitter. Wonder why? Now you want to know why I didn't ask about coming home? I had the heebee jeebees thinking about your not writing. I'm afraid I've lost you. If you no longer care for me, I'd rather be here. I've been gone five weeks and already you've found somebody else? Is that why you didn't call? Unless you talk or write to me, I have no idea how you feel about us. Now when I imagine my wedding, I get a knot in my gut that won't go away.

I am soo afraid, Donnie! I don't think I can live if you don't love me any more!

Excuse me again while I go puke.

(Later again . . .) I doubt I'll sleep, so I might as well jabber to "you" all night. If I had any guts I'd call your dormitory and leave a message that it's an emergency and for you to call me immediately.

When I finished talking, Sylvia took the phone and sort of cussed Mom out in a kidding way for not reminding her—she remembered my birthday was in June of course but thought it was later. I knew Sylvia wanted to yak about every little detail of my life because she turned her back to me, but I wasn't about to disappear and make it easy to gossip. When she hung up, she said we'd have a special birthday dinner Saturday night (tomorrow night, since it's already Friday), and she'd call Linda's mom and I could invite any friends who could come on short notice. She seemed embarrassed, as if it reflected on her, and that was gratifying, even if it wasn't fair of me to be gratified because I could've told her when it was.

I felt soothed that finally somebody had taken notice!

But how will I possibly get through my own birthday party on the night of Saturday, June 20th, the same night as the ROTC ball?

Stay tuned, I guess. If you haven't already changed the station, that is.

Yours or no longer yours?

MK

Wish I had the guts to send this letter!

TWENTY-TWO

FRIDAY MORNING, WHEN Sylvia left for work she gave Georgie a to-do list for Mary Kay's party on Saturday. Shortly after, he and Walter were in the kitchen drinking coffee before tackling the barbeque pit when his mother arrived with Marianne.

She'd popped in several times when Sylvia was at work. By arriving without notice and strolling the grounds with gloved hand to her brow as if assessing the rain gutters, she made it clear that he and Sylvia lived here thanks to her indulgence. From the kitchen table, he heard the screen creak, then—this was typical—while tapping the beveled glass pane with a knuckle, she turned the knob and opened the door to show she didn't knock for permission; the tap declared she was inside but would warn them out of courtesy. It perfectly expressed absolute authority and civility at once. She often pretended to be en route to other, more important errands.

She'd inspect rooms on the run, clucking her tongue, rolling her eyes at items such as the statuette of the Virgin Mary Sylvia had set on the mantle, fingering a drape, toeing a tear in linoleum, swiping sills with a glove—but never uttering a word. So he couldn't report to Sylvia that she *said* anything about how the house was kept. Once she asked if Sylvia had found the little Wedgwood cream pitcher that was missing, so he knew that in their absence she inspected the house like a landlord renting to an untrustworthy tenant. He hadn't told Sylvia this.

He invited her and Marianne to join them, but she wasn't about to sit with a Negro, even one as familiar as Walter; Marianne made a separate pot and they drank it in the parlor with his mother standing with cup and saucer in one hand while the other riffled the magazines and sheet music on the piano and unfamiliar books in the shelves. Walter went out to the back yard. Georgie watched his mother pick up a snow globe of a wintry London. She upturned it to read the inscription on the base thanking Sylvia for work in the War Bonds show and, judging by the lemon twist of lip, apparently thought better of a catty remark.

"I wanted to stop by and let you know I expect you and Sylvia and that lovely child for dinner Sunday."

"Sure, Mama." It came to his mind to mention the birthday party tomorrow night, but that would necessitate an invitation to the whole Kountze crowd and not even with Thelma helping could Sylvia manage that—even if she wished to.

"Georgie, you have so little time left I wish you'd spend more of it with your family." She dipped her head toward Marianne, as if speaking on her behalf and not her own.

"Sure, Mama. Next week, I promise. I'll take you both to lunch."

"I have a standing bridge luncheon on Tuesdays."

"Okay. Wednesday?"

"That would be nice."

Marianne said, as if they hadn't seen one another in years and were distant cousins, "Do you still know how to play croquet?"

"Croquet?" This baffled him, but Marianne frequently uttered this sort of *non sequitur.* "Hit the ball through the hoop?"

"We have a new set."

"We'll play then."

His mother set her cup on the coffee table, but to his dismay instead of donning her gloves next, she sat in the chintz-covered wing chair and crossed her legs. He itched to dig with Walter.

"How is Sylvia liking her factory work?"

"Fine. Mary Kay's working at Emerson's Drug, now."

"I understand your boarder has moved out."

"Yeah. Couple days ago."

"I'm glad to hear it. I'm not saying you have reason to be alarmed, Georgie, but it didn't *look right* for a lady whose husband is away to have a good-looking bachelor around the house."

He decided to ignore her insinuation. Then he saw a sure way to hasten her departure.

"Listen, Mama, long as you're here, maybe you could tell me about how the trust is set up. We're thinking about getting our own place, maybe buying and maybe building, and you know what I get on a regular basis isn't enough for a married man who might be thinking about raising a family."

He'd conjured up more grandchildren as an enticement. He watched her face. Staring into space, she pursed her lips as if judging a mediocre wine.

"You may be right. But it's premature considering that you'll be housed by the U.S. Army for the near future. And Sylvia certainly seems to have made herself at home."

She meant the changes in décor and furniture placement. She'd probably tell Marianne later that the snow globe was tacky, and that cheap statuette was something a Southern European peasant might've purchased on a bus tour to Lourdes.

"I'm in no hurry." He'd done enough by planting the seed. "Down the road."

She rose and tugged on her gloves. Marianne put the cups and saucers on the butler tray and carried it to the kitchen.

"I hope you and Sylvia can iron out your difficulties while you're home. It's hard to work on them long distance. And it's always best for a married couple to get things into the open."

"What difficulties?"

His mother smiled. "My word, Georgie! How would I know? But every couple has their ups and downs. You can always talk to the Reverend Allbright about them, you know."

"What troubles did you and Papa have?"

"We're not talking about your father and me. I know sometimes, honey, we learn things about our spouses that disappoint us."

"Well, that's not my case."

Walter had a good start on the pit. Georgie pitched in to help. They spaded up earthworms threaded through the soil. J.J., the half-starved stray he'd given to Mary Kay as a "learner" dog, pawed at the writhing pink Lumbricus, snorkeled dirt in his snout and sneezed doggishly while they bedded the worms in a coffee can. If they didn't fish with them soon, they'd toss them back to do their beneficial work.

Walter had negotiated a trade with a widow who was about to butcher two cows. In exchange for their labor, she'd give them a quarter side of beef. George and Walter drove to her farm in Walter's old truck. She wanted a large stack of lumber hauled off. They loaded 1 x 8s that Walter had pulled off her old barn and denailed already, then they loaded 4 x 4s and about a cord of live oak Walter had cut from a storm fall. They drove the loaded truck to Walter's house, and Thelma fixed lunch.

While pouring their coffee, she said, "Men come looking for you."

Walter was adding a dash from a Mason jar into their mugs. He looked up quick as a blink. "What men?"

"Two white men."

Walter grunted. "Whad they say?"

She shrugged. But Georgie read her worry on her face. "Said they lookin' for you. Dint say what fo'."

"Wha'd you tell 'em?"

Thelma stepped to the window and peered toward the street. "I said you gone. I said you *been* gone a good while. And I don't know where."

"What kind of white men they look like?"

"They wearing suits and ties and hats but they sure don't look like no preachers."

Walter frowned. "Um. They show anything?"

She shook her head. "But they drivin' a plain ol' Ford thaz new."

"Not outlaws, then, I reckon," said Georgie. He wanted to make a joke to get included, but Walter didn't laugh.

While they were unloading the truck in Walter's back yard, Walter said, "Sound like them damn G-men to me."

"What they want with you?"

Walter shrugged. "I suppose they reckon I know something they think they ought to know."

"Do you?"

"I doan know what they know." He grinned. "I doan know what I know half the time."

He wanted to pretend it didn't matter, but it was clear to Georgie he was worried—he'd brought it up.

"Have to do with being in jail down there?"

“Might be. They had me hoeing the sheriff’s cotton sunup sundown count of I busted a Pinkerton’s nose, just plain assault you know, I was doing a hunnerd-eighty days with some others. Started out simple with a bunch a pickers tryin’ to get a better wage then somebody tossed a big firecracker into a packing shed and the growers hollered *sabotage* ’cause they knew tha’d bring the gummint down to turn over rocks for *spies*. That was gonna make it treason and that meant hangin’, so one night six of us hauled ass outta there.”

“You think those men are here about that?”

“My guess.”

“What’re you gonna do?”

“Damn if I know. Hope they think I’m way to hell and gone and go lookin’ for me there.”

“You think they’re watchin’ for you?”

Walter nodded. “They wouldn’t come all this way they don’t hang ’round to see if I show up.”

They both looked around—Walter’s house stood elbow-to-elbow with other frame shacks, the yards packed dirt on which stood the hulks of decommissioned autos and appliances. Children were playing in the street and two women next door were hanging out their laundry. Across the way four old fellows sat on a porch in cane bottom chairs. No G-men.

“Hell, maybe they’re outta Houston. Maybe you’re jus’ one thing on a long list.”

“Tha’d be all right.” Walter sounded hopeful but not optimistic. “Rayette’s up in Portland workin’ in a shipyard. Maybe I oughta light out for there.”

That Walter was in trouble made Georgie’s heart skip. He blinked. Sometimes it seemed the past would never lie down and quietly die.

“You need a place to hide say so,” Georgie blurted out. “Since that damned old Aitch kicked the bucket and Aunt Mary moved to Kountze, that house is standing empty. Take Thelma and Scooter with you. Stay long as you need to. Or want to.”

“I ’preciate the thought. But I best stay with what I know, *who* I know.”

“Sure, I unnerstand. Just. It’s there, that’s all.” He wanted to say *I’m there* but didn’t believe Walter would count that as an asset.

Friday night, lying in the dark, he was pleased with himself.

He'd been useful and Sylvia had gushed about it, and it had been good to work with Walter and have that fellowship. They had reestablished a footing despite that ancient ugly business with his family. But, truthfully, until he proved himself worthy and wiped the past away, they'd never approach the easy intimacy that he and Rayette and Walter had as kids. Maybe as adults it wasn't possible. As they had grown, the line between their worlds had deepened into a chasm that often seemed unbridgeable.

Sylvia had her back to him. He eased his palm onto her upturned hip, felt the slick satin on his fingertips. He listened to her breathing. She was asleep. Having a wife was a truly wonderful thing. She kept saying *Oh I wish you didn't have to go to war!* And he'd murmur *uh me too!* It would be on his tongue to add *Truth is, honey, I got a medical discharge,* but then she'd say, *But I am so very proud of my soldier boy!* So he put it off. He had a week or so before the clock would force the issue, so he didn't have to think about it tonight.

He'd forgotten to mention his mother's visit to her. *Forgotten* wasn't exactly it. He hated to give Sylvia news that chafed her. He had brought up the matter of the trust, and he could report that tomorrow, at least. Hedge about his mother's reply. And not mention that junk about the boarder.

His mother's poison! *Don't drink it!* But it had seeped into his system already, as if conveyed by an airborne spore or burrowed through his epidermis. So hypocritical to pretend to be too righteous to listen to gossip. Hinting at what was said, she perpetuated it, though wouldn't be accountable. When she'd done it in her letters, he'd considered the source, shrugged off his suspicions, found the antidote in Sylvia's letters.

Planting these suspicions was outrageous. He'd caught himself watching Sylvia closely because he couldn't help himself, and each time he'd jerked himself out of that dark place with a curse aimed at gossip. What his mother didn't know was how *cold* Sylvia was to Robert compared to how she flirted with other men, even strangers. He wouldn't have offered that in Sylvia's defense, though Mama was surely aware of how Sylvia behaved at the USO canteen. She liked to be friendly, that's all. To judge by how she acted around Robert, she didn't care for him one whit.

But she hadn't said so, had she?

It struck Georgie that Robert had eaten more meals with Sylvia than he had, spent more evenings in the parlor talking or listening to the radio or to her playing the piano and singing. Undeniably, they shared *something* that excluded him, even if he didn't know what to label it. Robert could rise from the breakfast table and retrieve the milk from the icebox without asking and hold up his coffee mug for her to fill without a word exchanged.

This domestic intimacy that Georgie still didn't share with her distressed him because he didn't know its limits. He had too much pride to ask or to accuse. If innocent, she might be flattered by his jealousy—weren't females said to be pleased or touched by it?—but it might offend her. Such an accusation would profoundly insult a faithful wife.

And if she's guilty, why should she admit it? Any anger sparked by hearing the question could easily be caused by guilt and the wish to throw him off the scent. He'd never distinguish righteous indignation from hypocritical guilt if all he had to go on was her word. Her "no" could mean many things, and it wouldn't set his mind at ease unless he practiced utter denial of the darkest possibility. So as long as he'd wind up doing that anyway, why put the fragility of denial to such a strenuous test?

A "yes" would devastate him.

Since it was still a matter of choice, he took the high road—it afforded the most pleasure.

He snuggled against her warm back, fitting her soft hip cheeks into his loins.

"Syl," he whispered. He rocked gently, pressing his growing erection against her. "Syl, honey."

She stirred, sighed, squeezed his hand draped over her breast.

"What, Sweetie?"

He kissed her neck, nibbled at her ear lobe. She chuckled.

"You *are* a naughty boy."

"Are you too tired?"

"No. I'll get nothing but rest when you're gone."

She wriggled about to kiss his mouth.

"Oh, Syl, honey, do you love me?"

"'Course I do, Georgie!"

"Promise?"

"Cross my heart."

He wanted to say *and there's nobody else?* but she'd opened her legs and he'd slid between them so her puss was rubbing his naked belly and he wasn't about to spoil what was coming next.

TWENTY-THREE

Saturday morning, Thelma worked on a potato salad while Sylvia studied the recipe for "Spring Party Cake" in the *Good Housekeeping* laid open on the table. Luckily Robert had overlooked his ration book in his exit, leaving extra coupons for sugar. The men would barbeque when they returned with the beef, and a pot of pinto beans now simmered. They'd have tomatoes, cucumbers, and lettuce from the garden, fried okra, and Thelma's wonderful cornbread. Along with Linda and another girl, there'd be Mary Kay, Georgie, Thelma, Walter, Scooter and herself—plenty of food for eight.

She and Thelma were companionable, though she acknowledged Thelma's expertise. Sylvia enjoyed being the mistress of the house; she need only imagine, say, the okra, the cornbread, the potato salad, then ask Thelma to prepare them. Having an employee was an utter novelty for Sylvia, and today's work gave her a tantalizing glimpse of how life might be once they had "help."

Cream shortening; add sugar slowly; blend well. Add egg whites one at a time; beat well after each addition. Add vanilla ... While she was blending the shortening and the sugar, Thelma watched, as if *grading* her. Maybe it amused her to see someone crib a recipe from a magazine.

"Miz Karacek, you want sweet or sour pickles in this here salad?"

"What do you think, dear?"

"Sour, ma'am."

Sylvia smiled. "Sour it is." Thelma nodded, turned back to the crockery bowl on the counter. She was a taciturn sort, decidedly impervious to Sylvia's charm. Not impolite certainly, and not cold: just businesslike, maybe cautious and circumspect with her white employers. Her demeanor didn't encourage chatter, and when Sylvia volunteered opinions about the habits of local ladies, Thelma seemed deaf. If compelled to respond, she murmured a vaguely affirmative, *Yes'm, mm-hmm,* and Sylvia felt foolish to work so hard to be ingratiating. Perhaps Thelma was unaccustomed to it, and it unsettled her. That distressed Sylvia; she wanted to break through that wall of custom but feared making a fool of herself. When Thelma talked to Scooter, the mother in her emerged, playful and confident and certainly more voluble, but likewise earnest. Trying to "reach" Thelma left Sylvia feeling as if she were the help. She longed for Thelma to volunteer a crack about her husband, a gripe about the heat, a hope that a relative overseas stay out of harm, anything!

Of course, she might only be shy, respectful. After all, Sylvia was "Mrs. Karacek," and the name meant something in this town.

While Sylvia was washing pots and pans (wondering *Will this make me seem more egalitarian, more friendly? Or only like a patsy who doesn't know how to treat the help?),* through the window over the sink she saw Georgie and Walter walk through the yard with something big, pinkish-red, and bloody hoisted between their shoulders. Scooter and Buster and Billie and J.J. followed, the dogs yapping and dancing around the men.

"Good Lord! What in the world!?"

Thelma stepped to her side to look. She chuckled. "Thas a quarter side of beef."

"We can't eat all that!"

"No ma'am. I can't say for Mister Georgie, but Walter and Scooter might put away a goodly portion, though."

Sylvia snuck a sideways glance. Thelma was good-looking, with long lashes, bow lips, and skin the color of honey. She wasn't dressed like a "Negro servant" in an Aunt Jemima get-up or the black-and-white uniform with cap preferred by Port Farview ladies for their help. She'd arrived wearing flats and a cotton dress in a floral pattern with a wide yoke and had brought her own apron. Her hair had been marcelled, and Sylvia thought her lipstick was Patriot Red. Sylvia's guess was Thelma had dressed for the party and not the work, and she wasn't sure how she was supposed to feel about that.

After a few minutes, Georgie appeared in the kitchen door. He'd left the house wearing a yellow shirt and now huge ruddy patches of blood splotched the shoulders.

"I gotta change my shirt," he said. "What should I do with this one?" Sylvia was about to say run cold water over it in the bathtub, but Thelma said, "Bring it to me, Mister Georgie."

Ah! thought Sylvia.

"We ran into that fellow Robert at the ice house," Georgie said. "Hope you don't mind, but I invited him. I figured Mary Kay would appreciate having as many folks as she knows show up."

She turned back to the window so he couldn't read her face.

"I'm gonna go change."

He left. She kept her hands busy in the sink a moment, then said, "Excuse me a minute, please, Thelma."

She waited in the bedroom for Georgie to emerge from the bathroom. She was so livid and rattled she could hardly think.

He looked surprised to find her lurking there.

"Georgie, it's not right to invite people to this party or any other without checking with me first."

"I'm sorry. I just figured—"

"I did *not* want anyone but family here!" It sounded good but wouldn't hold up under even the slightest scrutiny, she knew. "*I* am in charge of things in this house! Putting on a party is *my* job! It's not for *you* to decide willy-nilly to include someone without checking with me!"

"Okay, I'm sorry. We were getting the ice and he saw that beef in the truck and asked about it so naturally I had to tell him what it was for, and then he said he'd go buy Mary Kay a present and drop it off, and—well, heck, it would've been really rude not to invite him. Next time I promise I'll check first." He smiled and leaned into her, kissed her cheek. "I'm just so happy. I'm in a festive mood! I want the whole world to enjoy being home with you!"

She burned, looked away. "Okay, honey. Next time."

When he sailed merrily off in a clean shirt, she lagged behind, eased the door to so she could collect herself. She didn't wish to see

Robert again. She sure shouldn't have allowed him that "good-bye kiss" Wednesday night—it just seemed then that not resisting would be the quickest way to get him gone from the house. But of course it stirred him up and next she knew they were saying pretty ugly things. *Of course* she felt guilty! And he kept insisting that she tell Georgie, as if he believed that she would run away with him rather than stay. Well, she didn't have to confess to Georgie because that's why she had a priest, and *he* says he's the only one who needs to hear my secrets. Robert scoffed. *Catholics!! Must be nice!*

I think you pull me with one hand and push me away with the other. You need me to make you alive inside, and you know sooner or later you and Georgie will call it quits and I'm your fall-back. He's money in the bank and I'm a ride on a roller-coaster when you're bored. That still stung like the dickens—he all but called her a gold-digging whore.

Having finally ousted Robert, she'd breathed more easily and believed she could now pitch herself whole-heartedly into her marriage. She wouldn't be tempted to stray. That man was some kind of … *delicious poison.* When he was within range, it was as if she split into two halves. She didn't love him. He'd been a friend until he turned so treacherous. They had a way of being together, though, that she'd never known—as if they two together conjured up a third entity—an *us* or a *them*—that did the talking and acting, and that *us/them* did unpredictable and terribly inappropriate deeds. That good-bye kiss for example. When she was with Robert she felt out of control, not exactly losing herself to *him* but to that third thing.

Tonight she'd avoid being alone with him, not give him an opening or a reason to think she approved of Georgie's invitation.

She loved Georgie. Yes, she did. With him, she seemed safe. He would never harm her, and he would think only of her welfare, her security, her pleasure. When she was down he'd picked her up. The list was long—when she was fired for having the flu for three days, he told her manager that was rotten, and that sorry bastard had driven all the way out to the Bide-A-Wee to apologize and offer her the job back. Her first inkling of how much that name meant here. Took her to the beach if she asked, took her to the Sky View where they let her do a couple numbers at the piano. A dozen generous gestures. And always a perfect gentleman, never pressing her for sex—so different. Such a relief that was. She'd trusted him.

And then the thing that made her know he treasured her: when she told him about Anthony, about how she hadn't been married to the boy's father, about how he had died of diphtheria out in Hastings, Nebraska, when she was touring with a tent show and how she'd had to bury him in a strange cemetery (she did omit the help she'd gotten from Josef) out in the middle of a frozen prairie and no money for anything but a simple stone no bigger than a bread box—Georgie had said, "Let's go up there and put a stone angel over his grave."

He stood up to his mother and married her anyway. It would've been nice to have a lavish church wedding, of course, but that would be pushing things—as it was, he gave her more money to piddle away in New Orleans on their honeymoon than she'd ever had at one time to spend on anything but necessities.

He could be counted on to *adore her.* It hurt to think she had hurt him. But wouldn't confessing only hurt more? How could it help? She would make it up to him now by being the best wife any man could ever have—she could promise him that!

She wiped her eyes on her apron hem. She peeked through the blinds into the yard. Georgie and Walter were trimming out the pit they'd dug last evening, Georgie joking between sporadic shovelfuls of the turf and Walter staying on task, steadily planting the shovel into the sandy loam and heaving it out of the pit. Georgie was obviously enjoying himself.

Two weeks left of his furlough. He still hadn't talked to that lawyer, and she knew it pained him to consider. But after he left, she could do that on her own. They were *married.* Texas was a community property state. So Lester Pratt was her family lawyer as well.

God forbid that anything should happen, but given the possibility, she wanted this house in her name as well. She hated to confront him with such things when his stay was so short, and so she hadn't pushed. But she did *deserve* to be considered.

Yes, she was ashamed of how she'd acted with Robert, but she'd given up both the sin and the pleasure now, and she wanted recompense for this sacrifice.

When she stepped from the window to return to the kitchen, Georgie's two-toned oxford tripped her, and she bent to lift and heave it and its mate out of her path. He wasn't good about picking up after himself, and she was tired of doing that, but soon she'd have "help"—whatever

Georgie wished to call it—to tidy up. He left the bathroom a mess after shaving and after a meal just got up from the table. He acted like what he was—a person who'd been waited upon all his life. Call them whatever, the Karaceks had had servants for *decades,* and being a Karacek herself now, she should not have to live like a pinch-penny wage-slave.

The doorbell chimed. Maybe Thelma would answer it, she thought (Thelma having somehow become her housekeeper), then, when she realized she'd have to do it, she hurried down the hall as the postman rang the doorbell again.

"My brother Bill will be 18 next month"

The kid means a lot to me. There's four years difference between us, but it never stopped him from trying to keep up with me. He's game as a banty rooster.

Last time I was home on leave we had a talk. Bill finished high school last June and he's been working — making good money. It's not a skilled job, but he's helping in the war by putting his pay into War Bonds.

Some folks would say that's enough, but I could see the kid wasn't satisfied. He wanted my advice. Okay, I gave it to him straight.

* *

"Bill," I said, "you're the kind the Army needs. You'll make a top-notch soldier because you're young and can learn fast. You haven't filled out yet, but a few months of Army work and Army grub will turn you into a bearcat of a fighting man.

"You know what would make me mighty proud? To salute you as a commissioned officer! I'm not kidding, Bill. If you enlist now you'll have a head start on most men of your age. You'll have first-class training and a fine chance of getting into an Officer Candidate School.

"But that's not the only reason for joining up now. Before you're twenty you can choose any one of thirteen branches of the service. I know how keen you are about radio, and the Army needs lots of radio men. We use it for all kinds of communication. You like to tinker with things, too. There are plenty of places in the Army where mechanical skill counts. Pick your service. You'll have a chance to get fine training for almost any career you want to follow. The Army is a good school, Bill.

"And one more thing. You'll sleep with a clear conscience, nights. You'll know you've done the right thing for your country."

Well, Bill went to the Recruiting Office his next day off. He's in the Army now!

> "It is not enough for our Army to be as big and as well-equipped as the enemy's — it should also be as well-balanced in age groups. The Army invites American youth to answer that challenge.
>
> "The privilege of electing their branches of the service can safely be given to the men in the younger age group for precisely the reason for which the Army needs them — their adaptability and ready response to training."
>
> LIEUT. GENERAL BREHON B. SOMERVELL
> Commanding General,
> Services of Supply

Men of 18 and 19 who enlist in the U. S. Army can choose any one of 13 branches of service: Air Force (including Aviation Cadets), Armored Force, Cavalry, Chemical Warfare Service, Coast Artillery (Antiaircraft or Harbor Defense), Corps of Engineers, Corps of Military Police, Field Artillery, Infantry, Medical Department, Ordnance Department, Quartermaster Corps or Signal Corps. Call at the nearest Army Recruiting and Induction Station.

"KEEP 'EM FLYING!"

U.S. Army

Recruiting and Induction Service

TWENTY-FOUR

When the postman handed Sylvia a package, Mary Kay was upstairs struggling with a sleeveless blouse she was sewing from a Butterick pattern. This morning she was near tears at anything that thwarted her, beginning when she dropped her toothbrush into the toilet bowl. She had a rough night; her hair felt sore from her head's violent churning on her pillow. She itched all over and wanted to scream. It wasn't biological (her "friend" wasn't due soon). She was muttering when Sylvia appeared with a package the size of a cheese box.

"What's the fuss?"

"Buttonholes!"

Sylvia set the box down and slipped onto the sewing bench beside her. Mary Kay watched dumbly while Sylvia easily scooted the fabric around as the needle flew up and down.

"You see?"

Mary Kay nodded.

"What's wrong, hon?"

Mary Kay felt the woman's soft warm arm drape across her shoulders. She looked into Sylvia's brown eyes. Mary Kay longed to lay her head on that ample motherly bosom and cry her heart out. But you don't ask a tramp for sympathy about losing your guy to a tramp. Knowing Sylvia's secret prevented intimacy. She was angry at them for that.

"Didn't sleep enough. Guess I'm excited."

"You can nap all you like this afternoon." Sylva smiled and patted her thigh. "King's X on any chores. In Texas, this is your birthday." Sylvia beamed, picked up the box. "Maybe this will pep you up. It just came."

Taking it, Mary Kay shot her gaze instantly to the return address but it offered a jab of disappointment followed by curiosity—not from Donnie, not from Mom—from Corporal Mills! Still, a gift from even a stranger was welcome. Had she mentioned her birthday?

Sylvia hovered, but when Mary Kay looked up as she carefully peeled back the brown wrapping, she said, "I better get back to the kitchen," relinquishing her curiosity to honor Mary Kay's privacy.

A smaller box was couched inside the bigger one. A letter was folded under its tie cord.

> Dear Goldilocks!
> Thanks for the cookies and the good news from home. Since we're one H*** of a long way from a store, I hope you'll accept this souvenir as thanks. It's all I could think of to send that might make you feel you were really here. The yellow slanty-eyed b****** I took it off of was dead, but I'm proud I got a couple dozen notches on my old M-1 anyhoo!
>
> Keep up your cards and letters!
> Yrs truly,
> Corporal Ernie Mills

The smaller container was the size of a kitchen match box and made of thin, olive-drab pasteboard. It had black numerals and letters in English, but they spelled nothing recognizable. She supposed it originally housed military equipment or C-rations. The look and feel of it inched her closer to the actual war.

She unfolded the tabs on one end and peered inside. Something wrapped in gauze gave off a powerfully medicinal smell, like Campo-Phenique, maybe. She slipped the object from the box and set it on her lap. She peeled back layers of saturated gauze until she was staring blankly at the thing inside. It was oval, a ruddy rust color, with ridges and curves, like a large dried mushroom or a strangely tinted prune. She bent closer, too wary to touch it, and squinted. Gingerly, she pinched it between thumb and index finger and brought it closer.

She shrieked, flung it as she leaped. It hit the wall and fell to the floor behind the table. Her heart thudded wildly in her chest. She eased back onto the sewing bench.

Was that thing what she thought it was?

Maybe she jumped to conclusions. Still, though, it was *nasty* for sure. She'd thought maybe it was an exotic food she knew darn well she'd never taste in a million years but might keep as something from a foreign land, and even as she'd lifted it into view before her glasses and was thinking, vaguely, of showing it at a Victory Girl meeting, it suddenly looked too much like a human ear.

Maybe. Surely not.

She skimmed the note. *yellow slanty-eyed b****** I took it off of* ... Took it off of? Took it from his pocket, slipped it off his wrist? Not ... well, not use a ... something sharp enough to ... *Souvenir ... something to make you feel you are really here with me.*

Trembling, she rose, tip-toed to the table, where she peered beyond the edge at the thing. It was lying in wait. It might jump like a tarantula. She used one end of a yardstick to inch it into the light from the floor lamp. She bent, holding her breath to avoid smelling anything.

It *was* an ear! And Corporal Mills had, she guessed, used his bayonet or a knife to saw it from the dead man's head—now she recognized the upper delicate curve, the inner ridges, but the center was a ragged opening where it had been attached. It appeared to have been ... *pickled!* Preserved some way. The coating substance might be blood, but it looked more like that dark red gooey grease they packed rifles in. It glistened and furry dust from the floor had stuck to it.

She froze, listening for footsteps. Without knowing why, her impulse was to hide this thing. If Sylvia asked, she'd say it was a trinket then evade showing it. She didn't want anyone to learn that the soldier she'd been writing would do this. She could imagine going about her trivial business, doing her algebra, while on the other side of the globe Corporal Mills was using his bayonet .... The Movietone newsreel showed the brave boys in the Pacific hiking haggard along a jungle trail with their chin straps dangling while the announcer said they fought *a fierce and fanatical enemy,* and she looked close hoping by pure coincidence to see Corporal Mills, then the announcer said *But GI Joe is tender too* as the film showed a soldier on his knees reaching under a tank to pluck a kitten to safety.

Then when the camera's back was turned he used his bayonet to hack off the ear of a dead Jap?

It happened thousands of miles away. So far that day was night there, and night day. So far that the numbers of the date and the name of the day are different—so it was like another world that coexists with this one, either behind or ahead, depending. That world was ocean, islands, jungles. This one was continents, rivers, and lakes. Mary Kay had never seen a jungle and didn't know anyone who had. Nobody there but natives in loin cloths wearing bones through their noses while they cooked missionaries in big iron pots.

Who knew what the rules were way over there? *The law of the jungle!* It meant beast behavior, survival of the fittest. *Fierce and fanatical.*

Should she be flattered? He took the trouble to "prepare" and ship it. He took the trouble to *get it.* He wanted to show his appreciation. It was a long way to a store. It couldn't have been easy to get. She was glad his powers of description were weak and that he didn't say more. Maybe it upset him to do it? He had to take the knife and set the blade ....

She shook her head, gazed out the window. The trash can in the alley. Or bury it? Did burying a human ear require a ceremony? Was it against the law to do that without notifying authorities? Or would anybody care? The Japs were *fierce and fanatical* fighters who flung themselves suicidally into battle for the glory of the Emperor of the Rising Sun. They didn't subscribe to the Geneva Convention. They were hypnotized, their eyes glazed over as they pointed their dive bombers into American ships and never considered bailing out. If you're a brain-washed zombie, it wasn't courage. If you lost an ear you wouldn't care.

Would Corporal Mills pay her a call and expect to see it on the coffee table like a knick-knack? Would he feel insulted to know she buried it or tossed it into the garbage can?

The word *souvenir* implied keepsake, not something to be consumed or worn out. *Souvenir* implied an obligation to dust it now and then, trot it out on occasions (like a birthday party?) to show. She couldn't tell people *I want you to see this ear a pen pal sent me* any more than she could tell them her Mom's boyfriend Clyde jammed his tongue down her throat and felt her up.

If she were a boy, maybe this gift would mean more. Donnie might laugh at how squeamish she was. She could picture his fraternity pals gleefully gathering around to even handle it and hear how it came to be parted from its original body. They'd shrug, say, *That's war, kid. Did you think it's a stroll in the park?* Maybe Corporal Mills wanted to *impress* her, the way boys in elementary threatened you with insects to let you know they weren't scared to handle them.

She scooted it a few inches with the yardstick as if testing for signs of life. She was both nauseated and horrified and could scarcely force herself to peer at it, though the fuzz made it almost comical, commonplace. It helped to compare it to a chunk of withered apple.

She was sorry she'd written to him and wouldn't write again. The thing made her shudder, like a shrunken head. She wanted to put it out of her mind, but she also needed to run tell about it—it was another secret to bear alone.

A glimpse of it sparked her to conjure Mills' features, but without an expression—for God's sake, what expression do you wear while hacking the ear off a corpse? She couldn't create one, and yet, all the same, his arms moved over the head and the big knife in one hand went down and the other hand held the dead man's hair stretched taut to keep the head still and maybe a boot sole planted on the forehead while the cutting was done … .

My god, how could anybody do such a thing?!

Would he be grim-faced and angry, or cackling like a mad demon, or calm as you'd be slicing baloney?

The difference between what she was inside and anything remotely approaching Corporal Mills's state of mind in performing this ugly act was so cataclysmic it boggled her mind. Between herself and her pen pal Corporal Mills was a black space of motive and intent so mysterious, a state so wholly foreign, that struggling to probe it with her reason was like being utterly blind and feeling your way forward in a strange location by using a cane that collapses the instant you touch anything.

"Mary Kay?" Sylvia called up the stairs. "Wash up for lunch, hon."

Startled, Mary Kay yelled back, "Okay!" An electric current of fear zipped through her, as if she was about to be caught at something shameful.

With the yardstick, she shoved the thing onto a piece of newspaper, folded the paper over it, then, pinching it between the yardstick and her toe, she crushed the ugly thing to fit inside the bigger box. Holding the box on the floor with one hand, she crammed the thing into the opening with the yard stick. It was how she'd dispose of a dead rat.

She let out her breath. Now it couldn't be seen, though the stench of that antiseptic laid over the rot still stung her nostrils. She used the original brown wrapping to pack it quick as she could, hoping the odor didn't leak through.

She crept quietly down the stairs. Sylvia was talking in the kitchen to Thelma. Mary Kay held the box down at her side, glided around the newel post and went trippingly on her toes down the hall, hearing at her back Sylvia coming into the foyer and, seeing her making for the back door, calling out, "Mary Kay?" and Mary Kay flung over her shoulder, "Just a sec, okay? Gotta go do something."

Billie and J.J. clambered from under the washing machine and rushed her, yapping and leaping, eager with canine lust to poke their noses into the smelly package—she'd learned that all dogs had a ghoulish penchant for dead things—and she was afraid their racket would alert someone.

"Down!" she hissed, then slipped through the screen door.

Wearing slickers and hats in a drizzle, Georgie and Walter stood leaning on hoe handles while overseeing a huge fire in their pit. She glimpsed the meat protruding from the tarp. Suddenly the world seemed all raw claw and bloody fang, everybody better sleep with one eye open and a grip on a club. The men passed a Mason jar between them of a clear liquid whose volatility they'd demonstrated by pouring a dash onto the ground and igniting it with a match. Sylvia said liquor didn't mix with his medicine, and he had a fit night before last while Mary Kay lay awake worrying about Donnie. She heard a terrible *bump bump bump* like somebody falling down the stairs. When she hopped out of bed and darted to the landing overlooking the foyer, Sylvia was dashing toward the parlor, saw her and yelled, "No!" to wave Mary Kay back, then a thumping and groaning went on below. Then it was quiet. Sylvia came back to the foyer, smiled nervously, "Everything's fine. Go back to sleep, dear." As if she'd been asleep. If liquor was bad for him, why'd he drink it? This morning, at breakfast alone with Mary Kay, Sylvia said, out of nowhere, *This war has just turned everybody upside down and inside out.*

Keeping the men in view, she hoped to dash between the house and the garage stairs unseen, and she made it almost to the alley gate before they spotted her. She then had to wave, trying to semaphore something like *hello but bye bye, be out of sight in a second, no need to keep watching!* then she strode to the garbage can and without pausing lifted the lid and plunged her arm with the box in hand down as far as she could. Got something nasty under her nails. She scooped up leaves beside the can and tossed them in. The box couldn't be seen if you just lifted the lid.

Relief. She straightened and took a deep breath, releasing it as a sigh. No sooner done than George stepped through gate and saw her. Sylvia had hailed him from the back door to retrieve her. She backed away from the garbage can, wiping her hands on her pant legs.

"What the heck are you doing out here, Slim?"

"Nothing."

He grinned. "You act like a person who's up to something."

"Well, I'm not. I'm just getting some air. It's stuffy in my room. In the sewing room. I'm just gonna go around the block."

"Sylvia's calling us to eat."

"I know. It's just half a block." She needed a minute to get herself together.

"I'll walk with you. We'll go fast so Syl won't get wacky."

They struck out, and Mary Kay thought of how Sylvia went this route the night Georgie called from California and she caught them together up in RB's room.

"Do you think war changes people, you know, ruins them?"

"Some more than others, I'd guess."

"Do you think it makes men more savage, even good men?"

He laughed, too loud. She could tell he'd been drinking. "All the good men I ever knew were savages before the war."

"No, dammit, I mean it!"

Her vehemence made his head roll back. "Well, I guess the war magnifies whatever's there, good and bad."

"Do you think that if a good man does really savage things in war he can come back and be like he was before?"

"I don't think anybody can be what they were before no matter what happens. You can't step into the river twice in the same spot. Why you wanna know?"

She shrugged. She was too churned up to go on; it wasn't the time or place to try to talk about that awful thing. The war had turned her into a vagabond, an orphan; the war had turned Sylvia into an unfaithful wife; the war had turned her husband into a poor sap who got cheated on; the war had turned RB into a jilted groom and home-breaker. The war had turned Corporal Mills into a savage. How could he return to civilian life and put that out of his mind? And if it wasn't out of mind, how could he live the way he did before?

All these months since the war began, she'd innocently imagined that it was a temporary interruption, and that come victory, everyone would be restored to their normal lives, take up the plans they'd left off. She and her mother would return to Ohio to be with Gram—or Donnie would marry her.

Now she had a horrific, chilling vision that even after a victorious outcome everything will have shifted and the jumbled pieces would no longer fit. Even if Donnie still loves her, will he still be "Donnie"—could he possibly turn into a Corporal Mills?

And will she still be "Mary Kay?"

That no longer seemed possible. No one knew who or what they would become.

"Happy belated birthday, by the way," said Georgie.

TWENTY-FIVE

THE MEAT, THE birthday cake, the punch and wine—they stewed in Robert's gut, heavy as wet dirt but bubbling hot. He watched Georgie chow down, giggling, his titties jiggly, calling to his Negro pal and crooning "Sweetie" and "Honey" to Sylvia to show he had her. God it galled him! One look and acid roiled in his throat and a zip like a shot from a car battery jazzed his shoulders. He grit his teeth to keep from screaming. Once Georgie caught him staring and his brows popped up in surprise, then Robert looked away, but not so quick he'd think Robert was afraid, just enough he'd wonder what was churning in his head. Her precious Blubber Butt. *Why sweetie you look so fit!* She had to be joking. He could fill Mary Kay's brassiere better than she did.

Did she believe this preposterous flattery would produce "passion?" She was poisoning Robert with jealousy. She made a show of purring, being playful, touching Georgie. A smoldering heat seeped up his spine and oozed over his neck, and he looked away, ignored her. A hundred dollars said she didn't do it unless he was there. If he did catch her gaze, she smirked—*eat your heart out!* He wouldn't give her the satisfaction. Georgie took her caresses for granted, looked blissfully vacant as a cow. Made Robert want to blab just to wipe that goony contentment off his porky face. He could say he knew her from way back, let her deny it. Anything to plant the idea that Georgie's tenure was temporary, furlough or no.

He felt feverish and demented about her. That one night, it was the first dose of the drug that hooked you. He woke up each morning this week hard as a hammer handle, and that made him plot. Get one hand curled tight around that thing, it was a joy stick steering the plane of his thinking, swooping down to strafe somebody. Some genie inventoried the contents of his mind—his memories, his knowledge of himself and the world—and replaced each item with something of Sylvia's. The capital of South Dakota was now the soft space behind her knees; once upon a time he was engaged to those sweet hollows at the base of her labia; the war they were fighting with the Japs in her twisted grin and with the Gerrys in her intimate sewing room where they danced and sweet-talked was not going well, and soon they would invade her black rayon slacks from behind. Ike was the Supreme Commander of her laughter, how her mouth opened to expel a lungful of smoke.

Did he need a psychiatrist or a voo-doo priestess? Somebody please tell him how he lost himself in two women in succession and lost them to other men. Bad luck, bad karma, or stupidity? A Darwinian struggle wherein he was the inferior male bested by biological superiors? He couldn't say for sure about Claire's naval officer, but surely he was as much a man as Georgie, to judge by Sylvia's hints. Maybe she believed it wasn't her place to choose—it was their duty to lock horns and the winner claim the spoils.

That'd be too easy. Despite Georgie's pork, Robert could kick his ass from here to Kingdom Come and heartily enjoy it. He could kick in his fucking gap-toothed grin without the slightest twinge of conscience.

He felt bruised and sour. He wanted to work Georgie over with a baseball bat. He wished Georgie'd look cross-eyed, say one wrong thing, smart off about his leg or being 4-F. Anything would set him off. But he knew Georgie wouldn't. He was pathetic. He was the fat kid everybody picked on and he just took it. Georgie made him puke. Even if Sylvia were to tell Georgie *exactly* what they'd done, how it felt and how she liked it, it'd just sail over his head. Pathetic!

His thoughts—they were really ugly. Callous and unbecoming.

Swear to God he'd never been a bully. His own bad leg made him a likely target so he always took up for the underdog. But injustice rankled him. Pampered Georgie Warbucks never had to live by the sweat of his brow. For God's sake, where'd he been the past ten years? Living on an allowance! Meanwhile, Robert's old man got laid off and wore out shoe leather looking for work and said *no, Robert! Don't give up school, it means too much to us!* To prove they weren't trash. When his dad had to take Roosevelt's relief it about killed him. Mom took in ironing. Soon as he got to Washington he sent money, then the war came and they found work, but you can bet they had *not* forgotten what life was like before that.

He knew those years were in Sylvia's head, too. She had no family to rely on, so what she found here was a long-term meal ticket. He couldn't blame her. Meanwhile, Georgie smacked his lips and wolfed down the beef and potato salad and beans and cake and wine. That drinking alarmed Sylvia, but he thought *Cheers, you blubbery fuck!* When he got tipsy he sang "Sweet Adeline," conducted them with the hand holding his glass and sloshed wine on his cuff, the fucking oaf. Made Robert want to puke.

When Mary Kay had opened her presents he went out to the porch, he was so sick of Georgie. He lit a cigarette and wondered how much of what he exhaled was smoke and how much was gas bubbling up from his sour gut. Fire burned his belly and his breath was hot and sour. The moonless sky was ink above the trees with star-pricks winking through the skein of city light and chemical effluent. Nearby houses were lit like huge lanterns, and music played over loud and happy voices; parties blossomed everywhere, it seemed.

Never in America had so many people had so much fun than since this fucking war began.

Wrangling this invitation had been a mistake. He'd wanted to get within arm's reach to take her temperature. That kiss before he left showed him just how much she wanted it.

He'd taken a room at the Bide-A-Wee so when word got around she'd picture him spraying his tomcat stench all over hers and Georgie's love nest. It was a squalid, noir-story place well-suited for plotting, say, a double murder. While he was at it he lined Claire against the wall, too. He didn't trust Sylvia—she could make a man lose his head. She might stir Georgie up. With every Tom, Dick, and Harry on the planet being issued a firearm by his government, Robert felt left out. He bought a .38 revolver like the G-men use.

Being expelled from Eden made him look around. The war was spilling over in the streets; everybody was snarly, fist-fighting on buses and in the taverns. They often lacked bread and milk, and many folks had no decent place to sleep. Only three days gone and already he missed Sylvia's cooking. They served swill in the cafés because they could. At Magnolia they'd put a few Negroes over whites on the job. One cracker told him "I never worked *next* to no nigger, and I sure as hell ain't workin *for* one!" Fights out in the pipe yard, too, and every park had too many damn people. He was one among thousands of alien, disgruntled workers sweltering in the Texas heat and humidity, going without enough food or sleep but drinking too much.

But it suited him, the way it suited for your shoes to pinch when you're already pissed off. Inside, he was just like this town: boiling angry energy and too many things zapping under his skin to peacefully accommodate them. He lay on the bed brooding and staring at faces on the wall. He'd point the pistol and say, "Blam!" He'd load the empty cylinder with one bullet, spin it, put the muzzle to his temple, put his finger on the trigger, and say, "Blam!" Once he even pulled it, cringing, his body tense as an electroshock patient's in a nut ward. He'd swear he was *not* trying to shoot himself. When the steely click snapped in the empty room, he felt that giddy rush. Lying there, panting, heart thundering, sweat rolling off his brow, he felt a weirdly feral grin curl onto his mouth.

He had in mind becoming a very noisy fence of mischief around the perimeter of their alleged happiness. He wasn't content to wait for that damned furlough to end: he'd spoil whatever time they had left. He drove by the house Thursday evening, saw her sitting at the piano bench, playing. He pulled to the curb to watch and listen, his heart aching so bad it felt like a pulled muscle. He wanted to knock on the door, but he didn't have the guts. He was afraid what her face might show. If he had thirty seconds alone, he'd remind her he was waiting, that he believed her choosing Georgie was only practical. Temporary. He wanted her to acknowledge that if she were to follow *what she felt* she'd come to him.

Last night he'd called her pal Betty supposedly to have a nice long chat. He wound up rogering her royal, without a rubber, on her bed, and she didn't even turn down the nightstand photo of a homely yokel in air corps regalia. Sure, she bawled after. He'd grown used to this, though. Women were utterly faithless but couldn't admit it. He acted full of remorse. Their mutual regret preserved the possibility of a relapse in a "moment of weakness," and he was pretty sure Betty looked forward with relish to the drama of (Act I) poignant yearning, (Act II) agonized ambivalence, (Act III) ecstatic surrender, and (Act IV) remorseful repentance.

He was dying for Sylvia to find out, but Betty wouldn't tell her: the story would do her no credit except as the victim of a lowly seducer, but maybe that role appealed to her, and they could make a pity party and rake him over the coals. He hoped so.

He tossed his butt over the porch rail and lit another. He took a slow drag and tried to calm himself. A couple weeks, Georgie'd be gone, and he could make his play, slow and easy. Things could be so good if she'd be willing to leave. They could hit the road in that Lincoln. Nothing but a rosy future for smart, able-bodied adults like them in these times. They'd make enough to ward off the old nightmare of being so down and out she had to fake a fortune-teller stunt, the nightmare of the bread line she stood in daily for two weeks running, the nightmare of something dire she hinted of about a landlord. He'd wanted to crush the bastard's balls in his fist.

Thrum of bass notes, someone leaning on the low side of the keyboard, then diddling and fiddling on the high side, and someone—Sylvia no doubt—pounded out an introduction. She sang: *That ole black magic / has me in its spell / that ole black magic that you weave so well* … then other voices joined with *those icy fingers up and down my spine/ that same ole witchcraft when your eyes meet mine. . .*

His theme song! He wanted to scream. This a joke? Through the lace curtains he saw Sylvia on the piano, Georgie bellowing beside her with one hand clutching a wine glass, Mary Kay behind them with her palms on Sylvia's shoulders, her pals seated on the sofa, the girl named Nancy watching the singers and smirking while Linda stared at her shoes. Not much for sing-a-longs, he'd say.

Maybe it was only the wine, but he felt sorry for them all. They were a pitiful lot, including himself. Not a one knew what he was doing, where he was going. Like Mary Kay said, they were all roaring down the road at sixty and nobody was behind the wheel. He had this pretty picture of him and Sylvia strolling a New Jersey shore and making whoopee, but, really, next year they could be German citizens or POWs or hiding in the hills.

Or dead.

It made him want to be religious.

This kind of mood liberated and frightened him—when there's no real reason to live but likewise no reason not to. When there was really no right or wrong, no clear plan for anybody, and they were marbles spilled onto a great big tray to roll and bump off the sides and one another.

He went in. The rag-tag chorus had vamped into *Blue Moon, you saw me standing alone. . .without a dream in my heart. . .without a love of my own ...* with the piano duties assumed by Mary Kay and Georgie, Georgie in the treble plinking out the melody and MK doing the bouncy *bump-da-bump-ta, bump-da-bump-ta* of the bass. She was missing notes she usually got. Her peachy cheeks were flushed, and her head wobbled. Drunk, he guessed.

He sauntered to the sofa. "What say, girls?" Supposedly Linda found him dreamy, so when she looked up shy and fawn-like, he said, "You girls want to cut a rug?"

New Girl rolled her eyes—*not a chance, buster!*—but Linda cooed, "Gee, Mr. Goforth, I'm not much good. I can waltz."

"It's all the same. Guy and a girl stand face to face, hold hands and move their feet with the music. I can show you."

He got the feeling she needed the pal's permission, but the pal had declared these proceedings officially Beneath Contempt, so Linda was torn between dancing with Dream Boat and keeping her ally. To him all she needed to do was be seen in his arms and let her crush be witnessed.

"What'll it hurt? Promise not to step on your toes."

With a becoming splash of rosé tinting her cheek, she let him tug her upright by her hand; she was tall as he in her churchy pumps, and they assumed a chaste fox-trot pose, her fingertips dabbing his shoulder and her hot moist palm smothered by his cold one. He set his hand lightly on her waist and felt her flinch.

Turned out she knew the steps. She was light on her feet but uncertain, and since he was tipsy and lame and inexpert, in a jiffy they were ensnared in a who's-on-first debacle where she expected him to lead but knew the steps better, so he tried to lead by following her. They went galumphing over the rug and bumped into the coffee table, but he wheeled them to the piano where Sylvia stood behind Mary Kay as they rounded the end of the tune. He bumped into Sylvia and said, "Back to the top, Mary Kay!" Mary Kay hollered, "Okay!" dived back into the bass line and Blubber Butt gave chase.

Sylvia's mouth was a twisted rubber band as they whirled about. She hated his being here anyway, and the second Georgie issued the invitation at the icehouse he knew Sylvia hadn't said diddly-squat about them.

Linda and he were wobbly as a top out of axis, and when he dipped her he had to shoot a foot out to keep them from keeling over. They bumped the china cabinet and set Wedgwood teeth chattering behind the glass. Sylvia frowned, but he thought *who taught me to dance?*

Soon he crunched poor Linda's instep and she yelped "Yike!" and winced, so they stopped so she could plop down on the ottoman and rub her injury.

"Sorry! I got a little carried away!"

She smiled weakly, murmured, "'S okay. I'm not much good at this!"

"You kidding!? You're smooth as glass compared to me." Sylvia had her eye on them. He eased onto the ottoman beside the girl. "Here, lemme look at that," he said, as if he were a doctor. He cupped her stockinged foot and gently massaged it.

"That feel okay?"

"Uh-huh."

Her cheeks heated up. She had slender legs and pretty gray eyes with nice long lashes. If he wasn't such a goner on Sylvia he'd cash in on Linda's girlish crush and usher her off to womanhood, and he'd do it to stir up Sylvia. He had that much poison in him.

They ended the tune again, and Georgie said, "Hey, let's everybody dance! We'll put a record on!"

In the dining room they scooted the table to the wall—mostly him and Walter, with clumsy Georgie pitching in too late—and he considered twisting New Girl's arm to try a step, but she wasn't budging from the sofa. She was almost flinging the pages of a *Ladies Home Companion* one to the next while smacking her gum, showing her disdain. He guessed it had to do with Negroes being guests.

Mary Kay set the needle down on the Harry James version of "You Made Me Love You," and though it was an instrumental he knew the lyrics to the goddamn song. A curse lay on him—everything this night pointed back to how he couldn't get Sylvia out of his system. So he said, "Syl, lemme have the first dance." Before she objected he hooked his arm around her waist, grabbed her hand in his, tugged her belly to belly, and they swayed side to side.

Nobody reacted. Walter slipped an arm about his skinny mate and Mary Kay and Georgie faced off like ten-year-olds in a finishing school class, though he wore a goofy grin like he was about to polka her down the yellow brick road. She kept giggling out of position before they could take a first step, and he saw they were both so drunk they could hardly stand.

He swung Sylvia close by and said, "Hey, Georgie, you know the words to this song?"

He said, "Huh? Uh, no."

He sang at him—almost right in her face—"*You made me looove you, I didn't wanna do it, I didn't wanna do it. You made me want you . . . .*" But he and Mary Kay were cackling and watching their feet as they tried to set off on a fox trot. He thought fuck him four ways, and he sang, trying to *croon* really—so pathetic!—to Sylvia, drawing her head over his shoulder, "*You made me haaappy some. . .times, you made me glad. But there were times, dear . . .*" whirling her close to the two morons, "*you made me feel so mad!*"

Still no reaction. Jesus, was he so blind? Did he care so little? He started in again, "You made me wannnntt you," and Sylvia said, sharply, under her breath, "Stop it or I'm not dancing!" so he shut up.

He held her tighter and tighter and took smaller steps until their "dance" could've been done on a square of typing paper. He pressed her to him with his hand against her back and ground against her belly to the music. He felt wrought up, as if he might explode or collapse onto the floor and bawl.

"Oh Syl," he whispered. "Oh Syl honey . . ." She squeezed his hand hard to signal *shut the fuck up!* or *I know you do, sweetie!* He brushed her ear lobe with a lip and he knew Walter's wife saw it. But now he did not fucking care. His hand draped lower and he pressed his thigh between her legs, held her there and rocked.

"Hey, Georgie!" he hollered. She tried to pull away but he kept a tight grip. He looked up. "Hey, try this!" he dipped her so that she was riding his thigh. Georgie laughed like he couldn't see that Robert was massaging his wife's quim with his kneecap, and said, "Hey, okay!" then yanked Mary Kay toward him, but the song was over, and Sylvia jerked away.

"Put it on again!" he hollered into the parlor. Linda got up from the sofa and went to the Victrola. Sylvia called out "Jersey Bounce!" to keep him off the dance floor, knowing even if he tried a jitterbug they wouldn't be touching.

What they got was "I'll Never Smile Again" with Tommy Dorsey and Frank Sinatra, but before he could snatch up Sylvia, she announced,

"Change partners!" and moved for Georgie. But he was looking green about the gills, standing with one hand flat on the table and dabbing his moist pink brow with a napkin.

"You okay, hon?"

"Yeah, just need a second to get my wind."

"I want to dance with you."

"Oh go ahead." He waved at Robert. "I feel too hot. I wanna get some air."

"You sure you're okay?"

"Positive. Go on, dance."

Weaving, he went out into the hall, and Robert said to Sylvia, "I *promise.*" She looked wary but after hesitating, she nodded, took an earnest step toward him and her right arm went up to meet his left, all stiff and serious as if they'd be graded on form. This was her demeanor when she gave him lessons, and it was intended to chasten him.

They were granted a spell in their own little Eden. His hate drained and he held her loose and sorrowfully tender as they danced through "I'll Be Seeing You" and "Mood Indigo" and "Serenade in Blue"—blue moon, black magic, blue serenade, indigo mood, they were all the shades of bittersweet, melancholy rue. He felt a drunk's compassion burgeon in his breast toward her and her pitiful hubby.

Thing is? If he hadn't believed that deep down she really preferred him over Georgie, he'd have given up, he'd swear. He would've honored their commitment, applauded it even. He couldn't justify wrecking a home merely to satisfy an itch. But he didn't believe this was the best home for her in the long run.

After a while, she relaxed and let herself sink into his arms, let her breasts touch his chest, her loins brush his own, and he lay his cheek gently against hers.

His anger evaporated, leaving sadness. Walter and his wife had gone without his noticing, and sometime during their dancing Mary Kay had disappeared. Sylvia and he were alone in the room; the lights were low. Seeing a window of opportunity, he couldn't squelch the impulse to push.

"How much longer is Georgie's furlough?"

"It doesn't matter, Robert, because you're never setting foot in this house again."

He smiled into her ear. The song was about to end.

“I understand.” He wouldn’t need to. He had a room off the premises now.

TWENTY-SIX

Robert and sylvia were necking to the music. Mary Kay's tummy lurched, so she scurried to the bathroom and urped a goulash festooned with bits of pickled crayon.

Swear to God I'll never drink alcohol again in all my life!

She splashed her face, rinsed out her mouth, and then eased onto the rim of the tub, dizzy and winded.

Best birthday present now? Have somebody shoot her.

Back in the hall, she averted her gaze from the dining room and went through the foyer into the parlor. Nancy and Linda were standing, Nancy with hands clasped behind her back and her feet spread like a soldier at parade rest, and Linda with her arms crossed loosely under her breasts, her purse swinging from one white-gloved fist. Mary Kay pretended she didn't notice.

"Hey, you guys, let's go back up to my room. I wanna take your pictures."

Linda cocked her head, sad smile drooping on her mouth. "Aw, we gotta go. My mom's gonna—"

"Aw, it's really early! We can—"

"It's been really fun!" crooned Nancy. "Thanks for asking me."

Linda said, "Yeah, me too!"

Mary Kay bit her lower lip to stop her chin from quivering. They were in such an eager rush to be alone without her. So Nancy could sneer about Mary Kay's wearing school clothes to her own party though her guests wore nice dresses, and because Nancy's a Baptist they'd phone around to say Mary Kay got drunk and danced; they'd tell how the grown-ups were immoral, were queer and crippled, and—the deepest cut—they were "nigger-lovers."

"Okay. Wish you'd stay."

Nancy piped up, "Boy, me too! It's been really fun!"

Linda looked wistful, downright sad. As if she were saying goodbye before departing for a long trip and not merely strolling up the street to her home. Which she *was* saying, Mary Kay realized suddenly. You might befriend a Yankee newcomer out of charity, but you didn't want to besmirch yourself by association. She shouldn't have told Linda about her father. Or spilled her guts about Donnie's being at the ROTC Ball right this minute.

Nancy and Linda awkwardly skylarked while Mary Kay blotted her eyes with the heels of her hands, all pretending she wasn't crying.

"Well, gosh, thanks for coming, you guys! Thanks for the perfume, Nancy, I'll wear it next time I'm with my fiancé, and, Linda, it was so sweet of you to get me a diary just like yours. I'm gonna go up and write about how wonderful it's been to have a really good friend."

Linda blushed. "You're welcome. And would you please thank your. . .thank Miz Karacek for us?"

Mary Kay might've suggested they thank her themselves, but she knew why they hadn't and it was just as well. Peering into the next room you could see a demonstration of upright coitus set to dance-band music.

Without her prompting, the other duo glided into the foyer, and, though she longed to pitch herself face-first onto her bed, she knew to play the gracious hostess. They murmured over their shoulders "Guh-byee, guh-niite, see yew." Mary Kay couldn't resist tagging along to the porch, retarding their leave-taking, tormenting herself by the desire to hug Linda goodnight, and that expectation collided with Linda's apparent wish to avoid it—she wouldn't turn and face Mary Kay even as Mary Kay spoke to her back, "Hey, Linda, can you come over tomorrow? We can work on the aviation flash cards or sumpin?" and Linda hem-hawed, "Umm, dunno, maybe, have to see . . ." and Nancy was already down the three steps off the porch.

"Well!" Mary Kay declared. And stopped. Linda hesitated, one step down, looked back. She smiled politely but with a hint of pain; Mary Kay bent to embrace her, but Linda wouldn't concede the necessity, and Mary Kay had to hug her sideways with Linda's shoulder cap like a fist in her breastbone.

"See ya!" Mary Kay said. "Call me. Okay?"

The girls went down the walk. Despite herself, she clambered after them, calling out, "Hey, uh, wait you guys, uh, Nancy, didn't you have gloves?" Still walking, they half-twisted to look back, clearly not the least desirous of stopping, "—and I just had an idea, uh, we could, I mean if you guys are, uh—" she stammered, yearning to invite herself along, when Nancy, walking backward, lifted both white-gloved hands, waggled them in the air like a minstrel darky, chortled, "Heah dey be!" underscoring it with a snotty grin, and Mary Kay, stung, stopped dead in her tracks.

She watched their backs recede in the darkness. They were taking care, she was certain, not to be observed whispering something catty. She couldn't take her eyes away, sure that the instant she did Nancy would whisper something snide to Linda, and, even worse, Linda would giggle and whisper back. Before dinner, when they were in her room, she excused herself to pee; when she came back they were looking at Donnie's photograph and stopped talking the second she entered. Nancy's tiny, supposedly hidden smile struck fear in her heart. "Is he eye-talyun?" she asked, deadpan. Though Mary Kay laughed it off and said, "McBride?" there lay under Nancy's question a rich vein of presumption about someone who she thought looked *foreign*.

Their whispering was inevitable, so there was no point in pretending that her gaze on their backs formed a force field that would prevent it.

As she padded down the dim hall past the dining room, she tried to resist looking, but the music was still going. Robert was nuzzling Sylvia's neck. Mary Kay grit her teeth, clenched her fists, flit past quick as she could.

The telephone cord was just long enough to stretch under the bathroom door. She pulled the chain for the light and got a facefull of herself in the mirror. She turned away with a groan. She sat on the floor with her back to the tub, the phone in her lap.

"Operator. May I place your call, please?"

"Long distance, please. Ypsilanti, Michigan."

Then she recited for the new operator the number for the dormitory and told her it was "person-to-person to Mr. Donnie McBride." She should've checked the time. Probably he and that girl were still at the dance or had gone for breakfast. Or were riding around sipping from a flask, and Donnie and she were necking or even petting in the dark back seat, the girl letting Donnie go below the neck, where Mary Kay had not, and that was a HUGE mistake! If she was with him tonight she'd let him go all the way—he was a good person and if he was her first he'd treasure that, she just **knew** that he would honor and cherish her *my god why didn't I do that!!* Because if he did this with Melinda Melissa Whoever she'd claim it was her first time...

The phone rang. She pictured it on the counter in the lobby. Somebody was always speaking on it or the receiver was lying on the counter while they chased down the callee. Maybe a thunderstorm or even a tornado canceled the ball; Melinda/Melissa got the flu; Donnie was sick or decided that if Mary Kay couldn't go, he wouldn't, either.

Finally—"McCracken dormitory," and the operator—her nasal clipped Michigan accent like a fresh breeze to Mary Kay's ear—said, "Person-to-person for Mr. Donnie McBride." The desk clerk, a student paid to be on duty, replied, "I don't think he's in but I'll check."

"We'll hold," she said.

The phone was an auditory window into Donnie's world. Whir, buzz, faint beeps, static that she learned in science was caused by solar eruptions, over it the muted voice, as if the operator had cupped her mouthpiece to continue a yarn to a coworker. Then the voice stopped, the air pressure altered as if the hand was removed, and Mary Kay heard tiny gum smacks and maybe breathing.

"Sorry it's taking so long," Mary Kay said experimentally.

"S'okay, hon," the voice came crisp and surprisingly loud. "I get paid the same."

"It's my boyfriend's dormitory. He was out tonight and I was worried if he got back. What's the weather like up there?"

"Hottern' Hades."

"Not a storm?"

"Had a shower earlier."

"I'm down in Texas." No response, so Mary Kay added, "My mom works at Willow Run—you know where that is?"

"A course. I'm in Detroit. Got a cousin works at Bomber."

"Thing is, we're engaged, so I'm *really* concerned if he's okay."

"I'm sure he is. Congratulations!"

"Thanks." Would this operator eavesdrop? She'd hear the sad tale of the fiancée who waited weeks for her future groom to call then finally gave in and called herself only to hear the gory details of his date to a ball with another girl. She imagined the operator shaking her head. *Poor kid. How gullible can you get?*

"Are you married?"

The operator chuckled. "Now *there's* a long story!"

Not a happy ending, guessed Mary Kay, wishing she hadn't asked.

Suddenly a male voice was saying, "Sorry, he's not in."

"May I leave a message?"

"Sure," said the fellow, but her question had been to the operator, whose silence amounted to permission.

"Say, uh, that. . . oh, heck, never mind!"

The fellow hung up.

"Sorry, hon," said the operator.

"Uh, thanks. Please—" Mary Kay knew the operator had to cut her off, but she felt panicky.

"You wanna place another call?"

"No. Guess not. I dunno who to. My mom doesn't have a phone. Could you talk to me?"

"Aw, sweetheart, they won't allow it. I'm awful sorry."

"Okay. Thanks, anyways."

Then the phone was an inert black block in her lap, heavy as a stone. She set it onto the floor, then drew her knees under her chin and hugged her shins. Ten deep breaths to get calm.

Okay, don't go wacky. That Saturday, in Price's soda shop, sitting in the booth, chocolate malts and grilled cheese sandwiches, Donnie taking her dill slices when she offered, far enough past the lunch hour the booth behind him was empty. Though the juke box was playing "Mairsy Doats" instead of "You Stepped Out of a Dream" and though it was broad daylight and not starlight, and though she was wearing her Victory Girls uniform and he work trousers and a chambray shirt, and though he didn't go to his knee and slip a diamond on her finger—though it was nothing like the movies, it *did* count.

Didn't it?

He was talking about this gruff ROTC drill master, and she was perched leaning forward with her chin propped on her fists and her eyes all gooey with love, she guessed, because he stopped talking, grinned, then said, "You're 'bout the cutest thing I ever saw, you know that, Mary Kay?"

She said, "Nope, didn't know it! Don't believe it, either! Tell me ten times in a row to make sure I hear it okay."

He said, "I'd be scared it'd go to your head."

"Try me! Take a chance!"

He laughed. "You're awfully cute!"

"Now you're going backwards!"

He laughed again. "You're heaps of fun, Mary Kay. Smart too. I guess you'll make somebody really happy one of these days."

She could barely get it out, but she said, not looking at him but at the mirrored wall behind the soda counter, "Think so? Golly, I hope!"

He fell quiet and she was afraid the subject would be set aside, but then he said, "With the war and all, it's pretty hard to think about permanent things, you know, since I'm going into the air corps when I graduate."

"I know."

"I wish I could think about them. A guy gets out of college and starts making his way in the world, well, normally, he'd be thinking of taking on more responsibilities."

"I know, I know."

"Mary Kay, if I could think about them . . ."

"Yeah?" She held her breath.

"I would."

"Sure. I understand."

"There's always after, you know?"

"Yeah. After."

"Will you write to me?"

"Gah! Donnie! If you go overseas I'll write twice a day!! No lie!"

This was before the big ruckus, before her mother exiled her to this godforsaken place, and neither had any notion they'd be separated before he graduated. She'd fulfilled her pledge—she'd written and written!

That was the only time he spoke seriously about his future. She had believed this was the message: *If I could consider marriage now, I would choose you. When I get back, I'll be the fella that you will make so very happy.*

When he paid their bill, he bought a cigar. She said, "I didn't know you smoked cigars!"

"Don't," he said. "I'll give it to somebody."

He slipped the band off the aromatic cylinder, then he lifted her hand and slipped that paper ring onto her finger. It sported a colorful cameo of an Indian princess. He grinned, winked. She held her breath. She was expecting to hear him say something, well, *marital.*

He said, "Don't say I never gave you anything!"

"Gee thanks!" she wisecracked. She waggled her hand as if admiring a diamond. "It's beautiful, though, it really is." She meant to convey that she understood the deepest intent of the gesture.

Naturally, Linda and Nancy asked about a ring. She knew that it made them suspicious that she couldn't produce one. She'd taped that cigar band to a page in her diary and wrote beneath it how she'd gotten it and what it meant. Her mom found it along with other evidence she needed to justify sending her only child into exile so that she could sleep with a filthy-minded Palooka without distractions.

She told Linda, "We've got a ring on layaway up there." She went on to describe a diamond engagement band she'd seen in the window of an Ypsilanti store, a ring she'd pointed out to Donnie as they strolled by, saying, "Isn't that one really special?" Just to let him know. She imagined him going in alone and asking, "My girl admired that one. Can I put it on layaway?"

But he hadn't. Not yet, anyway. Now she could imagine Nancy braying like a jackass. "God-a-mity! She dint expect us to believe THET bull, did she?" And Linda thinking it was a lie, as well.

But it wasn't a lie! It was a. . . distinct possibility!

A draft slipped under the door, snuck up her spine and splashed the back of her damp neck. She shivered. From where she hunkered on the linoleum, the underbelly of the wash basin and the toilet rim were visible. She caught her breath. She heard Donnie's voice in a new and sinister aspect as if the background music had segued from syrupy violins to organ-in-a-crypt. When he said she was the cutest thing he'd ever seen and she asked him to say it ten times over, his reply was *I'm afraid it'd go to your head.* What if he wasn't joking? What if he'd regretted blurting that out because she took it too seriously, took it as a sign he cared for her more than he really did? Maybe he was trying to warn her not to lose her head? Not let a casual compliment sweep her away on a romantic dream of marriage.

That explained why he immediately mentioned that she'd make some fellow a great husband! It's what you offer as consolation! He meant some OTHER fellow!

It explained why he gave her that long song and dance about the uncertain future, about the war and not making plans!

Could it be he *wasn't* saying "wait for me?" He was saying "you better NOT wait because everything's temporary and nothing's certain."

And that stupid cigar band! Play-acting! His "proposal" was no more real than that ring, and he was trying to say, *Don't misunderstand—this is the only ring you'll be getting.*

And it was!

This was why he hadn't written except for that long letter explaining too much about why he was taking another girl to the dance: he wasn't asking Mary Kay's permission!! He was letting her know he was dating others!

She groaned, loud and long, and the empty room with its high ceiling was like a sounding box. God! The truth hurt so much!

"Oh … oh … oh. *Piss* on you!" she wailed.

TWENTY-SEVEN

"OKAY, ACT LIKE ladies and gentlemen!" Georgie held a plate of bones like a waiter while the hounds leapt with joy, front claws raking his belly and back. "J.J.—sit!" The dog complied by half, dipping its haunches porchward while continuing to dance. "Billie! Sit!" She was more dutiful, and, setting the plate on the floor, Georgie stepped back.

J.J. was still so new to the place he wouldn't eat from the food bowl—he darted in, snatched a bone, scurried under the wash tub, gripped it between forepaws and snarled as his jaws worried it like a harmonica player in rag-time.

Georgie had come out to catch a breath because his noggin was a whirl-a-gig, but when he appeared the pups jumped on him. He'd stroked them to a relative calm then gone back inside for the bones.

He took in the bracing anodyne of the honeysuckle-scented air. "You're easy to please. I like that about you dogs. Behave yourselves and you'll be living in the house 'fore long. Might sleep on the bed, too, but you ought not get ahead a yourselves. Dogs here used to do that, but times change, my friends. You're on probation. The lady of the house doesn't like mutts dirtying her floors, and we don't abide *accidents* if you get my drift. Or runnin' in the house. Jumpin' on the furniture or barkin'. Got that?"

Shaky on his legs, he sank into the swing, closed his eyes and slowly breathed the fresh air. He leaned back, relaxed. The music seeped through the windows. *Gonna take a sentimental journey …* Useless to get worked up about their dancing. He encouraged it partly to act out what he wished he felt. He didn't want Sylvia to be denied a simple pleasure because he couldn't face down his jealousy.

Everybody was only having fun. That was all. In all the years he'd lived here he never dreamed life inside this house could be so busy and pleasurable. Even with the strain of being responsible for things. He liked sitting at the head of the table, being the patron on his tiny ranchero; he liked being served by Sylvia, liked having his pal Walter drop by to bend an elbow, liked feeling free to be a slob, liked *not having Mama here* to carp, liked sleeping with that good warm woman.

Tonight he swelled with well-being. Now the house contained a family he had chosen and made—he brought Sylvia, he brought Walter and Thelma, and Sylvia brought the boarder and Mary Kay, and even with the tension they'd cobbled together a circle more welcoming than his biological relatives. It was a good life even with a gray cloud over it—his old nemesis epilepsy, his *problem* in the bed, his struggle to meet the world head-on and *make something* of himself, his failure as a soldier. When he felt optimistic like this, his problems could be worked on one by one, and eventually the future Georgie would be a man Sylvia could admire and respect.

Feeling stronger, he vacated the swing, opened the screen door—the dogs looked up but not even bolting free could compete with bones—and stepped out to where the pit glowed under its cover of tin. Through the nail holes coals winked and glimmered. Ought to put it out. Without thinking, he stooped to grab the corrugated tin, instantly dropped it, hollered, "Youch!!" and licked and blew on his fingers.

Tin's hot! *What'd you expect, moron!*

With a stick he lifted the tin and heaved it to the side to bare the coals. When the breeze hit them they swelled like a brass section ushering in the finale. He retrieved a rake from the garage and dragged the garden hose from a faucet by the house. He cranked the tap and got a drizzle no bigger than a beer piss and aimed it at the fire, got a sizzle and white smoke in return. The coals were radiant, pulsing.

Mary Kay came down the porch steps.

"Unless you want marshmallows, I'm dampin' the fire."

They stood in a meditative silence as he prodded the coals with the ribbon of water. A breeze shot up momentarily to put them downwind, the heat hit in oppressive waves—the night was sultry already—and the skin on his face went taut. Hers was orange in the glow. Her brows were scrunched.

"Where's your pals?"

"Left."

The glum way she said it alerted him. "Y'all have a spat?"

Her shrug was a spastic jerk, so there was a story. "What happened?"

She swiped at her eye with her fingertips—maybe a bit of ash blew in it, but she was tearing up.

"Nothing. They don't like me, I guess."

"Aw, that's bull. Besides, you ought not care. That Nancy's a pure-dee moron. I've known her since she was no biggern a bucket, and she was born a moron."

Mary Kay showed a weak smile.

"No kidding. It's in the record books. People came from miles around. Her folks had a booth at the county fair right next to the Ten-Toed Woman, and they sold tickets, called her Baby Idjit. That's how they came by their money, and now they're puttin on airs like they're the same as you or me. It's enough to make you urp."

"I already have. I drank too much wine. In front of them. Nancy's Baptist. I shouldn't of drunk it."

"Me, either." A puff of breeze spiraled a tower of sparks upward, and they followed it with their gaze, chins lifting. "You wanna take the abstinence pledge with me?"

"Okay. Sure." After a minute, she chuckled. "Ten-Toed Woman! Ha! I just now got it."

"Have to get up early around here."

She laughed. "You sure are a nice man, Georgie."

"Aw, heck, Slim! That's a swell thing to say. The feeling's mutual. You're like a kid sister now. And believe me you're the best of the bunch."

She smiled wanly. If he kept on, he might dig her out of this Slough of Despond. Last thing he should mention was that fellow up in Michigan.

"What're they doin' in yonder?"

Maybe she hadn't heard him. Before he could repeat it, she said, "This sure has been a lousy day!"

"Aw, I'm sorry!"

"Oh, it's not your fault! I know you and… *she*… tried, you really did! And I got such nice presents, too! I really appreciate it! Just … things, you know?"

Maybe she *did* want to talk about it. "What things?"

She toed the turf with her saddle shoe. "You remember my asking you this morning about war making savages out of fellows?"

"Yeah."

"I got something from a GI I've been writing. He sent it in a package. I don't know why he picked me. When you saw me in the alley? I was throwing it away. I think it was an… *ear.* Somebody's ear. I'm pretty sure it was, I guess. A Jap's ear."

"Aw, for cryin' out loud! He oughta be horse-whipped!"

"You think so? I was afraid something's wrong with me that I didn't like getting it. I mean he's out in the Pacific risking his life."

"Give me his address, Slim. I wanna write his CO. What a sorry thing to send a sweet kid like you."

That turned on the faucet! He must've given her permission to feel sorry for herself. She stood stock still, upright, clapped her hands to her face and lit into a bawling jag like a hobo at a four-course meal. He grimaced, shuffled for a bit thinking he'd wait it out and let her rain on herself. But when it didn't let up, she sounded so heart-broken he slipped his arms around her. She smashed her face into his chest and clutched him so tight you'd think she was in danger of falling off a cliff. Helplessly, he patted the top of her head with a free hand. It went on and on; it was astonishing how much grief one skinny girl could store up.

Finally, her spasms let up until she was shivery and gulping.

"I'm gonna give Linda a piece of my mind, too." He meant to console her, but it cranked her up again. After a bit, her breathing was less shaky and ragged, and her shoulders went still.

"This about that Donnie?"

Her head bumped his chin.

"Well, I'll write his CO too, then." He was trying to joke them out of this awkward intimacy. Her head shook *no no no,* brushing his chin. Then, she inhaled, gently pushed back, letting him know she wanted to go it alone like a big girl.

They stared at the fire.

"I used your phone." She snuffled, swiped her eyes with the backs of her hands. "Hope you don't mind."

He was momentarily puzzled then realized she meant she called long distance. "'Course not. Reach anybody?"

"No, it was person-to-person. He wasn't there."

For P-to-P in that case, there'd be no charge, so her announcement was only a wedge into the subject. But Georgie didn't know what question to ask. He wanted to ask one that answering would help her feel better, not worse. There might not be such a question, he knew; it could be she'd only feel better after feeling worse first.

"You can try again. Mi phone-oh es su phone-o. And it dudn't have to be collect."

"Thank you." Meek teary voice. Sniffling, then she cleared her throat. "I shouldna called. I was just torturing myself. I knew he wouldn't be there. He's at the ROTC ball with another girl. He wrote me he was gonna take her. He *said* he would've taken me if I'd been there."

"He sounds like an honest fellow."

"It's a formal dance they have every year, and officers from the regular army come with their wives. It's real important."

"Sure. And he couldn't go stag, now could he?"

"No. Guess not."

"So this is probably the only time he'll ever see her. Sometimes you have to trust people."

They were silent for a bit. Georgie whistled "Old Black Magic" through his teeth, aimed the hose at the far end to see the water arc over the flame and smoke. Fireman.

His sage advice wasn't sufficient to set her mind at ease. She peered into the fire as if there was a horror movie playing down there.

"It's not just that. He's only written that one letter since I've been here, and he hasn't called me once! He didn't even send a birthday card!"

"Oh, gosh, Slim, you know fellows are notorious about not writing!"

"How hard can it be to just write I love you, Mary Kay?"

"For some, harder'n you might think."

"I guess! I think he doesn't want to have to say he *doesn't* love me—that's the hard thing!"

Midnight shift at the water-works! He didn't hesitate to reach for her, but she held one palm against his chest to stop him; muscles in her jaw throbbed as she clenched her teeth, her intake of air whistled between her taut lips, she sniffled hard and wrenched herself into control.

"You don't know that. Could be you'll hear from him tomorrow. You shouldn't give up on him. Like I say, sometimes you gotta trust—"

"I don't want to be a fool!" she snapped.

"Sure. Who does? But until you know for sure you oughta give him the benefit of the doubt. Trust is—"

"I don't HAVE any doubt, Georgie!" She gave him a hard straight look. "I'm not going to be a *patsy* any more!"

"I'm just trying to say that maybe your fella will—"

"I said I don't wanna be a fool! And you shouldn't, either!"

Georgie smiled. "Heck, I've been one all my life. My folks coulda had a booth beside Nancy's, but they were way too ashamed. Sylvia's the only woman I ever met who could tolerate it."

Mary Kay groaned. "Maybe it's not good to be trusting."

Georgie shrugged: he'd already had this debate with himself today. "You got the choice, you know." He tapped his temple. "Your happiness, it's all in here, kiddo."

"Oh Georgie!" she wailed. When he tried to catch her eye, she turned to the fire.

When Mary Kay didn't go on, he said, "Oh Georgie what?"

"Nothing."

"Come on, you can tell me."

"It's … I know while you were away you heard stories about, about stuff."

He shrugged. "Oh sure."

"But you still trust her?"

"Yeah. It's how you have a marriage. You don't listen to gossip, Mary Kay." It gave him a rosy glow to speak as an expert.

They were quiet but she was gnawing her lower lip and stood with her arms hitched tight over her breasts, rocking, clearly agitated. Maybe he should be more honest about wrestling the demon Doubt. Earlier it had swamped him like the flu but he rode it out and it slipped off him during the day.

"Georgie? You know the night you called from California?"

"Yeah."

"Know why I answered the phone?"

"Sylvia was out for a walk?"

"I went to find her. She was. . .was up *there!*" Mary Kay jerked her head toward the garage apartment.

"Well, that doesn't mean anything."

"I went up to ask Robert if he'd seen her. I didn't know she was there. And I *heard* them!"

When she fell mute, he asked, "What they were saying?" Maybe she misinterpreted it. He could turn their same words any way he needed.

"They weren't *saying* anything."

Mary Kay had created something out of air like a kid seeing a shadow in her room at night imagined a boogie man. "Like they were making conversation?"

Her face swung toward him, her expression pained. "No, they ... weren't saying words. They were making, aw, making those *sounds* people make."

Surely she was mistaken. You groan or moan when somebody hits you with a corny pun, or when you're tired and get up from a chair, or when a woman sobs the way Mary Kay had moments ago. Hearing that from a distance and not knowing the situation, you might misconstrue the cause.

"Could of been a lot of things."

"Oh, gosh, Georgie! I'm sorry." She jammed her fists into her skirt pockets and turtled her head into her shoulder blades. "Never mind."

He was expecting or hoping to hear *yeah, you're probly right.* What he got was *I heard them. You didn't. But think what you want.*

"Or cats or something. Right?"

She glowered at the fire. "Please forget I said anything, okay?"

"Slim, I'm not calling you a liar. But an innocent kid like you—maybe you only *thought* you were hearing something."

"Okay. I'm sorry."

He was exasperated that she agreed only to be agreeable. It seemed urgent to extract a sincere acknowledgment that she was *only hearing things.* Her sullen agreement implied Robert had put the horns on him. For the sake of their familial harmony, Mary Kay shouldn't bear the burden of this false impression.

"Now, I'm not trying to win a debate, Slim. But you probly haven't had experience about this, so you probly weren't hearing what you thought." He was aware he'd already made that point.

"I said I'm sorry." She sounded truculent. She kicked a little dirt into the pit. "I'm going to bed."

He stared dumbly into the fire, hearing the screen door squeak open then clap back against the frame. He wished she'd stayed; he wanted to argue the point until he'd won. Without her, it was too easy for his mind to play tricks. He'd not yet doused the fire—they'd had it going since before noon and had fed it pretty steadily. The huge orange eye sunk in the turf blinked but kept on staring, the heartbeat of it thumping in the earth, and the stream from the hose seemed not only puny but somehow a *violation.* The fire lulled him into a trance, set him to mulling, and now he wanted to let it burn itself out without his interference.

He let the hose drop into a furrow in the garden and stared into the glowing coals.

Not much doubt now.

Robert had taken advantage of them both. Could be Mary Kay had heard him getting fresh. Maybe Sylvia had gone up there to speak to him about something, and he'd read her friendly nature wrong and grabbed her.

No wonder she'd been so cool to Robert! She was probably afraid to tell Georgie what the fellow tried, how he'd treated her. That must be why she'd made such a to-do this morning when he told her he'd invited Robert—she did *not* want *him* here! And that tale about his moving because of his bad leg—that seemed like hooey, too, since Robert's leg didn't keep him from dancing or using the front or back steps!

Why didn't she say he got fresh? Was she afraid he didn't have the gumption to stick up for her or that he'd play the hero and get hurt?

The heat beat against his face. Shame on you! The look on her face when Robert was dipping her, goading him, sneering *Hey Georgie try this!* and she was looking embarrassed.

Of course she was embarrassed! And humiliated!

Good God, man! You can't let somebody treat your wife that way! Especially somebody who's laughing at you and thinking you're a no-ball, no-brain wonder.

I don't want to be a fool, Georgie. And you shouldn't, either!

Each day brought a lesson in what it meant to be a husband. This was a hard one: you had to protect your wife, redress insults done to her good name, her honor.

He groaned, hissed through clenched teeth. He mashed his forearm against his mouth to stifle his sobs. Then he stamped out a circle, clomping, hopping. He knocked himself in the head with his fists.

That snide Yankee shitass! Did he think Georgie would just turn his head? Or his cheek? Was Robert a fucking idiot he didn't realize a person learns to use a firearm in boot camp? The M-1—he could clean it, load it, aim and *squeeezzzee,* until you get the *blam!* and the stock jolted your shoulder and made a bruise so the next day's firing was tougher to take. But he *had* taken it! He'd gone determined to prove he could march and fight like any man, and he had. He'd wanted them to be proud, yet now she was afraid to tell him what she'd endured because she feared he didn't have the *balls* to stand up for her!

He could damn sure use what he learned!

He slipped into an infantryman's mood; he glided through the back door and eased the screen to, then crept down the hall. No one was in the dining room, but Thelma was straightening up in the parlor. He went into the foyer. He rooted about in the dark, cluttered closet quietly until he felt the two cold cylinders of the old shotgun, pushed through hanging garments, groped for the stock, and lifted it out.

So far as he knew, it hadn't left this spot since the night some twenty years ago when Papa joined the men who beat Samuel and burned down colored town. To his surprise, when he broke it open, two bright coins of shell end showed in the chambers. Either they'd been there all along or Robert had loaded it! Did he plan to murder Georgie, too?

He'd half-hoped the gun would be empty and he'd only wave it, point it, scare Robert witless, make him light out running for fear of his life.

With the gun loaded—by accident? fate? chance?—events put their stamp upon him: he would not now *pretend* to be in control of a lethal weapon, not now *pretend* he had the power to smear his fucking face all over the walls, not now *pretend* to be someone whose honor couldn't be insulted! Fate egged him on—*You wanna be a man!? Then here's the gun—only it's loaded! It's a real man's gun, not a toy.*

He stopped at the entry to the parlor. Seeing the shotgun, Thelma got wide-eyed. "Georgie!"

He ignored her and went out onto the porch. Walter and Robert stood on the walk at the curb next to Robert's company coupe, their cigarettes winking like orange fireflies. It was as if he'd stepped on a midway carnival ride, the escalating whirl you can't get off until it stops, faster and faster—

"Shitass! Don't you have *any* respect for a person!"

They both spun about as he charged down the walk, the shotgun raised to his shoulder and aimed right at Robert. Robert's shock and fear carved a rich niche of pleasure into the moment. But his own chin quivered and his vision blurred, then the end of the barrel bobbled.

"Hey, now, Georgie," cooed Robert, the way you speak to a savage dog whose territory you've blundered into, "Hey now, just relax, all right?"

Robert took one step toward Georgie with a hand extended as if expecting Georgie to hand over the shotgun, but Georgie set him back by lifting the muzzle dead at his eyes. Oh how he'd love to blow this jackass from here to kingdom come! Just *squueezze* a little and this fellow who'd insulted his wife while enjoying his hospitality would be hamburger! His finger itched, twitched, tightened.

But he jerked the muzzle up.

"Just git! I want you out of my house! And you better not get it in your head to come around again or I'll—!" Despite himself he starting bawling like an angry, outraged kid, huffing and clenching his teeth and dancing in place and cursing as best he could with his jaw clamped shut, his heart pounding and the tears flooding so he could hardly see—only large shapes of light and dark.

"Goddamn you!"

He was about to explode. He aimed at Robert's face again and gritted his teeth thinking he'd count to three and yank the trigger; he went *one* in his head but his sight cleared and the face at the end of the barrel was wiped clean of its customary smirking irony, the sly arched brow, all the oily innuendo that had annoyed and worried Georgie: making this threat alone had reduced Robert to a frightened fellow holding up his palm as if it could stop twelve-gauge buckshot. Robert was wincing and cringing into his own shoulder, scuttling backwards around his car, whining, "Oh, hey, Georgie, let's slow down here, please, take it easy, I'm going, just take it easy with that, you hear…"

It was near enough to groveling.

"Git!" Georgie canted the muzzle over the car and yanked both triggers; recoil knocked him back on his butt to the grass. Shredded leaves rained down. While Robert cranked up his car fast and squealed away from the curb, Mary Kay, Sylvia, and Thelma rushed out onto the porch as Walter was giving him a hand-up to stand.

"What happened?" called out Mary Kay.

"Getting shut a varmints," said Georgie.

TWENTY-EIGHT

HAVING THAT SHOTGUN aimed at him was exhilarating, all right, but being spared a two-barrel blast between his eyes made him want to kiss Georgie's boots—or spit in his face. If Georgie were half a man, Robert would be bloody meat; since he was half a man, Robert was alive.

He jiggled his fingers and gloried at the wonder.

Maybe Sylvia had laid it all on him. The next day she hung up when he called, so he guessed she'd work the angles. She needed whatever a man had to offer more than she needed the man. If the well ran dry, she'd find another sucker.

He buried himself in work and spent hours at a pistol range and at honky-tonks, saw a couple dozen movies twice and read a shelf of books that wafted through his head like an invisible gas. He was groggy during the day and too damn wakeful at night, and often he struck out at midnight and walked several miles from the Bide-A-Wee to Acorn Street with his pistola tucked in his waistband under his shirt. He'd lurk in the dark and gawk at the house. Since he knew her schedule, he dogged her heels and hoped she didn't notice. He couldn't help himself. It was fucking pathetic, he knew. He wanted just five minutes to learn *what* she'd told and what she planned.

Marjorie returned. She'd put on a few pounds and when she came down the office hall her face was canted toward the floor and her brows were knit as if a nail had been driven into her forehead.

"Welcome back," he said. "Sorry to hear about your brother. They told me he was MIA."

"Yeah." She looked up. She looked older. Tired, a little bleary-eyed and bloated. "Oh, thanks, Robert," she added when she put a name to his face. "We're hoping."

"Sure. They get lost in the woods, you know, and it takes a while to get back to the unit and longer for the paperwork."

"Yeah. Thanks."

"Thought you were working at Higgins and living it up in The Big Easy."

She cracked a grin. "Life can't be all fun. How about yourself?"

"I've been pining away for you. I'm hurt you didn't send me a card."

"I sent my thoughts. Didn't you get them?"

"Must have been solar flare-ups. So are you living at home?"

"Uh-huh. But it's just temporary."

"Me too. I'm at the Bide-A-Wee."

She smirked. "I heard."

"It's true, every word."

"So you lied like a dog?" She was grinning. She didn't care one whit that he'd lied; she was having too much fun with it.

"Naw. There was nothing between us then, I swear to God!"

"Better watch out."

"It's actually a sad story. Her husband, well … ."

"He's a dope. Heard he got a medical discharge."

"Yeah?" *Mystery solved!* "He's a dope but she's a gold-digger."

Her eyebrows arched. "Tsk tsk. Last I heard she was up there with the saints." She arranged her face in a peculiar expression—her notion of how he'd looked when he said that. "'My gosh, Marjorie!'" she mocked. "'Don't even kid about such stuff! She's a wonderful, faithful wife who dearly misses her dear hubby.'"

"People wise up."

They pressed to the wall as fellows in overalls lumbered through going to the break room. Her skin looked flushed, overheated, and frizzed tendrils were sopped in sweat on her brow. One fellow winked and she sneered in a keep-your-distance way. After they passed, she pushed off from the wall and lurched into him. She fanned her face with the sheath of papers in her hand. The air coming off her smelled stale. It wouldn't have surprised him to hear she'd slept in that dress in somebody's car last night after passing out.

"I'm getting my own place." She slipped him a sly grin.

He smiled back, wolfishly, he hoped. "Nice to know. You don't like Mama's cooking?"

"I never had no chaperone down there, but I come home and all of a sudden her and Daddy want me to punch a time clock. Last Sunday I thought they'd never get off my back about going to church."

"So when's the house-warming? I'll bring you something."

"Don't have a place yet. You can hep me move, though. Say, here's a bright idea: let's the two of us go looking!" She winked. "Rent's cheaper split two ways."

"Aw, Marjorie, that's really mean to toy with me. A guy can only take so much disappointment."

"I am the devil in disguise."

"I won't argue."

"So where we going?"

"When?"

"Tonight."

"I know a road house." He was thinking of where he'd once taken Sylvia to dance, and he fleetingly pictured them all there "by accident." He'd have his .38 and his saucy young Marjorie on his arm.

She laughed. "I guess I know what you think of me!"

"You're the girl next door. Nothing Park Avenue. So when do I pick you up?"

"You don't."

"No?"

"I bought a car. What number at the 'Wee?'"

"Thirteen."

"Must be my lucky day!"

She ambled off, giving him an unstrip-tease with her hips and toodle-looing with her waggled fingers. For the balance of the afternoon, he conjured up vignettes—the purse dropped on his bed, her knees on the rug and her arms around his hips, or astraddle his lap in the chair. To rid himself of the distraction, he tossed off in the john.

Then his thoughts were melancholy, even compassionate: Marjorie had gone away a girl and come back a weathered and slightly weary woman, still a joker but now the humor maybe hid a secret sorrow she was bravely tamping back with wit (oh, he was doing a number!). She and he were underdogs teamed for mutual solace—the pairing he had pretended with Betty—though he knew deep down that was sentimental hogwash and a form of self-pity.

Marjorie's return—what could it signify but defeat? And they might lie down in sorrow together. Sylvia hadn't given her credit for a capacity to absorb her losses and turn lemons into lemonade. Together they could ally against the self-righteous, hypocritical Sylvias, who might pass themselves off as their moral superiors, but his and Marjorie's suffering had made them bountiful, large-spirited. So they belonged together. *Etcetera.*

That should irritate Sylvia no end.

Brazenly, Marjorie honked for him ten minutes late, sliding her five-year-old De Soto coupe to a halt a broken-leg's length of his door. The horn blared through that thin wood like a freight train closing on a dangerous crossing at tiptop speed. So much for lingering before dinner. He carried the foresight gin in a paper sack.

Her pink sun dress showed off her freckled arms and breasts, and her hair was combed out loose short of her shoulders. The car was tan, with white sidewalls. She had the radio going to hick music out of the hick state of Louisiana, a maniac sawing away on a fiddle and another lunatic warbling from inside his own nostrils.

"You wanna drive it?" she asked when he got in, as if afraid that being driven might insult him.

"Your car. I'll play bartender." He proffered the bottle. She nodded, slung gravel backing up, whanked the shift into low and peeled out fish-tailing onto the asphalt. She drove like a race-car driver but with none of the attention or precision. It perfectly suited his mood.

"Where's your mixer?"

"I recall you mix yours with spit."

"In a pinch. Let's get some 7-Up."

"Sure. Boy, that big city living made you hoity-toity."

"You don't know the half of it."

When he was inside the filling station rooting about in the water of the cold box he had the notion she'd drive off. He came back to the car with two green bottles of tepid 7-Up. He'd snapped their caps inside. She opened her door and poured off half the pop then filled the bottle with gin. She cocked a thumb over the mouth, turned the whole thing upside down.

"Very professional," he offered.

She took half in one big slug. "Ah! That hits the spot."

She looked like she might've spent the night worried about getting that drink if she hadn't had it right that instant.

He fixed one, though he preferred vermouth. He was easy to get along with. He felt liberated, though this odd inside voice urged *Faster!* but he didn't know why.

"Where to?"

"North about ten miles."

"Oh, I know *those* places. You don't give a shit about my reputation, then. What if my ma sees me?"

"What'd she be doing there?"

"That's the joke, dope!"

Dusk thickened and hid cars coming at them because not everybody had lights on. On the highway, she kicked it up to sixty-five in a 35-mph limit, and so they were passing four or five at a stretch. They got honked at twice by oncoming cars that barely missed them when she swerved back into their lane. That gin and 7-Up cocktail wasn't her first.

But he sat back cool as you please. The hillbilly music was far greater torture than any fear her reckless driving aroused. He took a half dozen straight slugs from the bottle to catch up.

"What'll this heap do, anyway?"

"Lickety-split."

"Show me. Come on, goose it!"

She laughed. "You men are all alike."

"Come on! You shouldn't own a car you don't wanna use the damn thing. It's good to know what's in reserve in case you ever need it."

"For what? Making a getaway?"

"You never know."

"I took it to ninety plenty of times."

"Prove it."

She planted a platform sandal to the floorboard so fast the coupe sprung forward and flung him back and cocktail sloshed onto his shirt. They got up to seventy quick but got blocked by cars ahead and some coming, so she fishtailed right and blasted down the shoulder to pass, spewing gravel against windshields, but they whizzed by so fast the honks of protest were only faint sheep-bleats. He laughed, slapped the seat.

"Thatta girl! Pedal to the metal!"

They ripped on a couple more miles, faster and faster. The hurricane blasting through the windows whipped her hair around her face. "Ninety-three!" she yelled, took her foot off the gas and they coasted down to cruise behind a bus spewing a noxious exhaust.

They seemed to crawl. It depressed him. He took another drink.

"That's the fastest ever!" She grinned, shaking back her hair. She pointed to the speedometer with a trembling hand. "I don't wanna break it. Was that fast enough for you?"

"For the little it lasted."

"You *are* a thrill-seeker!"

"I've come to it late in life."

"Well, it makes you less stuffy. Gets that cob out of your hiney."

"A left-handed compliment to be sure. But I'm glad you approve."

Then the Golden Spur glimmered out of the twilight like a festive stern-wheel casino anchored at a river landing. He'd forgotten his .38.

"Say, you don't happen to carry a pistol, do you?" Back East, this would've been an idiotic question, and how easy it was to ask showed him how far and to where he'd come.

"Not on my *person.* But Daddy give me Bud's .22 for pertekshun when I left for New Orleans. It's under my seat." She dipped her head. "Why? You got a yen to hunt?"

"Who knows? Maybe we can scare up a raccoon later on."

"I don't shoot coons," she sniffed. "They're cute and it's cruel."

"Okay. Possums?"

"Oh, they're ugly as all get-out! Like giant rats! Fire away!"

Since he was wearing slacks and a sport-shirt on this humid July evening, he couldn't carry a weapon and disguise it. It was absurd to expect Georgie and Sylvia to be inside—that Lincoln was not in the lot. He had Marjorie for the evening, and it was enough to imagine that Sylvia would know this by clairvoyance. Maybe her crystal ball would give her an eyeful. Or gossip could get around. Marjorie would tell her mother and her mother would relay the info at the train station canteen. He relished considering how jealous Sylvia would be. Marjorie was care-free, unattached, had her own money, her own automobile, kept her own hours; more to the point, Marjorie was young, luscious as a ripe peach, while Sylvia had lost her luster. Marjorie was dripping with *sex appeal.*

It should make Sylvia eat rat poison.

Unlike the night Sylvia and he had danced here, tonight the joint was jumping. That juke glowed like an asteroid. The jitter-buggers were jiving on the corn meal-salted planking. A lot of dogfaces and fly-boys from Ellington Field or Lake Charles, looked like. He was sick of running into these goons everywhere he went. He was up to his gob hearing about their sacrifices and untested valor before the fact. Civilians could be courageous, too.

"If you wanna rub elbows with riff-raff, here's your chance!" he yelled in Marjorie's ear. No free tables or booths, and stools along the bar were covered by khaki-colored asses. He went up to a lumberjack-sized fellow on one end and jabbed him with a forefinger. Fellow spun on the stool, irritated, half-expecting a familiar face, and when he saw Robert he darkened up like a summer stratocumulus ripe with lightning and hail.

"Say, Corporal, mind giving a lady your seat?" Robert hiked his thumb at Marjorie.

"Hell no." He exhaled sour beer breath into Robert's face. He winked at her. "Any time, good-lookin'. It won't cost you but a dance."

"That'd be twice what it's worth," she shot back. Count on Marjorie to turn on the Southern charm!

Robert said, "Don't mind her, Joe. She even talks to her mother that way."

He rolled his eyes and left carrying his smokes and his bottle and she slid onto the stool. Robert leaned on the bar. The guy on her far side said, "How about let's cut a rug, girlie?"

"You have to ask my fee-AHN-say."

Robert gave him a long-suffering grin of brotherhood. "Somebody needs to drain her energy," he said. "You're free to try. Don't bring her back until she's limp as a rag mop."

"Nobody has *my* permission," she told them. "I want a drink."

He ordered himself a beer and her a martini, and she said, "Oo la-la!" with a sneer but slurped it up when it came and semaphored the bartender for another while the head on his brew was still settling.

"Let's dance," she said.

"Something slow plays, I will."

"I thought you'd quickened your pace since we last went out."

"In some respects. Find a hero in uniform if you need to get tossed around."

She wagged a finger at him. “You sound bitter, Robert, that’s not becoming. Robert. Hmm. You need a new name. Robert’s got a cob up his hiney. Don’t you have a nickname?”

“No. I once had a ‘fee-ahn-SAY’ call me darling for a week.”

“What happened then?”

He shrugged. “Guess the mood lifted.”

“Wud you call her? Sugar-booger? Sweet Petunia?”

“Claire. Just Claire.”

“Sweet talker!”

“You think of something suits you, call me that.”

“Ashley.”

“Oh, for God’s sake, Marjorie! I take it back!”

“He’s a gentleman! Why would you mind that?”

“Never mind. Call me … Jake.”

She laughed. “You’re not a Jake.”

“You don’t know. I think my Jake’s gonna emerge any minute.”

“Does he dance more ’n you?”

“We’ll ask him when he gets here.”

She flagged the bartender down. She was a little unsteady, but that much gin would’ve put him face down on the floor.

“What was she like?”

“Rich. Blonde. Tall and thin. Had her own damn horse, and he wouldna known a plough from a pillow. You know a person’s an aristocrat when her horse is a *pet.*” He had a rush of discomfort to speak of Claire, but it passed and he felt like saying more. “She stabled him in Virginia and her family paid people to tend their horses so that now and then she could drive there to ride an hour. She had photos of him all over her apartment in sterling silver frames. She’d jumped him, had some ribbons. He was about the favorite mammal of her acquaintance.”

“What was she like, though?”

“Very persnickety. Had a lot of likes and dislikes about music and movies and books and people and food and clothing. It’d wear you out listening to her evaluations. She’d talk through a meal at a restaurant reviewing everything from the soup to the nuts and you’d think she was going on about world affairs. But I never saw anybody less interested in anything that really matters. I was pretty interested in politics. We had a group raised money for the war in Spain, and a couple fellows joined the Lincoln Brigade. I don’t think she knew there *was* a war in Spain.”

Marjorie lifted her cocktail glass to salute. "Remember the Maine."

"Not *that* Spanish war, Marjorie. Anyway, you could call her shallow."

"Eww! Bitter!"

"She had this laugh like a goose honk. Hee-HAW, hee-HAW! It embarrassed me in the movies because she'd laugh when nobody saw anything funny."

"How about your love life?"

"Geez. That your business?"

"Thought I could get away with it."

"Well, it's not."

She shrugged, indifferent.

"It was … fitful."

She choked on her drink. "Fitful?" she sputtered.

"I mean the frequency."

"So how you'd wind up with her?"

"Good question. She was up the ladder. I thought I wanted to stand on a higher rung."

"What'd she see in you?"

"Another good question. What do you see in me?"

"Who says I see anything?"

"Well, you're here."

She grinned as if she might smart-mouth him, but then she said, "You're good looking, you're smart, you know how to talk."

"I appreciate the flattery. Truth is, I think she was looking to soothe her wounded vanity. Fellow she'd known a long while broke off their engagement, and it helped her to have somebody like me to piss on."

"What a bitch."

He raised his bottle and she clinked it with her glass.

"How about your love life with the *Señorita*? Oh, sorry! That'd be *Señora.*"

"Like bunnies. Night and day. She couldn't keep her hands off me."

"You lie."

"You didn't believe me when I said we didn't do anything."

"That was then. Hey, there's something slow! Come on!"

The tune was "Dancing in the Dark" by Artie Shaw. They stood and embraced in the fox-trot fashion as he'd been taught by the master, but the floor was so crowded they moved only a foot in any direction. She hummed in his ear, and her hand was hot and damp on his nape.

She was smaller than Sylvia, lighter but not more nimble—Sylvia was a professional, and Marjorie's steps were not so quick to follow his clumsy lead. He might've gone all sour with nostalgia had not Marjorie been hunching his kneecap.

The big corporal he'd chased off the stool swung a local girl in saddle oxfords into their orbit and bumped them with his butt. It jolted Marjorie out of her upright intercourse position.

"Tight in here," she said.

He grunted and swayed in place, and no sooner was she settled on his thigh again than the fellow flung his partner at them like a projectile, and she about knocked them down.

"Hey, soldier!" he yelled. "You're as clumsy as you are ugly, you know that?"

Marjorie's laugh burst in his ear like a sneeze. The dogface was still twirling his girlie and gawking on the run. Encouraged by Marjorie's approval, Robert whirled them to watch his face. He hollered, "And you're as ugly as they come! Your ma a baboon?"

Marjorie snickered into his neck. "Shush! You're gonna get him riled up."

Since he outweighed Robert forty-fifty pounds and stood a head taller, he blinked and frowned like he couldn't believe a ninety-eight-pound weakling would speak to him this way. He squinted through the smoke and neon-lit gloaming as if unsure of what he'd heard.

"That's right," Robert mouthed at him. "I said your mother was an ape and your daddy such a sorry sack of shit he was proud to poke her!"

The corporal leaped onto his head and they crashed to the floor. He round-housed on his head and shoulders, and Robert flailed back and felt a satisfying jolt when his fist landed somewhere, but the dogface got him solid and might've done serious injury if somebody hadn't yanked him off and held him while Marjorie and he were hustled out the door.

TWENTY-NINE

"GEEZ, JAKE, you're a mess!"

His top shirt button was gone, his cheek stung, and his nose was tingly where he'd caught a glancing shot.

"Fucking apes."

"Come on. Let's get a drink."

She walked him arm-in-arm to the car. They drank straight from the bottle. She held it to the light from the road house and waggled it by the neck.

"I'm getting sad."

"We'll get more. You sure you got a pistol?"

Her brows cocked up. "You gonna shoot that soldier?"

"Worth considering."

"Get your own damn gun, then."

"I got one. At home."

She upturned the bottle then drained it. "You're a lot more dangerous than I took you for, Jake."

"And you're drunk."

She sighed. "At last!" She started the engine. "Where to?"

"California. I got fifty bucks, and they'll send my check. There's nothing in that damn tourist court I don't mind leaving. We'll split the gas and food, and when we get there we'll get a place together."

"Aw, don't tease! We'd get ten miles down the road and you'd wanna shoot a poor hitchhiking sailor, then I'd be a fugitive from justice."

"Okay. Let's go to my place, then. I wanna show you my itchings."

She laughed. "That's my choice? California or your place?"

"I'm open to suggestion. Except last time I let you choose you had me crawling around in the dark behind a colored juke-joint while you played Massah's daughter out front."

"Got something against coloreds?"

"Not in the least. You're driving. You decide."

Her lips twisted into a pucker. "I'm in a mood for swamp."

They slipped into a package store under the closing and got another fifth of gin and two bottles of White Rock with the perfect-breasted nymph on the label, one tonic and one ginger ale. Marjorie drove lickety-split but seemed sober enough, intent on operating the machinery, as if stewardship of moving metal was a skill she'd picked up at Higgins. She didn't object when he redialed to WWL in New Orleans, where the fare was Dixieland and Swing out of the Blue Room of the Roosevelt Hotel. The night air swam through the open windows carrying a scent of pine and the stink of burn-off from the oil wells.

A knot on his head rose and throbbed. He felt under her seat and tugged out the pistol.

"Is it loaded?"

"Clips are in the glove box."

"How about some target practice?"

"Atta boy!"

He held a clip up to oncoming lights, saw how it slid into the grip, and shoved it home. He wasn't sure what next.

"Here–" She shoved her knee against the wheel and reached over to peel the metal foreskin back, and the first shell clicked into the chamber

"Safety's on top the guard. Use your thumb."

"Safety first."

She laughed. "Too late for that!"

He gripped the thing in his right hand. It was lighter than his .38.

"Whatta you want for dinner, honey bunch?"

"Roast of road sign, I reckon."

A white speed sign loomed into their lights, already peppered—war inspired fellows to test their marksmanship—and he aimed out the window and got off a round as they sailed past. The .22 shell made a *snap!* like a damp firecracker. A letdown. His .38 made a robust *POP!* that stung your ears and the cordite stench was strong afterwards. It kicked, too. Bud's plinker had a mild spasm like an elderly preacher's hand shake.

"You get it?"

"Maybe."

He drew a bead on a billboard featuring a beaming Red Cross nurse with a Lucky between her fingers on its way to her parted lips, and he yanked a shot right up her big nostrils. The paper spewed like confetti.

"Gimme it. I hate these damn Burma Shave things."

She aimed out the driver's window at the second of four long red rectangles already riddled to the point the doggerel wasn't legible and, taking her eyes off the road, went *snap! snap! snap! snap! snap!* Splinters flew off the post.

She handed it back. The third line of the illegible stanza sailed by.

"I'll get that last one."

He scooted close and laid his left arm across the seat back. He bent his face close to her profile. Even with the wind rushing through the car she smelled of gin, dime-store perfume, and cigarettes. He deliberately brushed her breasts with his arm as he reached to aim out the window. She ignored it.

"Blast it, Jake."

He yanked the trigger three times. He thought his shots went high or wide. Fleetingly he wondered where the little slugs would go. Maybe somebody was there, at the crossroads of Wrong Place and Wrong Time. Tell it to the chaplain.

"Put another clip in."

He hated pulling away from her. He reloaded. On the shoulder way ahead, an armadillo, half-blind and full-frantic, reared on its hind legs and did a frenetic aimless jig in a tizzy over crossing or backing off.

"Wahoo! Yeea-hah!" he hollered. He shot twice figuring it would end up flat on the asphalt, anyway, but missed.

But live game was the thing! He waited for a rabbit or skunk or even a stray dog or cat to emerge out of the dimness beyond their lights.

"Come back."

He grinned, slid beside her. He set the pistol in his lap. His arm went around her neck and he draped his hand over her breast. He laid his right hand on her thigh. He could feel her firm warm flesh under the cotton. He wished Sylvia could see him now. He let his fingertips slide between her thighs.

"Ouch!" she said. He drew his hand back. "Those brights!" She was squinting. "The dope! Hey, Jake! Blast him!"

"What?"

She slammed her toe against the dimmer button and their lights flicked up high into the other driver's windshield. The challenge had no effect. His lights were piercing, and the radiating halo soon would blind them.

"Shoot him, Jake!"

He laughed.

"No shit! He's a dope! Aim for his lights! Teach him some manners!"

"Well . . ."

"Come ON!" She did a bump and grind. "Blast him!"

Was she kidding? His blood raced. His hands broke out in a sweat and her dress blotted his palm. *Was it a test?*

The opportunity was about to pass. The lights were glaring and huge now that the aura billowed out, and they couldn't see a damn thing as they hurled on through the darkness.

"If you won't, I will!" Her hand groped his lap for the pistol and got his erection, and she laughed. He already had the pistol in his right hand. He passed it to his left, pointed it tilted too far up to hit anything, he hoped, and pulled the trigger.

The car blew by with its horn blaring about their brights, and the driver must have seen the pistol. He looked out the back window.

"What's he doing?"

"Stopping looks like." Red tail lights bloomed up suddenly. He had to check an impulse to fire again. Then the lights dimmed down.

"Guess he's going on."

"He'll think twice."

Her right hand brushed over his lump, rested on his thigh. She chuckled. "Oh, Jake! You're a terror! First that brave soldier and now an innocent motorist?"

"I didn't really aim at him."

She laughed. "I'm sure glad! Killing somebody would spoil the rest of my evening!"

"You said blast him."

"You do everything I say?"

"Depends."

"You kill somebody for me?"

"If I thought he needed killing anyway."

"You're just talking, right?"

"And so are you."

It was great fun playing waterfront toughs out of a dime novel or like that evil duo in *Double Indemnity.* Holding the pistol hopped him up. He felt like a Jake.

"We take off for the coast right now we can hit hick-town banks on the way."

"If I thought there's half a chance you'd do it I'd turn around right now."

"There is," he said. "Half a chance."

They laughed. "But you just got home," he went on. "You liked it so much, why didn't you stay away?"

She cocked her head back, squinting ahead, and he looked through the windshield expecting an obstacle but saw only the black asphalt and the yellow arc of their head lamps rolling out over it like storm-driven waves on a shore.

"Guess I got restless."

Restless and coming home to Mama weren't compatible, but he wouldn't subject her to the third degree.

"Were you making good money?"

"Uh-huh. Couldn't save a dime, though. Melody and me and Jeanette were having a ball. 'Course I did buy this car."

"What were you doing at Higgins?"

"Welding for a while, then I got to be an inspector."

"Sounds like a perfect life. Where do I sign up?"

"Oh, you could get on, believe me."

"Could I live with Melody and what's her name?"

"You *are* a randy devil!"

"I wouldn't want to miss anything."

"You might not want everything."

"Why not?"

She shrugged. "It wudn't all a bed of roses."

"Yeah. How so?"

Again a shrug. "Situations. It's personal."

"Okay."

Then they jawed about the weather, rations, and nations. She mentioned Bud again, and he urged her to hope for the best. She asked him what he'd do when the war was over, as if it were a summer vacation. He told her he wanted to get into civil engineering, big projects like bridges and dams. She said she didn't know. She hadn't been on her way to anything in particular, so the war hadn't interrupted.

"Lots of girls wanna keep on working, but I'd as soon quit right now and get a house and have kids."

"And how about a nice hard-working hubby?"

"Let's don't get into that."

So they fell silent, and soon they turned onto a dirt road. They bounced over dried-mud ruts, flushing clouds of bugs that swirled like blown chaff into their headlights. They were deep in pine woods on the fringe of the Big Thicket, though he saw big sycamores and cypresses and flickers of light reflected off water through the murk.

They pulled into a clearing beside a slough leading into a lake. A half moon threw a pale light onto cypresses on the other side. Strands of moss dangled from their branches down to the dark still surface, and they stood with their huge knees submerged. He never liked swamps, and this one harbored gators and cottonmouth moccasins.

She shut off the engine and the lights but left the radio going.

"Bring that bottle."

She retrieved a blanket from the trunk. He tucked the pistol into his waistband and followed her to a ring of blackened stones at the water's edge. Tin cans lay about. She kicked something aside, spread the blanket on the trampled grass.

"Have a seat."

She tucked her knees under her chin, wrapped her arms around her legs. He sat, put the pistol on the blanket. He lit two cigarettes, passed her one.

"I like it out here."

"I'm surprised. Most girls would probably think it's spooky."

"Maybe that's what I like. It doesn't settle me down much. More like the opposite."

"Is this a favorite place?"

"Sort of. A girl I knew drowned here."

"What happened?"

"It was a bunch of families on a picnic. Barbara was my best friend.

We were twelve. We had a fight after she said something about my dress I took wrong. Next thing I knew she was missing, then they found her." She waved to the slough.

"You feel guilty?"

"Oh gosh no! We'd had lots of fights. She didn't kill herself. She was with other kids swimming and just went under." After a moment she added, "But sometimes it's like I'm supposed to live her life, too. We were really close. She'd lived next door since we were babies."

"So how's she like her life so far?"

"We're not exactly corresponding. But just guessing I'm not sure she'd like all my choices."

"Any one in particular?"

She looked pensive as if on the verge of telling him something important, but she said, "Nah. Just in general."

The ground under his ass was spongy, and moisture seeped up through the blanket. They smoked and looked at the dark water with the moonlight glimmering on it. The air was a sultry soup full of clicks and ticking sounds, little wings awhir, tiny claws scratching at rot. Sweat sheened his skin like a coat of machine oil. A carcass lay within sniffing distance.

"Did you hear Georgie was gonna shoot me?"

"Something like it. What happened?"

"He had me in his sights." He pointed his hand like a pistol at the water. "Blam! He shot a tree instead."

"Lucky for you."

"His mistake."

"How's that?"

"I'm still walking around. No telling what I might stir up."

"Is that your idea?"

"Maybe." They fell into a companionable silence. He wasn't sure what was on her mind.

"Look." She dipped her head toward the water. "Gator."

A V-shaped ripple glided through a patch of reflected moonlight, and a bark-like stump surfaced, dragging the ripples along. Furtive, calculated. He thought if they turned away it would heave up onto the bank and have at them. That infuriated him. He shivered with a delicious combination of fear and adrenalin and rage.

He jumped up with the pistol and strode to the bank. He drew a bead on the moving V and pulled off two rounds. They hit the water with a *ploonk!*

Marjorie laughed. "Bud says a twenty-two's like a gnat to a gator."

"We'll see about that. I'll plug the sucker right in the eye."

"Good luck."

She didn't know what he meant because when he stepped into the water without taking off his shoes, she jumped up and yelled, "Hey!" in alarm.

But he was in the grip of a fever that had slipped into his bloodstream when the war broke out. These days his blood was cooking like water in an overheated radiator, and his jaw ached from clenching his teeth. If something didn't break loose soon he was going to wind up a vicious thug or the world's most pious monk.

"What the hell you doing?"

"Killing gators!"

He had waded to his thighs into the warm black stinking water. It was full of claws and sticks, gristle and tiny skulls, submerged shrubs and leaves and tree limbs, fish fins, gills like sharp can lids, all churning like ingredients in a primeval stew. They brushed his legs as he waded deeper, following the widening V as it moved into the dark hollows under the cypress trees.

"You want an alligator bag?"

"Hey, that thing'll turn on you!"

"That's when I'll plug it!"

"You're nuts!"

He loved hearing her fretful twang. He felt dizzy with his own brash antic courage, and that crazy feral grin stretched his mouth.

"Cummere, gator boy!" he whistled the way you'd call a dog. "Come get your hot lead sandwich! Marjorie needs a new pair of shoes!"

He sent another round into the water where he'd last seen the gator. The commotion had made it dive. Destroyers and submarines. He'd lie and ready his torpedoes and he'd slog through the waist-deep water dropping his depth charges. He yelped and shivered when something bumped his hip, twirled and yanked the trigger and the round went *ploomp!* three feet away. It was probably a stick. Or a moccasin.

"Cummon gator-gator-gator! Jake's got a nice snack for ya! Try chewing on his leg!"

"Robert, get out of there."

He stepped deeper until the water crept up his ribs—he'd give the gator a chance. Ten seconds, and if he hadn't shown himself, he'd get out. He went one-Mississippi-two-Mississippi and so on to ten. He watched the water under the cypresses and caught a motion that might be a tail flicking or just a lapping of ripples.

He turned his back on it and waded slowly to shore, hair on his nape prickling, making enough noise that he wouldn't hear it glide up behind him, but he steeled himself against panic and didn't break into a run. The mud was thick and gooey, his shoes stuck in it, and he felt the tug and creak of his bad leg at the knee.

He stood on the bank dripping, mud coating his ankles.

"You're a mess," said Marjorie cheerfully.

He was pleased she was glad to see him out of danger. He tugged off his shoes and socks, undid his soggy belt and trousers, wrung out the tails of his shirt. He left his soaked underwear on.

He sat beside her. She passed the bottle and he swigged from it.

"Maybe I'll toss you in there for bait." He grabbed her shoulders and she squealed girlishly. So he grunted like a gorilla and slipped his arms around her waist and pretended to drag her to the water, and she squirmed and laughed again and tugged at his arms but not hard. They wrestled that way for a bit, him mock-tugging and her digging in her heels and laughing. Then she tried to tickle him, he tickled her back, and she was on her back thrashing and flailing and laughing, "No! Oh, God, no no no!" So he quit tickling and wormed his way between her legs. Her dress was to her waist. Their heads were close. Her eyes were shut. He could feel her breath on his face. Her arms went out and up as if he'd said, "Stick 'em up!" but their backs rested loose on the blanket.

She took what he did with hardly a murmur, as if she'd fainted dead away. He tugged her briefs aside, dabbed her with his spit, poked his way in. Her passivity surprised him, rang wrong to her character, and that puzzle poisoned his mood; he imagined her drowned friend rising like a weed-draped wraith from the water then he thought of the gator and his exposed back. He was going limp, and though he finished, getting there was only obligatory.

He rolled onto his back. Now he had to recognize neither of them had any real desire for the other. He was getting even with Sylvia, and Marjorie was—well, he didn't know her motive, but she wasn't swept away by romance. He wished he had it to do over again so he wouldn't.

"I'm sorry," he said.

She sat up, rearranged her underwear, her dress. She lit a cigarette.

"Where was your safety kit?"

"I didn't think of it."

She smoked for a moment and looked out over the water. "What if you knocked me up?"

"Maybe you should, uh, *wash?*"

She snorted. "Think it's that simple?"

He took another slug from the bottle to keep from having to say anything.

She chuckled. "Gee, Robert, you look so bumfuzzled! Don't worry. I'm probably not pee-gee, my cycle's not ripe for it, you know?" She smiled. "And if I am, my husband will just think it's his."

"Your husband?"

"Yeah." She leaned back on her elbows and crossed her ankles, oh so cool! *What a performer!* "I got married in New Orleans. He shipped out."

She was toying with him. "Must be true love."

"Well, that fifty-dollar allotment every month comes in mighty handy."

"And there's the life insurance in case he doesn't make it back."

"It's always at the top of my list."

THIRTY

As GEORGIE WATCHED Robert's car peel off the night he pulled the trigger on the shotgun, he ballooned inside: he'd grown into a man at last! His training hadn't been for naught even if it ended prematurely. As a kid he'd been insulted and assaulted, but he'd always endured it meekly and slunk away stripped of dignity and burning with humiliation. This time he'd locked horns and driven the challenger from the stomping grounds, by God! Protected his home and his family.

When he turned, trembling, to grin at the audience, Sylvia was no longer on the porch. Thelma and Mary Kay drew back as he bounded up the steps.

"Where's Sylvia?"

Nobody spoke. He went into the foyer and stood catching his breath. The barrel was hot in his hand, and he didn't want to hold the shotgun any longer, so he pushed through the thicket of coats in the closet and set it upright against the rear wall. Now that it had been fired, it didn't seem to belong there—it stunk of cordite and seemed too foul. He was shocked at himself for shooting it and horrified by his rage. The gun seemed the cause of it.

He poked his head into the kitchen, strode through the parlor, the dining room; the bathroom door stood open and the light was on, but the room was unoccupied. Their bedroom door was closed. He looked in—the room was dark but she wasn't there—then he went down the hall and to the back porch, where the dogs greeted him as if they hadn't seen a human face in hours.

"Sylvia?" he called.

Back in the hall, he noticed that the bedroom door he'd just come out of had been closed. He opened it. The room was still dark. He flicked on the overhead fixture, and it cast a pale skein of light the hue of moonlight but without the mystery or romance, draping his parents' old walnut furniture like mold.

The closet door was fit flush to the frame. It stuck so they normally never shut it all the way. This seemed odd. He stepped to the closet, heard a noise from inside, and tugged open the door.

Sylvia cowered on her haunches under hanging clothes, her arms wrapped about her head.

"Georgie, please don't hit me!"

He reeled back from the closet and fell into a sit on the bed.

"Hit you?"

She scrambled out of closet on her knees, grabbed his hands.

"Oh Georgie, I am so sorry! Please forgive me! I'll do *anything* if you'll forgive me!"

Sobbing, she told him she'd been *so terribly lonely* when he left. Robert had been *so friendly* and sympathetic. She'd had no friends and everyone had been so set against her and their marriage *oh honey once you left I felt so horribly alone!*

"I was only gone eleven weeks. How long was I away before it happened?" He thought—three weeks? Nine? Does it matter?

"Oh honey, there was only one time, I swear to God Almighty!"

"The night I called?"

She nodded. Oh, she'd give *anything* to have that night back to do over, she was feeling so blue and needed cheering up … .

He remembered standing in the lobby of the Paso Robles Inn and flashing her photo with such pride. When he called, Mary Kay had gone looking for her, and tonight when Mary Kay had said she'd heard *sounds,* he simply hadn't wanted to see that square on for what it was.

"Didn't he make you do it? I mean push himself on you?"

She shook her head sadly. "Yes. But I can't blame him altogether."

"Are you just a," he sucked in a breath, feeling the sting of tears, "a dirty *whore?*"

She buried her face in his lap and flung her arms about his waist. "Oh, Georgie, I tried so hard! I *really* did! Please believe me! I went to confession. I prayed and prayed for strength."

While she quietly wept and clung to him, he replayed the phone conversation that night and recognized her lies, replayed how she'd been so eager to stop at the tourist court instead of coming home—Good God! She'd only wished to distract him from the truth! And she pretended to be cold to Robert!

"Do you love him?"

"Oh, God no, Georgie! I *hate his guts!* I wish you'd shot that bastard!"

This startled him. "Do you want to leave?"

"Oh no! Please don't think that!"

"Do you want a divorce?"

"No, no." Meek little voice.

The longer they sat, with her clinging to him and burrowing her face in his thighs, the more his fury built. He was afraid he'd start bawling.

Suddenly he flung her off onto the floor and stood. He fought down an urge to slam his foot into her gut.

"You're pretty damn sorry, you know that? You're a pretty damn sorry excuse for a wife!"

He stormed out and stomped up the stairs. He spent the night in his old room, lying on the bed fully clothed, not sleeping a wink. His brain was in a whirl. He thought he had a fever, then chills. His stomach cramped, and he had to puke in the wastebasket. She'd knocked his wind out like getting slammed in the chest by that mock bomb-flour sack in boot camp. His skull was scoured clean of any useful thought and the space was filled with a poisonous crud like a ball of water moccasins writhing there, each one another version of the same thought. She betrayed me, cheated on me, lied to me, everybody's laughing behind my back because they've known it all along—why *wouldn't* she make the two-backed beast with the slick Yankee dandy, wasn't she trash from the start? *If that numb-nuts has no more sense than to trust a woman like that, he gets what he deserves.*

What was he supposed to do about it? Where did honor lie?

I wish you'd shot that bastard! That response was fully authorized; no jury in Port Farview would convict him for killing a man who screwed his wife. He could probably get away with busting up her face so bad she couldn't show it in public for a month. It was a possibility to relish. Picturing himself slugging her in the kisser or slamming her nose with a bat made his pulse pound hard and his hands sweat and his gut ache and he went literally breathless from it. He had to coach himself back down, counting slowly and relaxing his chest as his lungs sucked in air.

If they were Comanche, he could cut off her nose. If they were Japs, he could toss her into the street with his sword so she'd fall upon it.

He screamed into his pillow. He wept and ground his teeth. He muttered to the darkness: *Cunt! Whore! Bitch! Tramp! Slut! Cunt! Whore! Bitch! Tramp! Slut!*

When his anger had evaporated, he felt so sad he thought he'd die from it. No way could he endure this, survive it. He wished she hadn't done it; he wished he hadn't discovered it.

What was he going to do?

In the morning, her gentle tap at his door woke him. When he didn't respond, she eased it open and stuck her head through.

"Georgie," she whispered. Her brow was knotted as if to show remorse. "I'm going to Mass then I'm working at the canteen."

"Somebody down there need their dick sucked?"

He'd never uttered such a thing to anyone, let alone a female, and he was shocked. But when it crossed her face like the lash of a whip, he savored it.

While she was gone, he drove to the beach with the dogs and let them run. Couldn't bring himself to report to Sunday dinner at his mother's, though their absence would kindle a blaze of questions. Walking barefoot in ankle-high surf and tossing sticks for the mutts into the waves partly restored him. He imagined a future time when they could frame this as a rough patch they'd gotten through. But he was a long, long way from being there.

Had he gotten the full story? One time? Why believe that? Could be more than one fellow, who knew? Now her past was only what she said, and she was a fucking liar. A lying cunt whore tramp slut.

He felt ragged, wrung out, and he fretted about pitching a fit on the road home. That pissed him off. She was no good and she was no good for him.

Worse yet, his mother had been right.

At a diner he got take-out burgers for himself and the dogs and ate one that tasted like damp cardboard while sitting on the running board with the dogs milling at his feet.

The Oriental carpet from their bedroom was rolled up in the hall. The furniture had been shoved about. Sylvia was on her hands and knees. The soles of her bare feet, heels up, were charcoal with dirt. She wore an apron over an old house dress and a scarf wrapped like a turban. A dish pan with soapy water sat beside her. He smelled damp wood. She was bearing down on a rolled-up towel with her fists like a washer-woman, to and fro. Her ass jiggled under the thin cotton and something tore inside him. Sorrow slammed him between the shoulder blades and he had to lean against the door frame.

Hearing him, she raised up on her knees. She composed her face into a semblance of wounded piety, brows pleated like muffin cup paper. *I accept my guilt. Tell me my punishment.* The air of victimhood emitted by her little tableau annoyed him.

She was apparently waiting for him to curse or interrogate her. When he didn't, she said in a high, trembling voice nothing like her vibrant alto, "Georgie, may I stay, please?"

He couldn't stand those woebegone brown eyes. "I dunno."

"I promise I'll make it up to you."

When he didn't respond, she said, "I made your dinner," with the faintest interrogatory curl, as if she wished to know if that would help.

"Not hungry."

He managed to stare her down, and she went back to scrubbing, but he didn't want to see *that* again, so he said, despite himself, "How will you make it up?" His inflection made it clear he didn't think it possible, but she saw a hopeful sign. She eased back on one hip and braced herself with her palm on the floor.

"I'll be the best wife any man could ask for!"

She wiped tears from her cheek with her fingertips.

"Any man who asks?" He was discovering he had a mean streak and was learning to enjoy exercising it.

"You know what I mean." He saw a flicker of annoyance, quickly squelched. As if she felt guilty even for that, she added, "Georgie, honey, if you let me stay, I want to invite your mother to live with me while you're gone."

He scoffed. "She wouldn't do that in a million years and you know it."

She looked hurt; he knew she'd played her trump card right off. He had to admit it surprised him, but who could believe her?

"Would you tell me what I can do?"

"No. I don't want to talk to you."

After she'd gone to bed he rummaged in the icebox, scooping butter and jam from the containers with a spoon, ignoring the plate covered with a dish towel on the stove. He wouldn't deign to lift the cloth. He wouldn't allow her to make amends so easily. If he indulged her measly efforts he might be tempted to give an inch. He didn't trust her. He wanted her to *prove* she was sick with remorse, but she had no means to do so since the words of a fucking liar were useless, and any deed short of flinging herself off the Port Farview water tower was too easily come by. She claimed to want a chance to show she was contrite, that it wouldn't happen again, but who could believe her? She *hated* Robert's guts and wished Georgie *had* shot him? Easy to say now that her secret was laid open for the town to snicker at. And she said it wasn't his fault altogether but she hated his guts? That didn't add up. Why would she cock-tease a guy whose guts she hated?

They weren't to the end of this story yet. So it was impossible to entertain the idea of letting her prove her remorse. Talk was cheap. And so was she.

He refused to speak to her for several days. He avoided her and she him. He didn't get up until after she'd left for work; he made sure to be away when she returned home, and she hid out in their bedroom in the evenings. When exchanges were necessary, Georgie took great pleasure in insulting her. Once he waited for her to vacate the bathroom, and when she emerged, he said, "Sure you got it clean?" Unexpectedly encountering her in the kitchen one morning, he said, "Oh, sorry! I figured you were already at those hards at work, oh I mean hard at work." When she asked where she should get the Lincoln serviced, he said, "Our bedroom I guess."

Until he decided upon a grand task for her to "make it up to him," he'd inflict her with these smarting bites. See how much she could take. He was seldom quick enough to deliver a truly clever remark and had to settle for something so vulgar and clumsy he cringed with shame to rehear it later. ("I guess you're getting tired of these nasty cracks but that's cause you already got one.") And when he saw the pain in her eyes, it didn't help him feel better. He'd imagined that being as mean-spirited as his anger inspired him to be would soothe him. But every time he uttered an insult and saw it sting, he felt worse. Sad. How could he insult this woman he'd loved so dearly and deeply? It only underscored how far apart they were, and he had no idea how to get back.

As the days trudged toward the end of his faux furlough, he guessed that she was thinking *only a few more days!!* because however guilty she might feel, no normal human being welcomed nonstop insults in her own home. If he told her he had a medical discharge and planned to remind her every day of an infinite future that she was a lying slut, that would surely be a nasty surprise.

But he couldn't keep it up much longer. It made him so horribly sad to be at odds with her that he considered pretending to go back, going off and taking a job in a grocery or a radio repair shop. Let Mary Kay send reports about her behavior. If time proved her to be faithful as Penelope, then he could return. Besides, telling her he'd been discharged was tantamount to admitting he'd lied and he'd have to surrender the moral high ground.

But when he pictured himself going away, it was far too easy to imagine Sylvia off the leash. No telling what (or who) she might do.

THIRTY-ONE

Dear Mr. McBride,

How're you? Fine, I hope.

So much for polite chit-chat. Now I wish to declare that you are no longer missed. So if you've felt the slightest guilt over reading letter after letter from a girl pouring out her heart on the pages while you never once wrote back—don't fret. (Okay, you did write once.) The girl is cured.

Maybe you were telling yourself, "Gee, I don't want to encourage the poor thing, so silence is the wisest course and kinder in the long run. And I did tell her about my date to the ROTC ball."

Okay, not guilt. But would you be a tiny bit curious about how long the cure took and what the treatment was? It could be useful if God forbid! the same happened to you, and I do mean God forbid! because I wouldn't wish this grief on my worst enemy. Or if you're lucky enough to have the handle end of that stinger again, you can dispense advice. "Say, darlin', don't carry on like it's the end of the world! A girl down in Texas had just such an injury and knows how to heal it!" I'm sure she'd find it consoling to hear she's not the first to be stabbed in the heart by you and that another has survived the blow.

My secret recipe?

Have her chant this until she feels hypnotized: "Donnie is a bed-wetter! Not a wed-better, a bed-wetter!" If repeated one hundred times daily, it will soothe the chanter's dashed dreams of a rosy honeymoon.

You didn't know I knew? Even when your mattress stunk of pee though your bed was hastily made right before I came in? And you'd obviously been trying to dry it out?

In addition to "Don-nie wets his beeh hed!" (sing-song like they probably did in grammar school), suggest to your new victim that she take a gander at your Latin notes to see how you cribbed from your redheaded pal and how much "help" you're willing to get, like pinning a crib sheet to your cuff. So she can sing, "Donnie is a chee-ter!" and thank her lucky stars she didn't get hitched to a fellow who would abandon her and her children when he's sent to jail for embezzlement.

She'll also be spared the experience of having a wonderful dream of being on a sailing ship hand-to-hand with you at the railing gazing at the moon and feeling the fine mist of salt spray so cool against her skin—only to awake and find the ship is nothing but her marriage bed and you have hosed her down with stinky pee.

More stanzas—how you don't quite close your mouth when you chew and how you say, "Hey hey!" greeting a fraternity brother (it's so corny and way too much like "hip hip hooray!"), and how you point your chin in the air when you blow cigarette smoke like a prissy society dame. These few facts will get your new victim started in the right direction. I'm absolutely one hundred percent sure she'll come up with material of her own. We could compare notes. Who knows, she might not mind that icky way you kiss.

Besides the chants and such, though, no balm is quite so sweet and soothing as the adoration of another.

His name is Lawrence. Every time he sees me he says, "Well, hello there, honey! Darn if you're not a sight for sore eyes!" Then he smiles and blinks as if I've poured eye drops in them, kidding around. He's already out of college. He's a pharmacist. He hired me to help him at his drug store because his former employees ran out on him and went to work in war plants where the money's better, but he knows they'll come crawling back. He says he can't blame them. He'll probably hire them back. That's the kind of man he is. He wanted to join but personal reasons prevented it. He's tall, taller than you, and he's got wider shoulders. Not as much hair on his chest, but to me that's good because he never has a curly black sprig poking out of a buttonhole. He says things to me such as you never could bring yourself to say.

"You're just as cute as a bug, you know that?"

"Oh my gosh, kiddo, you're just as sweet as Christmas candy! I can't believe you don't have beaus lined up outside your door!"

"You know I swear you are just sharp as a tack, Mary Kay! I know you're going to be at the head of your class in college!"

And here's my personal favorite. I was looking at a picture of Lana Turner in a movie magazine and I said I thought she was really beautiful and I wished I looked like her, and he said, "Ohmagosh, Mary Kay! Tell me that's not true! You know, fellows don't go for a glamour puss like that—they go for the girls who are truly beautiful the way you are! Inside and out!" Of course I wanted to ask How am I beautiful? Please, please, please tell me! But all I could do was say, "What do you mean?" And Lawrence said, "You're beautiful the way a hay field in sunset is beautiful. Your kind of beauty makes fellows feel at home, and I meant your personality, too. A girl like you with big blue eyes and a really big smile and a warm personality—well, who'd want a Lana Turner?"

I knew he was joking and exaggerating. But, still, it made me feel good. He makes me feel good.

That's good medicine, you betcha!

So long forever, sucker.

Mary Kay Wainwright

THIRTY-TWO

LIKE THE STATIONS of the Cross, Sylvia's path to penance required arduous stops for ceremonial abasement. The injured party could interrogate her as the mood struck. Even dog-tired from walking the factory floor, she accepted being jostled awake.

"What is it, honey?"

"You say you love me and you like, uh, *being* with me in a wifely way, right?"

"Yes." The white Big Ben on her nightstand might show one or two or even three. She had to get up at five-forty-five. She didn't resent this punishment, though she wondered how long she'd have to endure it. They'd drawn no contract.

"I just wanna know what Robert *does* because I can do it too, I swear."

"Georgie, honey ... it's not like that."

"Not like what?"

"Not like you do anything *wrong*. I love making love with you."

"Okay, but are there things I could do, things maybe Robert—"

"Hush, honey! Please forget him."

A sigh. "Wish I could, believe me."

"He never did anything you don't do," she would be forced to declare. Knowing what came next, she steeled herself.

"Is his ... you know?" He sounded miserable.

"Honey, I've told you. No."

"Then—"

"I *told* you. I was weak. I am so sorry. I will *never* let it happen again! I made a terrible mistake, and I'm just lucky enough to have a man who's willing to accept me despite it."

The first few times she gave this speech, she moved herself almost to tears by her own deep shame and gratitude. But countless repetitions rendered it dull, like the Hail Marys murmured by order of Father McNally long after the penitential mood had passed.

Eventually pacified, he'd fall quiet. Often while she waited for him to continue, he'd slip into sleep and leave her chewing these things until dawn. Much about what had happened with Robert she didn't understand, though she understood more than she let on. It wouldn't help to let herself be badgered into detailed descriptions. Poor tortured Georgie seemed to believe that Robert had a *special irresistible technique.* If this were true, it would let her off the hook, and if he were to learn it, he must be thinking, then she'd have no reason to stray.

She wasn't lying when she said she hated Robert's guts. Something about him worked her up and set her off, and she couldn't *explain* it. She couldn't be frank about it. Her hope was to ignore this itch, squelch or bury it. Renounce that part of herself. It wasn't fair to feel a tender love for Georgie and such hostility toward Robert and yet Robert's touch singed her skin and aroused a delicious ache. She was the victim of an inexplicable perversity in the scheme of things, and the best she could do now was consider it a test of her mettle and her vow to chastity. She thought—*when he goes back, I'll be like a widow or a nun. I will chasten myself. I will not see that man; I will not speak to that man; I will not speak of that man; I will not think of that man.*

Worse yet—Georgie's interrogations often evolved into wanting to make love. But his manner and method now were rough and hasty, almost desperate, wholly unlike the playful and tentative way he'd approached her before. This told her he hoped to *outdo* Robert. She feared he might blurt out *is this as good as what he does?* He made Robert a third party in their bed, and this made her miserable for a score of reasons.

Such was the midnight-hour Station of the Cross.

Daytime version:

"Where'd you go?"

"How come it took you so long at the store?"

"Didn't you work at the canteen just yesterday?"

"Why are you wearing that to go to the drug store?"

Being with Josef had accustomed her to jealous interrogations, though Georgie would never fly into a rage; he took the punishment, each doubt hounding him mercilessly. She tried to tolerate his inquisitions with a cheerful forbearance appropriate to her self-imposed penance. Fortunately, Georgie was not dogged in trying to control her comings and goings and didn't extract minute accounts of her time. Nor did he secretly record the mileage on the odometer, and so far as she knew he never followed her. He didn't lawyer her testimony, catch her in a contradiction and worry it to death. Her simple answer sufficed to quell his anxiety, or else he knew that if she lied it was useless, really, to trip her up. He wanted reassurance that his suspicions were only waves of doubt; he wasn't seeking to confirm his worst fears. Nevertheless, she hardly set foot off the property that she didn't face questions on returning.

She unconsciously gravitated toward clothes she had before becoming Mrs. Karacek, blouses whose collars were dingy where her dirty neck had soiled them, slacks whose waistbands forced a belt of flesh to pooch above them, dresses so tight through the hips zippers were tugged from their stitching, and stockings laddered with runs. She washed her face and combed her hair but let her eyebrows go wild and only applied makeup for the sake of the Karacek family name. She had to give up her egotistical dreams of performing. She looked in the mirror and embraced her wrinkles as stigmata. She willed herself into old age prematurely so she wouldn't be tempted by "those" feelings.

It pained her to recall how Georgie had treated her with such tender respect and adoration during their courtship, and how she had grown to appreciate him. After he'd forced the manager of the White Blossom to come to her bedside at the Bide-A-Wee courts and, hat in hand, almost beg her to come back to work, Georgie quickly became a daily part of her life. In her room they'd play Parcheesi, Gin Rummy, and Chinese checkers. They listened to soap operas on a dome-topped Philco he said she could borrow as long as she wanted. He brought *Photoplay* and *Life* and bestsellers from the library, such as *Saratoga Trunk* and *Mrs. Miniver.* He told her to kick off her shoes and lie on the bed, then he read with gusto, reciting the women's dialogue in a quavering falsetto and the men's in a raspy bass, making her laugh. He memorized ragged swatches of "Hiawatha," the closest thing to "love" poetry he knew.

Every morning, gazing earthward,
Still the first thing he beheld there
Was her blue eyes looking at him,
Two blue lakes among the rushes.
And he loved the lonely maiden,
Who thus waited for his coming;
For they both were solitary,
She on earth and he in heaven.

And he wooed her with caresses,
Wooed her with his smile of sunshine ....

He'd arrive in his dented Chevy coupe bearing something—covered plates he'd gotten from Thelma, or cans of soup and soap and whatever she needed from Kline's.

He took her to movies—*The Magnificent Ambersons, Pride of the Yankees, Road to Morocco,* and (oh, how she sobbed!) *Random Harvest.* Her introduced her to Port Farview store clerks as "my friend Sylvia from the White Blossom." Their pairing seemed to arouse a droll or satirical thought the clerks didn't feel free to express, and she wondered what it was.

If Georgie expected sex as a quid pro quo, he never showed it, and she was grateful. She did feel warm toward him, very friendly, because he seemed vulnerable and green as well. He struck her as boyish, charming, harmless. But she didn't have *those* feelings. He was a gentleman—opening doors, sliding back chairs, always deferring to her preferences and whims. They didn't talk much about themselves. While they chattered about the books and movies and his dogs and things that happened at work and in the news, about themselves they only had one-sentence exchanges like the tennis volleys of amateurs.

He cheered her up. When he was a few minutes late she worried something had happened or that he had lost interest. She'd be itchy to secure him, not like a prize, more like wanting to slip into a favorite old robe after spending all morning dressed for church.

One day three weeks or so after they'd been running around, she waited almost an hour—he'd promised a quick outing to the beach. She was standing at her screen door watching when a gleaming black '40 Packard with white-wall tires pulled slowly into the courtyard, the big tires popping gravel under their substantial rubber. The sparkling chrome grill came within a few feet of her cottage and eased to a halt. The huge thrumming engine went off, and for a minute the metal creaked from the heat.

A Negro in livery emerged from behind the wheel, opened a rear door, and Georgie's mother stepped out. Sylvia's heart stumbled on a beat. Was he okay?

Evelyn was wearing a grey suit and a matching small grey hat with netting and carried a grey leather purse and white gloves. A gold floral brooch set with gems was pinned to her lapel. Sylvia envied the sharply formidable impression the woman made by wearing a fine wool suit custom-tailored to her diminutive form. *Must be nice.*

Sylvia stepped through the screen door before the woman had to knock.

"Mrs. Karacek? Is Georgie all right?"

The older woman stopped the way one steps up at a midway booth to pitch a ball. She hooded her eyes with a gloved hand.

"Yes, I think he'll be all right, just a little frazzled by too much excitement."

Apparently something dramatic had occurred in the family realm or in town. She back-handed the screen door to push it wider.

"Won't you please come in? I just brewed some fresh coffee for when Georgie gets here."

"It's not something he's supposed to have, but, yes, I'd be pleased to take a cup if you can sit a spell."

Sylvia pulled the chair from the corner and ushered the woman into it. As Evelyn pulled off her gloves with tidy little tugs on the finger ends reminiscent of thread-tightening, Sylvia turned her back and lifted the saucepan from her hot plate and poured two mugs. She knew Evelyn was getting a gander of the surroundings and felt flush with discomfort. Had she known the Queen was coming, she'd have found flowers and cleaned more thoroughly. At least her undies weren't hanging in the bathroom.

She handed a mug to Evelyn.

"Sorry I'm out of cream," she said, aware that Evelyn could easily see that no icebox was present. "Sugar I do have."

"Straight is fine," said Georgie's mother. "I've always drunk it the way cowboys do."

"Uh, I don't seem to have napkins at the moment, either." She blushed deeply as Evelyn plucked a handkerchief from her purse and draped it atop her thigh before settling the mug there.

Evelyn smiled. "This is where Georgie's been spending his spare time?"

"Well, Mrs. Karacek, he picks me up here and we've been going a lot of places. We don't spend much time in this room. It's pretty small—" She smiled and waved to dismiss it. "There's not much here by way of diversion."

Evelyn's gaze passed to the richly varnished radio sitting in a sunbeam atop the vanity; Sylvia wondered if she recognized it as an item gone missing from her household.

"Is everything all right with Georgie? I've been expecting him the past hour or so."

Evelyn Karacek took a tiny sip then lowered the mug gently to her thigh.

"He had a seizure earlier this morning."

Instantly Sylvia pictured Georgie keeling over from a heart attack. "A seizure? My God! Is he okay?"

"He's resting now."

"Oh, I am so sorry! Is he in the hospital?" Even as she asked she was mobilizing, thinking of what she might take, how she'd sit by his bed, hold his hand, read to him, and then the phrase "resting now" resonated back to a wintry night in Nebraska and a doctor saying that to her. "Where is he?" Sylvia blurted. She had an urge to leap up. "Can I—"

"At home." The older woman watched Sylvia with her head canted and one eye squinted the way you might scrutinize a museum offering you weren't sure should be there.

"What happened? I mean, how?"

Evelyn stretched to set her mug on the vanity, then she folded her handkerchief. It had an embroidered edge and a monogrammed letter Sylvia couldn't read.

"Has Georgie told you about his illness?"

"No," said Sylvia. Did saying no cost her a point? The coffee. Evelyn's saying *it's not something he's supposed to have.* His mother had come to inventory what he'd been doing with Sylvia to endanger his health. This was terrible! A heart condition? Besides the coffee, what was there?

"But I wish he had. I sure don't want to … well, I could be a help, if I knew. He's been so kind to me. He's very sweet. He's truly a gentleman, Mrs. Karacek." Against her will, her chin trembled minutely and she had to dig her nails into her palm. Poor Georgie! She'd not known anything was wrong and had gone along taking selfishly, never dreaming it cost him anything.

"Is there *anything* I can do, Mrs. Karacek?"

She dabbed at her eyes with the heels of her hands.

Evelyn nodded slowly, deeply. "Georgie has epilepsy."

"Epilepsy!"

"Yes. Since childhood. I supposed he'd told you that he was schooled at home and spent some of his adolescence in a sanitarium in New York." Evelyn seemed quite calm, as if to underscore the contrast between her long experience and Sylvia's apparent shock. "He does take medicine—Dilantin—and it allows him to live in more or less a normal way, but only if he keeps to a regular routine, and … well, stays *calm* is the best way to put it."

Sylvia nodded, absorbing the information as if being briefed on a nursing regimen she might follow.

"He didn't say a thing. I wish he would've," she murmured. "And the medicine. I could've been, you know," here she shot Evelyn a weak smile, "nagging him about it." She wanted to insist that *she could be on the team!*

"He needs to stay calm more than anything. The less uproar, the better."

"Sure!" Sylvia said. "Of course." She nodded, twice. "I understand." She was glad to have this information; she meant to imply that she wanted these lessons and would dedicate herself to applying them. The fact of *epilepsy* was a little scary, true, but having known Georgie before she knew of it, and having never witnessed a seizure, the condition seemed remote but still welcomed now as constituting a *mission* she could undertake. Though the parallel was murky, she imagined a connection to her own dear little Anthony—after all, she was talking to a mother whose son was ill—though now there might be the chance to make amends.

"I'm glad you do." After a moment, Evelyn rose, plucked her gloves from her purse and dressed her fingers, covering up a ring with a diamond big as a pea. The ring made a lump like a swollen knuckle.

"Thank you for your time and the coffee."

"You're welcome." Sylvia danced in front of her to open the screen. The news was so sudden and shocking that Sylvia hadn't digested it. She had an urge to detain the woman. When would he be well? What things upset him, threw him out of harmony? Other than making sure he took his medicine, what else might a nurse do?

But Evelyn was already treading toward her car. Of course Georgie could answer these questions.

"Mrs. Karacek," Sylvia sang out. "I'd like to help. I'd like to come see him, if I may."

Evelyn paused in the maw of the gleaming black automotive behemoth. She smiled as if in deepest sympathy. "I'm sorry, dear. It would probably be best that you don't. I'm sure you understand?"

"Oh, yes," Sylvia said, nodding so much she went almost dizzy with it. "Certainly. But please tell him I said get well."

By then the chauffeur had already swung the black door shut with a solid *thunk!*

Soon as she could, she thought, she'd take him the Parcheesi and a Hershey's bar (oh, wait! Is that all right?), cards, a magazine (he liked *The Saturday Evening Post*). She pictured herself beside his bed, but the picture was hazy because, she realized, she'd never seen his bed. Or his room. Or the house except from the street as they passed. And it was only one of their homes ... The family had a farm and owned saw mills and lumber yards and oil wells and who knew what else? Perhaps private hospitals! Sitting by his bed, are they alone in the house? The older sister, Marianne, lives there too, same floor? She'd never asked. Things she didn't know: now they seemed to constitute a long list she couldn't spy the end of. Seizures. She guessed they weren't frequent—at least not daily ... . She'd sit by Georgie's bed, bring him juice and water, his medicine. She would be his mother's personal assistant, because she and Evelyn were mother-to-mother, though Evelyn didn't know it, mothers with sick sons.

Imagining herself devoted to nursing Georgie back to health (overlooking that his disease was chronic), she was grateful for this maternal visit. She'd been so self-centered, and he'd been so self-sacrificing! She told him she'd been fired—he got her job back. She told him she missed listening to music—he got her a radio. She wanted to see the ocean—he planned to take her to the beach. It had been so strange to have a man be so eager to please her; it had made her fairly drunk with her own silly little whims.

She was *delighted* to have had this visit from Georgie's mother, glad to have the chance to earn the good will he'd showered on her.

Then she wondered how long until he was up and about. After all, this was old hat to the family, so surely they knew what to expect. Yet Evelyn hadn't mentioned it. She hadn't told much at all, really, aside from the offhand comment about the coffee and the vague references to "staying calm." You'd think she might've cited a list of things to watch for that caused his seizures. Just so Sylvia would know. Maybe Mrs. Karacek was embarrassed to discuss the illness to someone not in the family? It wasn't something you wanted known, though surely people in town had been aware for years—and maybe that lay behind the strange expressions when they were out and about together. Were people wondering *does she know?*

Maybe Evelyn meant to draw a line between "in the family" and out of it. And, sure, Sylvia could understand, but then Evelyn didn't know her heart. Evelyn didn't know how deeply she wanted to repay Georgie's generosity. So far as Evelyn knew, Sylvia was …

This turn in her thoughts came as she was dressing for her evening shift and she spied a coffee stain on her white blouse, and was simultaneously carrying the picture of herself in Evelyn's mind with the picture of having to wear the blouse tucked a little askew to hide it.

… was a hostess in a hotel dining room who rented a room in a tourist court by the week.

… had been entertaining her son there without a chaperone.

… was only passing through town. A tramp, maybe. One of those newcomers causing friction for the long-time residents, according to the *Enterprise.* Too much traffic now, too much litter, too much carousing, too many strangers—so the litany went.

She groaned. She took the blouse into the bathroom, spread the material on the lip of the basin and scrubbed on the stain. To think Evelyn might believe that! That hurt! Despite her circumstances, she had pride! Yes, she was a working woman. But only a snob would look down her nose at somebody drawing wages.

That old bat! She didn't believe Sylvia was *good enough* to help Georgie!

That really stung! She eased down on the rim of the tub, trembling. Georgie's mother was *slumming*. Pulled up to her door in that damn car with the colored man driving it like she was royalty! Just popping in unannounced wearing a custom-tailored suit and Rockefeller's rock as pretty as you please because *you don't have to practice good manners with someone who's little better than a waitress and rents a room in a tourist court!*

Then came the embarrassment—to recall how she rushed out onto her stoop to "see Evelyn out" like they'd just had tea in Sylvia's parlor (My God, how you humiliated yourself!), calling after her *I want to help; may I come visit?* and that phony sweet smile and her saying *it would be best that you don't.*

At the time, Sylvia had presumed she meant "right now, anyway. Maybe later." When what Evelyn clearly meant was *It would be better if you never came to visit.*

Because *she* was the upsetting thing!

She leaned up from her washerwoman's chore. Her back hurt. The stain resisted her efforts; it might be blood.

"That bitch!" Sylvia spat. "Who does she think she is?"

Nothing wounded her more deeply than to have Georgie's mother imagine that *she* caused his seizure. Did she believe that she was getting Georgie *stirred up?*

While walking to the bus stop, she continued to fume, but righteous indignation was undermined by doubt: how much did she know about *epilepsy?* People said those afflicted went berserk. But she'd heard that was an old wives' tale. In any case, who the heck was she to say what made Georgie have a fit? His mother had dealt with this condition all his life. Maybe Evelyn was being kind, the way she'd handled it, never directly accusing Sylvia, just putting the hint out there to be picked up, giving Sylvia credit for being intelligent enough to see the point. She didn't lay down the law or shake her finger in Sylvia's face, had she? Wasn't it more as if his mother was trying to *educate* her while gently planting a seed? Georgie's mother had real *class.*

She'd missed Georgie. She'd argued with herself two days running about calling him. Doing so would violate Evelyn's request. But if his mother only meant "not a good idea right now, maybe tomorrow," then waiting beyond that "tomorrow" would seem negligent. Also, by being persistent and maternal, she might sway Evelyn's heart, sweep away her prejudice.

On Wednesday afternoon following her shift, she stopped at the Bide-A-Wee office. Her fingers were trembling as she looked up the number in the book. The wall clock showed 3:05. It was hard to know if this was a good time or not.

"Hello, Karacek residence." A woman's voice—not the mother, thank God!

"Hello, is this Georgie's sister? I'm Sylvia, a friend of his. I hate to disturb anyone, but I was wondering how he was. I've been worried."

"Yes, this is Marianne. Georgie is doing quite well these days, thank you," she said breezily.

It was hard to know if this was just the public face or whether he had indeed recuperated. The blasé manner hinted that maybe the sister had no idea he'd been sick. Maybe his mother's claim was pure bull hockey.

"I heard from his mother that he'd had a, a rocky spell."

"Oh, yes. He's quite satisfactory, now, though." Sylvia heard a little snickering giggle. "Up to his usual pranks."

"Well, I'm glad to hear it." The call was growing distressingly useless and disappointing. "Would you please let him know I called?"

"Hold please," she said, in the distant manner of an operator. The phone went *clunk clunk* in Sylvia's ear.

She heard a great rumbling (he was running down the stairs), then the receiver was snatched up, and he said, "Sylvia??" breathless and excited.

"Georgie! How are you? I was worried about you!"

"Oh, I'm—" and he was suddenly deflated. "Mama told you about me, I guess."

"Yes. I wanted to come see you, but she thought it best not to."

"You really *wanted* to?"

"Yes! You're my … my *friend*, Georgie."

"Can I come see you right now?"

She laughed. "Yeah, sure! Is it okay?"

"Sure! Never mind what *she* says, okay? I'll be right there. I gotta bring Buster and Billie along, though, 'cause I gotta run them to the vet. Stay right there, okay?"

She laughed. "Okay. Honk and I'll come running."

She changed out of her work outfit into loose cotton slacks and a blouse and cardigan, loafers. She'd just reapplied her lipstick and worked on her hair when she heard the Chevy's tinny beep out front. She went out the door waving cheerily and fairly leaped into the passenger seat like a schoolgirl, and, since he was beaming to see her, she swung over and smacked his cheek. Two skinny yellow mutts were leaping about and pawing at the backs of the seats.

"This here's Buster and Billie." He grinned, jittery she could tell. But she was nervous, too. Her knowledge of his condition sat between them like a somber chaperone. "We gotta leave them at Doc Randall's for some shots."

The veterinary practice stood along the highway out of town, and, though it was a short drive, they were ill-at-ease and jumpy and so they jabbered furiously about the dogs—where he'd found them, what he fed them, how old they were (Billie was Buster's mother), and she had had a dog herself once, how many he'd had over years, which was the best … And so forth until he was pulling off the highway and onto a graveled parking lot before a set of low buildings with pens and corrals attached. He parked and leashed the dogs before letting them out, and she said she'd wait.

She was glad to be alone. He seemed like the same fellow he was only several days ago, though she had caught herself *watching* for something. Twitching? Blinking? Jerking? Awareness of his disease had tainted the way she looked at him, and that was alarming. She vowed to shake it off, talk it down.

He came back without the dogs and walked toward the car with his head down, and when he climbed back in, he didn't start the engine. He leaned back and drummed his fingers on the steering wheel.

"Didn't you ever wonder why this car is so dented up?"

"No."

"It's 'cause I keep running into things." He gave her a small, sad smile. "I kind of," he touched his forehead with a finger, "fade out and next thing you know *wham!* I've bumped into something."

"Georgie! My God! Should you be driving?"

"Probably not. And I know it's not fair to other people on the road, either. Or to people in the car with me."

He sighed. "But I did *not* want to just lay down and die, Sylvia. You understand?"

She nodded, though she didn't.

"Are you afraid to be with me now?"

She grinned. "I'm about to become the world's most active back seat driver."

He chuckled. "Well, I mean otherwise, you know…" He shrugged.

"Well, a little. But only a little."

"Will you forgive me for not telling you?"

"Yes. Sure. I can understand about that."

"I hated that she told you. I didn't know she was gonna come see you. When I found out she had, I figured that was the end. I thought you'd be too disgusted and afraid." Tears sprang to his eyes; she leaned toward him and put her hand over his wrist.

"I'm here."

He swallowed and turned back to look out the windshield. His heel was jittering against the floorboard. He was—*not calm!* A sudden, cold weight hit her in the chest like a sack of wet sand.

"Georgie, do you think I'm bad for you?"

"Is *that* what she said?"

"Well, not exactly."

"Oh, I know her! Are you bad for me? Sylvia, Sylvia!" He shook his head. "You have no idea."

She waited for him to go on. A truck pulled alongside them, and two men got out of the cab and started coaxing a large spotted cow from the back.

He said, "I think we were supposed to go to the beach the other day. Marianne made a lunch." He looked at her and grinned. "We can have a picnic?"

"She made it—for us?"

He nodded. So Marianne had no objection to their being together? It was good to have allies and even better to know who they were.

"I'm game." She smiled. "But I'll be ready to bail out, of course."

"Well, stay alert and between the two of us we can get it done."

They drove past Port Arthur then through a seaside village where it appeared workers in the refineries nearby were living in camp trailers and tents back from the shore. Bait shacks and a few road houses stretched for a mile or two beyond the cluster of buildings that housed a café, a souvenir shop, a tourist court, a little grocery/gas station, then they were driving on the packed sand of the beach along the Gulf. The heady scent of the ocean with its damp salty fish tang swept through the car's open windows. The sky was streaked with high clouds that washed the sunlight out, but the breeze coming off the water was warm and gentle. Fishermen stood in knee-high surf casting into rollers, and a fellow with the Texas Defense Guard wearing an armband and carrying a wooden mock-up of a rifle waved them down to give them a card bearing the black silhouettes of German or Japanese ships. A squad of men in civilian clothes stood nearby pitching what appeared to be beer cans filled with sand over the dunes, maybe practicing grenade-tossing.

"Anybody seen anything lately?" asked Georgie.

"Two days ago fellow says a German sub surfaced a couple hunnerd yards off shore."

"Right *here?*" Georgie was sorry as a twelve-year-old boy to have missed this.

"Couple miles down yonder by the old pier."

They drove the beach until they reached the decayed pilings jutting out of the water. He kept peering out to sea as he opened the trunk and lifted out a large red plaid blanket and an enormous wicker picnic basket the likes of which she had seen only in the pages of a magazine such as *Town & Country.*

"Would you like to go up in the dunes where it's a little warmer and there's less wind?"

She grinned. "Wouldn't you be upset if you missed that sub?"

He blushed. "Aw, you know, I just wanna do my part."

She spread the blanket in front of the car so that they could keep an eye on the horizon's grey line. There were ships—tankers or cargo ships, maybe—but in daylight it was hard to imagine they were anything but friendly. The tide was going out, and the shimmering strand lay pocked with burrowing creatures hurrying to vanish before the circling gulls had spotted them. She unpacked the wicker basket, curious as to what another woman, a stranger, had selected for their lunch. The sandwiches were on store bread whose crusts had been pared, and a quick inspection showed their contents to be egg salad and lettuce. Two pieces of pecan pie were wrapped in waxed paper, and there was an orange and an apple. Cloth napkins, no less! A thermos of tea. A bottle of wine. The inside surface of the basket's lid sported elastic holders for utensils, including a corkscrew. Every time she turned around, she bumped into a new sign of the family's largesse.

"Your sis really made a spread here. Please thank her for me. You want some wine?"

"Oh, no. I can't. My medicine doesn't go with it. It was just for you. I'll take the tea."

She set about hostessing while he sat on the blanket peering through binoculars. She'd never had the wherewithal for good wine, and her meager experience had shown that the white was always bitterly astringent and the red either sickeningly sweet or very sour. She presumed it was an acquired taste. He opened the bottle of Bordeaux for her and she poured a finger into a tumbler, saying she'd just try it and that she really liked tea with her meals. That first small sip slipped right to some tingly receptor in the center of her brain, smooth, airy somehow, dizzying. Maybe she'd have a little more.

An hour or so later, she'd had half the bottle and corked it just to keep herself away from it. *Must be nice,* she thought—that everything you had was of the highest quality. *Must be nice.* The phrase was becoming a kind of silent chant when she was around the Karaceks.

The sun went down while they were lying side by side talking, and, inspired by the wine and her carefree feeling, she scooted into his flank, took the loose folds of the blanket and wrapped them in it. We can watch for planes, too, he said. She said she didn't know one from another. He said he had a spotter card in the glove box. She said don't get up, I'm too comfortable.

His bulk radiated heat and she boldly set her cheek on his shoulder. He said he could build a fire. She said just stay put, will you?

He laughed. "You remember asking me if you were bad for me? I wanna tell you why not. You know that night we met at the White Blossom? Well, a couple hours before I'd gone out into our garage and stood on a crate and tied a rope around a rafter and around my neck and hitched it up short and tight as I could."

"Georgie! You're kidding!"

He chuckled. "Naw, sorry to say. I know it was foolish, and I was just feeling blue. Really blue. Really *really* blue! I know this sounds stupid, but I'd just run out of hope."

"Hope for what?"

"Aw, I hate to even say it. Hope that I'd ever have, you know. Somebody."

"Oh, Georgie, that's so sad! What stopped you?"

"Promise you won't laugh?"

"Of course, I won't laugh!"

"Well, it makes *me* laugh. So I warn you. First of all my dog Mollie found me. She's a collie, really old, probably eighty-five in dog time, been with me a dozen years, anyway—she comes out and lies down and watches like she always does when I'm doing something. I'm her entertainment. I think she knew what I was up to. She looked very *sad* for me, just kept looking at me with these big brown eyes. I turned my back so I wouldn't have to look at her, but next thing you know this other dog, Pester, he's a lot younger and really sort of stupid, and he didn't have any idea what I was planning, but he's the kind of dog always wants to help you. He'll try to bite your laces while you're tying your shoe. He's not happy just to watch. He tried to jump onto the crate with me, so I had to run them both out of the garage before I could take another stab at it."

Georgie chuckled, and his chest jiggled her head. "I guess you'd say having those mutts interfere kind of gave me *paws.* Get it? Anyway, the longer I tried to work up the guts, the more I worried that Marianne or my mother might see it, and I understand that when you hang yourself you mess your pants—not that this would be a novelty for me—and your tongue sticks out all swollen and black, and I just couldn't, you know ... ." He sighed, deeply. "Marianne, she's pretty fragile and high-strung, and I got to thinking it might make her go to pieces." He snorted. "Elizabeth would just be annoyed that my funeral interfered with plans she'd made." He tried to laugh but it came out strangled, like a cough.

"So, anyway, I thought I'd put it off until I could figure how to do it without making a mess and so they wouldn't have to see it."

"Promise me you won't try that again!"

"I don't have a reason now. When I saw you that night I told myself that I was going to see you again and make myself talk to you—I was a dead man, anyway, what would it hurt? That's what I was thinking, anyway."

"What about when you thought I wouldn't want to see you again after you'd had a, you know—"

"A fit. Well, there was always the hope. That was new."

"Gosh, that makes me feel terrible that I waited so long."

He shrugged. "You didn't know."

"And what about *staying calm?*"

"Mama can't get used to me being grown up."

They lay in silence for a while. He was humming; he seemed content, *not nervous.*

After a while he said, "What I tried to do was really stupid. Even my dogs knew it was stupid. No dog ever killed itself. I'd never done that before. I didn't mean it. I was just feeling sorry for myself. I hope I didn't scare you with that story."

She snuggled closer. She could feel the heat of his thigh against her loins. She propped her head up with her elbow and leaned close to his face. He was the sweetest fellow she'd ever known. To prove she wasn't afraid, she bent forward and kissed him lightly on the lips. He turned his head toward her and kissed her back. Then they kissed with just their lips, not moving any other part of their bodies. His breathing hitched up a notch, but he made no move to take them anywhere else. *This is nice*, she thought. Sweet and innocent, like they were just schoolkids. His lips were soft and warm. Kissing him aroused a tender friendliness in her.

"I am quadruple glad now I didn't jump off that crate."

"Me too."

She lay back down with her head on his chest and heard his *not calm* heart pounding a mile a minute against her ear and sounding like somebody running down an alley in the middle of the night.

In her dark night hours of penance while Georgie slept fitfully beside her, twitching perhaps from nightmares of faithless wives, she recalled that friendly tenderness. She'd thoughtlessly thrown it away. She hoped something of it could be salvaged. She remembered her stunned surprise the night he'd brought her engagement ring and proposed while she was working the night shift, told her to take off her apron and just walk away, but she didn't want to leave them short-handed. She also wanted to think it over for a day. He insisted that she wear the ring until then.

During her break, she went to the pay phone in the hotel lobby and called Doris in Ohio.

She remembered holding up her hand and staring at the ring while the phone rang on the other end. A diamond like that said *I am treasured. I belong to somebody.* And as shallow as it might seem, a rock like that made people imagine you were hitched to a life of other luxuries.

You became *that woman over there with a big rock on her finger.* Not somebody on her feet eight to twelve hours a day slinging hash or smiling at idiots or bending over a sewing machine until your neck got so stiff and sore you couldn't turn your head.

Doris came on, and soon as she could insert her news, Sylvia said, "Hey, guess what? A fellow popped the question."

"No kidding? Who's the chump?"

They laughed. "A guy down here. He's super sweet, really a dear."

"What'd you say?"

"Said I'd think it over."

"What—is he a toothless old fairy? What's he do, anyway?"

This detail she relished. "Not much of anything." A beat. "He doesn't have to."

"Oh, sweet Jesus! Jackpot! So what's your holdup?"

The operator held off her answer by telling her to deposit another fifty cents, and while she slipped the ten nickels one by one into the slot, she wondered herself. *I want to go to Hollywood* was too naked an admission of her foolish dreams, and even *Los Angeles* put her too near to laying it out to be lifted up and tossed back like something from a bargain basement table.

When the line was clear, she said, "I was thinking of going out to the coast."

"Hon," said Doris. "You don't mean war work? I can't see you doing that. Me, it's another story."

"Don't sell me so short. I'm as red, white, and blue as the next person. Maybe I want a part in a war movie."

"He know about Anthony and Josef?"

"Not yet. I'll tell him about Anthony for sure."

She'd hoped Doris could help her decide, but too much would go unreported: the epilepsy, the mother, the town itself, though living a life of leisure sure could ease that pain. So she asked about her goddaughter and got an earful about girls her age being boy crazy and snotty, and when the operator cut in again, she decided she wouldn't spend those two quarters.

"I've run out of money, punkin'."

"Okay, hon," then just before the line was cut, Doris said, "Bird in hand, Syl."

When they'd hung up, Sylvia thought: Funny. Doris never asked if

I loved the guy. What if she had? Wasn't this crucial? *He's very dear, I'm very fond of him, I love to be around him* (most of the time), *he's charming and sweet, and …* He aroused long fallow motherly sensations in her, and a deep pleasure in the intimacy you have with a pal. With him, she was never lonely. And he would never hit her.

Does he make your heart go pittypat? Do his kisses make your knees quiver?

No. But fellows who had done *that* had proven to be worthless at best and harmful at worst. You didn't want to put too much stock in that. She *liked* kissing Georgie, *liked* being close and being held. It was more than plenty enough. And unlike most men drawn to her, he wasn't grabby or drooling slobber. She knew he had *those feelings,* all right, but he was a gentleman. That's what you get when a guy has class.

Now, though, with her marriage almost ruined, she had to face the truth that Georgie had too much class for her. She hadn't risen to his level. Her nature was soiled, tainted, her will weak. She had spoiled something wonderful and pure with her whorish desire; she had killed the trust a wonderful husband had in her; she had wounded him so deeply he hardly smiled. She had turned him into a worrier, someone sick with jealousy. When he went back to the army, he would gnaw on her betrayal; it might distract him at just the moment when he needed to be the most alert. She had crippled his ability to protect himself. She was bad for him.

She was a bad person, a bad woman.

Worst of all, his mother had been right.

All she could do was devote herself to him, to their marriage. She wasn't fit to be a singer and dancer or actress in Hollywood. She was *trash.* If she was lucky, truly lucky, Georgie might forgive her, though it would be hard for him to forget. He might never trust her, might always ache to know where she was when she wasn't in sight.

Another station of her cross could be called "kneeling before Evelyn." News that a shotgun was discharged in the yard swiftly reached Georgie's mother, along with hearsay details about the party. The following day, a Sunday, they'd been expected to drive to Kountze for dinner, but she couldn't face Evelyn. Georgie hadn't gone, either, and sure enough Evelyn called Sunday evening. She'd heard about the brouhaha in the yard. Days later, Sylvia worked up the courage to ask

Georgie if he'd told his mother about her affair.

"Are you kidding?" He glared. "I told her Robert was a masher and you asked me to run him off."

"Thank you."

"I didn't lie for you. I don't want to hear her say I told you so for the rest of my life."

Though Evelyn didn't officially "know," she *knew,* thought Sylvia, and Sylvia required herself to act accordingly. When Evelyn showed up unannounced after Sylvia's working hours, she felt duty bound to drop whatever she was doing and prepare fresh coffee and serve it on the Wedgwood china in the parlor, with a linen napkin, the little Wedgwood cream pitcher and sugar bowl, and a sterling silver spoon monogrammed with K. Evelyn might take two sips. She might not utter a word to Sylvia—she'd ask Georgie about his diet and medication or talk at him about people known to them though not to her. Nonetheless, Sylvia sat dutifully silent waiting to be addressed. If Evelyn noticed her daughter-in-law's self-abasement, she didn't show it.

Finally, she felt driven to throw herself at Evelyn's feet, if only to get the woman to acknowledge her existence.

"Mother Karacek," she ventured during a lull, "when Georgie goes back, I was wondering if you wouldn't like to come here to live. I'd love to have the company and I could stand to learn a thing or two from........" (how to phrase this?) " ... from a person with good judgment about things."

Sylvia deliberately avoided seeing Georgie's reaction, but she heard an involuntary grunt.

"Thank you. It's nice to know that when my grandchildren wear on me, I can take refuge here. But I thought," here her gaze swung to Georgie, "that the two of you were planning to build a home of your own."

She hadn't forgotten Georgie's push for more control of the family money, then. Or that she'd nixed it.

"*Some* day, Mama. I told you that."

After she'd gone, Georgie said, "Told you she wouldn't be interested."

"You don't know until you ask. I wanted her to see I mean well, Georgie. When you're gone, I want to be her friend. Or I want her to be *my* friend."

"What if I wasn't going back?"

She'd been rearranging the coffee service so that when she lifted the tray nothing would be jostled, and she instantly stopped and plopped down in the place on the sofa his mother had just vacated. Georgie eased onto the piano bench, put his elbows on his thighs, clasped his hands.

"Yeah. I got a medical discharge. Because of my epilepsy."

Automatically she skimmed her memory quickly for mail from the War Department, but nothing had come recently save for his allotment check.

"Georgie? When?"

"Aren't you happy?"

"Oh yes! Sure!" She fought back a spasm of resentment to be so tested this way. "But it's such a surprise. When did you find out?"

She sat poker-faced while he explained about his seizures and that the last one landed him in the infirmary at Camp Roberts. She didn't tune him out as much as she also listened to her inner voice running not so harmoniously under his narrative. He seemed sheepish to reveal this at such a late date. He'd known all along! He had lied about this furlough! She knew she should celebrate the news he wouldn't be in harm's way, but the impulse ran counter to capitalizing on his confession and winning a respite.

"Why'd you keep this from me?"

He shrugged. "Guess I wanted you to think I was gonna do something heroic. Guess *I* wanted to keep on thinking that." His gaze flicked up to meet her own; he was wearing the expression of a despondent child. "But aren't you happy?"

She leaped from the sofa and ran to hug him, clutching his head to her breast.

"Of course I am, darling!"

"I guess you like it that I lied to you."

"Why would I like it?"

"Maybe you think it makes us even."

"Well, I don't! You don't, do you?"

"No. But now that I'm staying, maybe we can, you know, get a new start?"

She kissed his head and held him close. Yes, hers was still the greater sin by far. But asking for a "new start" signaled forgiveness and that allowed her to ease up on herself. She'd consigned herself to a lifetime of marriage no matter how dreary, so renouncing her dreams to go out to California no longer seemed a necessary payment for her sin. Nor was that renunciation a gift like a dowry. It would be a sacrifice required for a decent marriage, and she found herself wanting compensation for the loss.

THIRTY-THREE

SATURDAY AFTER LUNCH, Mary Kay was eager to leave for work, but Sylvia waylaid her "just to catch up." Sylvia poured coffee in a Wedgwood cup then sat with her elbows on the red oilcloth, lit a Chesterfield, and used the saucer for an ashtray. Mary Kay sat back from the table with a bottle of Coca-Cola propped on her knee. As she suspected, after some chit-chat, Sylvia said, "Sweetheart, I don't want you to make mistakes you can't undo."

"Do you mean Donnie? Gosh, I know falling for him was a mistake. I hope he gets shot down! Oh, I take it back! I don't really mean that."

"I know you don't. But you've got every right to be furious. If I had that boy right here I'd shake him so hard his teeth would rattle!"

They laughed. "Get in line behind me!"

"Atta girl."

"That's why you needn't worry. I won't ever be so foolish again ... No kidding! Don't give me that look! I'm completely disillusioned when it comes to boys. They're not grown up enough."

"You tell me not to worry then say things like they're not grown up enough? Mary Kay . . ."

Mary Kay dandled the bottle on her knee while Sylvia took a long drag that sounded like the breath you take before you dive.

"Why?"

"Well, people talk."

"What in the world do they say that *pertains* to me?"

"Give you three guesses."

Mary Kay felt a sulk descend upon her. She wasn't about to make this a parlor game. If Sylvia had a criticism, let her volunteer it.

"Don't play innocent, Mary Kay," Sylvia was forced to add, and Mary Kay felt a twinge of victory. "I've been around the block when it comes to dealing with fellows."

She wanted to say *Don't I know that!* but kept mum. She'd poked her nose in Sylvia's business enough to last a lifetime.

"I mean this thing with Mr. Emerson."

Mary Kay snorted. "What *thing?*"

Sylvia went at her fag again like it was oxygen. Then Mary Kay watched with a tiny interior grimace as Sylvia smashed the butt into the blue designs on the Wedgwood.

"The two of you have tongues wagging."

Mary Kay narrowed her eyes. "It's just gossip!"

"I know. And I know how much trouble it can stir up."

"Mister Emerson is a friend! He likes me a lot. He admires me! I sure don't see anything wrong in that! It really gets my goat that some old biddies sit around and make up stuff! We're just friends, like I said. He takes an interest in a lot of young people, not just me. Besides, I have to take my friends when and where I can get them!"

"Honey, I'm sure sooner or later you and Linda will make up and—"

"They can all go to Hades! They're too childish!"

"You know Georgie and I are concerned about your future, too. Why do you think he told you we would help with college?"

"I know. And I am grateful, Sylvia! He's really generous. You both are. And I'm glad, you know, that—" She let the unspoken predicate waft over the table. Things were *so* much better now that they were sleeping in the same room again.

"So you don't want to do anything that might *spoil* it, would you?"

"Of course not. What did you think I might do, anyways?"

"Oh, things girls do to get themselves in a jam."

Mary Kay set her Coke bottle on the table. "Like getting pee-gee?"

"Well, yes."

"Aw, gee, do you think I'm just a brainless tramp!"

"Of course not, Mary Kay! I'm just being … *motherly.*"

"Well, you're not my mother!" Mary Kay blurted out. Then she leaned to pick up the Coke bottle again, though it was empty. "I didn't mean that to sound so harsh. I really appreciate your concern. In some ways you're a better mother than my mother."

Sylvia rose, carried her cup and saucer to the sink, washed, and rinsed them. Mary Kay wondered if she could excuse herself to leave for work—for God's sake, she was an *employee!* Larry was a friend she worked for. People had such dirty minds! Maybe people like Sylvia who did those things presumed others were guilty, too.

"Did your mother ever tell you how we met?" Sylvia's back was turned while she set the dishes in the drainer.

"She said you're old friends. That you were like my godmother."

"But she never told you more?"

"Uh-uh. What's to know? Were you school pals or neighbors?"

"No. I met her when she was about to have you. I was pregnant, too. She was farther along, though."

"Were you in the same hospital ward?"

"Something like that."

"So you knew my father?"

"I knew *about* him. Your mom talked about him. Are you sure she's never told you about that time?"

"Gosh no! I'm dying to hear about it!"

"I'm not sure I should be the one."

"If I wait for her I'll never hear it, Sylvia. Please!"

Sylvia smiled. "I can tell you she bawled the happiest tears you could imagine when they brought you in. She said you were really cuddly looking. She said you had your daddy's eyes."

"No kidding!? She never told me that! She said I have his eyes?"

"Yes."

"Did she say anything else like that? I mean, I'm as tall as she is now but I'm skinny and long-waisted, and I have bony knees, nothing like hers, and her hair's a lot darker. Did she say anything about those things?"

"No, just about the eyes."

"Like his, huh? I have my daddy's eyes?"

"That's what she said."

"Did she mean the color? Or the shape or the brows or the lashes or how far apart they are or what?"

"The, uh, color, yes."

"Huh. I have my daddy's eyes!"

She lunged across the table top and pushed her face close to the side of the toaster to inspect herself.

"I think I'd know him now if I saw him," she said when she was resettled. "I'd look at his eyes. Where was he while we were in the hospital?"

"Hon, I don't know for sure. I think she said he was working out West."

"Doing what?"

"I don't know. I'm sorry. You'll have to ask her."

Mary Kay expelled a huff of exasperation. "She'd just cuss. She's never had a good word to say about him."

"Well, I know she loved him then. You were special to her, Mary Kay."

Mary Kay chuckled bitterly. "Wonder what happened."

"Sugar, I'm sure she loves you. You're her only child. She's just worn out. She's a woman alone in the world with a child to raise. War times are hard on everybody. Try to see it from her point of view."

Mary Kay sighed, slumped in the chair, toyed with the bottle by running her fingers around the hole.

"So you guys became best friends then?"

"We were very close, yeah."

"Did you see us a lot when we left the hospital?"

"Not much. I went back to Worcester—that's where I was from, a town outside of Boston, where my father had a diner. You and your mom went back to Ohio."

Mary Kay frowned. "The hospital was in Philadelphia but Mom and I went home to Ohio and you went to Massachusetts? Was this a special kind of hospital?"

"Yes. It was one where girls went to have their babies."

"Oh, my God! You mean a home for unwed mothers! My mom and dad weren't married?"

"Hon—they got married right after. She sent me the announcement from your paper and wrote me about how happy she was. And you shouldn't worry. Most people are born under those circumstances. It's just nobody wants to advertise it. She never thought for one second of giving you up, either. And most girls did that. Besides, if it had been a regular hospital I wouldn't have been with her more than a couple days. We were together a whole month, Mary Kay, and we were expectant mothers together. You have no idea how that can bring two women together." She grinned suddenly. "I'm not eager for you to learn it any time soon, either."

"I'm not having sex *ever!*"

Sylvia smiled. "All right. Anyway, your mother and I promised we'd be there for each other when things went wrong."

"And you never met my father?"

"No, honey."

"Did she tell you why he left us?"

"No. You should talk to her."

"She'd lie. It was probably because she was such a bee-eye-tee-see-aitch. Or he took one look at me and I was too ugly to be any daughter of his."

"Mary Kay! Now I *know* Doris has never said anything of the kind!"

"Not exactly. It's more like he couldn't stand to be responsible for us. Same thing, really. If I'd been *adorable* enough he wouldn't've minded the trouble."

"You're plenty adorable, Mary Kay. You've even got a little more than your share. That's why I worry when people gossip about the attention a married man with two children is paying to you."

"I said he *likes* me! He's helpful. He gave our Victory Girls troop money for posters, and he's letting us use the back of the store to work on our float for the war bonds parade."

"So long as he's always above board, I'll try not to worry."

"You mean getting fresh? Never! He's always a real gentleman."

"Fine."

"Like one time when we were working I got paint in my hair and he helped me get it out." The instant she began this story she knew she should've kept her mouth shut.

"Helped you how?"

"Oh, don't make a federal case out of this. Other people were there, too. He just took a damp rag and swabbed at it, then used a brush off the shelf and gave it to me. I have it upstairs."

"You couldn't have asked a girl friend to help you?"

"If I had one I might. Since I don't, I didn't think of it."

"You've still got friends or those girls wouldn't still come to the meetings."

"They voted in Linda as the leader. I'm a peon now. And I started it! That's the way it goes around here."

"All right! I'm only saying that kind of thing makes people talk and gives men the idea you can be … be. . . *approached*."

"I'll have to take your word for it."

"Oh, honey, don't be snotty! Do as I say, not as I do! Don't repeat my mistakes just to learn what the results are."

"You haven't done so bad."

Sylvia gave her sharp look, and Mary Kay added, "I mean Georgie is as good and nice a man as anybody could want for a husband. I know you guys have had some trouble, and I'm sorry, you know, uh, about … Anyway, he's great! Really! You know how much I like and respect him."

"The road to here was pretty rocky. As you know. I've been very lucky."

Mary Kay wondered what "as you know" might encompass. Since that horrid birthday party, she'd never told Sylvia she'd been the informer, and she hoped Georgie hadn't, either. Despite the turmoil, now that things were more peaceful she believed she'd done the right thing—she'd recorded the consequences in her diary, as if building a case should someone accuse her of causing trouble. Now Sylvia was all lovey-dovey with Georgie, kissing and hugging and sweet-talking, and he seemed increasingly willing to succumb to it. Since he told about his discharge, he'd gone back to work full-time at Kline's. Sylvia got him to stop drinking. The cloud behind this silver lining was that when he came home and she wasn't here, he fretted about it. Did she say where she was going? he'd ask Mary Kay. How long has she been gone? Wud she have on? Wud she have with her?

Mary Kay got up and set her empty under the cabinets where they stored for-deposit bottles. She looked out of the corner of her eye at Sylvia. Any chance Sylvia told her about her being a bastard child to get even? No, Sylvia had been in the same situation as her mom.

"Hey!" she said, suddenly struck by this. "You and my mom were pregnant at the same time." She stood beside Sylvia, brow furrowed in puzzlement. Had Sylvia given up her child? "If I'm who mom had …."

"Hold on. I'll show you something."

Mary Kay waited while Sylvia took the drainer's few dishes and put them up, slowly, very slowly, in the cabinet—she seemed to dawdle. Maybe it was to make Mary Kay feel guilty for being nosy? Or Sylvia was reluctant to take the next step. Sylvia said "most girls" gave up their babies. If Sylvia had, then every time she looked at Mary Kay, she saw the child she'd given away. That would hurt. It offered a little twisted pleasure to hurt Sylvia this way. It also inched her heart back toward her mom.

"Come," Sylvia said finally.

Sylvia knelt beside her bed on the hooked throw rug, grunted, reached under and dragged out a large tan leather suitcase, which she then slung onto the bed.

"Sit." Sylvia indicated the bed beside the valise.

Sylvia sighed, then very slowly she unlatched the locks on the closed clam-shell halves. The latches made an audible *clack*. Sylvia lifted the top half. She sighed again then eased beside the valise herself as if suddenly out of wind.

Clothing, stuffed animals, small toys, a framed studio photo of a child—a boy in a little sailor's suit, dark-haired, with brown eyes and a beaming smile. The photo had been tinted so that his cheeks were rosy. He was holding a ball. He might be four or five.

"Anthony." She waved toward the valise while looking away.

"Gosh! Where is. . ." Mary Kay realized the answer even before Sylvia gestured vaguely as if to say "away" or "in the air" then raised the hem of the bedspread to her eyes.

"How did he, you know."

"Diphtheria." Sylvia shook her head, patted the clothing stacked in the suitcase. "He was just six. His birthday's in August."

"He would be my age now."

"Mmm," grunted Sylvia.

"I could have a sort of cousin." Mary Kay gently riffled through the valise with only the tips of her fingers. "I wish he hadn't died."

Sylvia laughed, one short bark like a cough. "Oh, honey." She shook her head. "Oh, honey!"

Sylvia removed items and handed them to Mary Kay—bronzed baby shoe, a cellulose rattle, a teething ring, a metal toy car, a picture of a house drawn using a crayon, a locket on a chain with a hank of dark hair inside. A book of nursery rhymes. She talked about each thing as if it were a place on a grand tour she'd taken earlier in life but hadn't forgotten down to the last odd coin spent in a market for an unheard-of fruit.

"Why don't you wear the locket?" suggested Mary Kay when Sylvia was tucking it back into its envelope.

"I'm afraid it might break or fall off and I'd lose it. Also, if you wear a locket, people always want to look inside, don't they?"

"Yes. I guess they'd wonder whose picture it was."

"I never want to have to explain."

"Why not?"

Sylvia shrugged.

"I hope you don't mind showing me."

"Oh no. It was time."

"Where was Anthony's father, if you don't mind my asking."

"When I told him I was pregnant, I never heard from him again."

"What a creep!"

Sylvia smiled. "That's the kindest thing anybody ever said about him."

"How'd you get by?"

"I worked in my father's diner until he went bust. Then I joined a traveling tent show that played at small-town theaters, and we performed stunts and songs before the features—they were still doing that then. But when we were in Nebraska one winter, Tony got sick. I didn't have any money, and I kept telling myself, over and over, he wasn't really that sick." Sylvia fell silent for a moment, and Mary Kay knew not to prompt her.

"I remember a moment when he was lying on the cot, and I *knew* he was sick and had been for days, but we'd all had croup and colds, and I just kept telling myself, over and over, he'd get better. I kept saying you can't run to the doctor every time. Not if you don't have money. It would've meant missing a show to take him in. They all depended on me. It was the *worst* decision I ever made. I stood there and told myself he didn't need a doctor."

"You couldn't know."

Sylvia shook her head as if to disagree or free the air of Mary Kay's utterance. "After he died, this fellow in the troupe paid to have a little funeral."

"That was good."

"Georgie's wedding present was a stone angel for Anthony's grave. We went up there to see it set."

She closed the valise and locked the latches. She absently stroked the leather top.

"Why don't you keep the picture out?"

Sylvia sat for a long time, then she smiled. "I think that's a good idea." She reopened the valise and took out the photo. She walked about, trying it on the dresser, her vanity, positioning it on the wall with her hands.

"Put it on your nightstand," said Mary Kay.

"You think?"

She stood it there, fixed just so, gazed at it.

"Thank you, Mary Kay." She hugged Mary Kay quickly but ferociously, and plucked a tissue from a box by the photo.

Pleased to have pleased Sylvia so much, Mary Kay basked in her own wisdom. "Do you think you and Georgie might have kids?"

Sylvia smiled. "Can't tell. You never know about the future. I do know that money makes a difference, don't let anybody tell you different. If I had had money my little boy might be alive."

She turned to look at Mary Kay. "That's why I warned you about Larry Emerson, honey. Before you know what's what, you could be knocked up and he might decide he's never laid eyes on you. Larry Emerson has a wife and two children and a business, and he's not about to risk that."

"But that's so, so *cynical!*" Mary Kay directed her outburst to the air so she wouldn't seem to be judging Sylvia. "I *know* that he has nothing but the best intentions toward *all* the people he helps."

"All right. But promise if *anything* happens you'll talk to me about it. Even if it means I was right. Okay?"

Mary Kay looked up; Sylvia was half-grinning, so she grinned back. "Okay. Just so long as you don't say I told you so."

THIRTY-FOUR

A LEAKY GUTTER seam had caused paint under the eaves to peel, and roots from the chinaberry tree needed cutting before they crept into the sewer line. While his mother marched about citing complaints, Georgie lagged back, saying "Got it." Billie and JJ irritated her grandly by raking at her stockinged legs, and Georgie said, "No! Down! Bad dogs!" in a half-hearted way that let them know they were free to cavort.

"Did you repair the garbage can stand?" They moved past Sylvia's garden where everything had wilted from the heat, and he reminded himself to water the tomato plants. Not on his mother's list.

"Uh, well—"

"Never mind! I'll send a carpenter over."

"I said I'll fix it! Quit worrying. I'm not letting things slide. It's our house, too."

He waited for her to react to this goad.

"Perhaps," she said finally. "It remains to be seen."

He followed her to the parlor where Sylvia sat on the sofa dressed in her dark skirt and ivory blouse of prewar silk, though the day was muggy and very warm. She looked like a guest and not the lady of the house, and she rose when his mother strode in.

"I've told Georgie I would *prefer* he wear his uniform," Evelyn told Sylvia.

"Mama, Bud was a *war hero,* damn it! He'll have a color guard. Nobody wants to see me in uniform! They know my story! I didn't *earn* the right to wear it!"

His mother turned to Sylvia. "Will you talk sense into him?"

Sylvia visibly reeled with surprise to be appealed to as an ally, and Georgie's resistance inched a notch higher.

"Well—" Sylvia glanced his way, and he rolled his eyes behind his mother's back. "I'll certainly *discuss* it."

"Fine!" His mother tossed him a stern look. She was pretending Sylvia's answer constituted a victory. She picked up her handbag from the coffee table. "The funeral is at eleven. It's—" she slid back her cuff with a white-gloved finger. "Already ten. I'm going to get Marianne and Elizabeth and the children over at the Monroes."

"Okay. They would've been welcome to get ready here."

"Georgie's sisters and the children are always welcome," put in Sylvia.

"I told them that, but they said they'd feel more comfortable among their friends."

They kept mute while her heels clapped smartly across the front porch. The grandfather clock bonged ten times, and Sylvia sat back down. "I guess I'm ready too early."

"Let's skip the church service. We'll go to the graveside ceremony. If that's okay."

"Sure. Why?"

"Too claustrophobic."

"Did you take your medicine?"

"Not you too."

Sylvia rose and he followed her to the kitchen. She turned on the tap to pour water into the percolator.

"What's this about the uniform?"

"She knows everybody'll turn out for the funeral. They'll close the stores. She thinks my uniform will fool people into thinking I served same as everybody else. She doesn't give a damn about what I feel; she's just worried about what people think of 'the family' or of her. She's *ashamed* of me and she can't stand it."

"What have you got against wearing it?"

"I'd feel like an imposter. Bud was a cretin who treated me like I was the hunchback of Notre Dame, but he did die wearing the damn uniform, and I respect that. If I was somebody close to Bud and saw me there wearing khaki, I'd want to strip it off me. I don't know why Mama doesn't see that."

Sylvia set the percolator over a burner and turned down the flame. She poured water into a measuring cup and tipped the spout over a glass that held a cutting of Swedish ivy in the window sill.

"There might be other reasons why you should."

"Such as?"

The red oilcloth on the table was sticky, and when he moved his arms, his skin peeled away with a tiny ripping sound. Sylvia looked at his face, then she turned on the fan posted atop the refrigerator, and soon the air moved across his damp brow.

"Well, so long as things are uncertain, we don't need to make her any more pee-ooed." She sat at the table and frowned at her fingernails.

"Hell with her."

Sylvia smiled; it pleased her to hear him openly criticize her. And it pleased him to please her.

"My sentiments exactly, hon, but if it turns out the courts don't compel her to offer your rightful portion, we'll have to rely on her good will."

"Her good will?" Georgie laughed.

"You *are* her son. She is a mother, after all, and despite how she gets under my skin, I know she really does want what she thinks is best for you."

"Oh yeah! What *she* thinks is—"

"Don't spit on it! There's a long history—" She left him to finish: *of worrying about you because of your condition,* and he flushed hot.

"And if we have to resort to a civil suit, who's going to be on the jury?"

He considered the question rhetorical then realized with irritation she wanted to play teacher. "You tell me."

"People from here. People you know."

"Maybe Robert," he said to show his annoyance. "That might work to our advantage. Yours, anyway."

Sylvia sighed. "Georgie—"

"Sorry. But what's your point?"

"People see you in the uniform maybe they won't forget it if they wind up on a jury. You think everybody knows your story, but don't you think you get credit for *trying?*"

"I'm not wearing it!"

"Suit yourself."

Sylvia left him to mull over his decision while she went to reconsider accessories for her outfit. He would not feel *right* wearing that uniform. So long as he'd perpetuated the fiction of his furlough, he might've gotten away with it, disarming his own internal censor by reminding himself of his completed training and ignoring the ignominious finish. Now everybody could count past thirty to over forty-five, and the whisper campaign had begun. Once he'd come clean about his lie, everything had shifted in his relationships: his mother behaved as if she'd always known it would come to this and was content with her disappointment; Sylvia seemed happy to have him home but the humility she'd worn like a cloak of shame for her infidelity had slipped off her shoulders. He'd wanted a new start. The one he got was not altogether to his satisfaction.

Credit for trying? He could get that by walking around in civvies. To parade about in uniform would undermine that credit because those who credited him for *trying* would presume he didn't imagine he'd *succeeded*—sympathy granted for "trying" is recompense for failing—and the second they saw him in the uniform they'd say he was "trying to make people think he'd really done it" instead of "trying and failing and facing up to it."

How could that *lessen* the shame his mother felt? It would surely sharpen his own. Once again he had let her down. Doubly. First by running off and failing, now by refusing her the balm of this idiotic pretense. It was a long, sad, familiar story—resisting her efforts to "do what's best" for him then trying on his own and messing up. Leading to her embarrassment and his guilt.

But he'd had his way in large decisions: he'd married Sylvia against her will and gone off to the army, then displeased her utterly with this fuss about the trust fund. Why thwart her now over such a small thing? Besides, for once his wife and mother were aligned, though not for the same reasons. It wasn't often he could please them both by one simple act such as wearing one garment rather than another.

If only the hard fights could be won by riffling through your wardrobe!

Jesus God almighty, he was sick of the conflict! Ever since he'd revealed he was home for good, he and Sylvia had argued with each other and with his mother through various agents about money. He never liked thinking about money, let alone talking or *arguing* about it! When he raised this objection, Sylvia said acidly, "Well, it must be *nice* to never have to think about money!"

His mother had cut off his allowance and refused to give him a meaningful role in a family enterprise. "Since you consider yourself adult enough to take a wife and start a family, you can do what grown men do to support them."

So long as his mother tried using money as a lever, he could foil her by relinquishing a claim. With Sylvia's job and his, they'd managed. Now, though, she was trying to kick them out of the house. Sylvia declared, "Go to the bank! You're a grown man! Don't take your mother's word about the terms of the trust, Georgie! It's your money, too!"

He'd known Lester Pratt all his life, which, he supposed, was why the lawyer and executor had flicked off his requests to see the trust documents so easily, as if humoring an annoying child. Georgie said, not even smiling, "Will it take a court order?" Lester looked shocked. "Oh no. Just get Miz Karacek to buzz me and everything'll be dandy."

So Sylvia hired another lawyer—from Houston, because "everybody around here's using the same spittoon"—and that lawyer called Pratt to say he had clients who demanded to see the Karacek trust—the documents were *public record* after all.

Hardly minutes later, his mother was standing on the porch speaking to Georgie in a way that would strip paint off the siding. Sylvia rushed out and stood beside him to weather that withering hot wind.

Recalling it made his stomach flip and quiver. Now at the kitchen table his palms sweat and he set his cup down when a tremor rose in that hand. At the time he was glad Sylvia stood beside him for support but was also vaguely ashamed, as if she personified his guilt and betrayal. It hurt to treat his mother as an enemy to her face.

She ignored Sylvia and railed at him, "How *dare* you go demand this or that when you know damn good and well I've been in charge of the family's affairs since the day your father died! Not that I wanted to, Georgie! But it was my duty as a mother, and I believe I've done a damn good job, too! And you go behind my back—"

She was outraged to the point of speechlessness—about to cry, he saw—and when she hesitated, Sylvia leapt in. "Evelyn, I know you never approved of our marriage, but, good Lord, you're trying to blackmail him, pure and simple! Georgie has rights."

His mother glared at Sylvia, then turned to him. "Georgie, everything that's mine is yours. You are your father's son. But I will cut my own throat before I allow a penny of our hard-earned money to slip into someone else's hands!"

On hearing their report, their attorney said the court would not require her to cut her throat, but a judge might insist she settle about his portion. Georgie said, "Maybe she'll have a change of heart." Sylvia scoffed.

He was shoved this way and that between them. It frustrated and disheartened him that Sylvia wouldn't let things cook slowly on their own; she had to turn the burners up. What happened to her desire to befriend his mother? And his mother made absolutely no effort to appreciate Sylvia. He'd always hoped that if everybody kept calm and let things mosey along, eventually things would turn out all right. If his mother tried harder to understand why Sylvia was important to him, she might relent about not only the allowance but also let him be privy to the family's business affairs. Treat him as not only an *heir* but also a successor. If Sylvia would only wait patiently, she could have a very capable and loyal mother-in-law and access to the security of the family's money.

But no! His mother delivered ultimatums, pushed them into a corner, trying to drive Sylvia off, and Sylvia fought back tooth and claw. There was no room for compromise or for a normal conversation. Now only the lawyers met to speak about it.

His mother's last pronouncement on the subject—one he didn't pass on to Sylvia—was, "If you want a divorce I'll make sure you get all the family papers you want to see, believe me!"

Blackmail. Boy, Sylvia had his mother's number!

He sighed. The uniform business seemed silly now. He went to their bedroom. Sylvia had pulled the shades, and the room was dim and stuffy. She lay across their bed with her shoes off and her arm across her eyes.

"I decided to wear my uniform," he announced. She lifted her arm, craned her head up.

"Yeah?"

"Yeah. Not because she wants me to and not because you want me to. I'm wearing it for my own reasons."

"Okay," she said mildly, as if his reasons weren't of interest.

"What I'm thinking is this," he volunteered when she didn't ask. "It's something you both want, and so you won't be at each other's throats about it, and so maybe doing it will bring you two a half inch closer."

"Oh Georgie," she sighed.

"What? Oh Georgie what?"

"Oh, you are so. . .wonderfully *naïve* sometimes. Some day I hope to be as good a person as you are."

He smiled. "And that's why you love me, right?"

She grinned. "It's on the list."

THIRTY-FIVE

MARJORIE RODE WITH Robert rather than family because she had a half-pint of gin in her purse. Between sanctuary and cemetery, she sucked it down and plopped the bottle into the floorboard.

"Fucking high heels," she griped as they tottered toward the gravesite. Her ankles buckled like door hinges, and he had to jack her up by cupping her elbow. "That fucking Bud," she mewled. She swiped her nose with the back of her gloved hand. "He was a heap of trouble. I'll sure miss him."

"I know," he murmured. Attending her brother's funeral made him worry about Jimmy. He believed his brother was still in England.

"It just doesn't seem *fair!* He was only twenty-one! He hadden even *voted* yet! You know what chaps my ass? How some people get off scot-free!"

"I know." Maybe she meant him.

"Or they're raking it in hand over fist. They ought to hang the bastards!"

The veil on her hat poufed from that outburst; ahead, a crowd was amassed around the awning over the grave, and heads turned as they trudged up the turf-carpeted slope.

"Honey, you need to be strong for your folks' sake." He meant be quiet.

"Mmm!" she choked back a sob. "Poor Mom!"

There must've been a couple hundred milling about. The funeral procession had arrived minutes earlier, and cars stretched through the grounds and out to the street. Along the cemetery's eastern border, the brown river carried sludge from chemical plants and refineries toward the Gulf. Somebody on a barge hooded his brow to watch them. Two olive-drab sedans were parked behind the hearse. A squad of riflemen in dress uniform stood by the cars preening like chorus girls—two fellows stood breast to breast straightening each other's collars and another jack-knifed to brush his polished shoes.

He steered Marjorie through the crowd, murmuring, "'Scuse us, please," and people fell back in an unctuous but hurried way, as if they were royalty with leprosy. They murmured condolences; her head stayed bowed, but he felt her biceps tighten in his grip. She was wound tight as a barbed-wire fence. It wouldn't surprise him if she jumped somebody who spoke a little wrong to her.

He escorted her to straight-back chairs where her parents were seated. Her mother stood to welcome her with an embrace, and both exploded into sobs. He melted into the crowd. It was sultry, and sweat trickled down his flanks. Funeral or no, she was determined to move later today, and he didn't look forward to helping. Her dad refused to lift a stick on such a mournful occasion, and Robert thought it insensitive of her to insist, but she said, "I told Mom I gotta keep busy or I'll go nuts." He'd signed on Walter Jenkins to help.

He spotted Sylvia. She was walking up with Georgie and Mary Kay. The mother-in-law and the two sisters were nearby. Georgie was wearing his army khakis, and Robert wanted to laugh in his face. He wondered whose idea it was. Mary Kay looked very adult in pumps and her hair bunned up. They lingered on the fringe of the crowd, then Sylvia made her way alone to express condolences to the family. He hadn't seen her except from a distance for awhile; his knees quivered a little and he swallowed and turned away to get his bearings.

After a spell of spying on her, he'd been determined to purge her from his system. He read nights until long after midnight, when all breezes died and the cicadas sawed the dark silence into shreds; he took cold showers. He jumped out of bed in the mornings before melancholy thoughts could sap his peace of mind. Quite a few nights he went to the Port Farview Carnegie Library because his Rutgers philosophy professor said the Orient had useful ideas about love and lust. The few books on Buddhism and the like were authored by Christian missionaries, but even at that the librarians eyed him as if he were a spy. He'd hoped to locate a source for Dr. Foster's lecture on Tibetan corpse meditation. Spending the night beside a ripe one with the flesh falling off the bone in putrefied tatters like a stewed chicken and the stench loud enough to blind you supposedly taught the novice about the illusion of beauty and the futility of lust.

He was still hooked; his heart was thundering in his ears. He sidled around to Sylvia's blind side while she queued gripping the handle of a purse with both hands before her loins. She must have been sweltering in that dark suit; he edged close enough to see fine filigrees moistened to her nape. She wore a large black hat. Her delicate earlobes sported pearls. The closer he got the less matronly and more *womanly* she seemed, and the scent of her cologne and sweat and musk nearly floored him. His eyes stung with tears. After she hugged Bud's mother and Marjorie and had pumped the father's hand between her own, she broke aside for the next mourner. When she looked up he was standing in front of her.

"Robert!" She was surprised. Misreading his tears, she lunged forward and hugged him lightly, bouncing him off her chest. "Isn't it awful? These brave boys!"

"It's terrible!" he gushed.

They waited out an awkward silence. Mesmerized, he couldn't take his eyes off her lips, her eyes. She looked behind him or at her feet. She clutched the purse before her pelvis like a shield.

"Look. The color guard."

At the olive-drab sedans, the riflemen in formation stood at parade rest.

"They won't come up until after the service," he said. "I think they'll fire a twenty-one-gun salute. Then I think they take the flag off the coffin."

"Fold it up. That special way. They give it to—" She was about to say "the widow."

"His mother, I think," he put in. "I went to one in Washington."

"Oh. How can they do a twenty-one-gun salute? I only count seven soldiers."

This was driving him insane. "I miss you." He tried to sound offhand, upbeat, as if they'd been coworkers.

"Well, I miss you, too." She tossed it back in the same spirit—*miss your jokes around the water-cooler.*

He grinned, suddenly nervous. "That's good." He might've said *I'll do something about that* but lost his nerve and the moment was wrong. "How's Mary Kay?"

"Oh, fine!" After a second's hesitation, she said, "She's working at Emerson Drug."

"She like being a working stiff?"

"Oh yes. Likes having her own spending money. I—"

He waited. "You were going to say?"

"Oh, just that I worry about her. She's very innocent and vulnerable. You know that boy in Michigan broke the poor thing's heart."

"People survive broken hearts. More than once, even."

"It's different with girls."

"If you say so."

She passed him a look that might have meant *don't take yourself so seriously!*

"I *do* say so. But in the end she'll make some lucky young man the very best sort of wife. She has so much *heart!*" She thumped her own chest with a fist, and a film of tears jiggled in her eyes. "She is *so* smart, Robert. And pretty! I don't see why *any* young man would be so stupid as to overlook her."

"How's the man of the house? Full of vim and vigor?"

She didn't like his tone. "Very well. I'll tell him you asked."

As if that'd make him quake in his boots! "Suit yourself. Tell him I said he's a very lucky man."

"He says so himself."

"At least we're in agreement!" He seemed to be babbling. She rocked from foot to foot and looked about—for Georgie? Worried he'd see them together? He panicked. He didn't want to lose his chance.

"Sylvia, can we get together?" He got a sour look. "Just for a cup of java, just to talk? No funny stuff! You name the place." Five minutes alone, maybe he could win her back.

"What's to talk about?"

"I dunno. Old times."

"Robert . . ." She clucked her tongue.

"I didn't mean anything by that, honest."

"What would your girl friend say?"

He presumed she meant Marjorie. "Why would she care? We're just sitting in a diner. What could be more harmless?"

"Not doing it."

He sighed. She'd knocked the wind out of him. "Never mind." He sounded very bitter. "You wouldn't want to hear what I had to say about you, anyway."

She took a step back, but he hooked her inner elbow. "Wait, please. I don't mean I'd say *bad* things, Sylvia!"

"I have to find Georgie and Mary Kay."

"No you don't!" He was drenched in sweat and felt as if he were wrapped in a horsehair blanket with the sun flailing his head. He tugged on her arm, and she let him drag her a few steps off from the crowd but regarded him in stony silence and glared at his hand. He let go. Every effort he was making to amend his mistake only compounded it, like water draining in the tub accelerates. "I'd tell you how much I still want you. I'd tell you I *know* deep in my heart that you still want me! I *know* it, goddamnit! How can you deny it! I'd tell you that no matter who comes along I can't get you out of my system, I have tried, my God, I've honestly tried! And all I can remember is how we kissed, how we—"

"Robert!" she whispered in alarm. "Shut up, damnit!"

He stopped, grit his teeth.

"I have to go. If Evelyn sees me, I'll be in more trouble than you would *ever* be worth! I'm going to be absolutely frank with you, all right?"

"By all means!" he huffed.

"I *did* feel a passion for you I never felt for any other man." Here she moved closer. "But it *does not* matter! That's what you've *got* to see! I had a life without it and I can make a good life without it again. So many other things are more important and I hope for your sake some day you understand that."

"So you're—"

"I'm not about to discuss this! If you try to talk to me about it or anything else again, I swear to God, Robert, I'll have a peace warrant sworn out against you!"

That stung. He pictured himself collared like a peeping Tom and led away in cuffs.

He tried to laugh. "A peace warrant? Are you serious?"

"Yes! You think I don't know you follow me around?"

She wheeled and strode off toward the crowd. "Peace warrant!" he barked. "Are you *that* scared of what you feel?"

She ignored him and vanished in the milling throng. He was sure people nearby had heard him because when he glared, they looked away.

He walked down the slope to the company car. On the far side, he heaved himself down on the running board and lit a cigarette. Peace warrant!? He was stunned. How fucking preposterous! A desperate measure. But it was so humiliating—like saying she *had* to sic the law on him because he had no pride and self-control! As if he were a *sex criminal* who made indecent telephone calls or exposed himself! He'd left when she asked before.

Jesus God, woman! I do have *some* pride!

He sat furiously stewing. The service started, and he heard the muted drone of the preacher. He considered returning but didn't want to see Sylvia with Georgie, even though he'd worked up a slew of retorts to that peace warrant.

But, more calm, he realized he'd felt uncomfortable there. Georgie wasn't the only mourner in uniform; dozens of old fellows had donned garrison caps and puttees, sashes and arm cords and such to affiliate themselves with America's past imperial adventures. The burial of a warrior offered a chance for old soldiers to strut their stuff with a sententious solemnity that turned his stomach. Young men such as himself in civvies were hardly better than women and children.

The first rifle report jolted him to his feet and he fumbled his cigarette. He peered over the hood of the car. The squad was aiming for the sky. There came a second "POP!" and a trail of smoke, a shouted order, and a third "POP!" Then came the bugle and the brassy lamentation of taps. He'd forgotten they played that.

Something in him at last responded like a normal decent human being to the occasion, so he stood at attention with his hand over his heart. A hard thumping knocked against his fingers as if an angry little man locked inside was flinging himself against the walls to get out.

What can a man believe in?

The cannon on the hill resounded through the early morning mists. Slowly a solemn procession—men with muskets, women with prayer books—marched to the simple meeting house.

There in humble gratitude the Pilgrims bowed their heads and gave thanks for the privilege of worshiping in their own way, for their homes, their meagre harvest, for life itself!

Throughout our land today the spirit of that first Thanksgiving is being born again. As we learn to do without, our hearts are rediscovering the real gifts in our hands. Simple things like friendship. The satisfaction of making the most of what we have. The opportunity to share with our neighbors. The nobleness of sacrifice.

And anew are we learning the invincible strength of a people united to fight for freedom of worship and of speech, for freedom from fear and from want.

These are the things that transcend all others. Give thanks that they are ours to preserve, to fight for, to believe in!

Every Squibb product—whether made especially for prescription by the medical profession or for proper everyday use in the home—bears an individual control number. It means that each detail in the product's making has been checked against Squibb's high standards and recorded under that number at the Squibb Laboratories. Look for the name and control number when you buy. You can believe in Squibb.

E·R·SQUIBB & SONS

Manufacturing Chemists to the Medical Profession Since 1858

THE PRICELESS INGREDIENT OF EVERY PRODUCT IS THE HONOR AND INTEGRITY OF ITS MAKER

THIRTY-SIX

He died a hero in the prime of his youth defending America from evil forces bent on world conquest. We gather to pay honor to Elmer Sinclair, Jr. ....

Georgie had one ear to the preacher's eulogy but half his attention was turned to composing his own.

Dear Bud,

It's strange to envy a corpse—the adulation and attention, anyway. So many ironies! There's how much I always wanted to trade places ever since you became such a sure-footed cocksman and athlete, all piss and vinegar. We watched you whack the old horsehide over the fence at the fairgrounds, hooray for you, hooray for us, then there you were toting and booting the old pigskin and catching it on the fly. The horsehide and pigskin, oh, having your way with the hides of beasts, dear Bud, like a tribal chieftain. That's how we measure a man, that's how we measure up.

And we cheered you on.

You let us cheer you right onto that battlefield. Right into this grave. We made you believe you were the invincible warrior, bearer of our banners, and, really, Bud, maybe you should've been skeptical.

I'm not gloating. But breathing is recompense for being the anonymous survivor and not the glorious corpse. You got your picture on the front page of the *Enterprise* so when we mount a statue on the courthouse lawn next to the one for our stricken doughboys from The Great War, your name'll head the list of those engraved upon its side.

We're holding back a bit because nobody yet knows the circumstances of your death. I am, anyway. Could be a trick. Right now as the riflemen ready themselves to send you off to Valhalla with the requisite gunpowder wreath about your neck, we're publicly proclaiming you did something extraordinary to get yourself dead. So we hope it won't come to pass that, while you cowered in your foxhole too timid to advance, one of our tanks ran over you; we hope you didn't trip and knock your noggin, didn't accidentally shoot yourself, weren't drunk in a Jeep that overturned. Don't cheat us. We need to get our juices going; we need to relish the horrid cruelties of the enemy and to wallow in the melancholy anger that comes with the good dying young. It's selfish, I know, but truth is we want (and need) the best Bud to have been killed by the worst enemy.

So no cosmic laughter from the wings, please. We home folk like our stories to have upbeat endings and clear moral lessons. We need the inspiration and distraction of righteous indignation. The tear in our eye. You were a jackass on your own home turf, so we need to learn you had a turn of heart, mustered up mettle. Say your outfit was beating a fast retreat in the face of an onslaught and your best pal took a hit that blew off his legs and you stayed behind even though your pal said, no, Bud, forget about me!

That's upbeat. We want to say you gave your life. Your little brothers around town won't rush to take your place unless what happened makes us especially sad and mad; we can't go without coffee and cigarettes and sugar and tires and gasoline and new clothes and meat and cars and washing machines if we believe our young men are throwing away their lives because they're too stupid or greedy or thoughtless or self-destructive to live.

So, Bud, my old nemesis, the boy I never was and always longed to be, my prayer is that the truth of how you died will turn out to be uplifting. And if it's not, my prayer is that we never learn it.

Nobody knew this—not Sylvia or his mother or sisters or the nemesis himself, but Bud Sinclair was almost single-handedly responsible for Georgie's having joined the army.

On last Valentine's Day—his and Sylvia's one-month anniversary—he had run into Bud at Emerson Drug. Bud was standing at the register holding a heart-shaped box of Schraft's chocolates in one hand and a little blue vial of *Evening in Paris* in the other. He was clad in his uniform, his cap neatly halved over his web belt like the tanned pelt of a rodent. Georgie considered dawdling at the magazine rack until Bud had cleared the store but that seemed cowardly.

Clutching his Dilantin in a white sack, he crept up behind Bud. One evening a couple years back Bud and Lamont Stickley and Ralph Givens (now in navy bootcamp) had depantsed Georgie at Magnolia Park during a very public July Fourth celebration and roughed him up. When Deputy Abbott braced them, they said it was all in fun, though when Abbott's back was turned, Bud hissed, "Don't hang around my sis, pissant." The warning burned him, as Marjorie had indeed starred in his masturbatory revels, but in reality he'd only chatted her up when she came into Kline's for that strawberry licorice she liked.

To Georgie's dismay, Bud felt someone at his back.

"Hey, Georgie Porgie, how's it hangin'?"

"You look right soldierly, Bud. I see you got a stripe right out of boot."

"Yep." Bud patted the dark green V on his left sleeve as if it were a beloved pet.

Having kissed Bud's ass into complacency, Georgie sought an opening for his own news. He wanted Bud to learn that he was now a fellow *who got some regular.* He said, "What's with the *candy* and the *perfume*, soldier?"

Bud almost blushed. "It's Valentine's Day, dumbass, ever hear of that?"

This *was* news, but Georgie didn't let it jostle him. "So who's the lucky gal?" Georgie winked. "Anybody I know?"

Bud said, narrowing his eyes, "It's for my sis." Did Georgie want to make something of it?

"That's good. She's real sweet. I better get something for my old lady." Lest Bud think Georgie meant his mother, he hastily added, "My wife. I got hitched."

"Heard that. She's that gal works down the White Blossom, right?"

"Did work, yeah. Not now."

Bud grinned and poked his shoulder with a knuckle. "Hubba fuckin' hubba, Georgie. You sure you're up to the job?"

Georgie's grin made his face hurt. Bud was chuckling. The insult was strangely comforting—it doubted Georgie's manhood but applauded him for grabbing the prize.

"Aw, you know, Bud, I keep *practicing.*"

Larry Emerson glided behind the register in his pharmacist's smock, and spying Bud with the items in hand, declared—more loudly than necessary—"Hey, soldier—these are on the house!" He fairly lunged across the counter to thrust his hand at Bud, who had to set the perfume down to take it. Georgie smirked at Bud's back. Not long ago Larry had caught Bud and Lamont stuffing cigarette packs under their letter jackets, and he had to be coaxed out of filing a complaint.

When Bud left, Georgie picked up a bigger box of chocolates and the largest bottle of *Evening in Paris.* Bud had the know-how, but Georgie's gifts were for a sweetheart, and the implication he'd left in the air was that he'd parlay these items into conjugal bliss while Bud could not.

Never before had he bested the likes of Bud Sinclair!

He slid the red box under the front seat to keep Pester from pawing at the cellophane wrapper. He stopped by Thompson's Florists for the roses. Then he had an unprecedented swell of expansiveness and had bouquets sent to Marianne and his mother.

Coming out of Thompson's, things had a dazzling electrical outline that distressed him, but he blinked it away. He cruised slowly by the train depot, and spying the Lincoln, parked. The station was full of milling military personnel, and he had to wriggle through the throngs to reach the USO kiosk. Sylvia stood behind the counter between Ethel Bainbridge and Helen Tyler, two doyennes of the PF Country Club set who regularly played bridge with his mother. Bud and Marjorie Sinclair's mother was working with other women operating the big percolators and washing cups. He stood back as a sea of khaki and blue beat against the counter like gentle surf, the women proffering platters of crullers and dunkers dusted with white powdered sugar and setting out the steaming mugs. He smiled with pride—how nicely Sylvia was adapting! In a white smock and fetching little volunteer's cap, she was indistinguishable from her coworkers here except for being much younger and breathtakingly beautiful.

A joking sailor wanted more than his two-doughnut allotment; Sylvia grinned, winked, tapped him on the nose with a rolled-up paper napkin *naughty boy!* This tortured Georgie. Ethel and Helen were friendly, but they didn't flirt. He'd learned that his wife was fond of joking with men in a way that might make them think, if they didn't know better, that she was encouraging an advance. He was as new to jealousy as to utter infatuation. He hadn't known that the anxiety over winning a woman could be equaled by the terror of losing her. As much as he imagined that Ethel, Helen, and Matty Sinclair thought of Sylvia as one of them, he also imagined they disapproved of her. Though they didn't know this, she was a woman with *a past.* He'd magnanimously decided to overlook it, but others wouldn't be generous.

To hell with them! She's just *friendly. They're* jealous. Tapping shoulders and murmuring "'Scuse me please," he wormed to the counter clutching the roses, and when he headed up the line, he said, "Surprise!" and almost hit her in the face. She had to stop serving, and Ethel gave her elbow room to take them.

"Georgie! How sweet!" She glanced around helplessly, as if for a vase, and meanwhile troops swarmed around him—he was like something fallen from a truck in the roadway—and Ethel and Helen struggled to take up the slack since Sylvia's hands were full. He felt sheepish that his timing was so awkward.

"It's Valentine's Day!"

Ethel did glaze him with a little eyelash bat, but otherwise his grand gesture failed to draw gratifying applause.

"Oh, I know! Thank you!" She stuck her nose into the bouquet rather perfunctorily, then held it out to him. "Could you take them home? I don't have any place to put them here." Her smile was sweet but patronizing. Where was that saucy grin, the *naughty boy!* nose tap?

He slunk away, struggling to maintain his dignity. Only a moron would've tried a stunt like that. At home, he stuck the bundle in a crystal vase and set it on the dining table. The chocolates and perfume he hid in the side buffet for when the time was right.

The house seemed empty. He carried the Dilantin into the bathroom and drew out the bottle. He'd been paring back his dosage as a private experiment. Would living as a normal man with a wife have a positive influence on his health? Who knew? Marianne, a follower of Mary Baker Eddy, believed in mind over matter.

He fed Buster and Billie, Pester, and Mollie, then went upstairs to feed his fish. He and Sylvia slept in the downstairs bedroom now—his parents' room—and he often caught himself coming up to get something he'd already moved downstairs. His books and the paraphernalia from his hobbies still cluttered this room, and the single self who had inhabited it these years was a goading ghost.

So many changes in so little time! His mother and Marianne had been replaced by his *wife* (still a thrill to use that word), and he and Sylvia now lived as *bride and groom* with all the privileges and responsibilities thereto. He still worked four mornings a week at Kline's and drew his allowance from the trust; he had given Sylvia control over their money and let her manage the household. Elizabeth's wedding present had been the permanent loan of the 1938 Lincoln, originally their mother's car, which she and Clarence had driven before they'd bought their new Cadillac. He knew Sylvia felt regal behind the wheel of the stately sedan and had wisely discouraged him from driving it.

She seemed happy. So he shouldn't worry about how friendly she was to fellows who might soon meet bloody death. He should be generous. He should be pleased she was so civic-spirited.

When she hadn't returned by four-thirty, he got antsy and played throw-stick with Buster and Pester. He was getting hungry; he'd long been accustomed to his mother seeing that meals were regular as part of his therapeutic regimen, but she had taken their long-time cook, Jemma, with her to Kountze. Sylvia took on the chore, but clearly she lacked the desire to learn Southern cooking and seemed content for the lowly can opener to be her primary utensil. When he praised Jemma's dishes, Sylvia said, "But your mother didn't cook it, right? And your sister didn't, either, right?"

Was she *especially* late today? He wanted to spring the candy and the perfume on her, since the flowers had fizzled. He recalled what he'd implied to Bud. He recalled their wedding night in New Orleans and the first night they spent alone in this house. Everything had worked out dandy both those times.

What was she doing, anyway?

The Lincoln rolled down the drive at five-thirty, and when she staggered in the back door with a heavy bag in her arms, he rushed to take it.

Unpacking it, she said, "Some things are getting hard to buy. That clerk at Kline's told me that if they didn't have sugar it was because they couldn't keep up with what 'all you new folks' want. He said it like I was being a hog."

"Was it Bobby Hewitt?"

"I don't know one from the other."

"I'll remind him who you are."

A stalk of celery emerged, followed by two potatoes, then a bulky package wrapped in butcher paper.

"Pork chops?"

She smiled. "A guy brings me flowers, I'm thinking of his favorite dish."

He laughed, delighted. He wouldn't ask why she was late. But that tap on the sailor's nose nagged at him. He had too many thoughts about how many men she might've been with other than the father of her illegitimate son. He wanted to pretend they didn't matter. Not knowing anything for certain was a torment but asking was out of bounds. *That* gal, said Bud.

He sat at the table while she pared the potatoes, cut them, dumped them into a saucepan. His stomach growled.

"Is it always that crowded at the station? You girls seemed awfully popular today."

"You get a big rush when the train's in, then it gets quiet."

"Did you know Ethel and Helen are in Mama's bridge club?"

"No." She suspended a chop above a skillet, gave him a look as if suspecting the question was loaded. "They didn't mention it."

"I saw Bud Sinclair at Emerson's today. He's Matty Sinclair's boy, and he's on furlough."

"I met him. He came to pick her up the other day."

Funny he didn't mention meeting Sylvia, thought Georgie. Ugly little snapshot: a leering, uniformed Bud gropes a dunker as Sylvia saucily taps his nose.

"His sis has kind of a reputation."

She lowered one brow at him. "A reputation for what?"

He shrugged, embarrassed. Gossip was beneath him, but he felt compelled to push on with his agonizing inquisition. "Well, they say she's a tease. I'm not saying she is. But old biddies like Ethel and Helen start clucking their tongues when somebody young and pretty gets attention from the boys. Or if they seem to enjoy it too much."

"What's on your mind, Georgie?"

"Aw, nothing. Just, you know—"

"No, I don't."

Miserable, he went into the dining room to retrieve the candy and the perfume from the side buffet. He set them on the kitchen table.

"I got these for you today," he said, sorrowful as a hound. "I wanted to be your Valentine. That's all. So when I went to the station, it looked like you were, well—" Helpless, he shrugged.

"Oh, hon, I was really busy! I'm sorry." She set down her cooking fork, wiped her hands on her apron. "Cummere, you big dope!" The sensation of her warm breasts pressed to his belly made his knees weak. "You are my Valentine!"

He chuckled nervously. "And those fellows down there? You're just being nice, right?"

She leaned away to study his face. "You think I'm too friendly?"

"Aw, *I* don't think so. But those old biddies . . ."

"Georgie, it's sweet to worry about me that way. But I know how to take care of myself." She tugged him close and squirmed against him with an urgency that shot tingling thrills right to his groin. "I love you, Georgie. And you are my Valentine," she said in his ear.

After she'd cleaned the kitchen, it was full dark and they sat in the parlor on the sofa listening to "Fibber McGee & Molly" and the war news with Gabriel Heatter who, though he said as always "there's good news tonight!" had to report that the Japanese had invaded Singapore. Thinking about those fellows out in the Pacific made her weepy, and when Georgie asked what was wrong, she said, "Oh, those brave boys!"

Then it was time. She wore her new burgundy satin robe into the bathroom. He waited in bed for her. Nothing had been spoken, but he figured she knew what he wanted. He hoped she wouldn't come out with her face smeared with cold cream and her hair up in a sleep cap.

She emerged wearing the negligee she'd bought in the shop in the Garden District on their honeymoon. It had a lacy top trimmed in silk ribbon and a long sweeping flow over her hips, the silk so fine it was a little sheer, in an ivory hue that shimmered when it caught the light. She'd said it reminded her of one Jean Harlow wore in *Personal Property* and that she felt special in it, as if her very skin were more expensive. It cost more than she'd earn in a month at the White Blossom, she'd told him.

Boy! he gushed, *You're gorgeous! You look like a movie star!* He was sitting up in their bed. After he'd scanned her up and down while she turned on the oval hooked rug beside the bed to model, he jumped up and doused the lamps.

They cuddled beneath the covers and kissed. He murmured *Boy oh boy!* like a kid who'd been granted his most fervent Christmas wish. He gingerly caressed her breasts with a stroke that suggested they were extremely fragile or extremely dangerous. His breath hitched up a little ragged and his legs got fidgety, so she shifted to lay him between her thighs. *Move up.* She guided him with her fingers, and he began to rock.

Oh honey! Oh I love you so much!

Then he went rigid and groaned *awwnoo* then his arms flailed, an elbow jolted her chin, then dimly he heard her scream as if down the long stone hollow of a well, *Geooorrrorgie!*

He awoke alone in their bed. Sunlight shocked the bedroom like a photographer's white flash. He shut his eyes. He could read the signs in his nerve-ends, his muscles, the bruises and such, and they all said he'd had a fit, but it took a minute to come back. Here, in the bed, last night, while—

"Aww!" he groaned.

She must've changed him. He squinted against the glare and heaved himself up on an elbow. He palmed the sheets. Dry. He sniffed. He ought to get up—supposed to be at work, but—

The Baby Ben read half past ten.

He collapsed back, depleted. Flung an arm across his eyes. So he'd given her the full-bore deal last right in the middle of their lovemaking. For crying out loud! Why couldn't she have been spared that, and *while* he was … .

She'd wiped his ass. Must've been her, because he sure as hell hadn't done it. He pressed his arm to his mouth to stifle a sob. *Take a deep breath, there, Sonny Boy.*

It was only a matter of time. He'd had Eden for a month. She was sure to bolt on him.

Buck up. Be thankful for what you had. It's over.

Cradling his head between his palms, he sat up cautiously on the edge of the bed. He looked about for packed suitcases. On her vanity, her brushes, combs, vials, tubes, and jars were unaware of a change in plans.

The door was ajar. A tinkling, a hinge squeaking, water rushed, then stopped. She was in the kitchen. He sank back against the mattress and drew his eyelids over the starkly insistent furniture, the clamorous light, the laughing mirror on the dresser. Then her lovely alto, rich and lilting, wafted into the bedroom. Singing while she went about her chores. That's reassuring, he thought. Then the words emerged from the lullaby murk. *From coast to coast / in this great na-shun / Each man... has got a class-uh-fuh-cayshun ...* One of those goddamn war songs, the girl left at home pining for her soldier or sailor. Helen Forrest. *They tell me / Pray tell me ... What's yours ...*

His head ached something awful. *I got a guy ... who's really sumpthin' / This man of mine he ain't missin' nothing.*

The Greeks had it right—a little pride will bring you down. Way down. He'd been humiliated by a seizure many times before, but it was especially cruel that this one came after a day feeling proud he could act like a man. Bud's revenge. *Well, Georgie-Porgie, I might not get some off my sis, but heh heh heh I ain't gonna pitch a fit in her bed!*

Even if she wasn't leaving, a dime would get you a dollar that she was sure rueing the day ....

Haven't slept a wink last night / wondering if he'll be all right ... The woman in the song yearned for her man in his absence. Stood at the door looking off into the far beyond, to the Pacific. He was long gone to war. He was a hero. Nothing about him could be disgusting.

The sergeant of Bud's color guard barked an order, startling Georgie into attention. (Had the order been meant for him, he'd have responded late.) The seven spit-shined soldiers lined like the crossbar of a T across the top of the grave snapped audibly to attention and hefted their rifles to port arms. Another order and the rifles were shouldered, then came "Fire!" and the first volley. The sharp crack jolted everyone. The two successive volleys produced no reaction, but Georgie's nose twitched as the smoke from the rounds drifted back over the mourners.

The guard stacked their rifles in a waist-high bristling teepee then filed forward one slow footfall at a time to stand beside the coffin. They removed the flag and folded it, passing it so lugubriously from man to man that it was like watching a team of zombies make a bed.

Inexplicably, Sylvia took his hand, squeezed it once, held it. He turned to her. He got a quick, sorrowful glance. He didn't know how to read this. A sudden *frisson* of horror to think the corpse could be his? An apology?

Minutes ago he'd seen her and Robert talking, and for the thousandth time he'd fought the question of his honor: was it being insulted? Should he make a public display while they were in a tête-à-tête before the whole fucking town? Stomp right up to Robert and, what, slap him with a glove?

It took him right back to the night he'd hadn't pulled the trigger when he had Robert's face at the end of the barrel. Not *couldn't.* Hadn't.

Bud would have.

He was glad he hadn't. Or she wouldn't be by his side squeezing his hand and giving him a look that said *we have something, Georgie.*

But it was hard to show his face about town knowing people knew about them and knowing he had apparently forgiven his wife. The Sap. And just when he'd thought it had died down!—here he was in his fucking *uniform* like a pretend-soldier while she openly made plans to meet the turd whose life he spared and who apparently held Georgie in contempt for not demanding satisfaction for his tarnished honor.

Watching them, he'd hoped they'd break off before he had to acknowledge he was aware of them, and so he'd turned away and counseled himself to breathe slowly and deeply. When he'd impulsively turned back, he saw Sylvia cut off their talk and, scowling, hurry away from Robert about as fast as a woman toe-heeling across soggy sod in pumps could go. If this was a playlet wherein The Unfaithful Wife meets her Former Lover, then the gist of the scene was that they were no longer singing the same tune, and she'd been offended.

Did *that* require a manly response? Send by messenger a *billet* of challenge: *Sir, you have insulted my good wife! I will have satisfaction!*

Bud would have.

In the face of Bud's triumph, Georgie felt like a sheepish supplicant or one of those faceless ordinary cowards in a Greek chorus whose only act is providing useless commentary. A motif like a harmonic overtone had been running through his life, and he hadn't really heard it clearly until now: It was a sense of shame and dishonor and a yearning to discover what he might do, what he could do, to prove to everyone—his family, his wife, the people of Port Farview—that he was worthy of their respect.

Sylvia said, *Don't you think you get some credit for trying?*

With one gloved hand, a soldier raised a bugle to his lips. The mournful triplets of taps sang brassy in the sunlight about their ears. Georgie blinked back tears. He *would* prove one day that he too could be a hero. Sylvia reached for his hand again, gently pressed, and held it. It was as if she were saying: *you can do it, Georgie!* It might not come as easily as it always had to Bud, but the fight to conquer himself eventually might be won.

THIRTY-SEVEN

MARJORIE RODE HOME with her parents and told Robert to pick her up at six. He hoofed it to her house to find Walter waiting at the curb in an old truck. He was dressed in suit pants and a white shirt with black suspenders, to show respect, Robert supposed, though they'd be stevedores in this blue-blazes heat. He had his coat slung over his shoulder.

"So, Walter, looks like we're the stand-by pack mules for ladies in town. Maybe we oughta charge more."

He laughed. "Aw, they nice enough."

"She tell you to wait out here?"

"Umm."

It could've meant yes or no.

"I'll see if she's ready."

He moved through a crowd milling on the porch and let himself into the foyer. To his left, women were carrying dishes from a cluttered dining table into the kitchen beyond. In the parlor on his right Mr. Sinclair stood with two women whose purses hung from their elbow crooks, and Robert stepped forward to offer condolences.

He went down a hall past a couple of closed doors and to one cocked slightly open, showing Marjorie supine on a bed in her stockings, shoes spilled onto the floor. He knocked on the frame.

She sat up and waved him in. She yawned. Her hair was mussed and her makeup smeared.

"Damn my head hurts!" She vised her temples between her thumb and fingers.

"Maybe you oughta rest, forget moving."

"My damn *rent* started today, Robert."

She startled him by jumping up, bounding to the door, and closing it. She sat down on the bed.

"I don't wanna be here."

"But maybe your parents need you."

"They've got *scads* of sympathizers. *Oodles.* Everybody in town's *dyin'* to let us know they're so thrilled to have a dead hero in their own backyard."

"Those people are here for you, too. They know you lost a brother."

"If those people knew the first thing about me, I'd be on my rump outside the city line wearing a tar-and-feather coat. Having a brother killed in the war would just be something else to hold against me. I wouldn't be near good enough to be *his* sister."

"Oh, for God's sake, honey, that's ridiculous."

"Honey? Since when are you so sweet on me?"

He shrugged.

"It's just pity." She lay back. She spread her legs. "So console me."

"Don't be silly."

She started crying with her hands pressed to her face, then she was clenching her teeth and, well, *growling.*

"It's okay," he murmured, patting her knee.

"Oh *fuck you!*" She pounded the bed with her heels like a two-year-old in a tantrum.

She carried on with her sobbing for a while, her breath eased into a regular bellows rhythm, then she sighed. She sat up again. Her face looked as if it belonged to a woman who had just given birth and hadn't enjoyed a second of it. She sniffled, blew her nose on a tissue.

"Are you ready to do the heave-ho on this pitiful shit?"

"Sure. If you wanna."

They silently inventoried the room. Several cardboard cartons labeled with a crayon scrawl—"cloths" and "toys & bks" and "memores"—a tall chest painted green with eight drawers, a scarred kneehole vanity with bubbling veneer and a cracked mirror, a pine student desk.

"This bed was Bud's. Actshully, it was mine then I went to biness school and Bud stole it and wouldn't give it back. I got another one. But I left it in N'awlins. By the time everbody . . ." She shuddered. "It *stunk* to high heaven."

"Is this everything?"

"More in the garage. One day I swear to God I'm gonna have new French Provincial and it's all gonna match and I'll drag all this pitiful shit into the yard and take an axe and a torch to it."

"That hubby a big-time spender?"

"He's a prince. When he gets back we're gonna party till the cows come home."

"We all have postwar dreams, I guess."

"What's yours?"

"A good job, a house, my own car, a family. You know," he added, smiling, "what you have right now."

"Don't make me laugh. You don't know the half of what I got and don't got."

He and Walter carried a dinette set and a Morris chair and an old hassock out of the musty, dirt-floored garage, then from her room they hauled boxes and furniture large and bulky enough that they whacked several paint chips from the doorframes.

She stayed back to bid her folks good-bye, and Walter and he drove to the appropriately named River Street in the lower end of town where the city had left off paving. They rumbled past swampy woods where various kinds of homemade housing peeked through the interstices in the stands of pine: a travel trailer with a plywood addition, a tent, a piano crate covered with a tarpaulin. Smoke from hobo cooking fires curled up through the green darkness of the treetops. In the 1920s, an entrepreneur had a spate of inspiration and had knocked up a string of frame duplexes. You couldn't see the river from the tiny porches because of trees and unkempt brush, but you could smell it: they were downstream from the mills, the shipyard, the fuel depot, the refinery, downstream from where aging septic systems bled their fecal tea into the sluggish water.

Each little Monopoly-house might be stuffed to the rafters with humanity deep in the night, but on this hot, wet Saturday evening everybody had stayed out of doors hoping for a bit of breeze. The grownups lounged on the accommodating surfaces of broken-down vehicles or on chairs dragged outside for the evening. The street was a sandy-rutted playground with screaming children and barking dogs. They drove through a ball game and passed over a hubcap home plate while the players hollered "New meat!"

They parked in the yard of number five and got out. He heard a guitar and fiddle, laughter and hollering, singing, but nothing organized like an ensemble. Down at the lower end of the string where the last house melted in the twilight into the forested swamp, Negroes were in the yard.

"Whites and colored in the same block?" he said to Walter. They each held an end of the green chest and were inching it toward the stoop. A gaggle of snotty-chinned urchins stood gawking in their path—Marjorie's next-doors, it turned out.

"Pore is pore," Walter said around the cigar. "And they's a line, too. Everbody know where Jim Crow lives."

Marjorie had three rooms in the classic shotgun configuration. A tiny front room led into a tiny bedroom that had a tin shower stall and sink and toilet cobbled out of one corner and curtained by an evil-smelling pink sheer showing a wavy brown water line along its hem. Hardly bigger than a closet, the last room had a sink and a gas two-burner hot plate and a wooden icebox.

They were trying to guess where Marjorie might want the unloaded furniture placed when they heard her holler, "Get outta my way, y'all!" to the kids on the stoop. She toed the screen door open and kicked it aside then came barging in on a wave of curses, carrying an apple crate packed with kitchen utensils. She weaved and knocked her shoulder against the wall, and Walter took the box from her.

"Thanks. What a dump!" she said, doing Bette Davis. "Those damn kids better get out from underfoot or I'll stomp 'em like roaches!" She had changed into a cotton house dress, sleeveless and low-yoked, and her arms and breastbone glistened with sweat. "Put that in the kitchen, Walter. Damn, it is *so* damned hot!" she whined. "I bet that box dudin have a bit of ice! I'm thirsty!"

She snatched open the flaps of a carton and pulled out a bottle of gin. "Aha! You want a drink? I've got 7-Up in the car. There's glasses too in a box somewhere."

"I'll pass." He smiled. "Weren't you just griping about a headache?" What he wanted was a cold shower; what he wanted was the solitude to replay his conversation with Sylvia at the cemetery. Had it set him back or inched him forward? He felt sympathy toward Marjorie, but her form of mourning was a bigger strain on his patience than he could muster. He'd served his time.

"Hair of the dog." He caught a fleeting expression—suspicion, resentment, irritation—then she seemed to choke it down. "You're welcome to that 7-Up anyway."

"I could stand a long drink of plain old water."

"Fine. Let's whip it up."

Six steps through the bedroom and they were in the sink-locker, you might say. At the back door Walter looked through the screen and mopped his brow with a big red bandanna. His white shirt showed gray sweat patches under the arms and across his back. He'd rolled his cuffs to his elbows. From a box Marjorie pulled out glasses and set them on a table. She poured one full from the sink's sole faucet and handed it to Robert.

"Walter, you want a drink?" She waggled the gin bottle.

"Don't reckon. Too wahm. 'Preciate the offer, though."

"Oh come *on!*"

"I thank you but it mess up my haid with the heat."

She looked at him. "*Nobody's* gonna drink with me?"

Robert tried to ignore that she seemed on the brink of spontaneous combustion. She seemed to *dare* them to refuse her. He raised his glass and *tinked* it against the bottle she held. "Cheers!"

She snorted and set the bottle on the table. The breakfast set they'd brought hogged most of the available floor space in this cooking cell. She pulled a chair out and sat with her legs crossed and her elbows on the table. He followed her gaze across the sagging, water-stained ceiling. She made a face, wrinkled her nose.

She was about to weep and clenched her teeth. "This is an awful shit hole." She grimaced. "You should of seen the place we had in the Quarter. It was classy. High ceilings and all. That made it cooler, you know. They do that."

He thought *you didn't have to come home and you didn't have to move out of your parents' house.* And she didn't have to live here—didn't she get her husband's allotment?

She uncapped the bottle and gave them a stagey wink. "Here's to y'all. May you git to where you're goin before you slow." She upended the bottle and took a whale of a belt, making a production. Walter tried to swing his grin out of her view, but she caught it.

"You ever see a white girl stinky potted, Walter?"

"Time or two."

"I bet. How about you, Sir Robert Goforth?" She snickered.

"You."

She ignored him. "Come *on!*" she said to Walter. "What, I got leprosy or something you won't take one drink with me? Believe me, Bud was here he would. It's where I learned it. I'm askin' you, one drink. For Bud."

"Tell the truth, Thelma made me give it up. Made me stand up in church and swear to God Almighty."

"You're pullin' my leg! Big strong fella like you? Little bitty thang like her?" She looked at Robert. "What's *your* excuse? Some missy got a hold of your cojones too?"

"All right." He held out his empty glass. The second she started pouring he said, "Ho!" and had to pull the glass away.

"Here's to Bud."

"To Bud," he said. Walter sidled toward the door as if to slip away unnoticed, but Marjorie said, "You too, Walter." She pointed to the water glass he'd set on the table.

"Y'all go on. I'll get them other boxes."

He went out the back door.

"He too good to drink to *my brother*?"

Robert kept quiet.

"Really, can you believe the nerve? The war's about spoilt everything in this damn country."

"To Bud." He held up his glass.

"To my Bud." They clinked and drank. "He was a damn good brother. He watched out for me. Now there's nobody."

"How about that husband?"

She snorted. "He's in Siam or some damn place."

"There's your dad. And me."

"Okay. To you." They drank. "And one more for our baby that's on the way."

She almost caught him there. He put on a poker face. "Cheers to the little tyke!" He tilted the glass again, but it was empty.

"You think I'm kidding? You knocked me up that night you dint have no protection."

"It's about time I was a daddy. This place could be a honeymoon cottage if two love birds live in it. It's cozy as all get-out. You could sew curtains and plant petunias. We could elope and I'd make you an honest woman. But—darn it all!—- you're already married."

"Maybe I'll get a divorce. He might come to an unfortunate end."

"You never told me what branch he's in."

She snickered. "You'd be surprised by things I could tell you about him."

"I'm all ears." He leaned against the sink, poured a splash of water into his glass.

"What if he was colored?" Her mouth was slanted in a mocking challenge, and he couldn't tell if she was kidding.

"Then I'd wonder where you two obtained a marriage license. I understand Louisiana has laws against what they call miscegenation."

"Oh, Sir Robert, you are *such* a damn know-it-all! Who said anything about Lewzee-fucking-anna?"

Walter came back through the rear door. "I got them boxes in the front room yonder."

"*Thank* you, Walter!" She beamed him a saccharine smile. "Such a hep!"

"I need to be going," Robert said to Walter.

"Fine," Walter said. "I be- —"

"Hold on! Y'all *both* can't abandon me! I need hep moving that damn furnichure!"

"Tell us where—"

"I don't know yet! Don't *hound* me!"

"How about we decide?"

"Oh just go *on!* Walter can stay. Can't you, Walter?"

After a sidelong glance at Robert—a plea for help?—Walter nodded.

"Take my car," she said to Robert. "I'm sure *Walter* won't mind bringing me by your place to get it when we're done. *Will* you, Walter?"

If Walter had a wristwatch, he'd have checked it right then. He blotted his brow against his bicep, looked up. Finally he nodded.

"I don't mind walking. The air will clear my head."

"Last thing *I'd* want is clearing my head, but suit yourself. There's a radio in my car—bring it in before you go?"

"Aye-aye."

Robert carried the Philco table model in like a big bag of groceries. The only wall socket was in the front room, so she had him set the radio on the floor beside it. She bent to plug it in. Then she straightened, leaned back with her hands chocked in the small of her back, stretching and yawning; his eyes went to her belly. Could've been just extra pounds from the good life in the Crescent City, but, then again.

A crooner was warbling "My Blue Heaven" out of Houston; she swayed and snapped her fingers, her eyes closed. *Just Molly and me, and Baby makes three . . .*

The irony was too rich.

"Good night, folks!"

"So long, sucker. See ya in the funny papers."

In the smoky dusk, he started up the sandy road for the heart of town. He was glad to get loose—he'd been her companion all day, and he was eager to waste his energy fruitlessly ruminating about Sylvia.

TO PROPERTY OWNERS

who have not yet purchased

WAR DAMAGE INSURANCE

FIRST, let this be understood: that in writing War Damage insurance we are acting in behalf of the Federal Government—as are the agents and brokers of the country through whose offices you can purchase a policy. Consideration of War Damage insurance is urged upon every householder and business man. Its purpose is to protect the property owners of America, and it is to them that this message—this warning—is addressed.

Not whether, but IF...

You own a store in New Hampshire, a farm in Illinois or some furniture located in an apartment in California. *It isn't a question of whether or not there is going to BE a bombing or an invasion. The question is how you would be fixed without any insurance protection IF there WERE one.*

You don't buy fire insurance with the idea that there is going to be a fire, nor windstorm insurance* with the idea that there is going to be a tornado, nor automobile liability insurance with the idea that you are going to injure someone.

Think this over...

If an attack comes, no one can say when or where it will come or what damage will result.

It is a shorter distance by air from Tokio to Salt Lake City than from Tokio to San Diego.

Two incendiary bombs might start a conflagration that your regular fire insurance policy wouldn't cover.

Bombs don't always drop on their objectives. Planes crash wherever they happen to be put out of commission.

Part of the strategy of attack is to do the unexpected. The unexpected might mean a raid on *your* community.

See your Insurance Adviser

The purpose of this advertisement is not to scare you but to tell you that War Damage insurance is available—to warn that losses can not be paid *unless you have an insurance contract.* The way to get such a contract is to see an agent or broker. He will be glad to tell you all about it—will explain how little it costs. (You can insure a $5,000 home for only $5.) After a raid will be too late!

**By the way, ask your agent or broker to tell you about "Extended Coverage."*

Buy War Bonds!

HARTFORD INSURANCE

Hartford Fire Insurance Company • Hartford Accident and Indemnity Company

THE TWO HARTFORDS WRITE PRACTICALLY EVERY FORM OF INSURANCE EXCEPT LIFE

HARTFORD, CONNECTICUT

THIRTY-EIGHT

EACH DAY AFTER Emerson's closed, Mary Kay helped Mrs. Rainey wash soda fountain dishware and utensils, and she restocked the napkin and straw dispensers. Then she helped old Ned sweep, take out the trash, and dust window displays.

Her favorite chore was helping Larry. He walked the aisles to inventory shelves, and she'd follow, writing on a pad as he called out reorders for cod liver oil or Noxzema or Woodbury cream, Feen-A-Mint, cough drops, or playing cards. He'd be wearing his pharmacist's white smock. She felt like a nurse.

Wednesdays they closed at six, and the Wednesday before Bud Sinclair's funeral was no different except that Larry sent Mrs. Rainey home at five, leaving Mary Kay to clean the soda fountain alone.

Ned said, "Be seein' you tomorrow," as he left around seven. The steamy July daylight was thick despite the hour, and a hot amber glow suffused the street outside. Larry relocked the door and as always left the key inserted in the cylinder. She was drying tulip-shaped soda glasses and setting them upside down on a towel before shelving them. Kids from her school strolled by on their way to the picture show, she guessed, and she stifled a pang of loneliness with this thought: *she* was no frivolous child wasting a summer's night while our boys dodged bullets or shivered sleepless under ponchos in the rain. One girl looked in at her.

She felt on display, as if she and Larry were actors, and passers-by saw a play in progress. The theme was Hard Work Is Your Patriotic Duty.

Larry swung his slim hips onto a stool opposite her. He yawned, stretched, shot the cuffs of his white smock.

"Man, these long days are tough!"

"Can I get you something, sir?"

"A martini?"

She laughed. "Does it take milk and chocolate syrup?"

"No. There's a drink like that, though. It has vodka."

"Oh yack! That sounds urpy!"

He laughed. "How about a Coke with crushed ice and a cherry?"

"Coming right up."

"Let me buy you one, too, missy."

She played professional bartender. She handled two clean glasses with a towel, inspected them for spots, packed them with crushed ice—luckily some was left—poured the Coke, and added stemmed maraschino cherries.

She left hers on the counter while putting away the glasses. He drank his meditatively. When he raised the glass, his cuff fell to expose his broad, hairless wrist. He had gentlemanly hands like a virtuoso pianist's, she thought. Unlike Donnie, Larry was light-skinned and fair-haired and the backs of his fingers had almost invisible thatches of blondish down.

He got up and turned off the lights. The daylight saved through the governmental manipulation of clocks had been spent, and the sky had turned a deep orange. Enough glowed through the recessed entry to illuminate the front of the store, though the pharmacy was lost in murk.

He slid back onto the stool. "Come sit like a customer, drink your drink. Let's sit and contemplate the pleasures of a summer's evening."

Contemplate the pleasures of a summer's evening. Larry could sound educated without sounding prissy, and she liked that. Also, though she didn't know where he was from, he didn't sound Southern, and she liked that, too. They were fellow outsiders, and she enjoyed his jokes about his wife's family, who claimed a kinship to a doomed defender of the Alamo.

She took the next stool closer to the windows. She poked a straw in her drink and sucked up half the liquid. More kids went by, hurrying. Probably the movie was about to start. She recognized Birdie Thompson from her Texas history class. She was wearing two-toned oxfords, white bobby sox, and a plaid jitterbug skirt.

Mary Kay involuntarily snorted, and Larry said, as if reading her mind, "You ought to be out with them."

"They're dopes."

"I worry about you working like an old maid and not taking advantage of your youth and beauty. It goes by quickly, I warn you."

"What does—youth or beauty?"

"Sweetheart, they're one and the same." He leaned close and inhaled deeply. "You smell like—"

"*Shalimar.* Powder. It was a box that broke. You said—"

"Sure! I didn't mean you shouldn't have. I was going to say you smell like a grown woman."

She was allowed a discount or got damaged things free. She realized she'd grown cavalier about helping herself without permission, though he clearly wasn't reproaching her.

"Look at that young buck."

Two boys with a girl between passed by. The near-side boy wore pegged pants and his dark hair gleamed with Vitalis. "That's Leroy Higgins. His mother teaches French."

"Oh. Louise. I didn't recognize him he's so dandified."

"He thinks the girl's interested in him and not in the other Palooka—I forget his name, but *he's* the one with the car. He parks at school where everybody can see it coming out."

"It's Bill Pritchard's boy, has eczema couple times a year. He came in late one day and hung around the magazine rack waiting for everybody to leave, then he came back to the pharmacy and started hemming and hawing, and finally he asked me if I had any 'French safes.' I thought Good Lord, what veteran of the First World War did he learn *that* from? But I said, just as innocent as a lamb, 'safes? French safes? Have you tried John's Hardware?'"

She laughed, uncertainly, guessing he meant condoms. Having a man tell her an off-color story both embarrassed and thrilled her. But, after all, it was *occupational*—there were no vulgar words—a joke a pharmacist's helper could appreciate where others might not. Being Larry's chosen audience made her feel very adult.

They exchanged remarks about people who went by. Larry identified them by their prescriptions and ailments. She was snotty about their attire. Where before she had felt on display, now the sidewalk was the stage and the passersby, fools in a comedy.

"You hungry? Let's go to the Holiday and get a burger."

"Won't Mrs. Emerson expect you for dinner?"

"Her sister's here visiting from Fort Smith. I'm pretty sure they went out to Julia's folks' farm, so I'm batching it."

Sylvia and Georgie would've already eaten, and on Wednesday and Saturday nights when she worked late, she made do by rummaging in the icebox.

"Okay. I need to freshen up."

"Meetcha in my office."

She went into the darkened, barny space in back where her Victory Girls troop had built their War Bonds float. A bathroom with a toilet and sink for employees had been fashioned with partitions and a ceiling lower than the surrounding interior. In it, she slipped off her work apron and dabbed with a damp washcloth at a tear of chocolate syrup on the lapel of her blue cotton blouse. The washcloth was sour with mildew, so she splashed water on her face with her hands and dried with the one clean corner left on the communal towel. She kept a hair brush in the medicine chest; she undid the red ribbons that tied her braids and brushed out her shoulder-length page boy.

Looking back years later, she recognized the undercurrent present all along. The "drinks," his comment about "batching it," the joke about the French safes, going out to "dinner," his plaintive remarks about losing one's youth. He'd been courting her. And she'd felt courted, but as a *protégée.*

She bubbled with a subdued glow—the pleasure of *being chosen.* The prospect of being on his arm out in public, if only to a diner for the well-earned reward of labor, seemed delicious yet innocent. She *wanted* to be seen with him. Surely it wouldn't make tongues wag as Sylvia claimed. Sylvia's behavior had provoked gossip, but if a person were innocent the talk would only *bounce off.* To be seen with him would be like being seen in her Victory Girls uniform gathering scrap. She belonged; she was approved of, sought-after, even.

He was seated at his desk with only the banker's lamp illuminating the small room where he did the books. He rolled his chair back a little using his heels. He still had on his white medical smock. A small foil-covered box on the desk gleamed under the light. He smiled.

"C'mere. Wanna show you something."

He swiveled so that when he took her wrist and tugged on it, she wound up sidesaddle on his knees facing the desk. His arm went around her waist. He tapped the box with a long index finger.

"Look at this."

She picked it up and lifted the lid. Over a pillow of cotton lay a silver charm bracelet with painted metal hearts and teddy bears.

"You like it?"

She guessed it was a present but didn't want to be presumptuous. She held it up draped from her fingertips.

"It's very darling." Her mother sometimes used that word, and employing it, she felt grown up.

"Try it on." Before she could pretend to be puzzled, he took it from her and fit it around her wrist. "Looks good on you. I knew it would. It's why I bought it for you."

"For me?" She blushed. "Aw, gee, Larry."

"For working so hard when you should be playing with kids your own age." His lips were curled in a little ironic smile.

"Thanks!" she gushed, and without thinking, leaned into him, slung the braceleted arm around his neck and hugged him. His arm went around her shoulder, his free hand glided across the front of her waist, and he hugged her back. "Mmm, you smell good, kiddo! That *Shalimar* suits you!"

She sank into a daze of adoration, loving the warm secure feeling of being like a child in his lap. Like a daughter. This was how it would feel to be close and friendly with a dad who thought you were someone special.

"Mmm, I could eat you up!" he murmured in a clowning way. He kissed her neck. That surprised her a little. She thought *this wouldn't look right* to Julia Emerson if she walked in. But it was just horse-play. He hugged her tighter, hooking her hips with his arm and pulling her deeper into his lap. The hand on her waist dropped listlessly onto her thigh, somehow eased under her skirt, then after a moment, fingers dug under her briefs.

She bolted up.

"Hey!"

"I'm sorry, hon! Is something wrong?"

He sounded so *surprised* she hardly knew how to answer. Maybe she'd been mistaken, just jumpy. Could be he didn't realize where his hand was. He wouldn't try to touch her *there*, he wasn't that kind of man, not like Clyde, so it was best to pretend she didn't notice his mistake.

"Could we go eat now?"

"Don't you like your bracelet?"

She leaned against the desk, legs quivering. She held her wrist to the light.

"Yes. It's adorable. Thank you," she said, though with less enthusiasm. She was afraid of what gratitude could provoke.

They went for the burgers, but she couldn't eat. His appetite was hearty, though, and he spoke to her solicitously, as if she were recuperating. *Sure you can't eat something, Mary Kay? It's on me. You worked awfully hard! Come on, honey, how about some French fries?*

She didn't wish to be seen. She hung in a strange suspension. She felt troubled and uncertain as to how to act. She stayed quiet while Larry tossed jokes and tidbits of news at other customers, gassing on about the war, the price of meat and coffee, the weather. He had blue-green eyes behind rimless spectacles like those of a doctor or teacher, and nice thin lips that hadn't until now looked threatening. She scanned his features looking for the man she'd known or thought she knew. She was frightened by his display of devotion and kept the hand with the bracelet in her lap. She felt ashamed but didn't know why. She shouldn't, should she? He was a pharmacist. That was like a doctor, and they often did unusual things to people's bodies, examined them, probed them.

Soon as she arrived home Sylvia spotted the bracelet as if it were as conspicuous as Hester's A.

"That's cute. Where'd you get that, hon?"

"Work."

"Get a discount?"

She considered telling Sylvia, though she wasn't exactly sure what happened, if anything. When her mom's boyfriend Clyde jammed his tongue in her mouth, that was crystal clear. But Larry wasn't anything like him.

For a day or so she had a knot in her stomach. She lay awake wondering if what Sylvia warned her against was about to happen and if Mary Kay should tell her. But that would make it incontrovertibly actual, and she couldn't then deny it to Sylvia if she needed. Malicious talk like that harmed innocent people, and she couldn't do that to such a good friend. Besides, if it *was* true, they could no longer be friends.

She'd no longer have a job. Since Georgie had gotten her this one, she was obligated to him, and it would be horrendously embarrassing to reveal she gave it up because of something like *that.*

She'd never felt so alone. The truth of her life fell on her like earth thrown into a grave: no one cared enough about her to protect her. The friend who was Larry might have, and now he certainly spoke to her as if he cherished her, but what happened so frightened her she needed *him* to protect her from it. She hoped to think it away, whittle on it, reason off its raw edges until she'd reduced it to a harmless state. She was just plain wrong about where his hand had been or that he was aware of it himself.

If it was *possible* he was aware, did she invite it? Sometimes she'd been very affectionate and friendly, and she'd joke-punch his shoulder, or if he was seated at a booth or at his desk she might slip up behind him and ruffle his hair or put her hands over his eyes, or grab him around the neck like a wrestler.

Had he misunderstood those things?

After Wednesday night, she tried to keep as much distance between them as humanly possible. Not because she'd *decided* he'd done something wrong, but because she couldn't decide. The torment rising from the experience constituted such a powerful toxin that she needed to nurse herself into equanimity and couldn't risk re-infecting herself before she'd found an antidote. If Larry entered the fountain corral as if he meant to pass behind her, she scooted out by the opposite end. She wouldn't go into the back unless he was occupied with a customer at the pharmacy counter.

On the day of Bud Sinclair's funeral, they didn't open until three, and that put them behind. She had hoped not to be last out the door. She hurried through her chores but noted with dismay that Mrs. Rainey and Miss Vickers and Old Ned managed to get away before she could. Since the store was closed, the front door had to be unlocked and relocked with each departure, so if she was last, she had to let Larry know so he could lock after her.

When she finished, Larry was busy in the back, and she hoped she could just yell, "I'm going!" and be out the door before he could stop her. She whipped off her apron and was draping it over a counter stool to avoid hanging it in the bathroom when he came to the front.

"I was just leaving," she said.

"I'll see you out, madam."

Her heart beat wildly and her hands were slick. She stood beside the front door itching to go through it. Though he still had on his smock, she knew he'd take it home to be laundered. Almost frantic with anxiety, she watched him set his black lunch pail down on the counter, check the register, straighten a display of headache powders, performing little departure rituals that previously seemed endearing but at this moment seemed sinister, as if their ulterior purpose was to toy with her.

"Everything look right to you?"

"Yes."

He turned out the store lights. The key was in the lock. She pressed her shoulder to the glass and wondered if they could be seen from the street. He came up beside her. She knew the ritual: he'd unlock the door, slip the key out and tuck it out of sight under the carpet in the display window, then, once outside, he'd use a key from the ring that held those to his house and car to lock the door.

They stood side by side in the dim light from the waning dusk. She waited for his hand to rise to the key that protruded from the lock. It always looked incomplete or useless that way—what good is a lock that has a key inserted in it?—but also *ready* for service, as if it had gone part of the way toward doing its duty on its own. It could lock or unlock. Once Larry had the key in hand, he could easily slip it out instead of using it to unlatch the bolt.

"Mary Kay, is everything all right?"

"Yeah, sure." She was afraid he'd ask why she hadn't worn the bracelet since that night.

"You've seemed so distant. Are you worried about something?"

She looked into the street. *Open the damn door!* It crossed her mind to mention the funeral, but she heard herself say, "No. Well, my mom, she hasn't been well."

"I'm sorry to hear that. Anything I could send her?"

"No. She's got a pharmacy. I mean, no, she doesn't need anything."

Still he wouldn't open the door.

"Say, before we go for the night, maybe I oughta show you something I've been working on." He ducked his head toward the dark office.

"I gotta go!" She sounded panicky, and his eyebrows lifted. "Sylvia's waiting for me."

The instant she told that lie she remembered Sylvia told her to watch out.

"She warned me!" she blurted out. Tears welled up. Her jaw quivered.

"Warned you?"

"About … being late and all."

"Well, honey, you seem so upset! Anything I can do?"

She violently shook her head and stared at the floor. She was trembling, and when he reached for her, she flinched and took two stumbling steps backward.

"Aw honey," he crooned. "Is this about what happened the other night?"

"Please open the door!"

"I will. But talk to me first. Are you upset because we were so, so intimate?"

She nodded.

"I wish you wouldn't be! You are so sweet! I think you're so precious! I don't mean anything by what I do. You're so very special to me. I just get carried away by my feelings sometimes. Doesn't that happen to you? You were sitting on my lap, and then you hugged me. I was just overwhelmed. And I thought because of how close we were that you cared for me, too."

"Sure! As a friend."

"You're not going to stay upset, are you?"

"Guess not," she said in the voice of an injured child, hoping he'd reach up and twist that damned key to the left and slip it out. Then she could dash through the door and toss a "See you Monday!" over her shoulder as if all her discomfort had been erased by those sugary words.

"Well, can't we—" he chuckled—"shake on it, maybe have a hug?"

She nodded; he skipped the shake and looped her into his arms and despite her stiffening he embraced her so tightly her face was crushed in his chest. His hand slid over her hip and between her legs then away so quickly she couldn't protest; he leaned down, pecked her cheek, and she knew that if she didn't struggle he'd try to kiss her mouth.

She pushed against him, so he released her.

"There!" He had a disturbing look in his eyes. "All friends again!"

She walked home in a daze, and when there she hardly knew what to do with herself: being alone made her think too much, but being with

Georgie or Sylvia made her afraid she'd say something that would arouse their suspicions.

She sat in the kitchen absently leafing through a magazine, half in a trance, yearning for somebody to wonder what in the world is wrong with this child.

THIRTY-NINE

Hours after they'd been home from the funeral, Georgie whiffed smoke. He said, "Somethin's burning" to Mary Kay. She was leafing through a *Life* and drinking a Grapette. The radio was playing a program from the cafeteria of the Magnolia plant—a band composed of employees.

Everybody had a burn barrel, and when people had time to keep an eye on them, the barrels smoked and smoldered. But that odor had a tang of wet garbage scorching and the hot light smell of flaming cardboard. This stench was more woody, like when you set an iron down on a plank or like the smoke from a fireplace. Since it was so hot and humid, he doubted anybody had a blaze in their hearth.

"I think I should check," he said to let Mary Kay know he was in charge. Her face turned up slowly from the magazine as if her attention had been on a long ocean cruise and hadn't quite reached the dock.

He strode to the back stoop and sniffed. Evening had come, though a faint glow that could be ambient light from the city or dregs of a sunset oozed through a haze of chemical fog. Billie bounded up from her post under the garage staircase and stuck her muzzle in his crotch, and he caressed the yellow hound's silky ears. She whined. She wanted to be taken for a walk. The property was fenced only along the back, so she was free to roam like J.J. and Buster were, but she rarely left the lot without a human. He'd fed them already; J.J. and Buster were doubtless out crapping in a neighbor's flower bed, and Georgie would probably hear about it.

Billie sneezed. Georgie inhaled hard and deep, testing the air. The smell hung in the air like an olfactory fog, stronger now and tinged with a chemical taint or maybe kerosene or rubber. Maybe newspapers in a garage caught fire or an ember from a barrel fell to the grass.

With Billie at his heels happily (and incorrectly) presuming they were embarking upon a stroll, Georgie went through the gate into the alley. Nothing seemed amiss up and down the narrow rutted lane, only the usual prowling cats, a brace of ambling mutts (not his) down near the mouth where the alley intersected Pine. A phone rang twice somewhere. Two backyards down, a badminton racket struck a shuttlecock with a muted *tunk*.

As he peered toward the lighted street, two cars sped by toward downtown, honking at one another, it seemed. Then two more. Kids, most likely. Hot-rodding. Wasting gasoline. He heard more honking elsewhere in the distance.

He had to coax Billie back through the gate. Mary Kay came down the back stairs calling for him. When she spotted him, she hurried into the yard. She put her hands on her hips like a coach.

"Georgie, the radio is saying stuff."

"What?"

She beckoned and vanished into the house. He scurried up behind her and down the hall into the kitchen. Fred Clark the news man was talking on the radio, but Georgie said, "What's up?"

Sylvia was at the sink lighting a cigarette with a kitchen match. "They stopped the program a minute ago to say that some kind of ruckus is going on downtown. It's about a Negro and a white woman. They're telling people to stay away from the River Street area and Jones Street because they're looking for a suspect."

"They know who it is?"

"Maybe. The suspect was driving a truck registered to Walter."

"The woman's in the hospital," said Mary Kay.

"Maybe he loaned it out."

Sylvia nodded.

He called the Cloud Café on Jones Street and it rang several times before a male answered "Yeah?" rather than the customary "Cloud

Café." In the background were shouts and car honks. "That you, Marcus?" asked the voice. "You gotta—"

"Is this the Cloud Café?"

"What? Uh. . .yeah. We not open. We getting outta here."

"Wait. Is Thelma there?"

"Thelma? She gone."

He could sense the speaker was about to cut him off. "Is this Louis? This is Georgie, Georgie Karacek."

"Aw, uh. Yes, Mistah Georgie?"

"I'm looking for Walter."

"You and everbody else, suh."

"Where—"

"Excuse me, suh, but people are goin' wild and I gotta get home to my famly."

The line went dead. Georgie set the receiver into the cradle and took in several deep breaths. The burning smell. The racing cars. This kind of rumor—*something about a Negro and a white woman*—was bad enough in normal times, but add the tension since the war started . . .

Back in the kitchen, he announced, "I'm goin' to Walter's."

"What did you find out?"

"Walter may be in trouble."

"We better leave this to the police, Georgie."

"Surely you don't want me to do *nothing*."

"No. Of course not. I'm just . . ." She leaned over to stub out a cigarette in the ashtray on the table. "Never mind." She shook her head.

He walked out of the kitchen, and Sylvia was right on his heels.

"What will you do?"

"I don't know. I need to talk to him. Maybe he needs food, I don't know. Money, whatever somebody needs who's lying low or planning to run, I guess."

"I'm not sure that's a good idea. You know for sure he didn't do something? I mean, we don't, do we?"

"Look, this all goes *waaay* back."

"Can't you let the police take care of this?"

"You've gotta be kidding, Sylvia! The *police?*"

He plucked the Chevy's keys from the tray on his dresser top.

"Well, there is a thing called aiding and abetting."

"I can't aid and abet 'cause I don't know he's done anything."

Sylvia raised one hand to swipe at her brow, closing her eyes momentarily, sighing.

"I need to go with you, Georgie. I'm afraid for you to drive under such nerve-wracking conditions. I don't want you to wind up in a ditch. Surely you don't owe Walter your life."

"Oh yeah? Don't worry. I'll be fine. I want you and Mary Kay to lock up down here and go upstairs. Take the shotgun."

"Surely you don't think. . ."

"Better safe than sorry."

The scene from the past played in his head even as he tried to shake it off—men running by in the street brandishing torches, Papa sending them all upstairs to Marianne's room, and Mama clutching the butcher knife for hours while they waited.

She looked balky. "I might talk Walter into giving himself up, let the police take care of it," he added, though he'd rot in hell before even *suggesting* surrender, given their history. "That way, people would think..." He shrugged. "You know."

"Promise you'll be careful? You won't take any unnecessary chances?"

"Sure." He smiled. He billowed inside, expanding to fit the role suddenly cast upon him—man with a dangerous mission. "I'll call soon as I can."

He picked up the half loaf of bread from the counter, swept up a peanut butter jar and tucked it under his arm, and went to the garage, fending off both J.J. and Billie as they leaped for the bread. He set the loaf and the jar on the roof while he fingered the keys in the murk to find the one that fit the ignition.

His breath felt ragged in his chest and he was minutely trembling from anxiety. He didn't think these were prelude to a seizure, but . . .

He turned the key, the engine caught, he backed out of the drive; when he reached the street he could see people standing in their yards looking off toward downtown. He turned onto Pine heading toward the port. Traffic was heavy coming his way, drivers honking and waving people back. His heart stumbled then whacked in his chest; the wheel was slick from his hands and he had to grip it so firmly his fingers ached. Other cars moved in his direction but most were laden with white male passengers brandishing axe handles and baseball bats out the windows.

Moments later he turned onto Main, the boulevard running through downtown to the river and the commercial landing, and then he saw the glow over the rooftops in the Negro business district. The fire was near or at where the Cloud Café, the Dew Drop Inn, and the Royal cleaners stood. The smell flooded through the car—powerful, acrid, a roiling odor-stew of brick and box, timber and tar, wiring and stuffing, cloth and paint and wax, beams and rafters and shingles. His headlights fuzzed in the fog of smoke drifting across the thoroughfare; the smoke gingerly boosted bits of winking tinder and papery shards of char. Far down the street, a crowd milled, and shouts rose like an alarm.

Georgie pulled to the curb. Two men carrying hanks of lumber trotted by the car heading in. Georgie leaned out his window. "What's going on?"

"Niggers!" yelled one over his shoulder.

It was aural shorthand. It meant "they" were "out of hand" and had done something these crackers deemed worthy of punishment. Maybe Walter and his supposed offense were part of a larger uprising?

The men ran on. The courthouse and jail were scarcely a half block beyond the intersection where the crowd surged along the avenue heading south, and, beyond that lay the Negro residential district that had been set ablaze by white townsmen in 1919—provoked in part by Walter's uncle Samuel. Damnation! These Jenkinses will not be beaten down, he thought. And once again the Karaceks are in the middle of it!

No point going to the café now. He could charge straight through that mob and race through those blocks to Walter's house or he could go around and hope to avoid the rioting. He swallowed. Walter might be down there now getting thrashed or worse, but he also might be hiding in his own house. In any case, if Georgie had anything to do with it, Walter was going to slip out of this noose.

His hands shook. Now he was obligated by the sins of his own and his family's past to step in and face down people who had no respect for him and took him for hardly more than a drooling oaf. Now he couldn't *volunteer*, he was stuck with the task like someone who'd drawn the black bean, and once it seemed beyond his volition, it was so frightening he found his jaw clenched tight as a vise and his calf shook like jelly when he pressed the clutch to get the car into reverse.

The gears ground. He cursed. He took a side street that ran parallel to the river but lay on the outskirts of the business district. He zoomed by a burning auto pushed onto the sidewalk, and behind it, windows of a Negro store showed jagged holes where stones had shattered the glass.

He stepped on the gas and saw figures moving about inside the stores' dim interiors. Looters, must be.

He ran a red light even with traffic approaching from his left, got honked at, heard tires squeal, worried it might be a police car, but pushed the battered Chevy up to fifty, soon sailing through quiet streets where the houses were eerily dark for a Saturday night, as if everybody had turned off their lights and crawled under their beds.

His pulse clicked down a notch or two now as he headed away from the rioting. He was free of that mess, at least. But every foot closer to Walter was another foot probed into the heart of this inferno.

Surely you don't owe Walter your life. Sylvia had a short memory, or else getting hauled out of the river like a drowning cat didn't count for much in her book. Beyond whatever was between Walter and him as boyhood pals, there was the other thing—he was a Karacek and Walter a Jenkins so there was no way to *get free of that mess* because they *were* the mess.

This town! *Goddamn you, Papa!*

FORTY

HE REACHED HIS room so exhausted by the five-mile walk from Marjorie's and the long day that sleep cold-cocked him before he could shrug off his clothes. A horrendous pounding rattled the bed frame; he stumbled up not knowing if ten minutes or ten hours had passed, and he opened the door before he was fully awake.

At the police station a tornado swirled around him, with hollering, ringing phones, shouted orders, whistles, sirens, squealing tires, doors banged shut. He had a headache, but he was cold sober, and while answering questions he drank six cups of coffee. He'd done nothing and had nothing to hide. They told him Marjorie said she caught Walter stealing her wallet, they fought, and he raped her. She'd staggered about in the street, bruised, her clothing torn, then shipyard workers found her and took her to the Hotel Dieu. They'd rushed to the Penn shipyard to spread the news. Hospital staff had called the police.

His head reeled. The story was bizarre. He told the police everything from loading at her parents' house to bringing in the radio. How much gin had he drunk? "Couple snorts." How about her? "About the same," he hedged. And that nigger? "None." How much did she say she'd pay? "Nothing for me—it was between friends, and I don't know about him."

How did Jenkins act? How was she acting? He hardly knew what to say, though considering the characterizations they later released to the public, he knew they looked to blame Walter.

He said, "Look, this is a surprise. I sure wouldn't have guessed anything like that would happen. Walter was moving furniture and was the soul of civility, and Marjorie was just trying to get this done. She was pretty broken up about her brother."

A man in a rumpled linen suit and a straw boater—he wore a bow-tie so Robert guessed he wasn't a local—said he knew that Marjorie and he worked at Magnolia and wondered if Walter ever asked about the layout of the refinery or the operations, who did what where.

Robert laughed. "He's a native. I'd say he knows more about it already than I do."

"He said that?"

"Oh no. I mean he wouldn't need to ask me."

"He ever talk about unions there?"

"No."

"Did he ever talk about what he did in Florida?"

"Apparently not, since I have no idea what he did."

Now this fellow handed him a look—*we can put you in our book, too.* "He never said anything that called his patriotism into question?"

"Like what?"

"Oh, like who needs Nazis when you've got the KKK, that sort of thing."

He had to smile. "No."

"Something hit your funny bone?"

"No. He's never said anything remotely seditious. Unless you count griping about Daylight Savings Time. Will that get a fellow in Dutch with Hoover?"

They released him, but the bureau's man was making notes. In '33, when Robert was in high school, his dad got laid off from the ceramics factory and the town shut down the branch library where his mom worked part-time. They slipped behind on the rent. One day he came home from school and their furniture was piled on the curb. His mother was sitting at the kitchen table, on the street, bawling. The landlord had sent Pinkertons armed with billy clubs and a court order. His dad went looking for the landlord, but he wouldn't answer the knock. Robert was no John Dillinger, and he knew they needed men in blue. But the Red-hunters, Pinkertons, and union-busting constables who played toady for powers-that-be, they could fuck themselves. He was willing to cooperate to his utmost with local constabulary, but the idea that Walter might spy for a foreign nation would be laughable if it wasn't so dangerous.

The uproar was a huge bonfire sparked in that squalid shotgun shack. Despite how cool he'd seemed giving his statement, he was alarmed. Marjorie was at the hospital and Walter was on the lam. Since he'd been mixed up in it involuntarily, somebody owed him the straight story. He seriously doubted she'd given the police the whole truth and nothing but the truth.

The hospital lay six blocks south, and fortunately the melee of rioting shipyard workers and lounge jockeys who joined them had buzzed off to the west like a bee swarm. Along this main thoroughfare, state militiamen stood at the curb and formed in the cross streets to block unofficial vehicles. They were smoking and bantering as if this were a weekend drill. He strolled along whistling and nobody minded him.

At the hospital, he tipped the elevator operator a dime to learn they were keeping her on the fourth floor, and when he stepped into that corridor, a portly law man was speaking to a doctor outside a door. Another officer lounged in a chair with a magazine. The doc left, the sheriff spoke to the deputy, who set his *Field & Stream* with the cover's moose face down on the floor beside his hat, then he left with the sheriff.

They'd return, he guessed, so he was quick to slip into Marjorie's room. She was lying under a sheet. The sash windows were open, and distant shouts and a hint of acrid smoke tainted the air. A table fan went to and fro. Her eyes were closed.

"Marjorie," he whispered, and she came awake. Her pupils were dilated, and she smiled weakly. Her cheek was rounded and red, and she had a bandage high on her forehead.

"What the heck happened to you?"

"Tripped." She gently pressed the bandage with her fingertips. "I think. I was loaded." She blew out a long breath and licked her lips. Her focus was fixed to a point a foot over her head. It made her cross-eyed. "I gotta stay away from gin. I got the worse fucking headache. They gave me a shot. Knocked me out."

"They're saying you said Walter did something to you."

She frowned. "I tripped. I—" She scrunched up her face, wincing. "I got myself in a hell of a pickle here, Bobby."

"How's that?" Nobody but insurance and encyclopedia salesmen called him that, not even his mother.

"Well—" She squinted at him. She was rising into full awareness. "You got to promise to keep it to yourself."

"Okay."

"You remember I said I was married."

"Yeah."

"And you never believed me."

"No. So are you?"

She snorted. "Hell no. But a fellow in N'awlins knocked me up sure as shootin'."

"He know that?"

"Wouldn't care if he did."

"How long you known?"

"Why I came back."

"For a lot of girls that'd be good reason to stay away."

"You know what they say—home is where they have to take you in when you gotta go there. I was gonna take care of the problem before it got to this."

"You know somebody?"

"Supposed to be a doctor in Orange did it on the sly. But it didn't pan out."

"You'd think New Orleans would be a good place to find that."

"Maybe. But I was really scared."

"*You* were?"

She nodded. "Thing is, it gets worse."

"How so?"

"Fellow who did *this*," she softly patted her abdomen, "is colored."

Now he *was* surprised.

She pressed her fingertips to her eyes, and her shoulders trembled. "Oh, it just gets worse and worse! I went and fell for him. And he just—" Her eyes opened wide and she glared—"He threw me out like trash! Can you believe he had the *gall!*"

He said, "Mmm."

"Don't be thinking he's a common field nigger! He's *handsome.* High yellow. He's part French and kinda dandified. From one of those islands, you know. Sweet talker. He played the piano in this club we went to in the Quarter, so his hands were … you know, manicured, nails better shape than mine most of the time. He seemed like, uh, well, a *foreign gentleman* to me, an artist. I've never known a colored man like that, besides Elrod Johnson the undertaker and all the preachers and a few doctors, but they're just uppity, not really *cultured* like Ernest." She scoffed. "Ernest. Not Ernie. He'd get snippety about it. He really put on airs like he's a prince of wherever he claims to be from, which I don't put no stock in now for sure. Just like I know all the *junk* he said to me was just a *pack of fucking lies!*"

Her fists clenched and unclenched.

"Well, you're not the first girl hoodwinked by a rascal."

"He never meant a *single word!* He just wanted to get into a white girl's panties. I don't know who I'm madder at—him for fooling me or me for being fooled."

"I know how you feel."

"I doubt that! When Lady Ascot booted your butt she didn't leave you with a pickaninny in your belly."

"Okay. You win. Nobody knows de trouble you've seen."

"You said it, buster."

Prodding her ire restored Marjorie to her combative self. She seemed more alert now.

"But what about Walter?"

"Oh, shit, I don't know! I was really drunk."

"The police told me you said he tried to steal your wallet."

She shook her head. "I was scared shitless when they talked to me."

"It's not true?"

"I swear to God I can't remember. I was *that* damn drunk. I gotta stay away from gin."

"But do you *think* he hit you?"

"Oh, no. I was runnin' through the house and tripped and slammed my damn face right on the fucking floor. They must of got that all mixed up!"

"Why were you running?"

She closed her eyes, those woolly brows crinkled, as if to see images on the backs of her eyelids. "I was trying to catch them damn kids that was spying on us."

"Did you tell the police that Walter had sex with you against your will?"

He was looking at the dim orange glow of the fires over the rooftops, hearing the sirens, thinking of how this destruction resulted from one drunken female's confused account of an experience that she couldn't say for certain had occurred.

"Did they say I said that?"

"Yes. And you signed a statement." Possibly she'd had a black-out.

"I remember the oddest thing. I know I was drunk and was weepy and sad, and I was glad he was there. We've been kind of friends and enemies all our lives. But things were different, too, because of Ernest. I feel like an outlaw, like I don't really belong. I ast him to be my friend and said I was sorry I'd been such a bitch all my life. And I meant it."

"Did he ... *take advantage* of that?"

"I dunno. I told him about Ernest. Next thing I knew I was half-nekkid and them damn kids were at my window hollering and laughing, and I looked down and saw my dress up, and I just felt ... *confused.*"

Her story *confused* him. "You mean you passed out and he did something? And those kids saw it?"

"I don't know. I guess so. I was real drunk. I can't drink that damn gin any more."

"Marjorie, this doesn't sound like the same story you told the police."

"Like I said, I was scared shitless."

"What were *you* scared of?" All over town, Negro householders were cringing under their tables and beds as white mobs blitzkrieged through their neighborhoods.

"Somebody would think I'd *ast* for it. They say that about women like me."

"Not when there's a Negro involved. I don't think they can allow themselves to believe that."

He wanted to grab her head and force her to look out the window. He said, "Are you gonna tell them different? Your statement says he raped you."

She sighed. "Maybe. If they catch him."

"Well, I hope for his sake you do, Marjorie! Because they might lynch him before you can speak up."

She didn't answer. She closed her eyes. Robert could tell the police he had good reason to believe she was lying. But recanting her own testimony would go the furthest toward stopping this madness.

"You hear me?"

"I'm tired. I'm gonna ring for the nurse. My mama's supposed to be on the way, and I don't wanna see her."

"Okay. But will you think about it?"

She was silent a moment. He got the impression that right here and now would be all the thinking she'd do.

"What I'm worried about and what everbody else is worried about, they're not the same, Robert. Me, I'm thinkin' that when this little black bastard pops out, everbody'll think they know where it came from."

FORTY-ONE

Georgie maneuvered the Chevy through debris on the last paved street before turning down the sandy lane that ran before the homes of Negroes. People were huddled, standing, on their porches, while others scurried to and fro loading vehicles with bundles and boxes. Car doors slammed, shouts were exchanged, headlights jutted sharply as vehicles wheeled about.

Walter's house was dark. Georgie went onto the stoop; the solid door behind the screen was shut—unusual in the summer. He tugged the screen aside, tapped on the frame.

"Hershey!"

He stuck his head inside, yelled again. The interior smelled faintly of bacon frying. The windows were closed; that too wasn't normal. He hollered once again, waited, thought of traipsing through the four rooms to see if anyone was hiding but didn't want to invade their privacy.

He was making his way through the yard to the house next door when the door of a shed in the back creaked open. Walter said, "Yo. Tater." Georgie looked about, then slipped inside.

"Here you are. Where's Thelma and Scooter?"

"Down the lane with some folks."

Walter eased back onto a lumber pile and pressed his face to the siding to peer through a crack.

"You by youself?"

"Yeah."

Georgie sat on the lumber. "What the heck happened? The radio said somebody assaulted a white woman. They seem to be lookin' for you."

"Bitch!" spat Walter.

"I know you didn't do nothing."

"Nothin' she didn't ast for way she was actin'."

"What did—"

"She yanking my chain all my damn life, Tater."

"Who."

"Marjorie Sinclair."

Georgie said, "What *happened,* though?"

Walter sighed, wearily. "Aw, hell, she hired me to hep her move, and that white boy Robert was there, and we got it moved in my truck to her new place down on River. She been tootin' a glass horn 'bout all afternoon far as I could tell. She was worked up, you know, 'cause her brother just passed, and she and that white boy put away damn near a whole bottle a gin by the time we got her settled. Then he took off. If I'd a been smart I woulda too, but she said she wanted me to hep her move things around. Well, I did. She plugged in the damn radio and tried to git me to drink with her but I wouldn't. But she keep hounding me then tells me all about the big time she had in N'awlins. Says she got lot a new friends down there."

Walter paused, shifted about. "She say she got *colored* friends."

"Marjorie?"

"Oh yeah, I say *aw-haw* just like you do, but she go on about it. She say she had a *colored boyfriend,* some cat play piano in a club. I just say *do tell, aw-huh, mm mercy,* I act like she's telling me her auntie's having a garden party at the country club."

"Thad seem wise."

"Then I say well I best be getting home, and she say, aw now wait a minute have a drink with me, just one drink, and I say naw better not, and she say her *colored man* likes his gin same as she does and he likes his chocolate and his vanilla, too. And she say that the way she is now. Likes her vanilla *and* her chocolate. Rolls her eyes at me, you know."

"Uh-oh. No kidding?"

"She drunk as a skunk by then. Still on her feet but looking for a spot to lie back on. She say *I miss my colored man something awful,*

Walter, I miss him bad. Plopped down on her bed and started blubberin' 'bout how lonely she was."

"Aw, Lord's sake!" Georgie waited for him to go on. After a bit, Georgie said, "You leave then?"

"I shoulda."

"You stuck around? That wadden smart, Hershey."

"No shit."

"But whut—"

"Aw, hell, Georgie! I thoughta all the times she'd called me out, tryin' to cut me down. Now here she was throwin' it *at* me or throwin' it up *to* me, hard to tell which."

"You wanted to get back at her?"

Walter bristled in the darkness. "Soon's my knee hit the bed she had her dress up her own self."

Slut! Despite himself, Georgie was repelled by the picture of Walter between Marjorie's splayed knees. "But if *she* wanted to, then why—" Georgie began, but Walter held up his hand.

"We not at it ten seconds 'fore I hear gigglin' and I look up and it's some damn kids from next door, looking in the winda like we're a pitcher show, and when I see 'em they start hollerin' and laughin' and raising a hell of a ruckus. Marjorie, she pops up clutchin' her bosom and screams at the kids, and they *gone* in a second, then she say to me *git out! now!* like she want me to get away clean. So I light out running for my truck, and no sooner do I get backed out in the road than I hear her screaming her head off, just *screamin'*."

He groaned, sagged back against the wall. "I'm thinkin' *you the biggest damn fool ever lived, Walter Jenkins.*"

After a minute, Georgie said, "They're tearin' up the town lookin' for you."

"That *my* fault?"

"No!"

But things weren't as simple as Georgie had imagined. He'd presumed Walter would be, well, *innocent.* Not that he was *guilty,* exactly. It was hard to put your finger on what to call it. Walter had crossed a line, flouted a deeply held taboo, deliberately; even with a clear invitation, though, he hadn't been prudent. He should've shucked and jived, said *M'am* and *Miz Mawjoree* and got the hell away before she made trouble.

But as much as Georgie might look for an excuse to beg off sticking his neck out for Walter, he hadn't found a good one yet. Walter had done a dumb thing: not a hanging offense.

"Fuck them mothafuckahs!" spat Walter. "Yeah, that bitch had her damn chocolate sundae! She want a *coluhed man,* she *had* herself one."

Georgie let him fume in silence; Walter twitched and knocked his fist against the lumber, put his head in his hands and rocked.

"Where's your truck?"

"Police got it I reckon. I didn't get a hunnerd feet 'fore the crackers who live on River heard her hollerin' and took out after me and the damn thing stalled and I had to hot foot."

"You gonna hide here?"

"I doahn know yet. Just got here. Had to get Thelma and Scooter safe. I didn't 'zactly sit and talk it out over dinner. I figure they'll show up here soon and wreck the place lookin' for me. You probly oughta scat."

"You should too."

"Too tired to run."

"I don't see you have a choice."

"Oh, I got lots a choice, but not if you wanna be *choosey.* I'm thinking I'll walk into the jail house and say here I am, mothafuckahs, that white gal's a lyin' bitch, and I want my day in court!"

"I probly got rope in the car if you wanna skip to the end of *that* chapter!"

"No shit, Tater. I'm not jiving."

"You got a hole in your head, son."

"They can't do more'n kill me."

They sat in silence for awhile; Georgie didn't want to further agitate Walter by interrogating him about Marjorie or by insisting his only sensible option was to run. Walter had put his head in his hands and was rubbing his temples. Georgie cracked open the door. Cars were streaming out of the block and people were fleeing on foot. They expected rioters to torch their homes. His heart fluttered with momentary panic. He didn't want to be caught in a burning building.

"Let's go out to the farm."

"I said I ain't goin' nowhere."

"What're you gonna do?"

"Damn, Tater!"

"All right. Think about this. You want your day in court, you oughta wait till things cool down to declare yourself."

"I need to stick by Thelma and Scooter."

"We'll all go. Let's go now."

The smell of smoke was stronger and police and fire sirens were rising up and bearing down on them. "Y'all stay out there and after a day or two we can negotiate you coming in when everybody's calm."

Walter sighed. "Yeah. You right."

Georgie was anxious to get away, so he and Walter drove to the house where Thelma and Scooter were staying. Walter darted inside to fetch them but shortly came out alone and got in the passenger seat.

"Something happen on the road, I don't want them with me. They be safer here."

Georgie nodded. He was about to put the Chevy into gear when two squad cars pulled into the lane ahead and slid to a halt before Walter's house. Doors popped open and beams of flashlights jittered as troopers swarmed over the yard.

"Shit."

Walter looked as if he might bolt, but Georgie said, "Get in the trunk!" Walter tumbled out of the car and a moment later his weight dipped the vehicle and the trunk door slammed. Georgie sucked in a long breath. He considered a U-turn, but the lane deadheaded into the river two blocks east. The way out required passing those squad cars. To sit here would eventually attract their attention once their business at Walter's was done.

He could only drive past and hope he didn't snag their notice. His knees were Jell-O jiggly and his arms dripped sweat off his elbows. He huffed a breath out his lower lip past his cheeks to cool himself. Last thing he needed now would be a seizure.

The clutch needed a ton of weight to press it, and his trembly foot had trouble keeping it floored enough to shift into low. The gears ground but popped into place, and his foot slid off the clutch. The car lurched, stalled and died. He cranked it up again, dabbing his damp forehead against his shirt sleeve. The red lights atop the squad cars burned in the smoky mist looming over the street.

"Hang on, Hershey!" He released the clutch and the car eased forward into the sandy lane, the tires weaving in the ruts, and a sudden fearful fantasy made him picture slamming into a squad car as he tried to pass.

He crawled closer and tried not to look or seem curious; every light in Walter's house was ablaze and blue-garbed forms moved inside and stood in the yard with their flashlights. The screen door had been ripped from its hinges and hung askew. A trooper with a flashlight stood on the shoulder watching the Chevy approach, and when the light was aimed at his eyes he winced and his heart shuddered; he squinted and hoped he wasn't too blind to keep the car on course. The trooper waved him down, so Georgie stopped in the lane to let the patrolman cross over to the driver's side, but the trooper bent to get a closer look at him—at his white face, Georgie guessed—then waved him on.

He was so afraid of being whistled back that he couldn't look into the rearview mirror until they'd driven another block, and when he did, the red lights were small, like ordinary warnings at a railroad crossing.

But back on the pavement, he drove up on a roadblock. They'd cordoned off the neighborhood. Two cars and an old truck ahead carrying Negroes had been pulled aside and the occupants stood outside the vehicles being inspected. For an instant, he thought of gunning the engine and detouring up an alley on his left, but there'd be a barrier that way too, no doubt.

Though they were searching the Negroes' cars, they might not his. If they did find Walter, he could claim to be taking Walter to the station as he'd asked and that he'd hidden in the trunk from the lynch mob. More likely, Georgie would be accused of aiding and abetting a nigger rapist, and things wouldn't go well for him and his family for years to come.

Too late to turn back. He eased the car up to the barricade, and two troopers, one on either side, probed the car's interior inquisitively with their beams. He hoped they'd be locals he might know, but these fellows looked like Rangers.

"What's goin' on, officer?" he asked the one at his elbow before the officer could speak.

"Any reason you're in colored town?"

"Sure. I brought our maid home. Same as every Saturday night. Ask anybody."

"What's wrong she don't take the bus?"

Georgie bristled. Since the trooper didn't know he was a criminal, the interrogation seemed entirely out of bounds, but he stifled an impulse to get sassy.

"Officer, my mammy's been with the famly since I was a toddler, and she's gettin' on. With all this mess, we didn't want her to fret."

The other Ranger at the rear was worrisome laggard in his inspection. Georgie set his hands on the wheel at ten and two and looked ahead beyond the barricades as if any second he expected to be on his way, and, to his relief, he heard the officer say, "All right. But you'd best stay clear of downtown."

He drove a route out of the city that took them west along farm-to-market roads and country lanes then north into the industrial outskirts on the upper reaches of the river. On the highway north, the lighted honky-tonks were doing their usual business, and no sign showed here that anything was wrong.

It took another forty minutes to where he pulled off the highway and went up the lane to the main house at the farm. He stopped before it and opened the trunk.

"Damn, my laig went to sleep." Walter clambered free and stomped about to restore his circulation. He looked up at the house.

"Nobody here?"

"No. You can stay here. Or wherever you want. You know the place as well as I do."

"I'll stick close by. Somethin' runs me off I'll be at Uncle Roy's old place or at the mound."

"Okay. Just don't do anything rash. I'll bring you some grub first chance, then, soon's things cool down . . ."

They were silent while Walter stretched his arms and jogged in place, rolling his neck. Georgie pulled out his pocket watch. It was just after midnight.

"I had a loaf a bread and a jar of peanut butter but I set 'em on the roof and forgot 'em when I drove off."

Walter chuckled. Georgie felt very tired suddenly now that they'd reached safety. Driving back through the gantlet, even without Walter, seemed daunting. He sat on the running board to forestall having to leave.

"Wish I had a cigar," said Walter.

"Wishes were horses."

"Yup. Thing I need is a Sherman tank."

"Thing you need is a good lawyer," said Georgie after a moment.

FORTY-TWO

ROBERT HAD NO confidence Marjorie would tell the truth: she had nothing to gain, and he could only hope the friendship she'd claimed to feel for Walter would win out.

He'd have been foolish to rely on that, though. Right away he felt pushed to do *something*. When he left her, the deputy was dozing in the chair outside her door. Robert shook him gently and he jumped.

"Whut?"

He couldn't say he'd talked to Marjorie because the deputy's job was to prevent that. "I'm the fellow with her earlier? I helped that Negro move her?"

"You cain't go in there. Sheriff's orders."

"Okay. How's she doing?"

"Fair. Considerin'."

"Thing is, I talked to her before they brought her here."

He looked at Robert—*so?*

"I hate to doubt her word, but I don't think she told the gospel truth."

He yawned. "That right? You see what happened?"

"Well, no. But I talked to her. At the station."

"She done give a statement."

"Yeah. But she might not've said everything."

"Whud she leave out?"

"She and Jenkins have known one another all their lives. She could've given him the notion she was willing."

"She said *thet?*"

"Not exactly."

"Whut then?"

He sighed. She could easily deny words he put in her mouth. "She was drunk."

"Boy, you ain't whistling Dixie."

Robert added, "So her statement's got to be taken with a grain of salt."

The deputy looked at the door to her room. He stuck a finger in his ear as if to clear his hearing. He checked the nail of that finger. He shrugged.

"She said whut she said."

He picked up his magazine, opened it, and mimed reading.

Robert thought he'd try his luck at the police station, and he was half sorry he'd sassed the G-man. When he stepped out the door, shouts and horn honks cut through the hospital's hum, closer it seemed, maybe coming his way, and the odor of burning rubber was strong on the breeze.

He heard what he thought were gunshots in the distance. He dreaded pitching himself into this mess, dreaded talking to the cops again. His exchange with the deputy wasn't encouraging, and all he could do was cast doubt on Marjorie's veracity by telling them she lied about being married, had an affair with a Negro, and was pregnant by him. But would that get Walter off the hook? It was his only shot.

His watch showed two-fifteen. He felt dead on his feet, though adrenaline coursed through his muscles and kept him upright and twitchy-jumpy. His eyes burned. He longed to pitch himself into bed and say to hell with her, to hell with this Dixie shit-hole, to hell with Walter—why was this *his* problem? If Walter'd had any brains, he'd have left when Robert had. He knows the territory!

Probably ten blocks of Commerce stood between the hospital and the station. The boulevard was a long straight shot, wide enough for parking on both sides with two lanes in the middle. When he'd come that way earlier, it was peaceful, and state militiamen were mustering. But after he left the hospital and walked that way, they had vanished. It was deserted except for a fire flickering at the far end near or on the curb; the street lamps posted over intersections formed a ragged chain of globes for blocks, lighting up the strangely littered pavement—you'd think a parade had gone through, or a flood had left debris in its wake. The street was silent, like a long narrow canyon where an ambush might occur. Some stores had smashed front windows, but he didn't know if they were owned by Negroes or whites.

A dog trotted into a far intersection, looked down the boulevard his way, then suddenly whirled and scurried into the darkness; in his weird, exhausted state he imagined it was a canine spy.

He strode to the sidewalk and started north. The calm spooked him; he thought of his .38, useless back in his room. A big rock, he thought. Then he spotted a hank of 2 x 4 lying in a heap of lumber that might've been a traffic barricade pushed beyond its limit. He picked it up. A big nail stuck out one end. He swung it a few times like a bat, testing the weight. It would have to do if it came to needing something. He wasn't a fast runner.

Picking up that chunk, having it in his grip: he's thought about that since, again and again over the years. You feel naked in a situation where somebody might be out to get you, and you want to fill your hand with your fist or better yet something heavy and hard that will hurt or at least warn somebody off. All the better if it's long enough to put distance between you and whoever's after you. He remembered that the butt end was lumber-shaped and so didn't really fit his hand like a carved stock or grip. It felt awkward to hold, as if it might fly out of his hand if he hit something or swung it too wildly. But holding it, he felt a little safer in one way and not safer in another. With it, he was more ready for combat, but now combat *could be a choice.*

As he crept up that street half out of his head with the fear of encountering the mob, the Sunday-school solution didn't occur to him: *I am defenseless; smite me and I will turn my cheek.* You don't win wars sending your chaplain out to parlay with theirs. That's the thought he hangs to now. He was scared; he picked up something to protect himself with. It was that simple, then. That night he didn't see that by picking up a weapon, you might turn into the Whoever that's out to get you, that you might defend yourself too well. He tells himself he *had to.* Even if he'd puzzled it all out then he'd still have made that choice. Anybody would, he believes. He's sure of it.

So he scurried along hugging the storefronts for another block, edging close enough to the fire that it clarified into a blazing auto hulk.

It seemed odd the fire department either didn't know about it or let it burn. But fires had broken out all across the city and no doubt the crews were stretched beyond their means. Police, too. Looters could steal or even *murder* under the cover of the chaos.

The pavement was slick with sheeny puddles that gave off the stink of petroleum. Low-hanging clouds rolled overhead like a swiftly moving ceiling, reflecting the strange orange light, pushed by a fitful wind that kept tatters of smoldering paper aloft and flitting like fireflies. He went on cautiously; he thought the station was another four blocks dead ahead then two blocks west off the waterfront, but he didn't know this part of town, especially on foot and at night. He strode another half-block, not exactly whistling in the dark but stepping quickly as he could through shards from broken windows and the debris on the walk from looted interiors.

Shouts sprang up on the next street over maybe, and a heated tingle prickled his nape as his heart pounded. He gripped his makeshift club with both hands and moved on north along the walk. The hubbub sounded closer and between him and his destination.

Then a few blocks up, a crowd surged into the intersection from a side street, but the lights were too dim to tell if these were rioters or people running from them; he couldn't see if they were black or white, and when he caught himself trying to discern that, he realized he didn't want to be swept up by a mob of any color. The pack of shipyard hyenas howling for blood and brandishing their cudgels as they raced along looking to beat any hapless "coon" caught in their path—they wouldn't quietly assemble at his knee while he urged them to reconsider "new evidence." They didn't *care* who was right; they trudged through their normal lives simmering and itching for an excuse to go "nigger-knocking," and they did *not* want to hear *there's no excuse.* And if Negro men had somehow formed a troop of defenders or avengers, they wouldn't heed a white man's plea to let the law handle this. They already knew how the law handled riots.

The crowd swelled as people flowed in from adjoining streets; he stopped and slipped into the shadows, watched. His hands made the board slick and he wiped his palms on his pants. No one seemed to be holding a blazing torch. Maybe they weren't on the warpath.

He caught himself panting and held his breath to calm down. Then, as if the crossroad couldn't hold their numbers, the near edge broke like water over the rim of a filling bowl and they were coming his way, shouting. Gun shots—*pop crack! pop crack!*—screaming. He was halfway in his block and if he ran back the way he'd come he'd be spotted, maybe chased, just for running. He couldn't make it safely up to the next intersection, either.

Panicky, he pressed inside an alcove. This store had not been hit by the mob; windows and door were intact. He danced in place, shivering with fear, and all he could think to do was this: he raised his club and whacked the door glass; it exploded, raining glittering chips over his feet, and he hacked at the splintery remnants in the opening until he could stick one leg through without cutting himself, then he was in the dark interior. Haberdashery, he thought. Hats, coats, clothing, but he couldn't tell if for colored or white. A light seeped into the sales floor from deep inside the store, and his heart rammed into his throat—somebody's here? Maybe the proprietor was holed up with a firearm to protect his property. He'd presume Robert was looting and shoot him on sight. Robert would, if it were his store.

He was afraid to yell anything for fear the crowd would hear, but he was also afraid to be taken for a looter.

"Hello inside? Don't shoot! I'm here to hide. They're coming."

No answer. He kept to the darkness feeling his way through the standing racks of garments. The light was coming through a frosted pane of an office door—maybe an ordinary security light. He crept to the glass but ducked low, aware that the illuminated pane would silhouette him to anybody on the street. He tapped on it with a knuckle.

"Hello? Don't shoot, please!"

A phone there? He could report the mob's position. And report that Marjorie wasn't clear on what happened. A long time after this he wondered why he hadn't called from the hospital. But when he conjures up that deputy and how he tried to coax him to action, he pictures himself on a pay phone in the hospital, saying things about Marjorie in his "Yankee" accent, and he couldn't have recalled the names of the gumshoes who interviewed him. At least in person he'd recognize who'd taken his statement, and they might believe him.

With a mob trapping him in the store, a phone was his only hope. He stood to the wall and rattled the knob to the office door, but the lock was latched. He heard fast footfalls on the sidewalk and turned just as three figures darted past for an instant, then were gone. He thought they were white men.

He *had* to do something fast! He was jumpy, about to leap out of his skin, so he followed through with what he'd begun: he smashed the door to the office, groped inside to unlatch the lock. The banker's light with a green shade shone down on a clutter of papers. He thought he had to turn off that damn light quick as possible, otherwise anybody passing could see it or him. But no sooner had he scrambled to the desk and was fumbling to find the switch than he heard a racket. Now the crowd was rushing past, and rather than duck and hold his breath and stay quiet, his brain had already sent the message to his hand to shut off the light, and when it happened sure enough somebody hollered, "Hey!" loud and close by the front.

In the darkness, he crouched behind the desk praying that they'd move on. But there was scuffling and more voices and tinkling, and he knew somebody—one, two, several?—had come through the smashed door. White or colored didn't matter—to whoever found him in the dark, in their worked-up state he was an enemy.

He couldn't step out and declare himself. He had to stay hidden, and, doing that, he couldn't avoid a fight if they found him. The *situation* demanded it. He heard voices in the store, men's voices, maybe white maybe colored he didn't know because Southern brogues ran together to his ear. He couldn't raise his head to look. And it didn't matter. He comes back to that, again and again. The mob looks for the lone man, and if he's not eager to join, he becomes their prey. He believes anybody who'd been with him there would come to the same conclusion.

When it sounded as if someone was moving toward him, he thought they knew he was here and would drag him out by his neck to hang him as a looter or a nigger-lover or a white man. He trembled from head to toe and had a flash of what his brother might go through elsewhere on the globe; this *utter fear* welled up and swept over him, froze him cold as being dipped in a winter ocean, squeezed his bowels until they cramped, and his breathing wouldn't catch air. He crouched holding the club, blinking back sweat, hearing the sounds grow larger, hoping it was only his runaway imagination. But then a far-off voice said something that ended like a question and a sudden booming voice right at the office door yelled back, "Yo!" sharp and decisive.

The man took a step into the office. The floor creaked beneath his shoe. Then he stood stock still. It was dark, and though Robert couldn't see the figure because he himself was crouched behind the desk, he had the advantage of knowing the dimensions of the room and where the furniture was placed, though his hurried glimpse before the light went out hadn't given him much. Then the other man crept about the room, slowly and deliberately, or that's what Robert thought he heard, with strangely muffled sounds higher up as if he were feeling his way. He thought thank God he has no torch or flashlight, at least the man didn't know for sure he was here, and Robert knew where the door was.

Then Robert could've sworn he felt the stranger's heat, smelled his rank sweat and the tobacco and liquor taint on his breath. Robert slowly bent his head up, and there was a figure in the dark standing not three feet away but making no move, saying nothing, as if waiting. His heart boomed like a bass drum in his ribcage, and he was afraid it could be heard; his bad knee ached because he was hunkered on it with the other foot to the floor; he was afraid it would give and he'd tumble out at his feet and all the other man would have to do is plant his boot on his neck and shoot him in the head or club him like a fish in the bottom of a boat. The soldiers back from the war, they had this mantra, he's heard it a thousand times over the years: *it was me or him.*

All of a sudden he was smothering and trapped and he *had* to get out that door, so he bolted right up and was trying to scramble over the desk with one hand still clamped on his stick, when the fellow hollered, surprised it sounded, "Hey!" Robert tried to run through him, but when he tried to shove him aside, something whacked his shoulder hard, and he guessed the guy had a club too, and all he knew to get free of him and out of that office was swing his own club and hope it knocked him away, gave him room to run. But when he swung—at the darkness, at the formless shape—he hit something but the man grunted, and something else, the guy's fist he thought, smashed Robert in the left ear, and that sent him into a wild panic so he swung his club, hit the fellow once, he went *uhhh!* and whatever he carried banged Robert across his free forearm and the pain was so sharp he saw blinding white and his head rang. He tried to spin and lurch for the door, felt the other man right behind him, whirled, and with all his weight and strength two-handed that chunk of wood, swinging it from over his head at the darkness, at the *hole in the light,* having no idea if anybody was there, flailing for freedom with that frantic burst of wild fear such as you feel when you discover a spider on your neck.

His club connected, something soft, he heard a grunt and a yell, just a "huah!" nothing you could respond to; a hand grabbed at his shoulder, a big strong hand, and he swung crazy and furious again and connected. The hand released his shoulder. He would've sworn he heard the fellow lunge at him, and so he swung hard again, this time hit something more substantial, and the man went "Owwwuh!" loud and angry. Hearing this *anger*—it lit something up in Robert like a bomb—so he went at the figure again with his stick, furiously, insanely, not even thinking of getting out the door because by now he was closer than the other was. He hit the fellow again and again until it started to feel *good,* and when he realized the guy wasn't hitting back, a sensation of triumph swept over him like a blast of heat and he went at him double-time and eager, making him pay (he knows now but not then), for having stolen Claire, making him pay for the insults to his manhood because of his leg, making him pay for being the Pinkerton who said to his ma, "Quit cher pissin' and moanin'. Yer lucky yer stuff's so sorry they ain't takin' it, too," making him pay for being bested by a big pink blubbery fuck handed everything he wanted and earning not a smidgeon of it.

The rage overwhelmed him. He struck again and again. You ask him was it necessary, he'll have to say no now. He could've left then, and the man wouldn't have chased him. Couldn't have. But Robert was possessed.

The figure fell to the floor and Robert added savage kicks to his body along with the drubbing he was delivering with his stick. Then when he struck he felt the nail go in. All the way through the stick, down to his hands, the vibration of it penetrated, like a butcher knife plunged into a melon, it's *horrible* to remember. He pictured it puncturing the ear, piercing the eye, and the fellow howled with anguish. The sensation of *feeling* that nail in his club go in him made him let go of the stick like it was suddenly red hot.

He whirled thinking he'd run, then he remembered there might be others, but when he looked to the front, the mob seemed to have passed. Footfalls outside made him duck low for a moment. He peered intently into the shadows where the man had fallen; he didn't know if he was waiting or was out or was dead. He couldn't shake the kinetic memory in his hand and arm of the nail meeting a little resistance then breaking through and sinking in and the man crying out.

For the first time in many minutes a car sped along the street, honking. Its headlights flashed through the store, and he saw the man he'd struck lying by the desk, only for a second, but long enough to see his lips and nose and the nail end of the board stuck in his skull.

He crept quick as he could to the entrance. It was wildly urgent to get away from this fellow. He was far less afraid of what he might encounter on the street than he was of loitering in here. Afraid of what—it's something he's thought about many times over the years. He wasn't afraid the other would come to and get at him, and he wasn't afraid of being caught by his pals or the law. He was afraid that if he stayed he might have to acknowledge what he'd done; he wanted to run from that rage; he wanted to hide from what he'd felt when that nail sunk in and he'd flung the stick away like it was a writhing viper.

He got outside and ran to the nearest side street, and within minutes he was striding along an avenue where white folks were gathered on their porches in their night clothes, their lights ablaze, standing guard over their domiciles with family firearms, talking among themselves.

It took him a good while to reach the Bide-A-Wee on foot. When he got into his room, everything inside him turned to jelly; he tumbled into his bed fully clothed and lay awake trembling until just before dawn.

He awoke mid-morning, aching and hot and damp—he'd left the windows closed though it was stuffy and hot when he'd come in—and his filthy clothes were sopped with stinking nerve sweat. His arm ached, then he remembered it had been hit by something.

He remembered too he'd been on his way to the police station when he stopped to hide and that it never occurred to him to resume his mission. *Not one thought about that crossed his mind.* He wanted to get "home" to this squalid room and hide. That thought was so large it crowded out everything else in his head. Then his stomach churned when he had a sudden memory of the nail sinking in, and he stumbled out of bed to puke.

The memory plagued him for days. Sometimes he'd be sitting in a chair and had to grasp the arms as if it were about to take off like an airplane; he'd grit his teeth, lay his head back, close his eyes, and hang on while ugly pictures and sensations flooded over him. The rage that swept over him was so huge and furious that if he'd had a machete he'd have hacked at that man until he was raw meat and chopped bone. Feeling it, he'd been horrified and flung down his stick.

But was that thing really much larger? Had he only let a little of it out? It was there inside him; it might be small, this thing, something the situation allowed to grow, and it might recede never to be experienced again. But he didn't know for sure. He didn't know if or when it might strike again.

FORTY-THREE

Coaching himself to behave like a law-abiding citizen, Georgie drove back to town on the main highway. He was dog-tired, trembling with the dregs of adrenaline that swept through him earlier. His vision was blurry, his head ached, and despite the heat he had a chill. His tongue lay huge and dry like a chunk of frayed rope. Maybe it portended a seizure—or merely how it felt to be up too long on too little fuel with your heart hammering a mile a minute for hours. He steeled himself, hoping his conscious self would remain in charge.

At the Commerce Street bridge, they'd blocked off the road. A line of cars crept to the head for inspection. Most were denied entry and were turning back. Thank God Walter wasn't in the trunk. But he had a frightful sense that word was out and the sole reason for this blockade was apprehending Georgie Karacek, who'd aided and abetted the Negro rapist Walter Jenkins.

The bridge arched over the river just upstream from where the shipyard stood on an island like a city unto itself, ablaze with light like a grand industrial castle whose minions and serfs had flooded forth to lay siege to the countryside. The edifice was accessible to workers via a footbridge lighted by a string of naked bulbs. Beyond the commercial landing, fires glowed orange over the roofline like a strange late sunset on a distant ridge. As he poked the Chevy forward foot by foot in the line, he pictured the cuffs clicked shut on his wrists, a Ranger at either elbow. But they might be privately sympathetic and admire what he'd done, even though they had orders to arrest him.

Most would curse him as a traitor, a nigger-lover. There'd be an interrogation—*where's that damn nigger Walter Jenkins?* He'd never tell. How did police make people spill their guts? You heard stories about electrical devices hooked to your nuts, your nipples, or rough objects rammed up your rectum.

He shuddered. If it came to that, he hoped he'd pass out—or have a fit. If there was ever an opportune time to have a grandy, it would be while your balls were being zapped by wires plugged into a wall socket. It might scare them off. If they did manage to squeeze his secrets out, there'd be a trial—and with it the chance to tell the jury, the gallery, the citizens of Port Farview who jeered or sneered, that he was paying a debt, and he was damn proud of it! Walter's family had worked as servants in the Karaceks' homes and toiled in their fields. The family trust Sylvia wanted him to claim—much of it was built on the backs of slaves and then the vastly underpaid "free" men and women who worked the land for a bare subsistence! *Fellow citizens of Port Farview, it is high time we ALL acknowledge to whom we owe our pleasant secure existence …*

To say nothing of how Walter dragged him dripping from the river.

Full of the fervor of his good deed, he eased up to the barricade manned by two Jefferson County deputies. One was Buddy Allbright. Back in Elizabeth's brief heyday as fetching wench, Buddy had sat on their porch and drooled while she pranced in the yard in her majorette's skirt and practiced baton twirls; she was a lousy twirler, but every time she dropped it she had to bend over to pick it up. Georgie had felt sorry for the poor chump.

Buddy came to the window. "Hey, Georgie, how's it hangin'? What're yew doin' out here this time of night?"

"Been to Kountze to see Mama. She's been sick. I heard about the mess and thought I better get back to the old lady."

"Y'all still over on Acorn?"

"Yep."

Buddy scratched his chin. "We not suppose to let people in 'cept in uh 'mergency."

"Sure. It ain't. But I am worried, you know."

Buddy peered across the empty bridge to the burning city then back to the growing line of cars. Buddy was clearly on the fence. Georgie could say *Lizzy always goes on about you,* but it would seem contrived.

"Y'all sure got a mess on your hands, Buddy." He waved ahead to the empty bridge. "I guess I could tell you the old lady's about to pop one out. If that would hep."

"It's what I'll say if anybody asks," said Buddy. "Don't take Telephone to get home."

"Thanks, amigo."

Buddy stepped in front of the Chevy to remove the yellow sawhorse, and just as Georgie eased beside him and was about to goose it, Buddy asked plaintively, "How's your sis?"

Georgie decided to reward him for his kindness. "Fat as a fucking pig, Buddy. Hadden you seen her lately?" He grinned and Buddy sheepishly grinned back.

He plotted a route along quiet white residential streets and made it home without incident. Sylvia had been waiting on the back porch and ran to greet him as he emerged from the garage. She hugged him.

"Oh, I'm so glad you're back! I was so worried!"

He basked in this reception. "Aw, everything went fine. Couple times I was a little rattled, though."

"What happened? Did you find Walter?"

He held off answering until they reached the parlor, where Mary Kay lunged and gave him a hug so light and quick it was as if she'd tossed her skinny self at him and bounced off. He sat and Sylvia brought him a glass of fresh lemonade with chipped ice. When he swigged it, the sugar gave him a needed boost and the cold liquid melted over his parched tongue like a medicinal balm.

He gave his report; he couldn't resist wringing a little extra drama about the close call at the barricade with Walter in the trunk and made sport of Buddy's asking about Elizabeth at the next one.

"So you left him at the farm?"

"Yeah." He handed his empty glass to Sylvia. "Could I have some water, please?"

Mary Kay said, "The radio says the Texas State Guard is camping on the library grounds."

"I didn't go by there. Amazing, idden it? All this just because Marjorie hollered rape."

"Marjorie Sinclair?" Sylvia was returning with his water. He nodded.

"Well, I know enough about that girl to have my doubts."

"But what if it's not a lie?" said Mary Kay. "If it really happened then shouldn't Mr. Jenkins be caught?" She'd uttered this perhaps without realizing to what extent Georgie was complicit, and, seeing it, blushed and added, "I mean, maybe he did and maybe he didn't, but isn't there only one way to find out for sure?"

"Yes. He's not running, Mary Kay. He's just lying low until people calm down. He wants to turn himself in." He started to add, *I've got a plan.* But until he worked it out, he didn't want to subject it to anybody's scrutiny.

They were silent for a bit. Mary Kay yawned.

"Go on up to bed, sugar," said Sylvia. "It's almost four."

When she'd gone, Sylvia said, "What now?"

"I'm gonna rest a bit. Make a few calls later on."

"Who are you calling?"

He finished the water. He was still thirsty. "Walter needs more help than I can give him."

She nodded. He sighed, rubbed his temples, then lay on the sofa and closed his eyes. He felt Sylvia's lips on his forehead.

"My sweet hero," she murmured.

She turned out the lights and left the room. He fell into a drooling heated slumber but was awakened shortly after dawn by fire truck sirens in the distance. The kitchen radio came on, and he roused himself. Sylvia was making coffee.

"They declared martial law," she said. "Everybody has to be off the streets by eight-thirty tonight."

"Good."

She served him coffee and a hearty breakfast of bacon and scrambled eggs, slices of tomato from their garden, grits, and toast. The food propped him up like four lumberjacks hoisting him onto their shoulders. He took his Dilantin, then. He stretched the phone cord into the bathroom. Since Sylvia had apparently approved of his helping Walter hide, she might not object to his next step, but, then again, the subject of money always awakened their differences. He didn't want to argue about it. It wasn't appropriate for a wife to argue about such things.

He called two lawyers in Port Farview who'd worked for his family. It was difficult to reveal enough without revealing too much, but they got the drift: would they represent the suspect if he surrendered?

Both turned him down. One said, "Look, Georgie, no attorney in town would stick his neck out like that. Open-and-shut case of rape on a colored boy with testimony by a white woman whose brother's a dead war hero? I'd spend the rest of my life making bail for colored D & D."

The Houston lawyer Sylvia hired to work their trust case said he'd consider it for a $2,000 retainer plus bodyguards to escort him in and out of the county on court dates.

When he left the bathroom, Sylvia was waiting in the hall.

"What're you doing?"

"Walter wants to demand the justice that's owed him. He needs a lawyer."

"What'll it cost us?"

"Only one I could find was your fellow in Houston."

"What's he want?"

"Two thousand dollars to start."

"Two thousand dollars! That would buy a house! Good honk! Does he think we're made of gold?"

"I reckon he doesn't care."

"Did you bargain with him?"

"I told him I didn't have two thousand."

"And?"

Seeing the parlor was empty—Mary Kay was still sleeping—he strode into it with Sylvia on his heels and flung himself onto the sofa. It was irritating that she had so little confidence in him. She perched on the piano bench.

"He said I should feel free to call him when I did."

"Lawyers! What about offering him more contingency on the trust case?"

He blushed. "I didn't think of it." He wished he had, and now her doubt about his competence seemed reasonable. "He didn't bring it up, either, though."

"Are you worried?" Sylvia asked after a minute. "I mean about helping him? God, I know this is cheap and selfish of me, but I'm afraid, Georgie. Are you?"

"Well, no, I guess. Okay, some. A couple times last night I knew that if I was caught hauling Walter I'd be tarred and feathered. If not hung."

"It's noble of you to help, hon, it really is, but."

"I owe him."

"Georgie, what could you owe Walter that you're willing to risk *our home?* Even if nobody knows you're involved, won't they catch wind you're shopping for a lawyer to help him? Then there'll be a lynch mob in *our* front yard."

"Aw, Sylvia, nobody'll know I made a few calls."

"Oh, Georgie! It'll be all over town by noon, believe me."

He got up and walked into the kitchen, but she dogged him, expecting a response.

"Okay, you're right. And I am worried. But what else can I do?"

"I don't know. But I'm asking you don't be so hasty. Please don't be reckless and destroy everything we've worked for!"

"I haven't had to work for nothing, and I reckon that's the point."

"Please don't talk like a hillbilly and a moron."

"Don't be insulting. I'm trying to *do* something right, don't you understand?"

She swayed from foot to foot, considering. "Yes. I know. But you need to *talk* to me. Don't I deserve to have a say as your partner? I'm not your enemy, sweetheart, really, I'm not."

"Okay. You wanna know what's on my mind, right?"

"Yes."

"It's on my mind to ask Mama for the money."

"I'm sure you know what I think of *that!*"

"Yes." To avoid her ferocious dark gaze, he stepped to the drainboard, retrieved a mug from the cabinet, then lifted the percolator from a cold burner, but only a tepid finger drizzled out. A fix of something sullen and stubborn was slipping through his veins. A man stood up to his wife when things had to be done; a man resisted a wife's sometimes-angry, sometimes-sulky, sometimes-sugary efforts to shelter and cajole. Inasmuch as he'd learned to resist, he'd pinned a medal on his own chest, and if nobody else could see it, at least he could! And this was ironic: he'd rebelled against his mother's authority by marrying Sylvia, went up against them both to join the army, and now Sylvia was siding with his mother (though she probably wouldn't admit it), both seeming to be chanting the mantra he heard over and over in childhood: *Don't run! Don't get all heated up! It's bad for you! Play it safe!*

She left the room, and he leaned against the sink holding the mug of lukewarm dregs as if he intended to drink from it. Problem was—she was dead right, and, perversely, that made him balky. The local lawyers he'd called were thickly enmeshed in Port Farview politics and society—they attended First Baptist—and his efforts would be new grist for the gossip mill at fellowship hall coffees only hours from now. No "nice folks" would charge their home bearing torches—their ostracism would be subtle, more lengthy, more damaging—but when the word filtered to the hoi polloi, the Karacek front windows might be blasted to smithereens by buckshot, at best, and the house blown by dynamite at worst. He *did* feel a responsibility toward it, toward Sylvia, toward Mary Kay, and he had no eagerness to add bristling hatred to the bemused contempt he believed most locals felt toward him.

He'd worked for some time to grow up. He had no idea the road would be so rocky, or that there'd be so many stops or double-backs along the way. But he had reached the point where he could *recognize* an opportunity to take the next step forward, and so it was harder to mark time or pretend the obstacles in the path were insurmountable.

This could be done.

He presumed Sylvia had left the kitchen in anger, so he was surprised when she returned holding a black leather purse before her the way you would a covered platter—one hand on top, the other on the bottom. She set it on the table but kept a palm on it as if to steady it.

"Georgie, I want to show you something."

She gestured him into a chair, then sat across, opened the purse, dipped her hand in it, and brought out a stack of bills.

"I've been saving this since you left. I want you to have it. It's three hundred dollars."

"Three hundred dollars?" He was astonished.

"I saved it in case I had to leave. I don't mean you. I've always had a hard time trusting a situation, and this money was sort of an insurance policy in case…"

He smiled. "In case I turned out to be a blithering idiot."

"No, in case you never came back. Or in case you turned out to be a mean drunk."

"How did you—"

She shrugged. "A dollar here, a dollar there. I've always had the knack. Comes from growing up poor."

She slid the bills into his reach. "Here."

Confusion rolled over him. He was hurt she'd kept it from him until now, and that pressed the tender bruise of her secret life and her betrayal, so this news seemed drawn from the well of her still unknown history. But she *had* given it up, told him about it. She implied she was no longer hedging her bets. She was literally and figuratively investing in their union. Without this money, she had no fallback.

Supposedly. Was another couple hundred buried in a coffee can? And, damn it all, what did she *want* for it?

"I appreciate it, Sylvia. Not just the money, but, you know..." He smiled. She patted his hand.

"You could offer it to Walter."

"For a colored lawyer?"

She looked away. "I was thinking he might prefer taking Thelma and Scooter and leaving. They could make a new start with that much."

"We talked about it. He's too proud to run."

"He ran from Florida, didn't he?"

Georgie nodded. "His people are here. He wasn't just running *from;* he was also running *to.*"

"Maybe the money would be an encouragement."

A *bribe,* thought Georgie. She wants to buy my way out?

"I can't let you use your money."

"I just *gave* it to you."

"But I can't let you take care of my problem like this."

She looked surprised. "Why is it *your* problem? Couldn't it be *ours?*"

"I can't explain."

"Why not?"

"I don't feel right taking your hard-earned money."

"But you don't mind getting it from Evelyn!"

"She *owes* it!" he said hotly. "Besides, that's *my* money, too! If you've taught me anything, Sylvia, it's *that!*" He pushed the bills to her side. "Put it away, please! Keep saving and some day we can take a grand tour of Europe! Have a real honeymoon!"

The struggle riffled her features like a breeze on water.

"Or buy our own house," he added. "I'm proud of you for being so resourceful. I'm a lucky fellow!"

After a moment, she sighed, smiled wryly, put the bills back in the purse.

"I keep this in the closet in the hat box on the far left."

"That's good to know. But from now on, I'll try my darndest to put something *in* it."

"Then I guess it could be our 'Go To Hell Fund.'"

They laughed.

When she took the purse and rose, she said, "Give me a minute and I'll be ready."

"I better talk to her alone."

"But you—"

"I'll be fine!" he insisted. He rose quickly and felt several inches taller somehow, pleased to have asserted his will about raising the lawyer's retainer, pleased to have refused her nest egg, and pleased even more to have backed her down. Yet also made her happy! So it followed that he should insist upon driving himself to his mother's house. It's what men did—ignore the warnings their women gave them.

Though it was early, the humidity was high and the heat came with the sun. Traffic was very light; not even the buses were running. The city was shut down, the radio said. The rioting had been quelled; two hundred rioters had been arrested and were corralled at the county fairgrounds. But the suspect was still at large (said the reporter), "so this city is not resting easy."

His stomach churned all the way to Kountze. He played out scenarios like chess games: Walter walks into the station? No—Georgie talks Walter into being represented by a lawyer who walks into the station. Secret plans are negotiated to produce him, extra guards demanded to protect him while he's jailed .... There was the flight from Florida and the possibility the F.B.I. was interested in him. Was that good in the long run? Extradition to Florida would spare him from the heated outrage of the rape charge, anyway.

Since his call to his mother was unprecedented, apparently to her mind it signified a major concession or news detrimental to his marriage. She was quite pleased to see him. That was vaguely alarming, as if she knew something he'd forgotten or hadn't yet learned.

Clarence was in Tulsa; Elizabeth wouldn't rise until noon, and the children would be tended by a nurse. Marianne was roused from sleep. They had a new cook and housekeeper named Rachel, a young, light-skinned Negro with freckles and a quiet reserve that could be attributed to a love of reading or—considering the riot—to the patient, silent accumulation of information necessary to safely slit her employers' throats. She was put to work preparing breakfast for his mother and Marianne, and, to mollify his mother, Georgie agreed to eat a piece of cinnamon toast and drink a glass of orange juice the new girl would have to squeeze.

"He likes his toast with plenty of butter," Evelyn informed her.

Once they'd eaten, he felt itchy with the time passing. He said, "Mama, I need two thousand dollars."

"What in the world for?" Evelyn imitated surprise that money had inspired this trip.

He explained as best he could. Against his better judgment, he said he'd driven Walter to the farm to hide.

"My! I never knew you to be such a take-charge person." Acidic mockery underlay the compliment. He thought she was bitter to see it now; she could have used it earlier.

"What does *she* say about it?"

"She's not crazy about it."

"I'm sure she doesn't want *her little apple cart* upset!"

He bristled inwardly but hid his irritation. "She doesn't want anything to happen to the house, Mama. She has great respect for the family's property."

His mother smiled and her eyes glittered briefly, her sign she was leaving things unuttered. "I'd say that's wise."

"I'll pay it back."

"Pay *what* back?"

"The two thousand."

His mother smiled coyly. "What two thousand?"

It was a catechism: an object lesson. "The two thousand I need to hire a lawyer to help Walter."

"What about it?"

Marianne was almost mouthing the words to him.

"I'm asking you to loan it to me," he uttered.

"Ah! *Lend* it to you. Why didn't you say so?"

She shot up from the table and strode into the dining room where her walnut drop-front secretary stood. She acted as if she'd been *yearning* to help and had eagerly awaited the signal he wanted it. He didn't trust her for a second.

He fake-yawned, fake-stretched, got up to follow. Seeing her at her secretary, he realized he'd asked for a *loan*. He'd boldly told Sylvia he'd demand two thousand dollars of his own money. Now was not the time to provoke his mother, though, not if he wanted to accomplish something more than placating his masculine pride.

Before her was a business ledger. She hadn't opened it, he noted. One leg was delicately hooked over the other; one hand held a fountain pen in the air like a lit cigarette. She was going to make him grovel.

"I'll pay you back, Mama, I swear it."

"I heard you the first time, Georgie. And I appreciate the sentiment. I have no idea how you could possibly do that, though. Alfred Kline doesn't pay you much," she said sweetly, as if truly welcoming his ideas.

"We've saved some money. And I'm gonna get war work."

"That *is* good news! Doing what?"

She was so snide he wanted to thrash her. "Every place needs people to do about anything, Mama. There's a war on."

She didn't rise to the bait of his sarcasm. She played another old card instead.

"I would worry about your health keeping long hours, Georgie."

"I know. But I take my medicine. Sylvia sees to it. I've only had a few minor spells. I wouldn't operate machinery that could harm me if I couldn't pay close attention."

He looked her in the eye—pleading in a way, but also putting enough steel in his gaze to show he should be taken seriously, as an adult, as a man. She turned to the ledger and opened the leather cover, the gold embossed lettering of his father's name glittering briefly as it reflected the blazing chandelier, and his heart lifted. She laid the cover back. She uncapped the pen, set the cap carefully in a cubby, plucked up a tissue and wiped at the nib. Chinese water-torture, he thought. They oughta draft her.

Finally, she wrote the date. He let his breath release slowly and shifted his weight to his other foot.

Then she lifted the pen and turned to him. "To be truthful, honey, I don't have much confidence I'll get this money back. I—"

"Mama! I'm giving you my word! I'll pay you back something every week for the rest of my life if it takes that!" Fleetingly he considered mentioning Sylvia's three hundred dollars but thought better of it.

"I was going to say it doesn't matter to me."

Inwardly he reeled: she'd make this a gift? "Oh, well, Mama. I *want* to pay it back." Now they were fumbling for the bill, so to speak. He'd let her pick it up eventually.

She ignored him and continued writing. He leaned forward to spy over her shoulder. She wrote "$2,000" in the blank.

But again she stopped. He clenched his teeth.

"How much does she disapprove of getting *this* from me?" She tapped the ledger with the pen.

He said, petulant as an accused child, "She's not my master, Mama."

"Are you sure, Georgie?"

"Mother! Either give me the money or not and let me get about my business!" he burst out.

He almost instantly apologized. Her eyes rounded with surprise, but the tiny smile never left her lips, and before he could call his anger back, she nodded, turned to the check and made her florid quick signature, while he watched, happy not only for the money but also to have produced the result by showing a man's firmness and sternly dismissing her antics. He'd crossed a Rubicon with her; never again would he be afraid to call her down when it was right to do so.

She blotted the check then went to work on the stub.

"I'm noting here that this was a personal loan. I'm not going on record that this money paid anybody's legal fees."

"All right."

"If anybody asks I'll say I had no idea what you meant to do with it."

"I understand, Mama."

"And I'll expect you to do likewise. You're to tell people either that you lied outright to me or that you didn't tell me."

"Yes. Okay." She seemed to need to box him in.

At last, she tore the check slowly from its anchoring stub, notch by notch, making the most of it until he wanted to scream.

She held it up as if inspecting the accuracy of her cursive.

"It's a lot of money, Georgie."

"Mama, I said I'd pay—"

"And I said I don't care if you pay me back." She held the check out, straining forward to insist he take it. He did. Relief flooded him like a cascade of warm water.

"But even so, that doesn't mean I don't want something for it, hon."

He slapped the check down onto the dining table as if it had gone up in flames.

"What do you want? My God, you're torturing me! Can't you just give me the damn money without all this … this *rigamarole?* You know, it's *my money too!*"

"You need to calm down," she said quietly. "You want to be treated like an adult you'll have to follow the rules. We all make compromises in life as grown-ups. It's not a good idea for me to give you this money as a hand-out or like a graduation present. This is not the way the world works. You're not a child asking for a pony now. You—"

"So whatta you want, Mama?" His face felt hot, and he knew it was red; he could almost see his own reflection in his mother's dark, glassy eyes.

"Not much, really. I want you two to drop the suit over the trust and I want you to stop this nonsense about getting the house put in your names. You and she will have to be patient. You'll get the house when I'm gone, Georgie, and you'll get a share of the estate as well. But not until then. Not if you want *that.*"

FORTY-FOUR

THAT MORNING AFTER the riot, soon as Robert awoke he went looking for a newspaper. Downtown was like a war zone, streets littered with glass and stone and sticks, the stench of grilled industrial seepage in the air. A newsboy near the rail station bravely hawked *The Enterprise* under a sooty sky littered with bits of char like snowflakes dressed for a funeral, and the governor's troops patrolled the business district. He was compelled to drive past *the* store, "Peabody's Fine Apparel," he believed it was, thinking *the criminal always returns to the scene of the crime.* The windows were busted out, and garments draped the glittering, shard-sharpened sills and the sidewalk like the shed skins of humans who'd vaporized. The store was looted after he'd gone.

In daylight he could see the nearby stores had suffered damage. Negroes stood around scowling, shaking their heads and poking through the smoking rubble. He wanted to ask if someone inside had been hurt, but for all he knew they'd jump him the second he got in reach.

Back in his room, he scoured the paper. Since the rioting had started late last evening, the paper's coverage was hurried, incomplete, and probably inaccurate. Nonetheless, under this headline—*2 Dead, 60 Wounded, 100 Houses Burn in Race Riot*—the story said, "John Johnson, a Negro, died from gunshot wounds early this morning, the second victim to die as a result of rioting in Port Farview Saturday evening and early this morning. Several hours earlier, a white man identified from a card in his pocket as Ellis Cleveland Brown, 55, died from a skull fracture received when he was slugged by a group of Negroes."

After describing the damage, the account claimed that upwards of 200 rioters had been arrested and held at the county fair grounds.

Since Brown's death was apparently accounted for, Robert shivered to think that the fellow he'd hit with the board, over and over, was John Johnson. He thought "gunshot wounds" might prove he wasn't, but then terrible thoughts caromed off that: that he was *pleased* this man had been shot. It exonerated him. He felt like a wretch to be relieved. Possibly the story was wrong; possibly they'd misinterpreted that horrible nail puncture as a bullet wound. That didn't seem reasonable—a gunshot wound would be identifiable to a doctor. But he was unhinged and not rational. He *knew* he'd harmed someone; he didn't know how seriously. The uncertainty made him jangly with dread.

Although it was too late to make any difference to John Johnson and Ellis Brown, what he knew about Marjorie was crucial to Walter's future and his own. And he had to report his encounter in the store.

The station was still in an uproar, and it took an hour to find one of the officers who'd roused him from sleep the previous night. He told him he'd seen Marjorie in the hospital and described the conversation to a deputy guarding her room. Robert told him Marjorie wasn't married to a serviceman, she was pregnant by a Negro boyfriend—no, not Jenkins—she was so drunk she couldn't now recall what she might've said to Walter.

Robert said her claim of rape was probably false. They'd been caught by the kids next door while in the act, and she was afraid of what might happen to her if she *didn't* claim rape.

The officer's uniform was the hue of a mushroom, with cordovan piping on the trouser legs, and the shirt showed damp twin Rorschachs under his arms. He looked as if he hadn't slept since they last talked. Robert's news neither surprised nor interested him.

"Damage has already been done. I reckon if they catch him what you say will be good for his lawyer to know."

"Getting the word out might calm folks down," Robert insisted. "That mob thought they had to avenge an *outrage* done to Marjorie. They would've lynched him."

"They're sleeping it off now, and we got things under control," he said pointedly. "Rangers with tear gas bombs."

Robert told him he'd read about the two killed. "Anybody else die? Papers don't always get it right."

None he knew yet. Robert said, "Well, the paper said sixty were injured, too. Any of them likely not to make it?"

The officer wanted to know why he asked. Robert told him he'd gotten into a "scuffle" with somebody inside a store—

"What was you doing inside a store?"

"Hiding from the damn rioters." And a fellow came in, and they tangled. He hit him, hit him with a stick. Knocked him down, at the very least. And then he ran.

"This in niggertown?"

Robert nodded.

"What kinda store?"

"Haberdashery. Named Peabody's I think. Anybody found in there, you know, injured? I got worried about the fellow."

The officer said he hadn't interviewed people in the hospital, and a good many others were treated and released, and a bunch *more* probably treated themselves and wouldn't show up at no doctor's office.

"Colored or white?" he said.

"Negro."

First Robert thought the officer hadn't heard then realized the officer didn't care. And damn him if he wasn't glad, too. He waited for the officer to charge him with something, but the officer seemed too dog-tired to worry about it. Robert had intruded upon the officer's work, their conversation was interrupted by two phone calls and three officers separately who spoke to him, and when the officer realized Robert still occupied the hard wooden chair beside his desk, he looked blank. Then he said, "Whut?" as if Robert had something to add and it would annoy him to hear it. That Negro's life was worth less than a white man's; he was worthless.

The officer sent him to the Hotel Dieu and to the morgue. Robert could see he didn't want him to report back.

At the Hotel Dieu, he went to the Negro ward down in the basement and took a quick tour of the one open room available to the town's colored patients, each bed occupied by someone sick or nursing injuries, none a man with a head wound. He asked a black nurse if anyone fitting that description had checked in or out, and she told him no.

The county morgue below the annex of the courthouse was Jim Crow, too, and he was escorted through two rooms before he reached the one for Negroes. It would only accommodate a dozen corpses. A deputy told him, "Most colored folks go right to the undertaker 'less they got no family." He pulled the doors on two drawers—an old fellow with wiry grey hair and a stout young man with gold front teeth who'd been shot in the heart over a gambling debt.

As the days crept on, he watched the papers to get an update on casualties, but nothing showed up about his man.

He drove by the store several times. It reminded him of how he'd driven down Acorn in the evenings to spy on Sylvia; his victim had become his new stalked lover. He thought of the fellow endlessly. He went back over every little motion, every little sound the man had made since the second Robert became aware he was in the store, trying to arrange these details into a motif like a musical theme that could be definitively interpreted: *this is the way a looter sounds and behaves* or *this is the way a man who is also hiding from the mob sounds* or *this is the way a proprietor sounds and behaves* or *this is the way a man who is looking for a man who is hiding sounds and behaves.* He carried a stick, too, and had hit Robert with it. Was it a stick he'd meant and hoped to use, or a stick he'd picked up in case he *had* to?

He started having nightmares, but their images dissipated as soon as he awoke, leaving only their somatic consequences: sweating, heart pounding, panting as if he'd just run up ten flights of stairs. He thought maybe he was sick, that some strange virus was lurking in his blood. Its primary symptom was that unaccountable, awesome, and horrendously frightening rage. What he feared most of all was that it might return, that it was just dozing in his blood, maybe getting ready for a new thrilling ride, a nightlong romp in his big, strong human form.

FORTY-FIVE

By Sunday night, flames were extinguished, though char smoldered for days. On Monday a full-page ad in the *Enterprise* paid for by "the Pennsylvania Shipyard chapter of War Dads of America" declared that by rioting "We have played directly into the hands of Hitler and the Japs …. The evidence is strong that enemy agents have been busy in this district stirring up racial prejudice and hate." It was crucial for "every employee, both colored and white, to get back on the job, forget past difficulties and work together to build the ships that are so vitally needed at this time by our armed forces."

Tuesday martial law was lifted, but the suspect remained at large. So white men who had sent wives and daughters to distant towns balked on bringing them home, and citizens of all color stayed jittery behind locked doors. Residential mail carriers were mostly Negroes; they resumed service on Wednesday and noted that white patrons with whom they customarily chatted were skittish if encountered or peeked from behind curtains. Many businesses could not reopen while so many Negro employees stayed home.

Sylvia boldly motored Mary Kay to Sanger's to buy ankle socks, feeling armored by her superior moral worth. Her husband had saved a Negro falsely accused of rape, and her secret knowledge of his (their) role gave her an insider's disdain for what Port Fairview hoi polloi might think.

His return from Kountze with the check had been a turning point. He was beaming.

"How'd you get it?" asked Sylvia.

"Told her I wanted it," he said. "This is *ours*. To help Walter."

"What's the hitch?"

"Aw, Syl—damn! Come *on!*"

It meant—*trust me*. Okay. No strings attached? A cloud lifted. She'd been worried; with Georgie discharged, they wouldn't get his allotment, and he needed something more lucrative than a school boy's job. Wresting this money from Evelyn was a signal. Maybe their threat about the suit had shown how serious they'd been, and Evelyn had finally seen the wisdom of letting Georgie grow into his inheritance. God knows she didn't have a lot of choice, thought Sylvia. Elizabeth had no head for commerce or any interest, and her husband Clarence was a glorified go-fer. Marianne would be a lifelong invalid with an indeterminate affliction, too other-worldly to be practical. So Georgie and she were the logical successors to authority over the family's sawmill and timber lands, rice fields and oil leases and real estate. Evelyn must have seen that Georgie was capable if coached by Sylvia.

Having concocted this narrative in which her mother-in-law had surrendered in principle (details hadn't been hammered out), she felt the generosity of the victorious. She'd reward Evelyn by becoming a dutiful daughter-in-law. She could be a better wife too now that this storm had passed to leave them in a patch of sunshine. It was pleasurable to picture a future where you bought things without counting pennies or answering to someone. They'd buy or build their own house and abandon the dowdy old furniture pieces standing about here like mummies. A place on Pine had a "For Sale" sign; it had blooming oleanders and a second-story covered balcony festooned with wrought-iron like a French home in New Orleans—and she could imagine herself seated in a white wicker rocker up there crocheting and having coffee and chatting with a friendly neighbor; she'd have "hep" to cook and clean and tend the lawn. And she'd be beloved by her servants because she'd been an underdog.

Georgie noticed that she'd put Anthony's picture on her nightstand. "You don't mention him much. You think of him a lot?"

On their trip to Hastings to set the angel on his grave, she'd unearthed every memory of Anthony for his benefit. She kept saying *I just should've gotten the doctor.* He'd crooned, *Aw sweetheart, you couldn't know.* Waking mornings to see Anthony's face scarcely an arm's length away offered a bittersweet pang of adoration and remorse.

"All the time." She smiled crookedly and winked.

"What's so funny?"

"Nothing's funny. I like you, husband. That's all."

"And I like you too, wife."

With martial law lifted, she had to report to work. Georgie was on his way to the farm to talk to Walter, and she hummed "My Blue Heaven" at his departing back as a hint. *Just Molly and me. And baby makes three.*

All machines were back on line for the first time since the preceding Saturday, but she had the devil's own time keeping her girls bent over their bobbins. They were eager to trade tales of what they'd done during the riot. When she got home, she weeded the garden and was dousing the tomato plants with soapy water to discourage aphids—a tip gleaned from Edith Busby across the alley—when Georgie returned. They sat on the back stoop in the shade drinking iced tea as he gave his report.

Walter had changed his mind about surrendering. Instead, he wanted to take Thelma and Scooter up to Oregon where Rayette was.

She sighed. "To tell the truth, I'm relieved to hear that."

He nodded. "Yeah, me, too. Less chance he'll get lynched."

"I meant relieved for us."

After sundown, he planned to pick up Thelma and Scooter, drive to the farm to get Walter, and then he'd take them to Houston to catch a bus.

"Tonight?"

"Putting it off just increases the risk."

"Hasn't he got friends who could do this?"

"Yeah," said Georgie tightly. "He's got me."

"I know *that.* I mean colored friends. Thelma's got family here."

"Yeah, he could get somebody else. But I'm volunteering. I've got more wherewithal because I'm a white boy named Karacek."

"Haven't you done enough? I'm not arguing, honey, just wondering. You stuck your neck out really far by taking him to the farm Saturday night. And he's hiding on our property."

She'd chosen the pronoun deliberately, trying it out, but he didn't seem to notice.

"I can't measure 'enough' except by when I stop feeling obligated. I ain't there yet."

"I can see that." She winced inwardly at his grammar. "It just ... *scares* me, that's all."

He chuckled. "Scares me too."

She studied his profile. Suddenly her nose prickled and her vision blurred. He still looked like an overgrown boy, but he was a brave lad, a kind and generous fellow with, luckily for her, a forgiving nature. How could she have been so fortunate to have her life intersect his? To think she'd imagined this was a *detour* that Sunday the war broke out and she stepped off the train too rattled to go on to Los Angeles!

She kissed his cheek. "I'll make supper."

In the icebox sat a leftover macaroni-and-cheese casserole she'd made Monday after work, and she added small cubes of Spam and tomato slices to the recipe she'd read from *Good Housekeeping*. She slipped the dish into the oven, poured a can of peas into a saucepan and lit the burner under it. She had two nice ripe tomatoes and a big onion and a cucumber from the garden, and she sliced those onto a salad plate.

These ordinary domestic rhythms were particularly delicious now that Walter would not drag them into a protracted conflict with the police and the district attorney's office, to say nothing of the profound ostracism they'd have endured if Walter used the Houston lawyer. They'd done what they could.

What about the $2,000 now? Georgie would probably give Walter something for their trip. He could use the hat-box money. That would be good. But that would leave a tidy balance for themselves. Almost everything in her life, save the clothes she'd bought, belonged to the Karaceks, including the house, the car, the furniture, even dishware and utensils. The Karacek largesse that so recently seemed like a blessing rained upon her had shown its underbelly of obligation and submission, and she believed that their new relationship to the trust meant that a portion would be theirs without question or condition.

Georgie dried the dishes and took out the garbage, though his eagerness to help seemed more like a need to forestall his mission. When the last dish was tucked into the cabinet, she said, "Georgie, I want to go with you. Let me drive."

"I dunno. It may be dangerous."

"Let me take some risk with you, please? Besides, if you had a little spill in the car, it might call attention to everyone."

He stood at the table fingering the salt shaker as if it were a chess piece he was uncertain about moving. "You wouldn't mind?"

"I *want* to help you!"

He grinned. "Okay. Partners in crime, then."

She didn't want Mary Kay to know too much, but she didn't want her to worry if the clock struck midnight and they hadn't returned. She hoped Mary Kay wouldn't be afraid to be here alone. At the dinner table she'd been glum and when pressed about her irritability said, "I *abhor* the male race!"

Sylvia hadn't pried. But she did wish Mary Kay would talk openly with her. Gliding up the stairs to Mary Kay's room, she cursed those girls who'd been so snotty that Mary Kay didn't feel comfortable leaning on them at a time like this. Sylvia had considered calling Linda's mother's bluff about having lunch or coffee—see if any genuine warmth lay behind that saccharine façade of Southern hospitality—and encourage the woman to encourage her daughter to realize how *alone* Mary Kay was. But she'd had little practice with parental match-making and the impulse had passed without provoking an action.

She told Mary Kay they'd been called to Kountze to see Georgie's mother and might return late.

Mary Kay nodded. Wearing shorts and a rumpled pink blouse that once belonged to Marianne Karacek, she lay on her side atop her unmade bed flipping pages of the *Ladies' Home Journal*, ankles crossed, feet bare. The red toenail paint had flaked and a purple bruise welled on her instep. She seemed frail and child-like, perhaps because Sylvia was about to abandon her, and Sylvia felt a moment's hesitation about leaving.

"You won't brood about that boy, will you?"

"I won't. I *don't*," she insisted, as if she'd been insulted.

"If you need something to do, you can work on the sleeves of that blouse," Sylvia said, trying to sound cheerful and generous. "You're advanced enough you don't need me hanging over your shoulder." When Mary Kay didn't answer she said, "You sure you'll be okay?"

Mary Kay flipped the magazine closed to the back cover. Her pale blue eyes—magnified slightly by her glasses—peered at Sylvia with a disquieting directness.

"I won't kill myself if that's what you're afraid of."

"Okay. Good. But I wasn't thinking that. I wondered if you were scared to be alone with all the uproar."

"Nothing to be afraid of," said Mary Kay. "Since you and Georgie are transporting *him* out of the county."

Eavesdropping, Sylvia guessed. "Hon, we don't believe he's guilty."

"Fine. But that's what juries are for, isn't it?"

"Yes. In an ideal world, yes."

"I thought America was the ideal world."

Sylvia heard a door close downstairs; Georgie was waiting.

"Mary Kay, I can't discuss this right now, but I will, okay?"

"Okay." She sat up, shook her hair out of her face. She swung her legs to set her feet on the floor. She wriggled her toes.

"Maybe I'll paint my toenails. Can I borrow your polish?"

"Sure."

"Listen," Mary Kay said as Sylvia was turning for the door. "Would you and Georgie mind if I don't work at Emerson Drugs any more?"

The question so surprised her she could only murmur, "Fine, do what you like," and file it away to pursue later.

Sylvia drove the Lincoln. Twilight called for headlights; Georgie navigated so that she steered the stately black auto through downtown streets. The lawn of the library, previously occupied by a company of the Texas State Guard, looked like the calm surface of an ocean after a liner has been torpedoed and sunk, with flotsam and jetsam abob from a light breeze on torn green turf. They cruised cautiously through sparse traffic on Jones Street, past the gutted black hole where the Cloud Café had stood, past a clothing store whose plate glass windows had been shattered and were now boarded up. A Negro with a white bandage swathing his head like a turban stood on the walk with his hands on his hips talking and gesticulating angrily to another, older fellow on crutches, and they turned to watch as the Lincoln glided along the avenue. The hulk of a burnt-out car had been shoved to the curb. These signs of the violence shook her. Simply being in the setting of its occurrence set her nape tingling.

Down here you had the feeling that none of this was really over.

She'd never driven to the Negro quarter, and Georgie called out the turns one by one. When he had her halt at a shotgun shack with a picket fence enclosing a yard of packed earth, she didn't want to stop the engine. Georgie was about to get out and knock when a figure appeared behind the screen and waved. She kept the engine running and the lights on.

"Do they have tickets already?"

"I doubt it."

They waited. Georgie's toe tapped the floorboard in a jittery dance and he gnawed on a fingernail. He'd not had a seizure in a while—so far as she knew, that is—he didn't always tell her.

"How long does it take to get to the farm?"

"Hour maybe."

"And from there to Houston?"

"Maybe seventy miles. I've never driven it."

She checked the gas gauge. Thanks to Evelyn, in May when rationing started, they'd gotten a C sticker, normally reserved for use by doctors and ministers and mail transporters, and that caused some of Sylvia's coworkers and fellow volunteers to grumble.

"We'll need gas."

"We can't stop at a station," he said in a panicky rush. "That's not a good idea. Walter can siphon some from the tractor. Can we make it to the farm?"

"Guess so."

"Should've brought some sandwiches," Georgie said after a moment. "For later."

She thought they might explode just sitting and waiting. Any minute now, she thought, a police car will pull up, yank them out and cuff them, even though they were not breaking any law by merely giving Thelma and Scooter a ride, though certainly the local constabulary would be curious as to where the wife and child of their number one suspect might be headed.

Light from the waning sunset had seeped out of the horizon, and full night fell onto the street. She felt less conspicuous but no less apprehensive, since now when headlights appeared ahead she couldn't identify the vehicle.

Then the screen door opened and Thelma and Scooter, each with a suitcase, came quietly and swiftly toward the car without leave-taking hails from inside. Georgie jumped from the passenger seat and opened the Lincoln's rear door for them.

"Ridin' in style," said Thelma when she and the boy were settled.

"Maybe you oughta hide your bags," said Georgie. "Put 'em on the floor."

Sylvia was glad to be in motion, but she kept a hot knot right between her shoulder blades as she maneuvered the big car back through the littered city streets. When she looked in the rearview mirror, she couldn't see Thelma or Scooter. They'd slipped below the rim of the seat. But it seemed that at every stop she had to come to at an intersection, people in cars nearby were craning their necks to peer into the Lincoln's rear compartment.

"Hurry," said Georgie.

"I don't want to call attention."

"Yeah. You're right."

The route they needed to take put them on Main right by the police station, and Georgie said, "Thelma, maybe y'all ought not duck down so low, you know. Just kinda turn your head if anybody looks your way."

She heard a muted rustle and their heads were silhouetted in her mirror. They got caught in a jerky caravan behind an old truck filled with scrap metal, and had to stop twice when the vehicle coughed to a stop and the driver cranked the engine again. The second stop put them directly alongside the steps to the station, and Sylvia noted from the corner of her eye that a trio of patrolmen were huddled there jawing. One looked their way. If they had to stop here for any longer, he might just stroll down and chat with Georgie—or he might be curious as to the identity of their passengers. She could call Thelma her housekeeper, her "hep" that she was taking home. The patrolmen might just recognize her, of course.

"Come *on!*" she urged the truck.

It backfired once, belching blue smoke, and they all jumped.

"Godamity!" cursed Georgie.

But then the avenue cleared and they were on their way again. Sylvia seemed to hold her breath to the outskirts of Port Farview, and not until they were on the highway north to the farm did she relax and settle into the task of wheeling the big car along at the 35-mph limit. The pace made her fret, but she sure didn't want to be stopped for speeding. Thelma and Georgie and Scooter passed the time by singing "Old MacDonald Had a Farm" and "It's a Grand Old Flag," and "Shall We Gather at the River?," and she chimed in when she could spare the attention.

The farm house was dark, but as soon as they pulled in front of it, Walter appeared. He and Georgie filled a can with gas from the tractor in the barn and added it to the Lincoln's tank. They discussed whether Walter should hide in the trunk, and Sylvia said that if he did, sooner or later they'd have to spring him and that might be witnessed.

The drive to Houston took over two hours. Scooter slept while each adult assumed a different silence, and they reached the Houston city limits around midnight. No one knew where the station was; they had to park outside a honky-tonk on the outskirts so Georgie could get directions.

It was after midnight on a weekday and there weren't many cars in the gravel lot. Georgie walked past a pickup with its lights on and its engine running. Two men were in the cab, and Sylvia could hear loud laughter. Georgie's path took him right beside the truck and up the steps to the door, and he hesitated a moment when he reached the truck. She presumed he was going to ask the occupants for directions, but when the driver looked at him, Georgie just tipped an invisible hat, nodded and went on. The driver laughed. The door to the joint popped open, and a man in an oil worker's hard hat staggered out. The pickup driver honked at him. Weaving, he peered, brow shaded with one hand, against the headlights. He leaned too far and bumped into Georgie. Georgie gave him the invisible hat-tip and an obvious muttered apology, and passed inside.

The fellow in the hard hat stumbled down the stairs and to the truck and tried to climb up into the bed by clambering over the rear fender but fell off twice. The fellows in the cab cackled with laughter at him. He cursed them. He looked about the lot as if to see who else might've witnessed this.

Sylvia turned on the Lincoln's engine. She knew she was visible in the light streaming from over the door of the tavern. *Hurry up, Georgie!* The man in the hard hat waved at her grandly, bowing. She was afraid to ignore him and afraid to acknowledge him.

"Damn!" declared Thelma, which rattled Sylvia.

She settled for a cool nod. That was all the invitation he needed. He pushed off from the fender of the pickup and started across the lot for them. He was grinning and had one thumb stuck in his jeans pocket and was strutting as if he imagined he cut a dashing figure.

"Lord help us," murmured Walter.

Because the night had been warm and humid, she'd been driving with her window open, and now she could only wish it had been closed.

Rolling it up in his face might be an insult he couldn't tolerate. The engine was idling, still, and so all she could do was turn on her headlights as if to show she meant to back away any moment.

The Lincoln's front seat was bathed in a pale white light from the tavern, fortunately leaving the back seat in shadows.

When he reached the car, he put his palms on the top of the window frame and leaned toward her, pushing ahead of him a fug of beer and tobacco and stinking clothes.

"Howdy good-lookin'. Why don't you gimme a ride in yore fancy car? I can show you a good time."

She nodded toward the building just before her. "I'm afraid I'm spoken for already, cowboy. My hubby's inside and I'm waiting for him."

"Aw, we don't have to let him stop us."

The pickup honked and the driver leaned out his window. "Burl, goddamnit, git over here if you're goin' with us."

"I'm gonna ride with this perty lady."

He turned back to Sylvia. "They leave me kin I sleep in yore car?" He weaved forward and poked his head at her so he could see into the back seat.

"Hey! You got niggers back there." He addressed Walter and Thelma and Scooter. "Y'all bein' so damn quiet I didn't even know you back there."

"They work for me," said Sylvia.

Over the hard hat's head Sylvia saw the tavern door open and Georgie emerged at last. He came down the steps. The driver of the pickup started honking and backing out of the lot.

"Come *on,* Burl. We're leavin'."

"Go fuck yerself!" hollered Burl.

"Say, fellow, mind watching your language?" Georgie said mildly.

"Who the fuck are yew?"

Georgie kept strolling around the car until he was at the front passenger door.

"I'm the lady's husband."

"Come on, Georgie," hissed Sylvia. "Just ignore him and get in!"

"Damn! I see who wears the pants in this fambly."

Georgie got into the passenger seat and shut the door. The pickup was creeping slowly out of the lot. Sylvia gunned the Lincoln's big engine, yanked out on the clutch, and they fishtailed backwards on the loose surface. The one called Burl was yelling at them, reached down and scooped up a handful of chat and flung it, peppering the windshield, but in a second she had wheeled the big car back up to the pavement and yanked the shift into low and they were clear of the lot.

She got up to fifty in a 30-mph zone she was so shaken, but then she eased off as she looked in the mirror and saw that they weren't pursuing them.

"Nice place," she said to Georgie. "You find out how to get there?"

"Yep. And you shouldna worried. I was about to sic Hershey on that roughneck."

"Oh *hell* yes!" laughed Walter. "And I guess you coulda took them other crackers."

"Natcherly. I'm a trained killer."

They reached downtown Houston with no hitch, but when they spotted the sign of the white dog, Georgie said, "Go around the block so we can get a look."

She complied. At one A.M. on a Thursday, the station seemed in a lull. A bus idling in the bay was taking on passengers. When Sylvia parked at the curb, she looked through the windows into the waiting room. A couple dozen passengers sat in knots and singles scattered on the benches; an air of indolent boredom and exhaustion was fairly palpable even from this distance.

Walter, Thelma, and Scooter got out, and Georgie joined them at the curb.

"I'll keep it running," she said.

Walter stuck his head in the passenger window. "I wanna thank you, Miz Karacek. I'm in your debt."

"You're welcome, Mr. Jenkins."

She watched them. Inside, they stood as a quartet on the near side of the room, Georgie fairly dancing in place, saying his good-byes, and when Thelma and Scooter turned away, Georgie passed Walter an envelope. He nodded, slipped it into his hip pocket.

This is like the Underground Railroad, she thought.

When Georgie returned and she pulled away, he said, "We got 'em here, by God!" He grinned and clapped her thigh. "By damn! You and me! We did it, woman!"

She laughed. She felt giddy and light, almost too shaky to drive, as if she'd been holding herself up by adrenaline, and it was like a cord stretched taut about her that driving off from the station had snipped.

"I hope they make it!"

"Me too."

"God! I am exhausted!" she said.

They stopped at an all-night diner in industrial Pasadena on a boulevard girded by truck parks, pipe yards, and refineries. At this hour the only other patrons at the counter were a fat couple wearing sweat-stained straw hats, so drunk and laugh-happy they couldn't find their mouths with their forks.

Sylvia and Georgie sat in a booth and ordered eggs, biscuits, hash browns, and coffee. Georgie added a plate of grits. The waitress had gone home at midnight, and the cook set their plates on the counter for Sylvia to retrieve.

They ate slowly, the excitement of the day oozing through their veins and starting to clog. She had a headache and her eyes felt as if they had grit behind her lids. She yawned. The food boosted them and would fuel her for the two-hour drive home, but she'd been up too long.

They drank two more cups of coffee. The counterman brought their bill and stood by the booth while Georgie got out his wallet and paid.

"Did Walter have their tickets?" she asked as they were walking to the car.

"Not that I know of."

"Did you give them money for that?"

"Oh, yeah," said Georgie. "I gave him the whole wad."

"Whole wad?"

"Yeah. Two grand."

She blinked. She was so tired she couldn't feel shock. She groped to understand: the off-hand way he reported this—you'd think they'd discussed it earlier. Or that he'd talked about it. Or thought it was too unremarkable to require discussion. She felt too dopey and wrung out to feel anything except a desire to set this troublesome news aside for later.

"Well, *that* was generous," she did reply at last when she'd gotten the car back up to speed.

Georgie shrugged. "Least I could do."

FORTY-SIX

LATER, WHEN HER thoughts returned to the gift, she told herself *no need to fret.* Surely Georgie wouldn't have been so generous if they couldn't tap into the reservoir as needed now.

While Georgie was away at boot camp, she'd paid their household bills from his allotment and allowance, and she'd put away her salary since starting work. Once their conflict with Evelyn had sprung up, Georgie's mother had ceased the allowance checks, and Sylvia had used Georgie's last allotment to cover their normal monthly expenses. But soon after their moral triumph at the Greyhound station, she was faced with several bills and no cash reserves, and she was reluctant to dig into the hatbox savings. She hated talking to Georgie about money. He implied it was beneath him (or bored him), and he seemed to feel she should find it beneath her as well. To even raise the subject, she branded herself as a practical drudge, if not a gold-digger.

She waited for the most propitious moment—she'd fed him pork chops and mashed potatoes with gravy, lima beans, and dinner rolls she'd recently learned to bake, and pecan pie. They were enjoying a nice evening sitting on the back porch swing. A breeze had miraculously avoided carrying the stench of the refineries on its back and conveyed a hint of the ocean instead.

"Hon, do you think your mother will have the trust send us a monthly check again? I just ask because we have the light bill and the household insurance premium to pay, and I want to take Mary Kay shopping."

"Mama'll take her. For some reason she likes to spend money on her."

She waited. But he hummed tunelessly as if her question had drifted out of his mind.

"What about those bills?"

"Send them to her, I guess."

He got up hardly ten seconds later to find Buster, who he said needed a flea bath.

She was immensely dissatisfied with the vagueness of their arrangement now: the allowance had been no grand sum but was regular as a paycheck. Since he had no interest in these details, Sylvia considered approaching Evelyn on her own simply to clarify how she and Georgie were to utilize his portion of the trust. It was time to quit using Georgie as a go-between, too, she thought. She and Evelyn might get along better if they met face-to-face under friendly or even neutral circumstances, and they might even meet not for business but for, say, an afternoon movie, or tea at the hotel. Sylvia's treat. Win her over. *Bowl* her over.

Getting Evelyn to herself was tricky since Marianne usually stuck to her side like old gum. Also, she needed to signal she had no motive other than a desire to be better friends. Evelyn was usually driven to Port Farview on Mondays and Thursdays; she spent a few hours at the family's business office downtown and often lunched at the country club. She had a bridge date every other Tuesday afternoon at the home of Cecilia Richardson, wife of a shipyard owner. Marianne didn't play bridge and instead haunted the Christian Science Reading Room.

A late-afternoon tea on a Tuesday? Evelyn could come after bridge and before returning to Kountze, and Marianne would presumably still be occupied. But would she feel insulted if Marianne wasn't invited? And should Sylvia do more than wedge herself into Evelyn's schedule?

She could offer to drive to Kountze to take Evelyn to tea. Steel herself to spend time with Elizabeth and those brats, too. (Marianne was an utter mystery, but Elizabeth treated Sylvia as if she were a servant who had inconveniently picked the time they were together to declare herself off-duty.) But she'd have to take a whole day off work, and it would provoke their suspicions. Better keep it simple.

A phone call? No, more personal. She took a sheet of her best creamy stationary. *Dear Mother Karacek, Since Georgie returned from his service, it has struck me time and again how very thoughtful and solicitous you have been toward us ...* Good grief! A preacher would write that! She wanted to sound friendly but not gushy or common; she wanted to make Evelyn feel good but not *worked on. Dear Evelyn, Now that our dear Georgie is home for good, I have been thinking how nice it would be ....* Why Georgie? Isn't the point to stop putting him between us? *Dear Evelyn, Living in your home here has brought me to a deeper appreciation of your taste and judgment, and I would welcome an opportunity for just the two of us to get to know one another better.* There. That seemed straightforward, sincere. *I would enjoy treating you to afternoon tea at the Magnolia perhaps on a Monday when you make your regular trip to town.* Best regards? Fondly? No. Just *Sincerely yours, Sylvia.*

There ensued two days of quiet torment. She could picture Evelyn reading the note. Elizabeth might hoot about the stationary with the gold-embossed name and condemn the enterprise as pretentious. It was hard to know if imitating people who considered themselves your betters was appreciated or only mocked.

The reply was enscribed on her mother-in-law's own engraved note card, a heavy, grey-toned, glossless paper with a simple initial "K" in an Edwardian script as a watermark. *Dear Sylvia, It would be a pleasure to have tea with you at the Magnolia on Monday. Shall we say four o'clock? Sincerely yours, Evelyn.*

The reply's simplicity and directness heartened her. Between the reply on Friday and Monday's meeting, she gleefully kept the meeting secret—she'd surprise Georgie when she reported where she'd been. The exchange made her think of her own parents. They'd married late and died fairly young; Sylvia had lost her mother as a child of ten. Could Evelyn fill this role, at least in the casual way grown women have mothers? Evelyn already had daughters, and if she was dissatisfied with them, Sylvia never heard about it. She had grandchildren, too. But maybe Sylvia could become a friend in a way that a mother's own progeny could not, closer to being an equal.

What to wear! Evelyn would've been at the business office and wouldn't change for tea at the Magnolia. Evelyn would wear one of three skirted suits—the black, grey, or navy one. A white silk collared blouse buttoned at the throat and a pearl choker, most likely. Pearl earrings. A brooch, maybe the small golden peacock with ruby eyes and emerald feathers her husband brought back from France. Her public wardrobe scarcely altered.

Sylvia decided on her one good navy rayon dress with the white yoke and three-quarter sleeves with white piping and matching two-toned pumps, along with hat and gloves. Evelyn had seen it several times before. Wearing it would signal she held her mother-in-law in esteem—she often wore the outfit to Mass (not that Evelyn ever saw Sylvia inside a Catholic church or would set foot in one herself); it showed she was an earnest, sober person, capable of choosing decent attire for the occasion and was not extravagant.

She'd take the afternoon off if she could get away with it so she'd have time to bathe and dress and get the taint of factory off her skin and hair, out of her system, her head.

She beat Evelyn to the foyer of the White Blossom by five minutes, and she was glad it wasn't the other way around. Evelyn appeared in the navy suit, wearing her usual low-heeled black shoes, and greeted Sylvia a tad on the warm side of civility. Sylvia asked the hostess, thankfully a stranger, to seat them in the back room. They passed close enough to Barbara Franklin that the waitress waved at Sylvia, and Sylvia looked away quickly to avoid acknowledging her. Barbara would surely talk later about how stuck up Sylvia had become; Sylvia's sudden need to shun Barbara made her ashamed, but there was more at stake than a former comradeship.

"I'm so glad you can make time for me," offered Sylvia when they were seated. "I realized I've let time slip by without realizing how much time—" she faltered. Had she really said "time" three "times"?

Evelyn smiled, waved a gloved hand to dismiss the protest. "Oh, I know. For me, it's decades, though. As you get older, there's a certain … *compression*, you could say. How is Georgie?"

"Oh, he's fine!" Had Evelyn presumed the meeting was about him? "Same sweet boy."

"And his health?"

"His condition is stable. I'm afraid we've put a few pounds back on him, though."

"He likes his sweets."

"Yes! And he's fond of his meat and potatoes, too!"

The long silence crackled while Evelyn held her tea cup at her chin and stared thoughtfully into it (reading the leaves?) before sipping and carefully setting it back into the saucer.

"You know, I've had time now to get used to some things."

"What's that?" Sylvia asked as sweetly as she could—"things" could be sugar rationing or living with grandchildren or her son's having marital relations.

"Georgie's being grown and on his own."

Sylvia waited a moment, then said, "You did a wonderful job of raising him under really difficult circumstances, Evelyn. He has real *character.*"

For the first time in Sylvia's memory, her mother-in-law blushed. Then quickly cocked her head down as if spying a cracker crumb in her lap.

"Thank you. It's often hard to do the right thing because it's so much easier to do the easy thing. Oh, I suppose *that* sounds like gibberish!"

"Oh, no, I know what you mean. You love a child so much you want to let them have and do things they shouldn't just because they want to!"

"Exactly."

"I know because I … did have a child, a son."

"You did!"

She couldn't read Evelyn's attitude—surprise kept anything else at arm's length at that moment. Sylvia had no idea where the need to blurt this came from; it certainly wasn't planned. It was *the most she had to offer.*

She told Evelyn about Anthony—a short version—and killed off the paternal seed-donor in a car wreck rather than make a deserted tramp of herself. She didn't mention Georgie's wedding gift, nor did she reveal her part in Anthony's dying of diphtheria. Or exactly how she was employed when it happened.

"Oh, I'm so very sorry!" Evelyn reached across the table and took Sylvia's white-gloved fingers in her own white-gloved hand. Evelyn had tears in her eyes.

"Thank you," murmured Sylvia. She slipped her fingers out to retrieve a handkerchief from her purse, and Evelyn did the same, and when they caught each other discreetly blowing into them, they laughed.

"Well!" gushed Sylvia, to put an end to that. "I guess that leads me to letting you know Georgie and I are … are trying, you know, to …" She smiled sheepishly.

"Oh, so *that's* what this was all about!" declared Evelyn in a happy choral peal. "Well, I'm very pleased to hear it!"

Sylvia had not planned to reveal this, either. She'd had no plans except to accomplish what she delightedly recognized was happening: they were drawing closer.

Evelyn ordered teacake for them both, and when she removed her gloves, Sylvia did as well. The plain white cake with a light cream icing was the object of their discussion for a bit, and that led to talk of rationing and recipes and the difficulties of wartime conditions. They chatted about the sultry August weather (here Evelyn played the weary veteran of the Southern climate and Sylvia the vanquished newcomer), about working at the USO canteen and making up surgical dressings, about Marianne and Elizabeth and Clarence and their children, and about Mary Kay. Sylvia told Evelyn that Mary Kay deeply appreciated the attention and the gifts she'd received from Evelyn, and she revealed that she'd known Mary Kay since the child's birth but didn't elaborate upon the circumstances.

To Sylvia's pleasure, Evelyn ordered another pot of tea. This was going well. They had not said a cross or baited word since sitting, and she was discovering that Evelyn was, after all, a mother and not a just a harridan and autocrat.

But now that Sylvia had advanced the idea of a grandchild, she felt the weight of the expenses that went with babies. Having opened this door, wouldn't now be the time to discuss money? She steered the discussion back to wartime shortages, the cost of things. Evelyn commiserated about the scarcity of silk stockings and butter.

Sylvia said, "I suppose it's not the best time to consider bringing a child into the world."

"I suppose not. But there never seems to be an ideal time, does there?"

Sylvia chuckled. "No. If human kind had to wait for the perfect moment, I doubt any of us would be here!"

Evelyn smiled. "I'm very happy to think that Georgie might become a father, Sylvia. It's a good sign." She smiled—even more warmly—and Sylvia wondered if Evelyn were about to admit that Sylvia had been good for him. "I just hope it's not too difficult for you both."

"We'll manage."

"I am proud of him—of you both—for being so self-reliant."

Sylvia blushed. "Thank you." After a beat, she added, "It would be nice, though, to know if our child will have all the advantages."

Evelyn nodded, her head lifted and bent back slightly away from the table. Had Evelyn understood what she meant?

"It would be reassuring, I mean."

"No grandchild of mine will ever go hungry," Evelyn said coolly.

"Oh no, of course not! I... *we're* just, well, *uncertain* is all. About how things stand." Sylvia removed her hands from her tea cup and set them in her lap. This was *hard,* and Evelyn was not helping her.

Evelyn looked genuinely puzzled. Sylvia would have to be forthright. "If we're considering a child, there'll be necessities," she stumbled onward. "I could only continue working for so long, and Georgie's pay at the grocery wouldn't sustain us, I'm afraid. He's looking for war work, and that will help, of course." How much more plain could she make this short of begging?

Evelyn frowned. "He didn't tell you?"

Sylvia's stomach clenched. "Tell me?"

"Oh, I *am* sorry! I just presumed he had." She looked off toward the hostess stand. Then sighed. She lifted one glove and slowly redressed the digits of her left hand. "You remember our talking a while ago about hard things and easy things with your children?" She looked up, met Sylvia's gaze with an expression Sylvia read as truly sorrowful. "It wasn't easy for me to make demands on him when he came to me about that money, Sylvia. But I didn't think it wise to just give him a handout. People have to learn that life is full of sacrifices."

Where was Evelyn leading? The tenor didn't bode well, and Sylvia's spine stiffened. What *sacrifices* had Evelyn ever made other than, say, having to make her own bed when her maid failed to show?

"He didn't say word one to me about any demands you'd made. He said he'd told you the money was his to have." She clenched her fists in her lap. "And it is."

"I'd never deny that. It's only a matter of when. All my children are named as beneficiaries in my will. I'm sorry," said Evelyn. "Truly sorry. Please ..."

"What did—" Sylvia broke off, suddenly depleted of energy and so sad she couldn't pursue this without bursting into tears. Georgie had not told her the truth. She wouldn't subject herself to further humiliation by asking for details.

Beyond her outrage and humiliation to hear this now, she realized Evelyn was disappointed, too. Both had arrived thinking the other had surrendered, and it had allowed both to show their vulnerable sides. That had made friendship possible. But the truth brought the barrier shooting back up, and the possibility had been whisked away before they'd had a chance to savor it.

FORTY-SEVEN

WHEN SYLVIA RETURNED from that tea with his mother, she cried for hours. In the lulls, Georgie tried to comfort her as if she were ill, sitting on the bed, patting her shoulder. But since he was the source, he could hardly apply the balm.

"Just what will we do now?" she raged. "How do you imagine we'll get by?"

"Aw, she won't kick us out. She'll come around. I'm gonna get war work. You'll see. Everything'll work out."

"I just can't believe that you didn't tell me how you got that money! You plain lied about it! Then you gave every single penny to Walter! Without saying a word to me! Your wife!"

"He deserved it."

"That's not the point."

"Okay. Yeah, I guess I probably should've mentioned it. I'm sorry about that."

Apparently he didn't sound sorry enough because she burned him with a scornful glare. He tried to look ashamed, but something about her ferocious indignation was presumptuous. It irritated him. It wasn't her damn money to begin with.

"This was between me and Mama."

"You're just shutting me out like it's none of my business?"

She was too furious even to face him, and she bolted up and fled to her sewing salon upstairs. Through the walls, he could hear her bawl. Deep down, he was afraid she was right. He had lied about promising to drop the suit over the trust and about the efforts to have the house put in their names. His impulse to get the money at any cost had seriously crippled their plans to have an independent future.

He would have to renege on his promise to his mother. That was clear. They'd find a way to toss that "gift" back in her face then go in good conscience to their lawyer about the trust. Sylvia probably wouldn't get the house, but she had her eye on others, anyway.

When he no longer heard weeping, he went to her salon. She was lying on her chaise longue with her arm across her eyes and wouldn't look when he tapped at the door and crept in.

"Sylvia, honey, I was wrong. I swear as soon as I pay her back, we'll see about the trust. I'll swear on a stack a Bibles ten miles high, honey! I'll write it down. You'll see."

That had no immediate effect on her but he felt 100 percent better. It gave him hope to think he could amend his mistake, and so long as it hinged on repaying the loan, nothing was required of him save sitting at a desk and adding figures, making lists—expenditures to cut, things to sell. Odd jobs on top of the war work. He knew she was pessimistic, but in time she'd see his word was good.

The next day he acquired his job as an expediter at the mattress factory, and when he waved at her across the cafeteria, she smiled a little, waved back. Thing is, he felt proud of what he'd done. Walter had no idea the envelope contained more cash than he'd ever seen in one place, most likely. It was gratifying to imagine his surprise upon opening it while they were on the bus, counting the money. It would set them up fine. Sooner or later, Sylvia would recognize that this was best in the long run for everybody. It settled old debts. In the meantime, he'd exercise patience, plug away at his plan to make things right.

But shortly thereafter, Buster uprooted one of Miz Malone's azalea bushes. While Georgie was replanting it, she stood over his shoulder and complained about other canine transgressions on her property. She said, "Your old Mollie never was thet way. Shame your mizzes run over her," then, with barely hidden glee, told him the story, including how that prick Robert finished her off with the butt of the shotgun. All one day before he returned home from boot camp!

When he confronted Sylvia, she readily confessed and tried to explain it as an accident. It probably was. That wasn't the point! If Miz Malone hadn't piped up, he might've gone forever not knowing this. She'd *lied* about it.

"When were you going to tell me?"

"Truth is I *forgot* about it, Georgie. It was an accident!"

"I said that's not the point! You told me she died of old age! Is there anything else went on while I was away I haven't heard about yet? You got a habit of keeping secrets. I don't know if I can ever trust you again."

"You trust *me!* How about how I've had to learn things from your mother from the get-go? Who told me about your epilepsy? Who told me that you promised to drop the lawsuit about the trust? It damn sure wasn't you, Georgie."

"It just seems to me like every time I turn around I find out something that I don't want to. Like about Anthony. Like the money in the damn hat box. Like about Robert and you! I don't know any more what kind of ugly surprise from your past is gonna show up and wreck things!"

"Every grown person on this planet has a past, Georgie, except for you, because your mother kept you at home and so she kept you from *living.*"

Sylvia's duplicity and her capacity for doing him harm now seemed limitless. He believed that he might spend the rest of his life waiting for other shoes to drop. A cascade of them over the years, maybe. At every turn, a terrifying new revelation, a dirty secret.

FORTY-EIGHT

THEY LIFTED MARTIAL law, cleaned the streets and made repairs, and when the haberdashery reopened, Robert parked in front of it a dozen times trying to screw up his courage to go in. Finally, he did. A Negro in his fifties was the sole occupant, and, he guessed, the proprietor. He was on the chubby side, dressed in a double-breasted suit and with a natty handkerchief in the coat pocket. He was civil but obviously curious about Robert's presence—Robert guessed he didn't have many white customers—and, though he smiled courteously when Robert took off his hat upon entering, the way he lifted his chin and swung it a little sideways when they talked suggested suspicion.

Robert couldn't introduce himself as someone who'd broken the glass in the front door and knocked somebody in the head while hiding here. He said he worked for a government agency and was doing a survey of damage to the commercial district. Could the fellow estimate what the riot cost him in lost sales or damaged merchandise or property repairs? And if anyone was injured on the premises, their medical costs, etc.

"Aw, we hadden started totin' that up just yet. You gimme yoah card, suh, and we'll be in touch."

Left them in the car, said Robert, be right back.

Plagued by the uncertainty, Robert kept thinking he'd given everybody a decent chance to discover both the "crime" and the criminal.

Gone to the station and confessed, even. Except for his nightmares and the tender purple hematoma on his left forearm, the whole incident in the store with the other man might as well have never happened.

A few days later, he was brooding over a cold Lone Star at Meadows Ice & Packing, a tin-sided warehouse with a covered patio and picnic tables. It was walking distance of the Bide-A-Wee; the marketplace ambiance soothed his loneliness and kept him from gnawing at the bone of what he'd done the night of the riot. It was a popular place for politicos and cops, grocers and factory hands, and on Saturday afternoon when Robert had formed the habit of coming here, men at tables played an indigenous version of dominoes called 42. Even families came, though your high-toned ladies wouldn't be caught seated on a wooden bench hoisting a cold bottle to their lips.

So he was surprised to spot Sylvia. She was seated alone in another quadrant under the awning. A beer bottle stood in front of her. Had she been there when he stood at the counter, or had she come in since? She looked smashing. Very glamorous, her long hair sweeping across her face and tumbling over the shoulders of her dress—a white number with big red polka-dots matching red Bakelite ear clips and a string of neck beads like big bloody pearls. Sunglasses topped it off. Hollywood. She smoked like a starlet, her hand languid, elbow propped on the table, leaning over—if a button popped, her breasts would spill out like melons from a basket. Amidst those farmers in patched overalls, drovers and roustabouts, urchins and their haggard mothers, she had an air of someone watching a polo match. His hands leaked sweat but he also had a twinge of sickness in his gut.

He hadn't seen her in a while. He was surprised to remember that until recently she'd occupied all the space in his skull. He conjured dodges to get her attention—going for another beer and passing by her, or getting her one as a peace offering? If he sat long enough she might look his way, and he'd wave, casually. Thing is, seeing her even from this distance dolled up and so fetching, made his blood simmer. His memory went haywire and tossed up images like confetti of that golden time when it was just she and he living in the house and he kissed her pretty much at will.

She caught him looking and he blushed purple. While he'd sat mooning, he must've been ogling her. She wagged one finger to say either *tsk tsk* or *hello there*. His hand flew up in a wild wave and a weird exuberance crossed his face before he could keep it suave and aloof.

He wrinkled his brow and tipped his bottle with a finger. She nodded back, smiled, so he retrieved two cold bottles at the counter. He set one down next to the empty.

"Drinking your troubles away?"

She laughed. "Not mine. Thanks." She glanced at the cold one but made no move to lift it. "No, I've been stood up."

"Who would do that to you?" Without asking, he eased onto the bench opposite her, nonchalantly, as if just to tie a shoe.

"Georgie's sister."

"The nun or the shrew?"

She smiled a little but not much. Maybe he was making her nervous. "Marianne."

To justify the ensuing silence he took a long swig. Sylvia's head swung slowly as she gazed about the terrace. The dark lenses kept him from tracking her focus.

"I haven't seen *her* in a while," he said.

"They're all the same."

The hint of weary disgust encouraged him. A temptation knocked in him to ask if she were "the same" too, but he didn't wish to provoke her the way he had at Bud Sinclair's funeral. Also, she seemed a stranger—those glasses were a mask, and so many things had happened.

He smiled in a way he hoped was winning. "I'm glad she's late. It gives us a chance to catch up. You still working at the chute plant?"

She hesitated. "Um. I got promoted to division supervisor."

"Good for you!"

"Georgie's there too, now." Before he could ask, she added, "He's an expediter."

"What's that?"

"He expedites things from one department to another."

He pictured a hand cart like a kid's red wagon, Georgie tugging it across a factory floor. "So you guys must be doing well."

She shrugged. "And you, how are you?"

He laughed. "How am I what?"

"Do you want to chit-chat or not?"

"If it's my only option. It's better than not getting to talk to you at all."

"Oh, I'm not so formidable as that, am I?" Then there was that taunting grin: the invitation to play. Since he couldn't see her eyes he had to read her mouth like the fine print on a contract.

"I'm fine. How are you?"

"Fine. And your *friend?*"

He didn't want to banter. "Sylvia, I *hate* what Marjorie did. I talked to her in the hospital that night and she told me she'd had a fling with a Negro in New Orleans who knocked her up, and if people wound up thinking the baby was Walter's that was fine with her. And I told the police about that."

"My God!" Sylvia slipped off her glasses. Her dark eyes were nested in wrinkles—they were eyes of someone tired, and, well, older than he'd thought. "I am so *sorry.*" She reached to squeeze his hand sympathetically. Her sudden unguarded warmth almost unhinged him.

"But I couldn't get to the station to stop anybody because I got caught up in it and had to hide in a store until it was safe."

"That must have been terrifying!"

"Yes. Yes, it was! Some fellows came in and, I don't know, maybe they were there to loot, and I was afraid they'd find me, so when one got too close I hit him with a stick. Hard. In the head. He got me, too."

He turned his arm to display the injury. The grain in the old bleached pine of the table swam and waved like heat rising from a highway.

"What happened then?"

"I dunno. I got out of there."

"Huh! I'm glad you did!"

She didn't get the drift, but he couldn't say more. He'd garbled the story, he realized. It would have to come out a little at a time in the future.

When he didn't go on, she said, "White man or a Negro?"

"Negro. But it could've been otherwise. Didn't matter. It was dark. Too dark to tell. Beforehand, I mean."

They fell quiet for a moment. Then she said, "I hope Marjorie feels ashamed of herself."

"I wouldn't know. She might. She was a desperate person doing a desperate thing. There's a cautionary tale in it about drinking."

Sylvia gave him a wry half-smile. "So, are you a free-stepping bachelor again?"

"I have been all along, Sylvia."

"Oh, I'm sure! I was wondering who now."

"You have someone in mind? A friend?"

She swigged long and the muscle of her wonderfully white throat was exposed to the light; she held the bottle lightly between her thumb and three fingers, and the red polish on her nails caught his eye. She licked her lower lip.

"A friend? Now, Robert—tsk tsk!" Her grin showed she'd forgiven him for seducing Betty.

"I feel bad about that. It was unkind to take out my frustration on her."

"Oh, she got over it in five minutes. She does love her fiancé, you know. She's happy you never called again. You were a very small moment of weakness." She raised her hand to make a tiny gap between thumb and forefinger. "This small. That's all."

He blushed. "I'm happy to hear it." His spirits were sinking. He was sorry he'd swallowed his pride and walked into this humiliation. Was he such a glutton for punishment?

"The answer to your question," he said finally, "is nobody now. I've sworn off. I have bad luck. I don't have the knack for getting myself and some gal together."

She laughed merrily. "Oh, you have oodles of *knack,* Robert! Marjorie's mother said that if you'd asked Marjorie to marry you, she'd have said yes in a second."

"Sure she would! She was knocked up! That doesn't prove much, Sylvia."

"All right, have it your way. You have no knack." She smirked. "But you did get at least two spoken-for girls to cheat on their men. There could be others I don't know about. Give yourself credit."

He noticed she'd stopped looking for Marianne. Now he wondered if Marianne had been expected. Maybe she'd been waiting for a new lover who'd seen them and ducked out. Or had come alone and didn't wish to admit it. He didn't know how to take this confession that she'd been susceptible to his supposed charm, this insistence that he was such a dangerous temptation.

"I don't want to argue about how attractive I am," he said, smiling—he was recalling that the last time he'd seen her she'd threatened him with a peace warrant. "But I'm just leery of the business between a man and a woman."

"It's very trying, that's for certain."

She took another drink; drops of condensation fell from the bottle into her cleavage and she dabbed at it with a napkin, sending the red beads wildly askew. He wanted to offer to lick up the drops. He'd been so engrossed in the agony of what he'd done in the riot he'd all but forgotten the sensation of tumultuous desire. But after a moment he reheard her word "trying" and he recalled her "they're all the same," added that to her harping on the topic of his appeal. His pulse thundered: was she opening a window? If he stuck his head through it, would she slam it down on his neck?

"Is yours *trying*, as you say?"

She propped her elbow on the wood and her chin in her palm and looked away. Spread her free hand on the table, palm down, fingers splayed, drumming them slowly.

"Yes."

When she didn't go on, he held his tongue. He didn't dare suggest she might want him.

"I'm *very* discouraged. I don't know if I have the stamina to fight his mother. Especially when he's not on my side."

"Oh. *That* problem!"

She nodded. "I'll tell you something nobody knows, Robert. You have to keep it to yourself."

She waited. Finally, he nodded.

"The reason nobody can find Walter is that Georgie and I helped him get away."

"I'm glad," he said, though part of him was jealous that she and Georgie had strolled hand in hand down the lane of a worthy enterprise: how small could he be? That small. That's all.

"Georgie gave him a *lot* of money to set them up, but he had to get it from Evelyn, and what he didn't tell me was she put strings on it. She made him promise we wouldn't make any claims against the family trust or try to put the house in our name."

"Really? And he didn't talk to you about this?" He saw a chance to be outraged on her behalf, to egg her on. "He just took the money and never said what he'd had to promise? That's absurd! Did he think he could hide it from you forever?"

She looked down at the table, embarrassed. "Georgie's an ostrich, Robert. It's like when he got booted out of the army and couldn't tell us. If something's distressing to think about, he just puts it out of his mind."

"How'd he finally tell you?"

"He didn't. Evelyn did."

"What a terrible way to find that out!"

"It was *humiliating*. It pretty well robbed me of any hope I'd had that Georgie and I together could keep her at arm's length. But she won. She's stronger than both of us. Since he won't stand up to her, he really becomes her pawn, and I can't stand up to them *both*. If he's not on my side—*our side*—then he's dead weight."

"Will you make him choose between you?"

"Oh he's already chosen. When he agreed to her promises without talking to me, he chose her. When he never told me and let her spring it on me, he chose her."

"What can you do?"

She looked about. "I know myself, Robert. I need to feel safe and secure, and I want a man to make me feel that. But I need to feel a certain independence, too. I know it doesn't sound reasonable, but it's in me, and even while I try to fight it, I know it's there." She smiled a little in self-mockery. "What I seem to want is to be 'independent upon a man.'"

He laughed.

"Right now I have the worst of all possible worlds."

She wouldn't look at him while she said this. He wanted to jump onto the table, do a *schadenfreude* jig, shout with joy. But he kept a straight face, shook his head sadly, clucked his tongue. "I know you've tried hard to keep this marriage together. It's really a darn shame. Have you talked to a priest?"

She sighed. "Yes. But I knew what his answer would be."

"You made your bed."

"Yes. That sort of thing."

"Did he make you feel better about things?"

"Momentarily. Until I got home and found out that Georgie had moved upstairs into his old room and wasn't going to speak to me again."

"What?"

She looked directly at him. "Mrs. Malone told him she saw us kill Mollie, and I think she put it in his head that we did it on purpose."

"Oh, for Christ's sake!"

"So he's living upstairs with those two mutts and he says of all the things I've done, nothing hurt him more than learning how Mollie died."

He felt a laugh bubbling up, but he swallowed it back. "You told him it was an accident, of course."

"Yes. But I'd lied to him. It was about the first thing he asked me when he got off the train that night he came home from boot camp. I said she'd died of old age."

"He's not going to speak to you—ever again?"

She looked away—to hide her tears, he thought. "He didn't say that."

"Do you…" he couldn't make himself finish; the question was too probing.

"Do I what?" she sounded wary.

"Do you still want to be married?"

"I do love him, Robert."

"Then do whatever you can to keep it going," he said, much more magnanimously than he felt.

"My feeling for him, it's like the way you love a puppy who just can't seem to be trained. Or how you love a little brother who always needs your help. I feel sorry for him. I pity him. But that's not somebody you want to have children with. And I'm not sure he'll have me now. I don't think he could ever trust me again."

He let a long mental sigh release deep inside him. He relished hearing all this, even knowing that taking pleasure in it was callous. But he didn't know how to interpret her news. Did she regret chasing him off, or was she teasing him out of boredom? Maybe like her pal Betty she enjoyed the bittersweet combination of arousal and renunciation to the full opera of ecstatic fulfillment and sorrowful guilt.

Beyond his suspicions about her motive, he knew they were being more intimate than they'd ever been. Her candor wasn't calculated to injure him, only to share feelings she couldn't reveal to her priest or to Georgie. He let his left leg wander under the table, and finally his leg met hers. A coin of heat glowed right where their calves welded. She'd been looking toward the street, and her gaze swung back to him, deliberately, without haste.

"We're going to have a trial separation."

"Really!"

She nodded. He started making plans.

"I'm going to Los Angeles."

"For how long?"

"I have no idea. Maybe after I've been there a while he'll decide I'm more important to him than his mother."

He waited for more. She finished her beer. He said, "You want another?" and she shook her head. He was perplexed and in a kind of panic. She was not quitting Georgie; she was leaving as a strategy to make her marriage work on her terms. Or maybe she was being sent away.

"When are you going?"

"Tomorrow, I hope."

"Tomorrow!? Gosh, Sylvia, this is—*shocking!* Would you have gone without saying goodbye?"

She leaned forward and took his hand between her own. "No. It's why I'm here."

Damn him if tears didn't spring up and he yanked his hand back before her warm sympathetic touch blew him completely apart.

"What if I go with you?" he blurted out, despite knowing he was letting himself in for rejection. "Just as a traveling companion. Nothing more, I swear! I need to get out of here, too. I've been hanging around to … just to find out about that mess. Where I stand. If anybody wants to make something of it. It's dogging my every waking moment, to tell the truth, and keeping me up at night. Maybe getting to another place I can put it behind me. I could *really* stand a change of scene. I came here hoping I'd get over losing Claire and flunking my draft physical, you know, and I can say for sure that Claire's a long way from my mind."

She was still for so long he didn't think she'd heard him. Then she moved her leg away; the hot spot evaporated. His heart fell. She reached down and took up a white purse he hadn't seen. She rummaged in it and pulled out a compact. She opened it, looked into the little mirror. She brushed at her cheek with a free hand. She plucked a tube of lipstick from the purse upright in her lap and applied it to her lips while holding the compact. His mother always said ladies do not drink, smoke, or repair their makeup in public. Maybe Sylvia was cheap. That aroused him, but it was likewise distressing in a vague, undefined way.

She clicked the compact shut, capped the lipstick, dropped them into the purse and snapped it shut. She pressed her fingers tightly over the clam-shell halves as if something inside were struggling to bust out.

Then she looked at him. Her eyes were bloodshot, and pale, bruise-like hollows lay under them. She looked so *old* all of a sudden that he was half-afraid that she'd say yes.

FORTY-NINE

She wasn't leaving him—she's only going on a trip. She wasn't leaving him—she's only going on a trip. Going on a trip.

A *temporary* separation. A "trial" as in test run or something. Not trial as in lawyers and courts. And it's "separation," not divorce, and nothing legal, no judge or papers. Just the two of them thinking it out. Taking a break. A breather. Like when you're digging in the garden and you stop for a minute to mop your brow and get a drink of nice cold water—you're not stopping the work, really, just dividing it into portions.

She'd already finished packing two valises and was now working on the upper layer of a steamer trunk open on the bedroom floor. It was the one he'd lugged to Sonyea and back. It gave him a small but uncertain measure of reassurance that she would use his luggage.

He sat backwards at her dressing table, which she had cleared and dusted. The barren surface seemed forlorn after being festooned with glittery vials and pots of powder and cream all giving off their richly feminine scents. Except for a hat and gloves, she was already dressed to go. She had on what he thought of as her "matron lady" garb—that navy dress with the blue piping and a white yoke, a pearl choker and pearl earrings. She could easily take a chair at his mother's bridge table.

"Don't you want to take Buster with you? He likes you a lot. Better than he likes me, I know. He asked me why you were doing all this packing, and when I told him, he just started whimpering and carrying on something awful. I'm sure you could find a place out there that allows dogs. Everybody needs a dog. They're great company. Billie's sick of him."

He was only half-serious, but she said, "No telling what housing's like out there, hon. I just can't think about taking care of a dog on top of everything else."

"Well, I'm still thinking you could just, you know, rent an apartment across town. I don't see why you have to take your half of this trial separation all the way across the country. Mine's gonna stay right here in this house. I mean, I'd promise to leave you alone, if that's what you want. Honest."

"Georgie, we've talked about this. If I have to do war work, I want to do it where I can also pursue my career."

Pursue my career. Where'd this kind of language come from? All her recent talk along these lines was the first he'd heard of it. Well, not the first, but he sure thought she'd dropped that nonsense long ago. She was on her way to Hollywood when she got off the train here. If it meant all that damn much to her, why didn't she just grab a quick lunch and get right back on? *Pursue my career.* What career, for God's sake! She was taking herself way too seriously but he knew not to argue that point right now. She seemed sort of, well, *injured* about all this.

"I'm going to miss you."

She looked up and gave him a wry smile. "What will you miss?"

He didn't have an inventory and, in truth, had uttered that mostly to hear her say *I'll miss you too,* but it wasn't all that hard to anticipate the pain of her absence.

"Well, I'll miss hearing you hum and sing while you're doing things like sweeping or cooking or just puttering around the house. I'll miss getting to hug you and having you hug me back. I'll miss dancing to our records. And kissing you, too. I think I'll miss walking into these rooms and catching a whiff of your perfume. I think I'll miss how you sometimes kind of reach over and do something with my hair. And just having a pal to listen to the radio with or walk on the beach with. Remember when we used to read books to each other in your room at the courts? We haven't done that in a while. We ought to."

She turned away to fold a slip and he thought maybe she was about to cry.

"Won't you miss me?"

She nodded.

"What will you miss?"

"Just be quiet, Georgie. Please."

After a moment, she resumed folding the slip, laid it into the trunk. Then she took Anthony's photo from the nightstand and wrapped a towel around the frame and laid it atop the slip. That was alarming.

"Are you going to leave anything for me to remember you by?"

"Of course I can! What do you want?"

"Something you've already worn. That smells like you."

"Georgie."

"Aren't you worried I'll forget you?"

She stopped and turned to face him. "Yes. Yes, I am. But it's just a risk I'll have to take. There's a war on, honey. People everywhere are separated from those they love."

"Not by choice."

She sighed and went back to her packing. "You've left me no choice."

He still didn't believe that was true, but they'd already argued the point many times in the past few days. He could be as mulish as she—let *her* find out too late what she had here, by God.

He drove her to the station in the Lincoln, partly because it was big enough to hold all her luggage and partly to instill a little fear in her about his future. She might be worried about what could happen to this auto she prized so highly with him behind the wheel, and she might also see this as a sign that in her absence he might do any number of things that everyone believed to be injurious to his health and welfare. *What if.* While she sat in the passenger seat with her purse in her lap seemingly preoccupied with the sights out her window (he suspected she was fighting the urge to cry), he considered pitching a fit on the station platform right before she boarded. She'd be about to step up into the train and would happen to look back and there he'd be flipping and flopping and drawing a crowd and she was just too good a person to walk away from that.

Trouble was, despite the emotional turmoil and the stress and strain of the past few days, he didn't feel that tingly weird sensation in his limbs or the theremin music and bright colors of his aura. He could fake one, yes—he'd done it before—but the sad truth was that though it might deter her from leaving on this particular train, there'd be another this evening.

"What if you get out there and you can't get a part in a movie or something, or you can't find a band to sing with. Will you come back home then?"

"It's not just that and you know it."

"I told you I was going to work on Mama about the trust and what-not."

"Then I'll be really happy to hear when it's all settled in our favor."

"So it's like I have to bribe you to come back? I have to buy you? I'd have thought your marriage vows meant more to you."

He knew that would sting. She didn't reply for several blocks. Finally she said, "All I know is that I have to work for a living even though I married into one of the richest families in town. But I've done it all my life. If I have to do that then I want the right to decide when and where, at least."

"But you got a good job here."

"That kind of work I can get anywhere these days. Look, Georgie, I want to tell you something. You know when you proposed and I said I wanted a day to think it over? You never asked me what I spent that day doing or what I might've been thinking about, you know."

"I just guessed it had to do with marrying somebody with epilepsy."

"No, believe it or not."

"What, then?"

"And you probably don't know why I said yes."

"I didn't know then but I'm getting a bad feeling about it these days."

"You think I'm that shallow."

"Aw."

"You remember the night you took me to The Sky View and I told you how I used to sneak up there on my breaks and hang around just to hear the singers and the bands? You *know* what a fan I've been of Helen Forrest. The night you proposed to me she played with Harry James, and I snuck up there and got to hear her sing 'Embraceable You,' and 'I Don't Want to Walk Without You,' and a couple other songs. I mean she was really super. It's like she was living the life I always wanted."

"If you wanted it so much then why in the heck didn't you go to Hollywood, damn it!"

"I think it was because I was scared. I was low on money, and, I don't know, I was thinking maybe I wasn't so young any more. And going out there right then seemed dangerous with the war breaking out."

She took a couple of long slow breaths as if she'd just run a hundred yard dash. "So, anyway, next morning I had to take the breakfast shift, and no sooner do I get into work than I see there's Helen Forrest in a banquette by the front window with a couple of sidemen from the band. Everybody's traipsing over to get her Joan Henry on ticket slips and napkins and such. I thought maybe I could horn in just for a second and let her know how much of a fan I am and just, you know, maybe get some tips about how to break into the business. I grabbed a coffee pot just to look official even though she was at one of Jeanette's stations and Jeanette was right there hovering over them like a mother hen. The first thing I saw was, well, nobody's at their best first thing in the morning, and she just looked a lot smaller all hunched down. She didn't have any makeup on, and her hair was dirty I guess because she was wearing a bandanna, and her nose looked big and her eyes were bloodshot and baggy as old socks. I was really kind of shocked. When I was walking over, Jeanette picked up her plate of scrambled eggs and whispered 'too watery' under her breath to me and rolled her eyes as she took them back to the kitchen. I went to the table with the pot and warmed up the sidemen's mugs, and I chatted them up for a second, asked them where their next booking was and so forth, but I swear to God that woman didn't even look up. I might as well have been a piece of furniture. I said, 'I'm sure a great fan of yours, Helen,' and when she looked up at me finally, kind of annoyed, I poured a warm-up in her mug, and she just said, 'Damn!' and *glared* at it, you know. She said, 'I had that just right,' like I'd wrecked some project she'd labored all night over. Made me feel like two cents, I guarantee you that. I had to go stand in the restroom bawling for ten minutes before I came out again. I wasn't about to lower myself then to ask for her advice. She was about as sour as they come. I thought 'well, being Helen Forrest sure as hell hasn't made *you* very happy.' And I was so teed off about how she treated me that when Jeanette came back with the new plate of eggs, I stood there while she set it down in front of Helen Forrest, and I showed Jeanette that diamond ring and bragged about your proposal loud and clear right in front of them and told her I'd accepted it, and Jeanette bless her heart just raved on and on like I'd said my nag just won the Kentucky Derby."

She seemed to run out of gas. Or else there was no more to tell. He sorted among the various possible meanings and chose one.

"So you said yes to me because that singer had hurt your pride by ignoring you? It was just to show her up?"

"Oh, Georgie! Of course not. If that were it, then as soon as she left town I could've just given you the ring back. I'm telling you, she looked like a very unhappy person. I thought maybe I had a chance of becoming a happy one."

He couldn't help himself; he had to pull the Lincoln to the curb and bawl for a minute with his face in his hands, hating it but having no control over it. She reached across as if to pat his shoulder but he shrugged out of reach.

"I'm okay," he insisted, swiping at his face with his hands. "Dammit, I'm okay. Really. I'm sorry."

At the station, he found a porter to take her luggage in a cart, and they walked out to the waiting train. It had rolled in from New Orleans only minutes earlier, and throngs of arriving and departing passengers milled and shoved in waves against one another. They made their way past a few troop carriers until they reached the Pullman cars. He'd talked Marianne into lending him the money to secure her a private sleeping compartment for the trip.

They stood, jostled, by the car's metal step.

"Do you want me to help you find your compartment?"

"It's all so crowded. Maybe we should say good-bye right here."

"Okay." He steeled himself, clenched his jaw. "Good-bye."

She looped her arms about his neck and drew him into her, and he felt the gratifying pressure from her breast and her loins and he hugged her back, his nose in her fragrant neck.

"Bye, honey. Take care of yourself. I love you. I hope I get to come back, I really do."

He pulled himself free of her. "I hate it when you say things like that. Like it has nothing to do with what you decide. You can come back the minute you think you want to, I swear to God."

She had no answer, just gave him a tiny wave and slipped into the crocodile slithering its way up the steps and into the train. He walked alongside the car for a moment, peering up through the windows, wondering if her compartment was on this side of the train. The compartment doors stood open to the passageway, and he could dimly make out figures moving down it in jerks and stops as their hand luggage hindered them. He thought he saw her pass, jumped to the flank of the hissing train to wave, but then she vanished. He saw someone go past behind her that he'd have sworn was the spitting image of Robert the snide Yankee prick, too, but then he decided to decide he was only imagining things.

Hello Mom—What do I do now?
THE BRIDE: (tearfully) We've been married eight whole hours, and he hasn't so much as kissed me, and . . .
US: Tut tut, sweet bride, why worry your Mom? Hang up the phone and dry your tears . . . we'll solve your problem!
THE BRIDE: (suspicious) How?
US: Easy! Simply telling you the one thing you should have known—The Big Secret!
THE BRIDE: (more suspicious than ever) What secret?
US: The secret of personal daintiness, my dear . . . the secret of bathing body odor away, the feminine way—
THE BRIDE: The feminine way? That's a laugh . . . I've always thought a soap to remove body odor had to have that strong, "mannish" smell to be effective!
US: Not this one, honey . . . here's a gentle, truly feminine soap that leaves you alluringly scented—and daily use stops all body odor.
THE BRIDE: (skeptical) Well, right now I'll try anything! But can you prove all this?
JUST MARRIED
US: Sure we can prove it—and quick—because today's specially-made Cashmere Bouquet Soap bathes away every trace of body odor, instantly!
THE BRIDE: Sa-a-ay, you're not kidding! Such suds, and — mmm—I love that heavenly perfume! Smells like $20-an-ounce!
US: On you, dear, it's priceless! And remember—no other soap can get rid of perspiration better than complexion-gentle Cashmere Bouquet!
THE BRIDE: Well, I hope I'm luscious as I feel, I hope . . . 'cause I've got a date with my mate—I hope!
US: Oops, sorry . . . didn't mean to intrude!
THE BRIDE: (blushing) You're forgiven—this time! But tell me . . . does Cashmere Bouquet always make a groom so attentive?
US: It's you, who rates the attention, my pet . . . Cashmere Bouquet just insures the perfection of tender moments by guarding your daintiness!
THE BRIDE: Well, thanks a million, pal . . . how can I ever repay you?
US: Just stay as sweet as you are.
Stay Dainty Each Day . . . with Cashmere Bouquet
the soap with the fragrance men love
11

FIFTY

MARY KAY SPENT her senior year at Port Farview more or less in hiding. She dropped out of Victory Girls because she believed they gossiped about her and Larry Emerson and called her trash. She dug into her books, practiced piano, did household and garden chores, nursed stray dogs. She worked after school and on Saturdays at a women's clothing shop, in which, thankfully, men rarely set foot, and when one did he teetered timidly just inside with hat in hand to ask the nearest female, "Say, uh, I'm looking for my wife?" She liked working in a place that repelled and even intimidated men. She told her mother that in the letter containing a refusal to come live with her and Clyde in a new apartment big enough for three.

She filled out, and boys asked for dates. That she attracted notice alarmed her, and she wondered if they'd heard gossip. Larry could've lied or bragged, and these boys were trying their luck. Why would they ask, otherwise?

She gave excuses. She tried to sound credibly disappointed so she wouldn't provoke anyone to … well, it was nameless, a vague anxiety to imagine them as hostile. Georgie's mother lived with them her last semester, and she was a good excuse: *She won't let me. She thinks I'm too young to date.*

She went to North Texas State Teachers' College in the fall of 1943 on scholarship and on help from her mother and Georgie. There it was easy to avoid boys by staying in the dormitory. Too, the ratio of women to men was four to one. She went with friends to campus mixers to mingle in the crowd. It became obvious to her roommate she was date-shy. "Hey, come on," she urged Mary Kay. "They won't bite!"

Well, they could. But Mary Kay knew she would have to overcome her fear if she were to lead a normal life. She dated a few "bow-tie guys" she thought of them, not fraternity boys or athletes, just studious fellows who were 4-F and too shy to ask for more than being allowed to hold her hand. One tried to peck her lips goodnight and she bolted into the dorm. She wouldn't go deep in the library stacks where a guy might lurk. She wouldn't board an elevator unless it was occupied by others and never used a staircase that wasn't busy.

It didn't seem reasonable; after all, Larry hadn't grabbed her in a dark alley and raped her at knife-point. He spoke pretty words; he gave her the bracelet; he petted her. Sometimes she had trouble recalling *exactly* what he'd done. One morning near dawn she had a half-awake dream of standing at the sink in the drug store bathroom brushing her hair, and Larry was crouched behind her and had his hand up her dress touching her; in the dream she pretended not to know it was happening because it embarrassed her and made her squirm. She wormed herself to consciousness to discover that she was distressingly aroused.

Her residual anxiety over the experience seemed far out of proportion to the severity. She'd never told anyone and acted as if it hadn't happened, except, of course, that she quit the job. There seemed to be an enormous differential like the barometric pressure in adjacent weather systems between the outside world and what she carried under her skin. If he'd been a stranger, she'd have slapped his face and never given it a second thought. But she had *trusted* him. He had destroyed her confidence in her own judgment.

By the end of her freshman year, this low-grade but persistent fear of men and of the world had become an unwelcome obstacle she resented. It made her angry at herself. She shouldn't let what happened bother her this much! What's wrong with her that she can't just forget it?

Finally, her festering anger turned outward to Larry. She broke down and told her roommate, Carol. At a loss to provide evidence strong enough to indict him, she conflated what he did with what Clyde had done, and then built on it—the butt pat, the forced French kiss, "accidentally" fondling her breasts—and she sent Larry's groping hand all the way to probe her with a digit.

Carol said, "Let's let him know that hell hath no fury!" They hatched plans for revenge all night; the longer they talked, the better Mary Kay felt. That she had fabricated details soon became unimportant and then was forgotten. To Carol, Mary Kay was blameless and Larry was a cad. That gratified Mary Kay, and it was wonderfully liberating to have told.

They wrote sappy love letters to Larry addressed to his home in a flowery script with "S.W.A.K." and red hearts festooning cologne-soaked envelopes. "Janet Goodnight" wrote about how she and Larry had been lovers for ages and that Larry had promised to ditch his wife and live with Janet at her new home in Denton, Texas. *"Oh, my darling! I long for the day when I can walk the streets with you without fear of discovery!"* wrote Carol. *"I yearn for your familiar kiss, your familiar touch,"* added Mary Kay. In one letter, Janet told Larry that she'd be visiting their "mutual friend" in Port Farview and she *yearned* for them to be together, even if it meant sneaking around.

The first college summer she spent the month of June with Gram in Ohio (her mother came to visit without Clyde), then returned to Denton for summer school. She was eager to finish her BS in biology; the sooner she became a full-fledged adult, the sooner she could burrow into employment, enjoy her own money, her own life, be free of the torments about courtship.

Before the fall term began, she went to Port Farview. Georgie had moved to the farm, and she and Marianne drove out to spend a weekend. Marianne brought groceries and laundered clothing because a municipal judge had forbidden Georgie to drive, and a bicycle was his only transportation.

On the way, Mary Kay asked about Sylvia.

"Oh, she wrote Georgie for awhile. She was working in an aircraft plant in Long Beach for a time then moved to Hollywood. She sent him a photograph of herself in a saloon girl outfit. She had a part in some musical motion picture called *Belle of the Yukon* I believe. But it's never played here, so we haven't seen it."

"You think they'll get back together?"

"Back in April Georgie served divorce papers on her for abandonment."

"Are they divorced now?"

"I think the lawyers are still arguing."

"How's Georgie feel about it?"

"Oh, he's calling the whole affair 'Karacek's Folly.'"

"But how's he really feel?"

"He has diabetes now," said Marianne. "He has to inject himself with insulin every day."

Mary Kay had to settle on judging for herself. Although Georgie claimed in his letters to Mary Kay that he never got lonely—a half-dozen dogs had free run of the house, including J.J.—he was clearly delighted to have their company. "Gosh, Slim!" he yelped. "You've grown half an inch!" He snatched her up and bear-hugged her, spun her before she could prepare herself and thus was alarmed, but then he released her so fast she had only a fleeting memory of abundant flesh and dusty smelling clothes, his surprisingly strong grip around her waist. It was the first hug she'd had from another human in so long she couldn't recall when; her bosom and loins and thighs tingled with the unexpected stimulation, roughed up a bit, her muscles alive and expectant the way they were after a volley in tennis and you're waiting for the next serve.

Georgie hadn't tidied up. Issues of *Argosy* and *Collier's* and *The Atlantic* and the *Enterprise,* Baby Ruth and Oh Henry! wrappers and Superman comics littered the parlor floor about a Morris chair with a torn leather cushion. The room also contained a console Magnavox, and a wooden card table with two chairs.

Despite Marianne's belief that Georgie viewed his marriage as a laughable mistake, Mary Kay saw that the publicity still from *Belle of the Yukon* had been framed and hung on the wall where it would catch the eye the moment you entered the house. The film starred Randolph Scott and Gypsy Rose Lee, and the still showed a saloon scene where those stars were front and center while around them were arrayed bartenders, patrons, and dance hall girls. Peering close, Mary Kay spotted Sylvia standing at the bar in a Western saloon gal get-up, one arm about the shoulders of a cowboy with a cocked-back hat. Mary Kay felt a complicated spasm of admiration, envy, and indignation. Sylvia had autographed the photo: "To my dear husband Georgie from 'Lulu.' This was wonderful!" (One late night in 1983, Mary Kay was on call at the emergency veterinarian clinic in Dallas and caught the old movie on TV. Sylvia had one line. Just before or after the publicity still was taken, she turns to the cowpoke to say, "Howdy, wrangler! Buy a gal a whiskey?")

Under constant surveillance by J.J., Mary Kay and Marianne thoroughly scoured the kitchen, then they fried catfish they'd brought, and Marianne made hush puppies and cole slaw. Georgie's huge garden was wild with unruly tomato plants, flowering onion tops, eight-foot okra, and zucchini the size of baseball bats, and it yielded vegetables to stew. Georgie served tea in Mason jars.

"It's nice to have you two here," said Georgie during dinner.

"You need somebody to look after you," said Marianne. "Like a wife."

"I beg to differ. I got dogs. A dog makes the best kind of wife."

Mary Kay laughed, but Marianne looked frightened. "Georgie!"

"Dog won't ask you where you're going," he said. "Or how long you'll be gone."

"Yeah, but they'll wanna go too," said Mary Kay.

"True. But when you say no, they don't remember it long enough to hold it against you."

"But a dog can't enjoy the intimacy between husband and wife," Marianne insisted.

"Aw, I dunno. If you mean talking, well, I pretty much know what's on a dog's mind. It's not complicated, and that's another plus. You got 'bowl' and 'ball' and 'bone,' and you got 'go' and 'tickle me now' and 'no bath today!' That's about it. And believe me, they know when you're not in a good mood."

"And don't forget they don't care about fashion or jewelry."

"Or cars or fancy appliances. You're not out one thin dime for little pretties. And a dog won't say a word about how you spend your money."

"No bunch of roses after you've stayed out too late playing poker, either," said Mary Kay.

"No. And no worry about birthdays or anniversaries. It's a dog's birthday, you say, 'Happy Birthday, Archie,' and give him an old bone you just found under the hedge, and he's happy."

"Georgie, I swear! You sound like somebody who fell off a turnip truck!"

"It's a cold night you make the dogs get on your bed and if you get too hot you just kick one off. It's hard to hurt a dog's feelings. They don't collect little slights done them during the day then figure out ways to punish you without saying diddly-squat directly and make you have to *ask.* A dog's pee-oohed, you'll know it right off."

"Georgie."

"Dogs have no politics."

"Actually," said Mary Kay, "they have a lot of politics. Who goes first, who has what bowl and who gets the biggest portion, who gets what sleeping spot."

"But they can't even *think* about Democrats or Republicans."

"Marianne, I don't mean those politics. I mean human social practices, the ladder, what church a person goes to, or what color they are, or how much money they have. Or whether you're a thief or such. A dog's measure of human worth is plain and simple—a good human is one who will give a pore dog food and shelter and a kind word."

Marianne giggled. "You make them sound like monks!"

"Yeah! You got it! Let's start a church, Marianne. Oh brothers and sisters, will you bay with me now?"

Mary Kay laughed. Encouraged, Georgie went on. "And then there's that fine old hymn, 'Bark of Ages.'"

"Or the story of 'Noah's bark,'" said Mary Kay.

"Yeah. 'Course, the shepherds would have a little edge. And in the First Church of Dog, a ripe butt smell is the key to the Kingdom of Heaven."

"Georgie, honey, you shouldn't—"

"—O, Lord Dog on high, lift thy leg and showeth us the way, that we might lift our legs as well and anoint the lilies of the valley, the trashcans of the alley . . ."

"Georgie, please don't blaspheme."

"Blaspheme?" Georgie laughed. "Have it your way. But don't blame me when you're standing at the pearly gates and a bulldog named Butch won't let you in."

"Maybe the streets of dog heaven are paved with cats," said Mary Kay.

"I was gonna say beef jerky, but your notion is downright appealing because it's so *dark*, Slim."

"Animals *are* God's creatures, but they don't have souls, Georgie. That's how we're different."

"Maybe in your gospel. Not in mine. A soul is the part of a being that's in harmony with the universe. Did you ever hear of a dog committing suicide or killing another dog for fun or because some other dog told him to? No, in my Church of Dog, animals have souls. It's the people who don't."

While Marianne listened to the radio, Mary Kay helped Georgie feed and water the dogs and change the bandage on a cocker pup's splinted leg. He had chickens, too, and a pet billy goat named Mister Sam who stunk to high heaven and who shoved Mary Kay around with his nose. It was great fun being with Georgie again; she'd forgotten how playful and teasing yet gentle he was, self-deprecating, not bossy like so many men.

All through the meal, through the evening while they worked side by side in the waning summer twilight, her body retained the kinetic memory of the bear-hug, the swingaround, his chest against her bosom, the smell of his sweat and dust as he clenched her tight and her nose was jammed into his chest, all so brief but nonetheless persistent in her nerve ends.

The idea popped to mind to kiss him—purely as a therapeutic measure. She trusted him more than any man on earth; kissing him would let her inch back toward a world of normal humanity, might banish this wholly irrational fear of being approached and touched. The more she thought, the more she *had* to do it. If not, her fear might build and wreck her life; it was clear by now she wouldn't *wear the fear out* as she'd hoped: she'd have to do something about it, something risky maybe.

Georgie was like a brother, and he was a dear friend; she had nothing to fear from leaning over while he curried this horrendously odiferous goat and pecking his cheek. He'd probably say, *What the heck was that for?* like a sixth-grader, and she'd say, *Just cause, that's why!* Innocent and harmless. He didn't need to know it was meant to help her return to the living. The horse might throw you again when you got back on, but that's why getting back on meant something.

So as he brushed the goat's grey coat, she bumped into him to draw his attention. When he turned, she strained up and aimed her lips for his cheek but hit half his damp mouth instead, and jerked herself quickly away.

"What the heck was that for?"

He blushed deep pink on his suntanned face and grinned boyishly.

"'Cause I missed you."

"Aw, Slim, I missed you, too! Boy, did I miss you!"

He drew her to him and pulled her head into his chest, his arms around her shoulders. He held on. She caught her breath for a bit, then exhaled, finally surrendering to the embrace. The longer she was in it, the stranger it seemed but also the more familiar, and she was so relieved to not be afraid that she squeezed him back. They rocked in place for a while. About them the deep violet light was suffused with muted creaturely sounds—a distant lowing from a cow, the dogs snorting and sneezing about the barnyard, faint twitter from a chinaberry tree near the house.

After a moment, she gently pulled apart from him. She smiled.

"Thanks."

"For what?"

"For hugging me."

He snorted. "It wasn't much of a chore. I don't much get a chance living out here. Not that I feel sorry for myself—it's a life I'm choosing. I can say that about it, at least."

It was difficult to articulate why she was so grateful. "Georgie, I want to tell you something, but I need for you to promise not to do anything about what I say."

He laughed. "Is it okay if I don't hear it, then?" He sounded wounded.

"It's not about Sylvia."

"Okay."

"You promise."

"Sure, if you need me to. Swear on a stack a Bibles ten feet high."

They were walking toward the house, and she didn't want an audience for this. She moved from the path to a picnic table under a chinaberry tree where they ate in good weather. He sat across from her, but she sat straddling the bench, facing down its length.

"You remember when I quit working at Emerson's?"

"Yeah."

"I don't know if you wondered why I quit or not."

"No, can't say as I did. I sort of had my head up my hiney at the time."

"It was because—" All at once a solid hot core of pure rage surged up from her gut into the very top of her head, so strong and unexpected and overwhelming that she was momentarily dizzy and her hands started trembling. She expelled a shaky breath. "Because Larry Emerson," she groped for a verb, " ... *molested* me!" The word seemed paltry beside the months of agony she'd endured—it simply couldn't cover or account for his devious little speeches and his furtive dirty hand and how he tried to pretend nothing happened or it didn't matter and even would've tried again if she'd not been alert.

"He did?"

She nodded. She couldn't look at him. But his silence then was so intense—like something magnetic—she had to flick her gaze across the table. He was digging a thumbnail along a furrow in the pine-topped table. His lips were twisted like he'd bitten something sour, but his eyes were watery and sad.

"I guess I know why you made me promise not to do anything." He sighed. "He's one sorry SOB, Mary Kay! I feel terrible about—"

"Oh, Georgie, you didn't know! You trusted him, too! It's not your fault."

"Are you sure you wouldn't like for me to take care of this?"

"Please don't do anything! I don't even want him to know that I told anybody here."

"Well, I tell you one thing, you sure as heck shouldn't be *afraid* of what he might do if—"

"I mean I don't want him to know it made that much difference to me, that I'd be telling on him. I don't want him to even remember me or think of me or even have any idea at all of me. I don't want him to have the satisfaction, you know?"

"Seems like we oughta do *something*, though, Mary Kay. You might not be the only girl who's had that kind of trouble with him. Or could have."

"I know, I know." Then she told him how she and Carol had written half-sealed love letters to his home under the name of Janet Goodnight. He laughed.

"Don't you think he knows who sent them?"

"Probably."

"So truth is he's probably remembering you all right, and maybe he's more than a little sorry he took advantage of you. I'd like to be a fly on the wall when he's trying to explain it to Julia."

"You and me both!"

They fell silent a moment. It struck her that he had responded to this news precisely the way she'd hoped he would, just the way she'd want an older brother or a father to act. What she'd feared most was that he'd feel his own honor had been violated and that the grievance would require redressing through a violent act. What she'd wanted and needed was a sympathetic ear and for someone who knew them both to believe her story without question.

"I guess you've been down in the dumps about it all for a pretty good while. Wish you'd had somebody to talk to."

"Sylvia tried to warn me about him."

"Good for her."

She wanted to ease away from the ugly memory that seemed not to be receding but was rather swelling there as they mutually contemplated it. She told Georgie she'd noticed the framed photo of Sylvia in costume on the living room wall.

He said, with a touch of pride, "Got that a while back. I guess she'll be in other pictures now."

"Is there any chance at all, you know, of . . ."

He shook his head. "Nah. Next to none. She's a goner." His nervous chuckle was like a car not starting. "Good riddance, I reckon."

"You really feel that way?"

He shrugged. "It hurts a little less each day, I think. Some days are worse than others. But I don't like the idea of it never hurting at all. I'd like to always know I had a life with her no matter how short it was."

At the back door, Marianne appeared as a silhouette backlit by the lamp in the kitchen. Dusk had settled all about the yard, though the sky was a shade of violet lighter than the darkness about the trees. She called, "Georgie, have you had your shot?"

"Be there in a minute," he called back. To Mary Kay, he murmured, "That poor dear girl. She means well, but what in the world does she think I do about that shot when she's not here?"

After Mary Kay and his sister had left Monday morning, Georgie kept himself occupied. He was working on a pen where he could isolate any mutt who needed medical attention or who had trouble mixing with the others because the PF dog-catcher, Burl Simpson, had called to ask if he'd put a couple more strays up for a bit. Before noon, he saw Arnold Beasley's mail truck stop on the road up from the house. He hailed Georgie with a wave before moving on, and Georgie waved back.

When he walked up with Buster and J.J. at his heels to get the mail from the box that stood atop a cedar post, he found a note from Walter with a $350 check in it. The note said, *Tater, don't be sending it back again, you hear?* Georgie smiled. Sooner or later one of them would tire of pitching it back and forth across the continent, but Georgie was determined it would be Walter.

He was gratified that Walter appreciated his help. Sylvia didn't really appreciate what he'd done for Walter and Thelma and their son; his mother certainly hadn't; so far as he could tell, his mother had not told Marianne and Elizabeth, and it'd be hard to say what Mary Kay thought. No one white in Port Farview who mattered had any idea he'd been involved, and it was probably best that they didn't. *Local Man Helps Accused Negro Rapist Get Off Scot-free* was not a headline likely to inspire a Carnegie medal nomination, for sure. Not being publicly excoriated for it (or prosecuted!) was a blessing, of course; not being publicly praised for the act also underscored its true value—that it needed doing, needed doing by someone from his family.

He didn't much feel like a hero, but he felt he'd squared things a bit. *Local Man Faces Mirror Each Morning.* It wasn't dragging a family out of a burning house, but if he hadn't made himself help Walter he'd have had to get out that rafter rope again. Too bad the cost of it was his marriage.

The hard thing about being a grown man was that the world flung down the gauntlet every time you turned around. Yes, he'd promised Mary Kay not to act on what she told him about Larry Emerson. And she said she didn't want Larry to know that she'd even told. He'd have to honor her request and his promise, of course. But he was *outraged* that Larry had done that! An allegedly upstanding Baptist deacon and family man, Rotarian, member of the PF Country Club, VIP at the Chamber of Commerce, and so forth. This called for punishment. Any innocent young girl deserved the protection of her family—Mary Kay was an honorary Karacek; she had been under his and Sylvia's wing, and for Larry to have treated her that way was unforgivable.

For a while last night he'd toyed with the idea of slyly letting his mother in on what that sorry bastard had done. His mother's furious indignation would no doubt inspire her to make Larry Emerson's life a living hell for the rest of his days in Port Farview, and he'd probably have no idea where his sudden long run of terrible bad luck had come from. But Georgie hadn't been able to imagine how to let her know without violating his promise to Mary Kay.

Bud Sinclair was a hero. What would he do? Beat Larry to a pulp? That wouldn't please Mary Kay at all. Georgie imagined going into

Emerson's in a grand huff, striding back to the pharmacy counter, and when Larry looked up from his pill counting and asked, "What's for you, Georgie—the usual?" Georgie would stand feet spread, cross-armed, and he'd glare. Maybe mutter, "Scummy pervert!" do a neat, military about-face and storm out empty-handed, never to return.

But, of course, that would betray that promise, too. In the end, the best he could muster as a heroic act of redress would be … well, not showing up.

He'd filled his last prescription at Emerson's, that was for dead certain. He wouldn't set foot in Emerson's even if it meant he had to bike or hitchhike all the way to Port Arthur to get his medicine!

He laughed at himself. Here was the honorific headline:

Local man stops trading at Emerson's!

FIFTY-ONE

LOCAL ANIMAL LOVER SUCCUMBS

Sunday, June 12, 1954

Services for Georgie Karacek, lifelong Port Farview resident known as "The Dog Man," will be held Wednesday at 4 P.M. at St. James's Episcopal Church with burial immediately after in Greenwood Cemetery.

Mr. Karacek, 45, died Saturday in a local hospital after suffering complications from diabetes. Mr. Karacek was the only son of the late Herman Karacek, the owner of Karacek Lumber and Minerals, and he is survived by his former wife, Sylvia Karacek of Riverside, California; his mother, Evelyn Karacek of Port Farview; two sisters, Marianne Karacek of Port Farview, and Elizabeth Cordell of Houston, and two nieces and a nephew, June, May, and Calvin Cordell of Houston.

Mr. Karacek was educated at home by members of the family as ill health prevented his attending public schools. His mother told the *Enterprise* that teaching her son was among the greatest joys in her life. "He was always interested in so many things, especially as a young boy. He always loved animals, and he had a great fondness for the natural world. He also liked to put on plays and perform stunts and tricks for family and friends. He was a lively boy with a lot of personality." His eldest sister, Marianne, said that Mr. Karacek "had a soft spot for anybody or anything that needed help."

Despite his medical problems, Mr. Karacek served bravely in the U.S. Army during World War II, said his mother. He was a recruit at Camp Roberts, California.

Locals best knew Mr. Karacek for his fondness for canine creatures. In 1945, he turned the family's farm north of the city into a haven for stray dogs and other unfortunate creatures in need of shelter. At one point, according to a neighbor, Louise Allred, he had some 75 to 100 dogs on the property and "he gave every one a name." Although Mrs. Allred was among those nearby who often complained to authorities about Mr. Karacek's use of the farm, she said, "If everybody had a heart like his there'd never have been any need for what he did." He was often seen walking the streets carrying treats in his pocket for our local canine friends. Family members tell of the many times he went out in inclement weather to find and feed homeless animals hiding in the alleys downtown or in abandoned buildings.

"He had a way with them," said Port Farview animal control officer, Marion Hicks. "It didn't seem to matter how suspicious or snarly some old mangy cur might be, old Georgie could sweet talk him right out of a hole." Mr. Hicks worked with Mr. Karacek many times, he said, and called on him frequently when the city's pound had become overcrowded. "He was really good with the sick and lame ones, the ones nobody would adopt."

A longtime family friend, Dr. Mary Kay Larson, credits Mr. Karacek with inspiring her to become a veterinarian, and she and her family often visited the farm and assisted in caring for the animals there.

In 1950, Mr. Karacek became known as "The Dog Man" when he began writing letters to the *Enterprise* under that name urging local citizens to take proper care of their pets. He also formed a foundation to raise money for the Port Farview Society for the Prevention of Cruelty to Animals shelter and was active in all SPCA activities, serving on the board in 1951 and 1952.

The family has asked that memorials be made in the name of "Mollie" to the Port Farview SPCA.

Purple Hearts: a novel
ISBN 978-0-87565-362-4
Case: $27.50